SPIRITS OF THE EARTH BOOK THREE

CITY OF GLASS

MILO JAMES FOWLER

www.aethonbooks.com

For Sara

"No one remembers the former generations,
and even those yet to come will not be remembered
by those who follow them."
Ecclesiastes 1:11

PART I
AWAKENING

1. SERA
22 YEARS AFTER ALL-CLEAR

I run.

Through darkness lit up for my eyes only, thanks to Wink and Blink hovering above the scene and painting every rooftop, every ledge, every gap between buildings in lines of infrared. My ocular implants pick up each architectural detail and highlight them in shades of crimson and blue, adding perspective and glowing brighter as I close the distance. I charge headlong, my exo-suit punching into the roof and providing an extra burst of speed for my lunge across a two-hundred-meter drop, then cushioning the impact when I crash-land onto the next unforgiving rooftop and roll to my feet.

Always moving as fast as I can. Always with my quarry in sight.

Somehow, he's managing to stay ahead of me, dodging and weaving as he runs, covering the same elevated urban terrain without the aid of any detectable augments or an exo-suit. According to the readings I'm getting from Wink and Blink, the guy's adrenaline levels are off the charts, and the same goes for the current endorphin rush he's riding. He moves like no one I've ever seen.

That first jump, three or four buildings back, should have been impossible for him. Never mind the landing. Without exo-rods attached to his legs, launching himself from one domescraper to another should not have been possible. Any normal person would have landed in a crumpled heap of bone fractures. Yet here he is, dashing full-tilt across this rooftop with no injuries sustained, whatsoever.

"Take him down, Sera," the voice of my commander says in my ear.

Back at headquarters, where things are just a bit less hectic, she's watching the chase play out on a big screen in the command center via Wink and Blink's transmission. They always like to share everything they see and hear.

"I've got him." My voice is quiet, confident. Not even winded. I've chased suspects before—maybe not at this altitude—and I've caught them without the use of any shock rounds. This guy is no different. Sure, he's got some impressive skills, but so do I. And I'm not about to let him beat me.

"Target him before he reaches the edge of that rooftop," Commander Bishop orders.

I glance at Wink and Blink's topographical map hovering at the bottom of my face shield's heads-up display. Swiping one gloved hand through the air as I run, I bring the map into a full-frame overlay and pivot it to focus on the next building and the gap in between. Measurements appear instantly, along with injury estimates according to the guy's current velocity and predicted trajectory, once he takes his next flying leap.

I curse silently.

"That's a hundred-meter drop to the next building," Bishop observes. "No chance he'll survive that. Shoot him now before you lose him. Takedown authorized."

I grit my teeth. If I shock him, he'll go into seizures, and he's no good to me if I can't get a coherent word out of him. By the time he's able to string sentences together again, he'll be back at HQ under an interrogator's supervision. And I won't be privy to anything they discuss while he's in lockdown.

Because once I pull the trigger, my role will be over. Takedown successful. Wait for the medics to arrive, then call it a night, Enforcer Chen. Go home to your cube, take a hot shower, stream something mildly entertaining to take your mind off work, eventually fall asleep alone in your bed. Wake up tomorrow, rinse and repeat. Leave the real police work to the investigators and interrogators.

No thanks.

"Enforcer, respond." Commander Bishop's tone makes it clear that my lengthy pause was not appreciated.

"Yes, ma'am. Taking him down." I draw my shocker mid-stride with one hand and swipe the topographical overlay aside with the other, leaving my face shield clear for the targeting reticle. Holding the shocker out in front of me with my index finger braced along the gun muzzle, I activate the charger. It whines as it powers up, promising discomfort. Then I increase the volume on my external audio transmitters. "You can guess what happens next, buddy. Save yourself the indignity."

He keeps running. So do I. The edge of the rooftop looms a few paces away for him, a few more for me.

"You won't make the next jump. Stop right where you are, and I won't shoot you. We'll have a little talk instead." I watch him, but he gives no indication that he's heard me.

He doesn't slow down. Neither do I.

The difference between us is that he'll die as soon as he completes that hundred-meter fall, and I won't. Wink and Blink will record the whole mess, and I'll land in his blood somewhere between his brains and his entrails. My exo-suit might suffer a few stress fractures, and I might have to replace it. Worst-case scenario.

But I have to know what he knows. Commander Bishop will be irate, and a well-written reprimand will be included in my permanent record for disobeying a direct order. Worth it? We'll see.

I raise my shocker to give the illusion of following through. I'm about to signal Wink and Blink to descend and block his path with their quadcopter props, usually enough of a deterrent when they're spinning millimeters away from the soft flesh of someone's face. I've got this situation under control.

But that's when the guy casually tosses a grenade over his shoulder. My boots skid across the rooftop as I try to alter course and avoid the blast.

"Enforcer—!" Bishop shouts in my ear, her voice cutting out at the same moment I lose all the data on my face shield along with everything incoming via my augments. Adding insult to injury, my exo-suit locks up, freezing me in place, stiff as a statue.

No last words from my commander as the grenade goes off. No chance for her to tell me how proud she is of her top enforcer, even though my inability to follow orders drives her nuts at times. No opportunity to question the guy before he vaults into the air and plummets to his death. No final thoughts to run through my mind as a twenty-year-young veteran of the human race.

Because there's no concussive blast and no smoke when that grenade goes off. Instead, I'm blinded by a burst of neon-blue light, the type that sparks and sizzles as it expands outward in a localized shockwave, knocking out anything with an electric signal in its blast radius.

I curse as Wink and Blink drop out of the dark sky like dead weights and smash against the rooftop, plasteel drone components breaking off and skittering in all directions.

"Don't jump!" I shout at the top of my lungs, unaided by my audio augments now.

"No stopping me," he calls out jauntily, trotting backward as he approaches the edge of the roof.

Everything is so murky without my visual implants, but even relying on biologic I can make out his shadowy form. Why are his arms spread out to the sides? Are those his eyes glowing in the dark—the same blue as that damn grenade blast? Night-vision ocular implants, if I had to guess. Wink and Blink should have detected them.

Not to mention the grenade.

"Stop right where you are!" I throw down my shocker, useless now, and pull the emergency release on my exo-suit. I tumble out of the thing in nothing but my thermal bodysuit and take off running in stocking feet, straight for him. I should feel naked and puny without the added strength of the exoskeleton, but I'm too angry to feel anything else right now.

Who does this curfew-violating miscreant think he is? And where did he get his hands on an EMP grenade?

"Have a nice evening, Enforcer." He pivots and lunges off the roof.

"*NO!*"

I won't be having a nice evening. Not now, thanks to him.

Reaching the parapet milliseconds after his jump, I fall forward onto both hands, fingers splayed across the brick, and stare after him. Not that I'm going to see much without my augments. Not after curfew, with every light out in every building and along every street, pitch darkness filling every space between the soaring dome above and my Eurasian city below. But I can listen, and holding my breath, that's what I do, straining to hear the impact of his body slamming into a low-riser's concrete rooftop—bones breaking and guts splashing—after dropping ten floors through the air from the adjacent high-riser. In the utter black of curfew's impenetrable darkness, I wait.

Silence.

Until I hear rubber-soled shoes squeaking and then slapping against pavement down there, along with a grunt that echoes up the side of my building. The sound of someone who's made an impossible jump and landed on his feet, only to keep right on running.

This can't be happening.

But it gets weirder.

Goodnight, Enforcer! he calls up to me. Except I don't hear his voice, not with my ears. I hear him inside my head—thoughts that aren't my own. *We should do this again sometime!*

My hands clench into fists. I stare after him blindly, hearing the roof access door slam shut behind him.

Then everything's quiet again, like it's supposed to be this time of night. Lights out. Everybody home, where they belong. Not out and about, running around in the dark. Jumping off buildings like it's nothing.

It's something. It really is. And I have no idea what to make of it.

I exhale loudly, releasing the breath I didn't realize I was holding, and take a minute to calm down. I can't go after the guy. I have to stay here, where my commander expects me to be—right where all my augments went offline. The aerocar she would've sent to retrieve me should arrive in a couple minutes. Standard procedure when a connection is lost between an enforcer and HQ.

I need to stay put. I need to get my head straight.

Scratch that. I've got to get my *story* straight.

Nobody's going to believe this guy took a flying leap and lived through it. Just like they won't believe he made the previous three or four jumps from one building to the next. Honestly, I lost count.

Before my requisite debrief, I'll need to watch the footage Wink and Blink transmitted to headquarters prior to crashing. Bishop should allow me that much. I need to confirm what I saw. But there won't be a record of anything after the EMP blast.

What I heard after he landed that final jump? His voice in my head? Stress-induced psychosis. Nothing else makes any semblance of sense.

A stiff breeze hits me sideways, and I brace myself against the parapet, cringing in my bodysuit. It keeps me warm enough against the ambient cold, but wind chill is another thing entirely. If it keeps up, I'll have to climb back into my exo-suit until the aerocar arrives, just to stay warm.

I retrieve Wink and Blink, carrying one smashed drone under each arm. Crossing paths with my discarded shocker, I pick it up and give it a spin by the trigger guard. Crouching, I slide the muzzle through what remains of the EMP grenade. Not much more than minuscule shards of plasteel.

"You guys let me down," I mutter.

Wink or Blink should have identified the bomb and let me know about it long before we started running across rooftops. Maybe the guy had some sort of lead shielding in his jacket to block their XR capabilities.

The first question my interrogator will ask: "When does a curfew violation escalate into a dangerous foot chase, Enforcer Chen?"

Answer: When that curfew violator has information I need, and he refuses to share it without an idiotic foot chase ensuing. When he's high on dust and nothing can touch him, and he feels the need to prove it to me.

Which he did, in a big way. And I still can't wrap my mind around what happened.

The soft warble of the aerocar's ionic thrusters announces its arrival, as does the minor jet wash stirred up by its vertical descent, gusting across the roof. I back up against my exo-suit and give the vehicle plenty of room to land. It doesn't take up more space than a sedan would, parked on the street. No wings, no nacelles. A sleek flying car with a full complement of powerful engines housed under the chassis.

"Chen?" the pilot says as his door rises, activating the soft glow of interior lights. Two bench seats behind the pilot, cargo space in back. Plenty of room for my exo and broken drones.

"That's me." Judging by the shape of his lanky silhouette, it's got to be Drasko. Low man on the totem pole, the only pilot Bishop would send out this time of night. And the only technician I'd ever trust with Wink and Blink. "I need you to fix these." I hand them over and go back for my suit.

Drasko cradles the drones like babies. "They've looked better. What were you doing up here, anyway?"

"Routine curfew violation." I grunt, dragging the rigid exo toward his vehicle.

"Routine? Right."

"Weren't you watching the big screen back at HQ? We put on quite a show for a little while."

"I didn't fly out of HQ." He places my drones into the backseat and belts them in place to avoid further damage while in flight. "Been out on patrol."

"Didn't realize it was your shift." Maintaining curfew from the air, ensuring lights are out all across the city. Gotta save energy, folks; can't be selfish. "Any noise?" I've got my exo by the shoulder struts, but I could use a little help.

"Calm and quiet in Dome 1—until Bishop's hail." He grabs hold of the boot-braces, and we load the suit horizontally into the cargo compartment. "EMP grenade, huh? That's unexpected."

I pat Wink's frame. "I'm gonna need the XR boosted. These two had no idea the guy was packing."

Drasko nods, lowering his voice. Like it matters up here where nobody can hear us. "Patriot, you think?"

I fold my arms. Now why would I be involved in anything like that? "You know as well as I do, that high-level stuff's for the investigators and interrogators. I issue warnings. Maybe a ticket. Anybody gets unruly, I shock 'em."

"You didn't shock this guy." He sniffs the air. "I'd smell it, if you had."

"What is this? You get promoted to interrogator without me knowing?" I punch him in the bony shoulder and climb aboard the aerocar. Careful not to rattle Wink or Blink, I find my seat beside them and strap in. "I don't have to tell you squat, Drasko."

He grins as he takes his place at the controls. Flipping a switch over his head, he activates the door closure and dims the cabin lights. "I'm not asking you anything they won't back at HQ. Consider this your trial run."

The door seals itself shut with a low whir, and the aerocar lifts off, pitching forward just a bit as Drasko takes us through the night sky at a leisurely pace. Outside, I can't see much of anything with my augments offline. Shadowy forms of domescrapers rise up from empty streets lined by dark buildings of different shapes and sizes. Maybe half a klick away at about the same altitude, another aerocar glides through the night on patrol. A single point of light on the side alternately blinking red and blue gives away its position.

"So, you didn't shock him." Drasko keeps his eyes either on the glowing display before him or the transparent windscreen, using his visual augments to maintain our course and trajectory. "I take that to mean you wanted to have a word with the guy. Instead of the usual untalkative seizures and pants-crapping."

"Never fun for either of us."

"Took me a while to clean up after the last retrieval. When was that? A week ago?"

"Sounds right." A drunk and disorderly curfew violator. I warned him politely to return home. He didn't want to. Thought he'd prove to his buddies what a real hard-ass he was by taking a swing at me instead. I wouldn't say I'm a quick-draw artist, but I hit him with a round from my shocker before his fist got anywhere close to my chin. "Almost good as new in here."

"Thanks for noticing." He chuckles. "So, tonight's violator. High on dust?"

"Prevailing theory."

He curses under his breath. "Hard to believe, right? The stories are one thing. Myths and legends. Nobody takes them seriously, not until you see it firsthand. Then it's like a whole new world's opened up, right there in front of you."

Drasko's twice my age, at least. As far as I know, he's always worked in law enforcement but has never seen any reason to rise up through the ranks. He likes flying, and he likes fixing things. There's a lot he doesn't open up about. Take the scars that run down both sides of his neck like puckered seams, proof he battled the plague more than twenty years ago. I asked him about it once.

"I'm a survivor." That's all he said at the time, with half a grin.

Like that much wasn't obvious enough.

No idea if he's got any family, or if he lost them during the plague. Maybe they're still alive but relegated to Dome 6 with all the other *sicks*.

"We live only now," he often recites the Eurasian credo, "never looking back."

He's seen plenty over the years, and he's told me stories about some of his encounters with dust freaks: unaugmented people seeing in the dark, breathing underwater, impervious to cuts and bruises no matter what abuse they put themselves through. But the abilities are always temporary, active only while they're high on the stuff.

Like my guy who threw himself off that roof back there. I would've caught him eventually, if he played fair.

"Chen?" Drasko brings me back to the present.

"Yeah." I nod. "First time."

"Lemme guess. No exo-suit, but he could leap between buildings without any damage? Maybe even jump off one and live to tell the tale?"

"That's about the size of it. You seen this before?" If he has, he's never said so.

"Not a jumper. Nope, can't say that I have. Pretty sure nobody has." He pauses. "Your boys recorded it, I trust."

I pat Blink's frame next to me. As lifeless as a brick. "Transmitted the first few jumps to HQ, so Bishop will have a record of that. Got a feeling the memory storage on these guys is fried."

One of Drasko's shoulders hitches up noncommittally. "I'll see what I can do about that."

"Fried is fried. Can't undo what's been done."

"Sometimes," he admits. "So the EMP blast wiped out any potential footage of his final freefall."

"Right." As if the guy didn't want anybody knowing the extent of his abilities. Anybody besides the low-level enforcer doing her overzealous due diligence.

City of Glass | 13

"Why'd he wait so long? Could've knocked your eyes out long before he started leaping tall buildings and whatnot."

"Ask him."

"So he survived."

"Pretty sure."

"Just your run-of-the-mill patriot/dust addict/curfew violator on the loose. Another night in the life of Sera Chen." He shakes his head as he angles the aerocar toward the roof of HQ, lit up for his eyes only in IR grids and outlines across the full width of his windscreen. "Bishop's gonna eat you for dinner."

"Early breakfast." I note the time on his display: 0300.

She's there to meet us as Drasko touches down. The wind stirred up by the aerocar flaps her coattails, and she squints against the flailing gusts. She stands just outside the elevator doors with her coat clasped at her throat.

"Ma'am." I nod to her as I step out under the rising side door.

"Commander," Drasko salutes, already out of his seat and retrieving my exo-suit.

"Walk with me," Bishop says, turning on her heel. The elevator doors open automatically, sensing her change of direction—or activated by her sheer force of will. After tonight's weirdness, not much would surprise me.

I glance back at Drasko. He gives me a look that says he's got my equipment covered. He'll get my drones, shocker, and exo all up and running again in no time. My augments, on the other hand, will have to be reactivated by a trained professional of the MedTech variety. Or a robodoc. I'll have to wait and see who's on duty.

"Thanks." I nod to Drasko. Then I jog into the dimly lit elevator right before the doors close.

Immediately, I feel underdressed. Commander Bishop's black coat, high-collared uniform, and shiny boots look immaculate. I've never seen her wear anything else, and she always looks so well put together. Maybe a little severe with the shaved head and steely demeanor, but I've always admired her commitment to law enforcement and the hours she puts in. Not sure whether the woman ever sleeps.

I don't know where to look. I glance at her for a clue as to the direction my early morning is headed—how severely I'll be reprimanded, what I should brace myself for. But she's tough to read, standing with her spine ramrod straight and her arms behind her back, her face set like stone. Her eyes are fixed on the digital display over the polished plasteel doors as the floors count backward from thirty.

My gaze shifts to my dusty stocking feet and the skin-tight bodysuit I'm wearing. Also black, so we have that in common. But so unprofessional. Perfectly acceptable in the locker room; not so much in an elevator with your superior officer.

"Ma'am..." I'm not off to a great start. Because I'm not sure where I should.

"Tell me about your recent promotion, Chen."

"Uh..." I'm about to dig myself further into a grave of stupid comebacks when a lone neuron fires in my brain, alerting me to the fact that she's being ironic. Or maybe sarcastic. Either way, she's not happy, and I know why. "No promotion, ma'am."

"So you're still an enforcer."

"That's right."

"Not an investigator. Not a tracker."

"No, ma'am."

"Your job is to do what, exactly?"

I exhale as quietly as I can without it sounding like an exasperated sigh. "I enforce the curfew."

"Explain."

I join her in watching the digits scroll by. We've already passed the 15th floor, and we continue downward.

"No citizen shall be permitted to walk, ride, or drive about the city between the hours of 2400 and 0500, any day of the week. Lights in all residences, businesses, and government buildings must be off for the duration, along with any other electrical device or machine, unless directly related to life support. The only exceptions are aerial patrol vehicles whose sole purpose is the enforcement of the curfew and assistance in the enforcement of said curfew by officers on the ground," I recite my duty word-for-word from the academy rulebook.

"And why is this curfew in place, Enforcer Chen?"

"To conserve the energy required to keep the Ten Domes fully functional, and to ensure a prosperous lifestyle for all Eurasian citizens." To maintain that precarious equilibrium between the consumers and everything we consume.

Commander Bishop raises an eyebrow as she pivots her head to look at me. Simultaneously, the elevator reaches the 10th floor and eases to a halt. The mirror-like doors slide open automatically, revealing the HQ command center. The big screen mounted front and center displays an aerial shot in IR from one of the aerocars, but not much is going on out there tonight—or in here.

A couple analysts are seated at their posts, brainjacked into their terminals, eyes staring blankly at the screens of code populating and repopulating line by line in front of them as they monitor surveillance data from across the Domes. Otherwise, the place is silent and empty.

"So I don't need to tell Chancellor Hawthorne about your little rooftop pursuit?"

"No, ma'am."

Bishop nods to herself, pensively. "Remind me, Enforcer Chen. Why is it that you were assigned a position with minimal risk?"

Now this is getting awkward. I don't like talking about it. I don't even like thinking about it. If I had my way, I'd go about my life completely forgetting it.

Like I try to do, every freaking day.

"Chen?"

I duck my chin and mutter something I hope she'll assume is the right answer.

"Try again," she says.

"Because I'm one of the *Twenty*."

She nods once, crisply. Then she sets her eyes straight ahead. "My office. Now."

She disembarks from the elevator, and I follow behind, unable to quell the feeling that I'm a kid again, in trouble with the teacher. Bishop doesn't say another word as we pass through the command center, and it's not until we're in her spacious office with the double doors shut that she holds a finger to her lips and activates what sure sounds like a static disruptor. She sets the pen-sized device she withdrew from her pocket on her desk, and it whispers away, masking anything we say with white noise.

Because, apparently, the commander's office is monitored.

"Have a seat."

I'm still staring at the disruptor. "Ma'am?"

She shrugs out of her coat and drapes it over the back of her ergonomic chair, black like every other piece of furniture or tech in the room. The walls and floor are an industrial grey, the wide window behind her desk providing a view of the same urban shadow-shapes I saw from Drasko's vehicle.

"Sit down, Sera. Please." She extends a hand toward the two minimalist armchairs facing her desk. She doesn't take her seat until I collapse into one of them.

"You're monitored, ma'am?"

Chin raised, she lowers herself into her chair, and it molds itself automatically to support her. "You think a commander would be above the law?"

Of course not. I just thought the law would be more lenient toward those who've devoted their lives to protecting it.

"We have two minutes before the Chancellor's analysts will become suspicious. Audio glitches during curfew are not entirely out of the ordinary. We are running on very limited electrical resources at this time of night." She almost smiles, but her face quickly resumes its stoic look, as if pretending that momentary lapse never occurred. "What happened tonight will not happen again. You are too important to put yourself in danger like that,

Sera. All of you are too important. The Chancellor has allowed you to live normal lives—"

I scoff at that. But since time is precious here, I don't elaborate.

Normal. Right. Going to the doctor every month since I was twelve. Being one of only twenty people in Eurasia my age. Going to boarding school with them, growing up with them like siblings, only to be split up across the Domes when we became of age. Not being able to see them or even communicate with them for years now. What are they doing with their lives these days? Getting lectured by their superiors?

"—in time for the banquet."

I curse out loud. Then I cover my mouth.

Commander Bishop is not amused. "Don't tell me you forgot about it."

I've had a lot going on lately.

"Probably can't go like this." I pluck at my bodysuit.

"You can't go anywhere like that. It's indecent." She shakes her head. "Promise me, Sera, that you will be more careful. I would hate to lose you. But if the Chancellor finds out about your rooftop chase and decides the role of enforcer is too dangerous for you, there will be nothing I can do about it. Her word is law."

"And she only wants what's best for me," I mutter.

"For all of us." She gives me a direct stare until I nod. "Now tell me why you pursued that curfew violator."

I glance at the disruptor. Apparently, she wants this discussion to be off the record. "I was following a lead, ma'am."

"A lead. I see. And why did you fail to notify an investigator about this?"

I dry-swallow uncomfortably. "Because it...wasn't an official matter." I lean forward. "But now it is. That grenade was proof he's a dangerous criminal with access to illegal weapons. A terrorist, most likely—"

She holds up a hand to stop me. "Explain this unofficial matter."

Right. No way I could distract her from that.

"I've been looking into..." I drop my gaze. Pick at my fingernail. "My parents."

Silence. Can't tell if it's the judgmental or surprised variety.

She knows.

My heart almost stops. Then it lurches into overdrive.

Before, when I heard that jumper's voice inside my head, I dismissed it as a symptom of high-stress. But just now, I heard two words from Commander Bishop when she didn't say a thing.

Did I read her mind? Of course not. That isn't possible.

The EMP really did a number on Wink and Blink. It affected me as well, and I won't know how severely until I check in with MedTech. Could be just a glitch in my augments, that's all.

So why am I trembling?

"And you thought this curfew violator had useful information." Bishop's tone is flat, like always.

"He said he did."

I cited him for his violation on the street outside a lights-out cube complex and told him to go home. Standard procedure. He smiled casually and apologized with a lame excuse, in no hurry to follow my order. Also standard among some nightlifers who think they're too pretty to obey the curfew.

Then he leaned in to read my badge and said, "Chen? You don't look Asian."

I've gotten that now and then over the years. It usually doesn't bother me. But coming from a loser like him?

I was a professional, so I kept my act together.

"My dad is. Not my mom." Common enough in Eurasia. "Goodnight, citizen. Be on your way."

He winked at me. "They're not your parents, Enforcer Chen."

I should have ignored him, put on the cop face until he made tracks straight to his domicile. Instead, I ordered him to explain himself.

"Trace your DNA." He shrugged, backing away. "Then you'll know for yourself."

He ambled off. I ordered him to stop, but he picked up the

pace instead, grinning at me like an idiot. Then he charged into the complex, dashing up fifty flights to the roof and beyond—with me right behind him.

"Why did you believe what he said?" Bishop brings me back to the moment at hand.

I shake my head. "I didn't see any reason not to. What would he have gained by lying to me?"

"Was this before or after you realized he was a dust addict?"

"Before." I frown. "I had no idea..."

"Your first encounter with one of them."

I nod.

"In ten years on the force, I have never seen anything like that—what he was able to do. Dust addicts in the past have been known for certain...parlor tricks, for lack of a better term. Entertaining, but not altogether dangerous." Her gaze turns inward, as if she's thinking out loud: "It could be that more potent strains are now being produced, with longer-term physical abilities." She frowns pensively. "Or it could all be a lie...everything we've been told..."

"Ma'am?"

Abruptly, she deactivates the disruptor and pockets it. Turning her attention to her desk, she swipes the obsidian surface, and it glows to life, populating with multiple frames of data, images, and muted videos. Without looking up, she orders, "Report to MedTech, Enforcer Chen. Then clock out for the day. Dismissed."

I leave her office, unsure whether I got off easy this time.

2. DAIYNA

5 YEARS AFTER ALL-CLEAR

They're gaining on me.

I grip the steering wheel with both hands and floor the accelerator, squeezing out whatever juice is left in my jeep's solar batteries. A shot rings out, blowing the mirror off the driver's side. That's alright. I didn't need it anyway.

I don't have to look to know how close they are.

Sweat trickles down the inside of my goggles. The heat is oppressive this time of day, the sun a merciless tyrant hovering above. I bounce and swerve in my seat as I maneuver the jeep across a rough patch of lifeless terrain. Then I send up a fresh cloud of dust in my wake as I veer around a boulder and drift the jeep sideways, skidding twenty meters before I even things out and continue westward.

Another shot from one of their rifles, and I duck instinctively. But the round was wide, completely missing my vehicle. And me inside, thankfully.

I should have known better than to try anything in Sector 31. But I couldn't help myself. They've always had the best stuff.

Used to, anyway.

Keeping the jeep steady with my left hand on the wheel, I reach for the 9mm tucked into my belt and pivot to glance over my shoulder. There's nothing but billowing dust back there now hiding my pursuers. Aiming the handgun toward my completely shattered rear window, I squeeze off a couple shots. Not expecting to hit anything behind me, just letting the Edenites know I'm still in the race. And I don't plan on making this easy for them.

Twenty hydropacks. That's the current bounty on my head. Insulting, really—as if I'm only worth that measly amount. But maybe it's more of a reflection on their dwindling resources, how much they're able to pay.

Wanted on a silver platter: the head of the woman who killed their dear Captain Willard.

I can't tell whether they backed off after those shots I sent their way. If they plan on returning to Eden without any punctures in their tires or their special suits, they'd better be more careful. There's an unpredictable female driving this jeep. Not only is she armed, but she's got nothing to lose.

That mirage on the horizon is mesmerizing. If it wasn't for all the jostling around at high speeds and the nerve-wracking gunfire, I might find it relaxing. Stake my hammock in a patch of shade and watch the optical illusion ripple. Let it hypnotize me into a false sense of security.

I smirk at the thought. There's no security on this continent. Anybody who thinks they can make a life for themselves here is delusional. The Edenites are the worst, hiding in their underground paradise and hoarding everything worth having. I wouldn't shed a single tear if they all ended up like Willard, with seven rounds to the head and chest.

But not courtesy of the gun I tuck back into my belt. Ending Willard was one thing. I felt cleansed afterward, relieved, like a boulder I'd been carrying had fallen off my back. And I haven't felt the need to kill anyone else since.

It's probably helped being alone. Less opportunity for someone to rub me the wrong way.

But I'm not alone. Not really. I have my spirit-pal Rehana

riding shotgun. She's the best companion anybody could ask for. Always there during the tough times with an encouraging word.

"Not sure you've thought this through, sister," she says, arms folded as she lurches in the seat beside me. "What happens when you run out of power?"

"Hasn't happened yet." I keep my eyes on the terrain ahead, looking for an abrupt precipice to launch us off and lead the fools behind me sailing through the air—into a horrendous crash landing only I would survive, thanks to my gift.

"You think you can live moment-to-moment forever, Daiyna?"

"It's worked fine so far." My voice sounds raw, my mouth and throat dry. I need to remember to hydrate, but taking care of myself hasn't been my strong suit lately.

"What do you hope to accomplish here?"

Leave it to spirit-Rehana to start up a heavy conversation right in the middle of a challenging situation. It's not like her life's at stake. She's been dead longer than I care to remember.

"Well, for one thing, I don't want those idiots to catch me. In the process, if their vehicle goes kaput and they find themselves stranded out here, that would be a bonus."

"What if your vehicle goes kaput first?"

"Not gonna happen." I slap the dashboard confidently. I've kept this machine running for years. No chance it's gonna crap out when I need it most.

A warning light flashes on the console as the jeep decelerates without warning. It keeps slowing down, no matter how hard I jam the accelerator into the floorboard. I curse, pounding my gloved fists against the steering wheel.

"You were saying?" Rehana chuckles.

"Grab the Colt and extra clip—" I catch myself. "Never mind. You're useless."

Not real good with corporeal things, these spirit-types.

I lean over and pop open the dash compartment in front of Rehana's knees. Fishing around the few hydro and nourishment packs stacked inside, I find what I'm looking for. No, not the flask. That's for later.

"You plan to kill them?"

I've got the 9mm in one hand and the Colt .44 in the other. I must look like I mean business. Mission accomplished. "Only if they try to kill me."

"The bounty's dead or alive, isn't it?"

I face her as the jeep rolls to an eventual stop. "Can I assume you won't be lending a hand?"

She's been decidedly hands-off as of late, leaving me to fend for myself—particularly when I go looking for trouble. Not a single dust devil or whirlwind to help a girl out.

Rehana shrugs, kicking back in her seat. "Wake me up when it's over." She closes her eyes.

The Edenites' jeep slams into our rear bumper, throwing me forward. I curl into a fetal position and stay down as a hail of bullets tears inside through that open window frame in back. The windshield cracks under the impact and fractures, but it doesn't shatter. I swing the Colt forward and break it free, sending the wide piece of plastiglass sliding down the jeep's hood. When there's a brief lull in the gunfire, I lunge out after it, sliding down across the hood as well.

I hit the ground on top of the windshield and roll over, tucking the 9mm into my belt. Then, gripping the windshield with one hand, I hold it up for a modicum of protection and advance on the Edenites.

For future reference, a windshield covered in spider-web fractures is nearly impossible to see through, and this one isn't bulletproof. There are more than a few holes in it already. But it might slow down any additional gunfire that comes my way.

I can hope.

One of them is out of their jeep, standing there in a makeshift suit of armor decorated with old tires. That's the best these people could come up with as far as protection against the elements. After all this time, they're still dead-set against contamination, and without their collared daemons to do their grunt work for them, they've had to venture out of Eden's sealed-off environment themselves for food and supplies.

Score one for the good guys—that would be Luther & Friends. They managed to wipe out every daemon in a thousand-kilometer radius, both the collared variety and the wild. I don't miss those ugly freaks one bit.

But Luther? I miss him. And Shechara, Samson, even Milton. I ache inside when I think about them.

I've got to focus here.

"Drop it!" I shout at the dumbest of the Edenites. He should have stayed inside his vehicle with his buddies and shot me from there, or used a door as cover. Instead, he's out in the open with his assault rifle wavering, not sure whether to pull the trigger. "Right now!" I fire a round into the dust at his feet, and he jerks back a step. "One hole in that pretty suit is all it'll take, and you'll be stuck out here in the real world with the likes of *me*!"

Our silent face-off drags on for seconds that feel like awkwardly long minutes. I don't know how many rounds it will take to pierce his suit. Neither does he, more than likely.

"Shoot her!" shouts the suited figure behind the wheel. He revs the engine like he's trying to intimidate me. Only it's not working.

I send a couple rounds into his side mirror, blasting it to pieces. Fair's fair.

"Are you going to kill them?" Mother Lairen suddenly appears between me and the bounty hunters, her scarlet hair and pale face a sharp contrast to the dusty monochrome around us. She stares at me unblinking, not even squinting under the harsh sun.

"Get out of my way!"

She's blocking my view, even though she isn't really there. Just another spirit-manifestation, supernaturally pulling memories from my brain. Our bunker commander/den mother who turned into some kind of weird religious nut after All-Clear. I thought I'd seen the last of her a while back—but then again, I thought the same about Rehana.

There's no reason for either one of them to be here. I'm beyond their influence at this point. I gave up on the spirits of the earth a long time ago.

"I thought you got it all out of your system," Mother Lairen says with her customary sneer. "After you murdered Arthur Willard."

I fire another round, this time straight through Mother Lairen and into the jeep, shattering one of the headlights. "Your tires are next. Drop that rifle!"

It takes only a split-second for the idiot to do something stupid. He blasts me with a volley that bowls me over, rounds piercing the windshield and thumping into the cracked hardpan all around me. One rips across my shoulder, and I flinch with a groan at the burning sensation.

That does it.

I roll sideways and leap to my feet, kicking the windshield aside. In a single movement, I draw the 9mm from my belt and empty it at the idiot, also squeezing the trigger on the Colt with a steady rhythm, sending .44 caliber round after round into the windshield, the other headlight, the front tire, the driver's side where that Edenite is stupid enough to lean out with his rifle. My last .44 round smacks it out of his hands.

Both of my guns click empty. I stand there in a cloud of dust with the armored idiot lying on the ground in front of me, groaning and cursing. His ride is gone, the driver figuring he can still manage with three functional tires. He's taken off in the opposite direction as fast as he can go, back to Eden.

"Morons," I mutter, shaking my head. If they'd only waited until I needed to reload, they could have killed me easily.

"Is that what you want?" Mother Lairen stands too close to me with that blank face and those eyes as dark as charcoal. "Do you want to die, Daiyna?"

"Shut it." I tuck the empty handguns into my belt and scoop

City of Glass | 27

up the idiot's rifle. Releasing the magazine, I take a moment to survey the rounds. Half-full. Or half-empty. Depends on the day. I slap it back into place and aim the muzzle at his head. "What are you whining about?"

He looks even more ridiculous on the ground than he did standing up. He can't seem to bend his knees, so they stick out in front of him. He's got both of his gloved hands pressed down on his left thigh—apparently, the only part of his suit I was able to puncture after firing all those shots at him. That's what happens when I split my focus.

"It's-it's been compromised," he manages, sounding both terrified and furious. A dangerous combo, if he was still armed.

"That's right." I squint after his buddy's vehicle, tough to see behind that plume of dust it's kicking up. "So now we wait."

He groans, sounding like he just might cry. Because he knows the inevitable is on its way like some kind of faceless predator. All part of this quarantined continent's charm. The mythos, that is.

For Edenites, it's cut and dry. You breathe in the dust, and you get infected by a fast-acting mutagen. It turns you into a messed-up freak of nature, most likely a cannibal. For the natives, those of us who left our bunkers after All-Clear and embraced the survivalist lifestyle, it's less scientific and more supernatural. The spirits of the earth will look into your soul and decide what sort of gift to bless you with. An ability from the animal kingdom, like superhuman speed and agility, or long-distance sight, or underwater breathing—as if that's useful in these parts. Can't remember the last time I saw a body of water. The Pacific isn't too far away, but I've steered clear. Too many raiders crawling all over those shores, loading their loot onto freighters bound for Eurasia.

I shoulder the rifle by its strap and step over to the identical weapon I shot out of the driver's hand. Loose grips sink ships. The barrel's dinged up, thanks to my .44 round, but it'll still shoot fine. It just won't look as glamorous. The mag is almost full. I sling it onto my other shoulder and head toward my jeep.

"You're not leaving me, are you?" Sounds like it's his greatest fear, to be abandoned out here in the Wastes. Until now, it was probably second-place to his fear of becoming infected. Now he's afraid of what he'll become.

The unknown. I'll admit, it's scary. That's why I stick to what I know.

"Pay attention, genius." I nod toward the solar panels on the roof. "They need to charge up, and I need to figure out why the batteries died on me. So we're stuck here for a while, you and me. Might as well settle in."

I drop one of the assault rifles into the cargo area in back of my jeep, and it clinks against shards of plastiglass from the broken rear window. I keep the other rifle handy, swaying from its strap, brushing against my side as I take a breather in what little shade the jeep provides.

"You're bleeding," he says. Nice of him to notice.

"You nicked me. Feel good about that." I apply pressure, one hand squeezing my shoulder. I'll check it out later. Judging from experience, it's just a superficial wound, unworthy of too much attention.

"You're..." He weighs his words. "Daiyna."

"What gave it away?" My lack of an environmental suit. My head covering that wraps around my face, its tail flapping in the breeze. My superhuman ability to fire two guns at once.

"How long did it take...for you?"

"Until I knew I was a sand freak?" I shrug my uninjured shoulder. "Not long."

"How did you know? I mean, what could you do?"

"Nothing you can do about it." Once you're infected, you're infected. Or *gifted*. Same difference. But after a few seconds of silence, I realize what he's really asking. "I could see in the dark. Night vision without the gear."

"No joke."

"Do I look funny to you?"

He doesn't answer. Smart—for an idiot.

"How long do you plan to keep that suit on?" As long as the

air's flowing inside, I'm sure he'll be comfortable sitting in the sun. But once it runs out of coolant and O2, he'll be roasting alive in there. "Not like it's keeping you safe anymore."

He doesn't answer. Instead, he looks like he wants to get to his feet. He's given up plugging the hole and instead presses his gloved hands against the ground, like he's ready to launch.

"Nope." I've got my new rifle pointed at him before he can blink. "You're staying put."

He curses. But he follows orders like a good little Eden Guard. "My people will be back. They'll pile into an armored car and bring more guns than you can handle."

"I'm handling yours just fine," I remind him.

"You might want to get this jeep running again, if he's right," Rehana calls from her seat. "Better to keep moving, out here in the wild."

"Nobody asked you," I snap at her, but she's right. She usually is. I need to check the wiring, see where the battery connection failed. But I also need to keep my eye on this bounty hunter. Too bad I can't be in two places at the same time. "Get out here and watch him."

"I'm good." She stretches, perfectly content right where she is.

"I see how it is," I mutter.

The Edenite is watching me. Real still, like he thinks I might bite him. Or I might have something that's catching.

"Not exactly sane, are you?" he observes.

Well, that was uncalled for. Makes me think I've been too hospitable. No more Ms. Nice Girl.

"Take off your suit. Do it now." I advance on him, aiming my rifle at his head. "You've got ten seconds. Then I start punching holes in that helmet."

"It takes ten minutes to get this thing off—" he complains.

"Then you'd better get started." He doesn't move, so I scream, "*NOW!*"

He stutters backward on his rear end and starts fumbling around, detaching the helmet from the collar first, then unzipping the torso. When he gets up and climbs out of the suit, I see a clean-shaven man in thermal underwear who looks like he hasn't been eating regularly as of late. I suppose an Edenite can have all the electricity and running water a body could want, but when the food runs out, he's no better off than anybody else scratching out a living on the surface.

I know from firsthand scavenging experience: Sector 31, located above Eden, is no longer the land of powdered milk, honey, and treasure troves of goods, materials, and foodstuffs. The UW raiders have seen to that.

"Leave it." I don't change my posture.

He drops the suit to the ground with a thump and a puff of dust. Then he sets the helmet on top of it.

"Now what?" he demands.

I nod in the direction his buddy took, long gone by now. "Start walking."

He scowls, shielding his pale face from the sun with an equally pale hand. Unprotected like that, it won't be long before every patch of exposed skin grows its own crop of blister-bubbles that will eventually break, become infected, and—if he survives—permanently scar.

"You know they won't let me back inside," he says. "Not now."

He's a sand freak in the making.

"And you know he'll never survive such a journey." Mother Lairen reappears in front of me. I would have flinched if I wasn't already accustomed to her spooky antics. "You might as well shoot him. You'll be killing him, either way."

Same old story with her. She always wants me to kill somebody.

"I don't care where you go," I tell him. "But you're heading east, as far away from me as possible." I take another lunging step forward, my rifle ready to inflict some serious misery. "Get moving!"

He backs away, unsteady on his stocking feet. "I doubt your people would recognize you anymore."

That raises my hackles. "I don't have any *people*."
"You used to."
Luther. Shechara. Samson. Milton. My jaw trembles. I clench it tight.
"You think you know me?" I scream. If I didn't know better, I would think I sounded completely out of my mind. "You don't know me!"
"You don't know me either," he says. "Not if you think I deserve to die out here."
Deserve? Who deserves anything anymore? What is there to deserve? It's survival of the fittest. You scavenge, you keep your eyes open, you stay alive. You act like an idiot, and you die.
"Bounty hunters are trash," I grate out. "Twenty hydropacks, right? For my head on a pike?"
"The pike's optional." He thinks he's funny. "I wasn't always like this. Neither were you." He's still moving backward, but his pace is agonizingly slow. "When you killed Captain Willard, things changed."
I want this conversation to end, for him to be part of that ripple on the eastern horizon, for me to have the time I need to fix my jeep and get the hell out of here. Keeping my rifle and my goggles trained on him, I stoop to pick up his suit and helmet. Not happening. Too much for one arm with a wounded shoulder to carry. So I settle on the helmet and back toward the jeep, setting it down inside the cargo area once I'm in range.
"That bastard deserved to die!" I shout, and my voice hangs in the silence for a few seconds.
"Maybe." He has to raise his voice now across the distance. Fifty meters or so. "But not like that. You were his judge, jury, and executioner."
"Yes, you were," Mother Lairen whispers into my ear. "Someone had to make him pay. What he took from you can never be replaced."
"Maybe not," Rehana offers from inside the jeep, "but Luther has a plan."

"Luther always has *plans*." Mother Lairen scoffs. "But they never work out so well, do they?"

I hate the memories that resurface, of us handing over our unborn children in clunky incubators to the United World troops. Rehana never wanted us to be Mother Lairen's cows, the *fruitful wombs* of the future. But having your eggs extracted against your will does something to you. Changes your mind about some things.

"Don't you want to meet your children?" Spirit-Rehana knows just what to say sometimes.

The rage burns inside. My muscles tighten, shaking, but somehow my aim is steady as I fire a warning shot over the idiot's head. He ducks mid-stride, but he doesn't run away. He just turns his back on me and keeps walking.

"At least give him a fighting chance," Rehana says. "Throw him a hydropack."

He's not my concern. The jeep is.

I watch him until I can't distinguish his scrawny silhouette from the mirage in the distance. Then I drop my rifle into the cargo compartment and stuff his protective suit in there beside the helmet. Might bring me something by way of trade next time I pass through Stack.

After reloading the Colt and returning it to the dashboard compartment, I load the clip of my 9mm and tuck it back into my belt. Best to be armed at all times, particularly while I'm under the hood, spending some quality time with the battery array.

Which turns out to be a fruitless waste of time. There's nothing wrong with the connection. The roof panels are fine. It's the batteries themselves. Both the primary and secondary are dead. Annoying, since I checked them just yesterday.

Or maybe it was last week. Time's been kind of fluid for a while now.

"Stupid bitch," Willard sneers. "How have you stayed alive this long?"

He's standing there in his fake fatigues glaring at me with his beady eyes, his stupid little caterpillar of a mustache glistening with sweat.

I pop open the dash compartment, ignoring Rehana because she isn't really there. Neither of them are. Grabbing the flask, I unscrew the top and take a swig. Swallow the burning whiskey and follow it with another, then another.

"Take it slow," Rehana advises. "You haven't eaten anything today—"

"And she doesn't drink anything else," Willard says.

"Shut up! Both of you!" The flask is half-empty. It's all I've got until I can replenish my supply, and there's no way to know when that will be.

Sometimes I drink enough so that my spirit-friends disappear. Unfortunately, I'm not at that point yet. And with all the walking ahead of me, I better keep some part of my head clear.

I load up my guns, my hydro and nutrition packs, the flask, and the idiot's environmental suit, stuffing them all into my extra-large satchel. With my wounded shoulder, I can't carry both rifles, so I take the mag from the dented one. I put on the helmet so I don't have to carry it. I wish I could take the solar panels from my jeep. They'll be ripe for the picking should any marauders pass this way and decide to cannibalize the parts. But if I pick up a new battery over in Stack and am able to return in time, it should be alright. I hope so, anyway.

That's funny: I still have hope.

"So, Stack." Rehana walks beside me as I begin my trek, heading north by northwest. "That's where we're headed."

She can talk to herself all she wants. I'm not saying a thing. The spirit that alternates between manifesting itself as Mother Lairen and Willard has already vanished, probably planning to pop up again at an inopportune moment. Spirit-Rehana is welcome to follow them wherever they went. I really don't care at this point.

"Been a while," Rehana continues. "Sure you'll be welcome there?"

I've got this suit, and I'm willing to trade. I'm sure I'll be welcome just about anywhere there's barter to be had.

"Someone may have heard about Luther, whatever he's up to lately." She leans toward me. "Might be able to give you an update."

I don't want an update. Spirit-Rehana herself could give me one at any time. Her fellow spirits of the earth are active all across the continent, if what she's told me is true, and they communicate via some sort of ethereal telepathy. Even though she's trudging along here beside me, she knows what Luther is doing at this very moment.

Probably sticking his neck out for somebody. Or boring some unsuspecting survivor with quotes from his holy scriptures. More likely, he's trying to sneak onto a freighter bound for Eurasia, a place just as unwelcoming to our kind as Eden, but much more bountiful where food and other necessities are concerned. Rumor has it, the domed cities are as much like life prior to D-Day as you can imagine—and then some. The most advanced human civilization ever in recorded history, contained inside ten massive, self-sustaining biospheres. Millions of all-natural human beings who've never breathed the contaminated air of the outside world.

Or seen sun-bleached skulls like these, spiked into the lifeless sands on lengths of rebar. New territorial markings by the local marauders. Cannibals, if I'm to believe the rumors. Their dominion must be spreading.

As if we need any more dangers out here.

Daylight passes into evening, and the only sound is the rhythm of my boots. By the time dusk falls, I'm still drenched in sweat. I take a few gulps from a hydropack every now and then, just to keep myself coherent. It's already twenty degrees cooler than it was a couple hours ago. As soon as darkness claims the night, it will be even colder, and I'll be shivering with my teeth-chattering like crazy. Something to look forward to.

"She should have waited and traveled in the cool of the evening," Mother Lairen says. Of course she returns to make me second-guess myself. "Then she wouldn't be soaked like this. Her constant movement would have kept her warm. Now she'll get chilled and make herself sick."

Like she cares at all. But if I have to pick an evil ghost to haunt me, I'd choose her over Willard any day of the week.

Too bad I have no say in the matter.

"It would have been difficult for her to find her way after dark," Rehana replies. "She's almost there. She'll be fine."

I curse out loud, bringing them up short. "What do you want from me? Why won't you leave me the hell alone?"

"We care about you, Daiyna—"

"Worry about yourselves. After we're dead and gone, you'll still be floating around this hellscape with nobody left to annoy." I shake my head, depressed by the prospect. "Don't you miss it? Being what you were?" The countless animal species that once filled this planet with life.

Rehana nods. "We yearn for what it was like. In the beginning, the Creator intended for us to be companions of humankind—"

"And look what we did to you." I scoff. Why would they ever want to have anything to do with us after that? Maybe the evil spirits have had it right, all along. "We should be obliterated."

Mother Lairen smiles like a proud mother. "She's beginning to see reason."

Now that's a scary thought.

Almost there. Maybe a kilometer or two to go. Then I'll reach the pile of shipping containers repurposed as a post-apocalyptic trading post.

Stack has grown over the years, from only three of those seven-meter-long containers to over a dozen. The last time I stopped by, not sure exactly when that was, the original trading post had expanded to include a hotel and a bar. There was also a machine shop, apartments for the permanent residents, and storage for goods and materials to be traded. The standing army of twenty gifted guns keeps Stack safe from marauders, and as of yet, the UW raiders haven't seen a need to plunder their stores.

I'm sure that will change once the Sector ruins run dry. For now, those of us without a death wish keep out of their way, steering clear of their regular routes, and the raiders don't bother us.

But as I climb the last hill and approach Stack, even from a distance, I can tell things may have changed. The place looks different.

It's on fire.

3. HAWTHORNE
22 YEARS AFTER ALL-CLEAR

The sun shines through the blue-tinted surface of Dome 1, a warm, radiation-neutralized light that reflects from the mirrored glass of forty-three high-rise buildings and brings to life the lush, green leaves of every tree lining the streets. Sunlight glints from aerocars in mid-flight, hundreds of them floating by serenely in their well-organized lanes of aerial traffic, crisscrossing without incident, ascending and descending to and from various rooftop landing zones.

It's a new day in Eurasia's central hub, the largest of the Ten Domes, and from what I can see, we are starting out strong.

I stand at the glass wall of my office, fifteen square meters perched atop the highest skyscraper in the dome. One hundred fifty floors below, citizens smaller than ants travel on foot, going about their morning routines. This is my daily ritual. I gaze out over my favorite city and bask in the sunlight. My augments are turned off. I rely on biologic with a warm mug of coffee sitting cradled in my hands. I inhale the aroma, and I exhale any concerns I have about the day ahead.

Perhaps I should not have a favorite, but I can't help it. Dome 1 was the first, the biggest and boldest architectural design of its time. A self-sustaining artificial biosphere able to house millions indefinitely. Decades old now, but barely showing its age. The construction of Domes 2 through 10 followed in quick succession as D-Day approached, each connected via subterranean tunnels with maglev trains running between them. Each special in its own way, of course, with a specific purpose; but none of the others was designed to be the nucleus of Eurasia. Dome 1 is the heart, pumping life into every other dome. It is the biggest by far—half a kilometer high, covering over 780 square kilometers of urban cityscape—symbolizing all that humanity still has to offer.

Surrounded by the Wastes of another age.

I seldom look beyond the dome walls. The two-meter-thick reinforced plexicon protects us from the old world. Another world, where things that were once human somehow manage to survive to this day. Strange, alien things. Our missile strikes have failed to eradicate them. Like cockroaches, they scramble about, living in ruins or caves or derelict storage containers. Hiding themselves from the dangerous sun that we, here in Eurasia, have no reason to fear.

We are protected; we are alive, and we are thriving.

We live only now, never looking back. The credo we live by.

I slip my fingers into the front pocket of my tailored vest and withdraw the silver snuff box. It shines in my hand, the morning sun striking its polished, filigreed surface. Popping it open, I take a pinch of the dust inside and inhale it gently, first with one nostril, then the other.

I keep my augments off during these quiet moments to myself, so the effects are stronger. No distractions.

Instantly, I hear a conversation taking place down the hallway from my office. It is Emmanuel, my aide, speaking via audiolink with someone. Thanks to the effects of the dust, I can hear long-distance, tuning in to whatever sound I choose; but this early in the morning, only Emmanuel's voice comes through loud and clear. Perhaps the other support staff have not yet reported for duty. I am an early riser, after all.

I cannot hear whomever Emmanuel is talking to, but I can infer who it is. Other than myself, there is only one person he would be speaking to so earnestly at this point in the workday: his sister, Mara.

"I don't know what you're up to, but this has to stop," he says. "You might be able to fool an analyst once or twice, but not this many times. And you can't expect me to cover for you when you get flagged. The Chancellor will want to know what's going on."

Intriguing. Is Commander Mara Bishop keeping secrets? Does it involve that young enforcer she dotes on, one of the *Twenty*?

I send my supernatural hearing on a sweep of the other offices on this floor, but they're silent. Good. Perhaps it will be a quiet morning. I'm about due for one of those. I drink my coffee. I enjoy my view. I listen to Emmanuel until the dust's effects eventually wear off.

By the time he knocks on my door, I've lost track of the time. I'm not even sure what I've been thinking about. As I get older, I find a certain peace in allowing my mind to go blank—sometimes unintentionally.

"Enter." I set down my coffee and seat myself in the ergonomic chair behind my desk, a black faux-leather model that adjusts itself to support me while, at the same time, squeezing and relaxing various pressure points. At my age, it's quite wonderful.

Not that anyone can truly tell how old I am, thanks to Dr. Wong's regular gene therapy sessions.

The glass door, tinted grey, swings open silently as Emmanuel enters, tapping his temple to end the call with his sister. He is the same age his late father was when I sent him to the North American continent two decades ago. If that version of James Bishop were to walk in at this moment, I would be hard-pressed to tell them apart. But of course their appearance would be the only similarity. Sergeant Bishop was a military man who saw life in terms of mission objectives. Emmanuel is an intellectual in a tailored suit. His sister Mara is an amalgam of the two. I never met their mother.

When James was unable to return from North America a hero, I made it my mission in life to ensure that his two children would be well provided for. They wanted for nothing as they grew up, and once they were adults, I made sure Mara and Emmanuel received career assignments well-suited to their personalities. Prestigious, as well, guaranteeing that the Bishop name will never be forgotten.

As far as I know, neither child remembers being held in that prison during their father's mission. It is the Eurasian way, after all, to live only *now*. Our augments help to keep us in the moment—as long as we remain online.

"Chancellor, forgive me." Emmanuel's voice echoes in the expansive room, the heels of his shoes hitting the obsidian tiles in a hurried rhythm. His eyes have the glazed look of someone referring to information displayed on ocular implants. "I have your morning briefing ready, whenever you would like to begin. I'm afraid there isn't much good news to share, besides the usual updates."

So much for my quiet morning. "Forgive you for what?"

He blinks, restoring his vision of my office—and me, seated before him. "Pardon?"

"You requested my forgiveness a moment ago." I tilt my head to one side. "Explain."

"Oh. It's just that I…" He trails off. Restarts. He's not usually flustered like this. The conversation with his sister must not have ended well. "You look like you've been waiting for me. And I didn't mean to keep you."

"The reason we do not have a set time for these morning briefings is because I have full confidence in you, Emmanuel. You always arrive on time." I grace him with a grandmotherly smile that says I find him endearing as well as entertaining. "Shall we begin?"

He nods, and his eyes glaze over again, as if staring out the window behind me without focusing on anything in particular. Beginning with the regular updates, most of which are strings of statistics, he shares how well crops are growing in the agricultural domes, the percentage of water recycled and purified as well as desalinated from the Atlantic haulers, in addition to waste management, oxygen generation, carbon dioxide diffusion, and other aspects of life that are always important to monitor in a network of self-sustaining artificial biospheres.

Catching his breath, he proceeds to the areas of concern. "Threats in the outlying domes are increasing. The complaints haven't changed, but they seem to be gaining traction among the laborers. Dome 10, in particular, remains the most vulnerable to attack."

I nod. Dome 10 is located closest to the Mediterranean, where our freighters dock to offload the plunder they've taken from the Wastes and the haulers bring in thousands of gallons of ocean water from the Atlantic for processing. If terrorists were to blow the maglev tunnel connecting Dome 10 to Dome 1, nothing from those freighters would make its way in. Dome 10 would become a city of riches while the rest of us languish without access to raw materials, supplies, and saltwater.

"Have these so-called *patriots*—" I cannot mask my disgust at the term. Who do they think they are, naming themselves after the fiends who instigated the events leading to D-Day all those years ago? These people are amateurs. They don't know how good they have it. "—made any specific demands?"

He shakes his head. "The usual rhetoric regarding class structure, unequal pay and representation, labor disputes, and quality of life. They claim the outer domes are peopled with second-class citizens whose sole purpose is to provide for the needs of Dome 1."

Much like the North American Sectors did prior to D-Day. Perhaps they have a point.

"We all must do our part to ensure Eurasia continues to function as well as it has for these past decades. Did someone promise them paradise? A life of leisure? I don't think so."

He almost smiles. "In other news, we have illegal religious protesters stirring up citizens in Dome 6."

Illegal on two counts: being religious and protesting. "Let me guess. They want us to invite the diseased back to live among us, to spread them out among the Ten Domes so we can share their illnesses?" I curse under my breath. There is a reason we keep them isolated. When they show signs of improvement, their level of isolation is reduced until we can welcome them back into society. "Next?"

"One last item," he says, blinking again to restore his focus on the here and now. Apparently, he knows this news item by heart. "Underworld activity. There appears to be a new ringleader calling himself Trezon—"

"*Treason?* Fitting."

"—and dust usage is on the rise. Addicts are becoming a nuisance in certain areas. One led a local enforcer on a rooftop chase just last night. There's video footage I can show you, if you're interested."

The snuff box in my pocket seems more pronounced. But that's just my imagination. As far as I know, paranoia is not a side effect of consistent use.

I clear my throat. "Yes, please."

He swipes his hand through the air over my desk, and the screentop comes to life, projecting a three-dimensional holographic image of the Dome 1 skyline. Two small figures run across the tops of one domescraper after another. The enforcer chases someone obviously high on dust, able to leap from one building to the next without an exoskeleton to aid in either jumping or landing. When the criminal reaches into his jacket and tosses something over his shoulder, the holo-image collapses. My desk returns to its gleaming obsidian surface.

"An EMP grenade." I steeple my fingertips. "They have stepped up their game."

Emmanuel's brow wrinkles. "The dust addicts?"

"The patriots. Who else would have access to such contraband? A mere addict? I think not. No, there is more to this story..." I rise to my feet. "Contact your sister immediately. We need to get a handle on this situation before it spirals out of control. No citizen should have access to a weapon like this, and particularly not an unstable dust freak."

He reaches for his temple to link up with Mara, but he pauses, his hand hovering there. "I don't understand how it continues to breach our walls."

"What?"

"The dust. It doesn't seem to matter how many smugglers we exile. The stuff keeps getting through." He shakes his head. "As long as there's a demand for it, I suppose the supply will continue. And the Wastes are covered in it."

Yes, they are. And as long as I'm Chancellor, there will be no end to the dust trade. It's a harmless diversion. And a lucrative one.

"The priority right now is capturing that addict and quarantining him. Once law enforcement has him in custody, we can find out where he obtained that grenade—and who his dust supplier is." I give Emmanuel a short nod. "Now get Mara on the line."

"Yes, Chancellor." He taps his temple.

Once the audiolink is established, he flicks his hand toward my desk, and another hologram is projected upward. This time, instead of a skyline, the face of a severe-looking woman in a black, high-collared uniform rotates my way. Her head is clean-shaven, her eyes dark and intelligent.

"Chancellor Hawthorne," she greets me without a hint of emotion on her stoic face. A beautiful woman, if she cared to nurture that aspect of her appearance. "A pleasure, as always."

"Commander Bishop." I fold my arms. "Tell me what you're doing about our enhanced terrorist."

She doesn't ask how I already know. "He has been identified, and my operatives are closing in on his location. I will contact you personally as soon as we have him in custody."

"You do that. And delete the footage of his rooftop acrobatics. I don't want it leaking onto the Linkstream and inspiring more of his ilk."

She nods. "Already done, Chancellor."

"That fool wanted us to see him in action..." I tap my chin with an index finger. "We must assume he has associates in the city."

"If the sun smiles on us, we'll catch them all in the same den."

"I'll leave you to it." But I don't disconnect. I watch her for a moment, and she looks right back at me. "The enforcer who chased him down. Was it Sera Chen?"

Mara dips her chin. "Yes."

"I want her on desk duty until further notice."

"Yes, Chancellor." No expression. No alteration in tone.

I nod to Emmanuel, and he ends the transmission with a wave of his hand. Mara's image dissolves like mist under the sun.

"Delete your copy of that footage as well, Emmanuel." We can't be too careful. Such enhanced physical abilities are unheard of among dust users. I should know. "Send out a notice on all channels reminding citizens of the consequences for buying, selling, or using dust. Include images of their fellow citizens enjoying all that VR has to offer."

Why put themselves in danger when they can have the same experiences in a safe, virtual environment? Because it's artificial. The power isn't real, and the human brain knows the difference. VR is nowhere near as exhilarating.

And nothing is more tantalizing than an illicit substance.

It's unclear how the dust works exactly, why it endows its users with a variety of abilities—yet only one per person. I have never been able to breathe underwater, see in the dark, or leap from great heights. As Chancellor, the dust-enhanced ability to overhear any conversation is indeed helpful, and if I believed in a higher power, I might wonder if this ability was tailor-made specifically for me. If so, then the terrorist that Sera Chen failed to apprehend must have appreciated his personalized ability as well, necessary to elude such an ambitious enforcer.

One of the *Twenty*.

"Is everything in order for the banquet this weekend?"

Emmanuel blinks, but he's not emerging from virtual space.

He's confused by the abrupt shift in our conversation. But he covers it well, smiling the way he does when he wants me to know he has everything under control.

"Yes, Chancellor. The Twenty have been notified that their presence is requested. All but one have confirmed their attendance."

One guess as to the only invitee yet to respond. "Sera Chen."

He nods. "I can send her a reminder—"

"She doesn't need to be reminded. She'll be there." I return to my chair. "Well then. If that is all..."

With a nod and slight bow, Emmanuel backs away a few steps before making an about-face and exiting my office. The morning briefing now concluded, he can return to his regular duties: keeping tabs on the analysts and monitoring the data that pours in every hour by the bucket load. If there is anything worthy of my attention, he will let me know.

Or I will discover it myself.

Absently, I pat the snuff box in my pocket as my thoughts drift, pondering what I overheard earlier. Emmanuel feeling the need to *cover* for his sister's actions. What was that all about? Something to do with this enhanced terrorist? Or with Mara Bishop's favorite curfew enforcer?

I tap my temple while simultaneously wiping my left hand through the air over my desk. My neural implants activate another hologram, this one a rotating, three-dimensional diamond. Each facet displays the face of one member of the Twenty. Young. Attractive. High-functioning members of society. Ten male, ten female.

I can't believe it has already been two decades since we brought those incubation chambers over from the Wastes. All twenty of them healthy specimens who have grown up in Eurasia and now reside throughout the Ten Domes, living their lives and contributing to their communities. All of them turning twenty years of age this weekend. What a reason to celebrate.

The banquet will be revelatory for them. They've known they

are special, born at a time when no citizens were able to conceive. After a decade of sterility across Eurasia, they were the first births to follow the Terminal Age—the last generation we thought we would ever see. Emmanuel and Mara's generation.

But now the Twenty will finally learn why they have been so important to us, why there were so many doctor's visits once they reached puberty. I will share with them the joy they brought to so many married couples over the past eight years as Dr. Solomon Wong spliced adoptive parents' DNA with gametes from the Twenty, creating hundreds of newborns from artificial wombs. In so doing, he created our next generation of Eurasians.

Of course, the Twenty could never be allowed to reproduce with one another. Half of them are siblings, after all. Without Dr. Wong's genetic manipulation, the gene pool would be too shallow, with significant birth defects as a result. This way, the children we produce share some genetic material with the adults who raise them, as well as their original progenitors—two males, two females. According to Arthur Willard, all four consenting adults were uninfected residents of his subterranean refuge, and they willingly volunteered their sex cells to be harvested. Such noble individuals.

I reach for the hovering diamond with its twenty facets, displaying the faces I have watched from a distance ever since Dr. Wong brought them into our world. I've seen them grow and mature, taking their place in society, each an exemplary citizen serving an important role in every dome. All of them carefully monitored to ensure their safety. None of them ever placed in situations with even the remotest possibility of danger.

The diamond rotates to display Sera Chen's placid, attractive face. A curfew enforcer. One of the most straightforward jobs in Dome 1. If any late-night revelers give you any trouble, you shock them. Then you wait for a transport to pick them up. By no means do you ever go running after them. If they outrun your shocker, you tag them in IR and send your drones after them.

But that's assuming there are no EMP grenades involved.

I curse under my breath, shaking my head at Chen as if I can show her how disappointed I am. She won't be happy about her desk duty assignment, but then again, her happiness is not my concern. Her ability to continue producing viable eggs is what matters. So keeping her safe is one of my greatest responsibilities.

Why did I allow her to become an enforcer? Why didn't I assign her a role in data analysis or food service? Because the Twenty deserve to live rich lives. And they deserve to have a say in those lives—perhaps to balance out how often they've had no say at all.

They never asked to be our saviors.

When Sera Chen applied to become an enforcer, there was no chance she would ever be working the day shift. Too many variables. Too many people out and about. Too many opportunities for an accident to happen. Chen is ambitious. The best of us always are. But she must learn her place, and at the Revelation Banquet, she will discover why she and the others are so important to us. Why they must be protected.

The hologram collapses like a wave crashing onto shore. But I did not gesture for it to do so. I frown, looking around my office. Everything is silent and still. I tap my temple, but my audiolink is inactive. All of my augments are offline.

A warning klaxon wails down the hall—generated by someone manually turning a crank.

I'm on my feet and at my office door just as it swings open.

"Chancellor—" Emmanuel looks pale. "We need to get you off the premises immediately." He holds the door and backs up a step so I have room to exit.

Two security clones stand in the hallway outside, both wearing helmets with dark face shields and white plasteel body armor covering every centimeter of their bodies. They look like robots, but they are biological organisms able to think independently within defined parameters, planning for every contingency in a situation like this.

"Are we under attack?" I take Emmanuel's arm as he leads me to the nearest stairwell. One clone walks purposefully in front of us while the other follows. Both carry assault rifles at rest against their chest plates.

"Unknown. The power is out, and everyone's augments are down. No way to contact law enforcement or find out what's happening." He nods to himself, keeping calm with obvious effort. "So we follow emergency protocols. Get you up to the roof while the rest of the building evacuates downward."

"So much for a quiet day," I murmur as we enter the stairwell after the lead clone's cursory sweep. We start our climb up the three flights of stairs to the roof access door.

"Ma'am?" Emmanuel says, leaning toward me as if he didn't quite hear.

"The terrorists, you think? Another EMP blast?"

He blinks. The thought has crossed his mind; he just doesn't want to admit it and give them that much credit. They have never been this brazen before. "In order to take out the entire building..."

"Can we assume that?"

"Right. Stick to what we know. This floor is offline, so emergency procedures dictate removing you from the premises on the double."

He's starting to sound like his father, the military man on a mission. I don't mind it.

A cool breeze greets us as we step onto the rooftop. The two clones spread out, rifles at the ready, sweeping the entire area. Dr. Wong's creations, designed for a singular purpose: keeping Eurasia's Chancellor safe. My private aerocar sits on the launch pad like a display model. Sleek white with gleaming blue-chrome accents and tinted windows. But the electromagnetic coils aren't warming up as expected, sensing our approach. They're offline like everything else.

"We planned for this contingency, Chancellor," Emmanuel

says. "If an EMP ever took out all 150 floors, we assumed your vehicle would be affected as well."

"We?" I face him.

He nods, pointing as a black and white police aerocar makes its approach. It swings sideways in midair and sets down beside my vehicle with a gust of air that blows my hair back from my shoulders. I have to close my eyes for a moment. When I open them, the driver's side door is drifting upward, and Mara Bishop is stepping out.

With a gun in her hand.

The tails of her coat flap as she strides forward, firing twice in quick succession. Each round hits a security clone in the middle of its forehead before it has time to assess the situation. They collapse with a clatter, their rifles pointless accessories now.

"You're not safe here." Mara takes me by the arm as if to escort me to the waiting aerocar.

I pull free and retreat toward the stairwell, but Emmanuel is standing there, blocking my path. I bump into him and cringe. This isn't right.

"Chancellor, you have to trust us," he says in my ear. Too close for comfort.

Brother and sister Bishop working together—for me or against me?

"Explain yourself." I jab an index finger at one of the security clones with a bloody hole in its face shield. Mara did not use a shocker to incapacitate it. She used an actual *bullet*. "Why was this necessary?"

"I'll explain everything once we're en route to a safe location. Right now, we have to move." The morning sun shines from her pale scalp. She keeps a hand on the grip of her gun, holstered for the moment. With the other, she reaches for me again. "Please, Chancellor."

I step away from them both and glance back at the stairwell door. A woman my age wouldn't be able to evade these two and make it very far downstairs. It would be undignified. I must maintain my composure and whatever control of the situation I still possess.

Chin raised, I look down my nose at Mara. "How did you know to come here?"

Her stoic disposition falters a moment as she glances at her brother. "One of our analysts monitors your building at all times, Chancellor. If anything out of the ordinary happens, I am immediately notified."

"So when you saw we had lost power, you decided to show up and shoot my security? To make me even more vulnerable?"

"Right now, I trust only the three people on this rooftop." Mara advances a step. I hold my ground. "The localized EMP used on this building is unlike anything we've ever seen. It took out the tech on every floor, organic and inorganic alike. Yet it didn't affect any building nearby, not even foot traffic passing along the sidewalk outside. This means one thing: inside job. So we're getting in this vehicle, and we're getting you out of here. Is that understood?"

I refrain from blinking, instead holding her severe gaze. With a short nod, I walk past her and climb into the car's rear passenger compartment. Without a word to Emmanuel, she returns to the cockpit while he takes the seat beside me. The doors drift downward and lock themselves automatically. As we lift off, I'm unable to turn my gaze away from the two clones lying on the rooftop.

"They were only doing their job," I murmur.

"I suppose they...could have been hacked," Emmanuel offers. Covering for his sister?

"They're clones. They can't be hacked." The disdain in my tone is thick. "That's why we use them for security. Unlike bots, clones are impervious to EMP attacks. They do what they're trained to do after rigorous psychological conditioning."

Mara glances at me. "Once a brain has been programmed, it is susceptible to further indoctrination. Human brain, clone brain, doesn't matter. Either one of those things down there could have been triggered to turn on you without warning."

I shake my head. "It's never happened before."

"Terrorists have never hit Hawthorne Tower with EMPs before." She shrugs. "It's a whole new world now, Chancellor."

"Do you think this has something to do with what happened last night? With Sera Chen?"

Mara clenches her jaw. Have I struck a nerve? "Enforcer Chen's encounter was not an isolated incident. Over the past twenty-four hours, our analysts have recorded electromagnetic events across the Ten Domes. Hitting your tower was the culmination of their efforts, we believe."

"To what end?"

She doesn't reply. Instead, she swipes the display on the vehicle console, tapping in our destination. The gridlines and 3D infrared imaging on that screen are too confusing for me to comprehend. I look away and find Emmanuel staring at me. I give him a questioning frown.

"I don't know how they did it...whoever they are." He blinks, scratching absently at his temple. Unaccustomed to his augments being offline. "I should have known. I should have been more observant—"

"Perhaps." In all my dust-induced aural experiences, I never heard an inkling of anything being planned against my building. "We all should have been more observant."

I watch the streets below. The morning plays out like any other in Dome 1. Orderly. Immaculate. Neither the street traffic nor the air variety shows any awareness of disturbances occurring elsewhere. Everything is proceeding as usual, with no repercussions whatsoever following the recent terrorist attack. No riots in the street, no illegal protesting. Not yet.

It's uncanny.

Mara sets us down on the well-manicured roof lawn of a cube complex thirty kilometers away from my building. A man I don't recognize stands outside waiting for us, holding up a hand to block the gusts of wind stirred up by our landing. When my door drifts upward, I see that he is close to my age but without the genetic modifications that would make him look much younger. White hair combed back, piercing blue eyes. Scarred fingers he extends as if to help me down from a Victorian-era carriage.

"Chancellor Hawthorne," he says with a warm, genuine smile. "I've been waiting to meet you for a very long time. My name is Luther."

4. SAMSON
5 YEARS AFTER ALL-CLEAR

The tractor-trailer tears across an endless stretch of cracked hardpan heading west, sending up dust that billows in its wake. I grip the door's lock-bar on the back of the shipping container with one mechanical hand and wipe my goggles with the other. Glancing back over my shoulder as I sway and shake with the trailer's rumbling movement, I check Shechara's position. She's got her jeep running at full power, following close enough but not too close, keeping ten meters between her grill and my dangling metal feet.

The rig's engine roars as the driver shifts gears, and the gap between me and Shechara widens.

I dip my chin toward the radio clipped to my shoulder. "They've spotted us, Sweetness."

"So now the fun starts," she replies, her voice tinny on the small speaker. She sounds like she might be enjoying herself this time.

I'm a bad influence.

As Shechara's jeep gradually closes the gap, I rip the lock-bar off the adjacent door and pull it open. Immediately, I'm blasted by automatic weapons fire from the guards inside, most of the rounds pinging against my metal arm holding the bar. The rest would have hit the jeep if Shechara hadn't veered to the right in the nick of time. She knew what to expect.

A quick peek into the dark interior is all my enhanced vision needs to count how many raiders I'm up against. Only two. These people are getting cocky.

Think I'll knock 'em down a few pegs.

I toss the bar inside at shin-level, toppling the guards head-first as I step into the shipping container. Their spastic fingers send a few rounds clattering around the steel interior, but they miss my organic parts. Small favors.

"Enough." I disarm the first one within reach and grab him by the front of his armored vest. These raiders are always decked out in the most advanced protective gear I've ever seen, straight from Eurasia. The form-fitting body armor and oxygen-helmets are a far cry from Bishop's bulky suit way back when. "Start walking."

I toss him out the back of the container and don't bother watching him bounce across the ground in an impressive array of lateral somersaults. Seen it before. The lack of any metallic crunch means Shechara steered her jeep clear of the flying body.

We're a well-oiled machine. Our earliest attempts at highway robbery were downright comical in comparison.

"What are you?" The second guard has his rifle pointed at me, but my mechatronic hand is clamped over the muzzle, squeezing and bending it out of shape. His eyes widen behind his face shield.

Have to admit, I always like this part.

"I am *justice*," I growl, grabbing him by the throat and lifting him up to my eye level. His puny boots kick at my metal legs with a series of clanks and clunks. He's got real spirit. "Tell your superiors this road is off limits. No more pillaging."

"Road?" he scoffs. "There aren't any roads in the Wastes!"

"They'll get the idea." I toss him out the back to practice his acrobatics. The landing, in particular.

Two down, two to go: the driver, and the guard riding shotgun. By now, they will have radioed for backup. So we need to grab whatever we can before we're really outnumbered.

The container is piled high with crates of materials and supplies, things you can scavenge in just about every city ruin on the continent. Not sure why Eurasia needs this stuff—other than to make our lives more difficult. They've already fired missiles at the Homeplace and the Shipyard and every other campsite where survivors have gathered to start a new life together. Now, after trying to kill us and separate us, Eurasia is sending in soldiers to steal from us and starve us. Not surprising, I guess.

Hydropacks are worth more than just about anything these days, along with protein packs and vitaminerals. Standard rations. Nothing special to a Eurasian. From what I hear, those domed cities across the ocean have their own farms producing fresh foodstuffs every day. They don't need what we have.

But they take it anyway. Or try to.

"Anything good?" Shechara asks on the radio.

"Plenty." I pick up the lock-bar. No way to know for sure what's inside these crates without breaking them open. "More than we can carry."

"So we hijack the truck. Drive it off their route and bury what we can't take with us."

"Hijack it, huh?" That'll be a first. Usually we smash and grab, then run as fast as we can. "Their reinforcements will track this thing wherever we take it."

"So we locate the tracker inside and deactivate it. Then we leave the truck someplace they'll be outnumbered, where a shipping container like this might go unnoticed."

I can't help grinning. "Sounds like a plan, Small Fry."

Dropping the lock-bar, I thrust both of my arms out to the sides and rotate them at the elbows. One of the benefits of having Swiss Army hands: I'm never unprepared. The metal digits flip inward, and in their place, pivoting outward from each wrist, I now have two blades. I like to think of them as medieval broadswords. Close enough.

Squeezing between the crates and crushing a few inward as I pass, I make my way toward the front end of the shipping container. With two swipes of my blade-arms, I cut a gash in the corten steel wide enough to peel and punch my way through.

In case I didn't already, now I definitely have the attention of the pair inside the truck. The guard leans out of the cab and fires a few bursts from his Tavor assault rifle, sending rounds pinging off my forearms with sparks of light. I duck back into the cargo container and reach for that lock-bar. My right blade retracts into a compartment in my forearm as my metal fingers make a reappearance, gripping the bar like a javelin.

Usually, I try to avoid killing these raiders. They're not the enemy, not really. Their superiors have given them a job to do, and they do it. Efficiently. I've never gotten the feeling that it's personal, that they sit in dark corners during their off-hours and cackle gleefully at the thought of starving North American survivors to death.

But who knows? Maybe that's exactly what they do.

"Stop this truck!" I bellow.

The guard fires another few bursts in my general direction. The driver doesn't slow down one iota. Which is disconcerting, considering the terrain. Wouldn't take much to capsize this rig.

The next burst of weapons fire is too close for comfort. Almost hits my fleshy trunk—the part of me holding all the important wet works. Not that I'm overweight; I'm stronger now than I've ever been. Have to be, lugging these mechanical arms and legs around. Round-the-clock weight training.

"Pull over! Last warning!" I shout.

A few expletives from the guard this time, followed by yet another volley.

I've had enough of this little dance.

I hurl the lock-bar through the back of the cab, and it impales the guard. He slumps out the open window with his arms dangling, the rifle swinging from its strap.

Stepping forward, I plow my left blade through the cab's rear wall, right through the middle, and tear a hole big enough to see the driver. Can't make out the face inside the helmet, but the semiautomatic pistol aimed between my eyes is clear enough.

"We're not stopping," she says, keeping an eye on the barren landscape ahead. Smart, considering its unpredictable nature. One-handed, she steers us around occasional outcroppings of rock, ditches, and soft patches of sand that would send this tractor-trailer pitching off course if given half a chance. Without my mechatronic legs, I'd be having a tough time keeping my balance as we careen along the way. "Now you get the hell off my rig. Or I blow your brains out."

"I've got a better idea." I crush her gun with my right hand and pull it free of her grip. "You put on the brakes, and I'll let you walk away."

For a second, it looks like she's turned to stone at the wheel. Then she nods once and applies the air brakes, trailer first. As we decelerate into the dust she's been kicking up, I flip my left blade back into a mechanical hand and swing myself around the outside of her door. I watch her set the parking brakes.

Then I tear her door off and toss it twenty meters away. Just for show, really.

"Get out." I drop to the ground and wait for her to join me.

She moves slowly, keeping her hands where I can see them. "Why are you doing this?" Sounds like a bit of the fight has gone out of her. I can't see her expression behind the dark face shield, but I have a feeling she's spitting mad.

"I could ask you the same thing." Out of the corner of my eye, I see Shechara approach. She's got a 9mm in both hands, elbows locked in the tactical stance I taught her, muzzle trained on the driver. "You're stealing our food, our fuel and supplies."

"It's not *yours*," the raider scoffs. "It's *ours*. Always has been."

So she might actually be one of those bad apples who cackles in the dark.

"The world's changed," I reply. "North America doesn't exist for the benefit of the United World anymore. Maybe we did, once.

Manufacturing and producing everything for you. But as you can probably tell, now we need it more."

"There is no *United World*. There is only Eurasia." She holds her spine straight, like she's real proud of something. Herself, most likely. "We live only now, never looking back."

"And those who ignore the past are doomed to repeat it." I shake my head at her. She's old enough to know better. "Start walking." I point toward her sore compadres, indistinct shapes in the distance. "We'll bury him."

She glances at the dead guard with the lock-bar skewering him through the chest. A length of steel piercing his heart like that would have killed him instantly. I gave him a chance to cease and desist, and he declined. I'm not thrilled that I ended him, but at least he didn't suffer any.

"We'll find you." The driver side-steps around Shechara and backs away from the truck. "There's nowhere you can take this rig without us knowing about it."

True enough. We don't have the time or the equipment to scan for a tracking device. My arms can do a lot of things, but not that.

"Until we meet again, then." I stare her down, my unreadable black goggles going up against her face shield. Guess we both win.

She walks away without a glance back, in no hurry to meet her bruised and battered pals. That pristine suit of hers will be as dusty as theirs in no time. It's obvious she's been behind the wheel for a while, not getting her boots dirty.

"Bury him?" Shechara inclines her head toward the dead guy.

Not now. We've got to get moving if we want to reach Stack before the raiders' reinforcements show up.

"Once we get to where we're going." I shrug my shoulders of flesh and bone. "If we can find the time."

"You big softy." She turns her goggles toward the retreating driver and tucks the 9mm into her belt. She keeps one hand resting on the grip, just in case. "Sure you can drive this thing?"

My grin is lost behind the head covering wrapped around my face, but I can't help it. I smile anyway. She has that effect on me.

"Girl, there's nothing on this wasted continent I can't drive. You know that."

"Have you driven one of these before?"

"Well, no."

"So this could be the first time you're stumped?" There's a playfulness in her tone.

"Let's get moving."

She skips toward me and stands on tip-toe, and I bend at the waist. Takes some effort, but we've figured out how to deal with our height difference. She's fun-sized, I'm cyborg-monster-sized, but somehow we make it work. Once the sun goes down, we won't have to kiss like a pair of mummies, pressing our lips together with these dusty head-rags in the way.

"I'll follow you, big guy." She pats my chest and returns to her jeep.

She'll keep an eye on our six while I steer this rig twenty klicks north, toward the only place other than the coast where shipping containers are a common sight. Once we're there, the locals will slide it off the flatbed to sit beside others of its kind. Then I'll ditch this tractor-trailer as far away as I can in the opposite direction. The last thing I want to do is draw any unwarranted attention to Stack. So far, they've managed to survive without earning the enmity of the UW raiders. Or *Eurasian*, if that woman's right about them no longer thinking of themselves as hailing from the United World.

Must be nice to be whatever you want to be. Reinvent yourself.

My gaze falls on my mechanical hands, metal digits curled around the rig's steering wheel as I sink into the driver's seat. I suppose I've gone through a couple rounds of reinvention myself.

"Strongman, this is Eagle Eye, over," Shechara's voice comes through the radio clipped to my shoulder.

I'm grinning again. "Trucker names?"

"Thought it was appropriate, considering."

"My thoughts are somehow inappropriate at the moment, Eagle Eye." I release the brakes and rev the engine, allowing the truck to roll forward as I get a feel for how it handles. Starting out slow before I ramp things up. "How about you and me schedule a passionate tryst in this here trailer, say 1500 hours? Clothing optional?"

Her laughter is music. "How about you keep your eyes on the road, Strongman?"

Probably a good idea. But I'm already thinking back on our most recent delightful encounter—when was that? Yesterday morning? Last night? It was dark out, either way. She was incredible, as always. Said I warmed up my metal parts to the perfect temperature, just the way she likes it. Then again, she always says that.

She's never cringed away from my inorganic limbs. And I've never looked away from her eyes. Because they're beautiful, like polished silver and diamonds. Rare. Valuable. Unlike any other eyes on the planet. When she looks at me, I feel—

The engine makes an awful grinding noise as I shift gears, and the rig shudders so much I'm afraid it's going to stall.

"Is that a normal sound, Strongman?"

"Not a good one, Eagle Eye. Maybe I should call you Eagle Ear."

"Pretty sure everybody over in Stack heard that."

"Then they'll know we're on our way." The truck lurches forward, and without warning, it's off, rolling right along and gaining speed. "Hope you can keep up."

"Roger that, good buddy. Eagle Eye out."

I glance at the side mirror but can't see her jeep. Probably in my blind spot. And the screen of dust I'm kicking up isn't helping the view any. Best to focus on what's ahead.

I take the rig at half-speed off the beaten path traversed by the raiders on their trips to and from the coast. That unpaved road-of-sorts was uneven at best. This is untamed wilderness, and it's downright bumpy. I have to strap in just to keep from bouncing out of my seat.

"You go much slower, Strongman, and we might be able to welcome the raiders' reinforcements in style. Just the two of us."

"Thought you said *out*. That usually implies an end to the conversation."

"Am I distracting you? Does my big, strong man need to focus all of his attention on driving right now?" She's using that pouty voice she reserves for my grumpier moments. When I'm taking things too seriously.

Like when I'm hijacking a UW tractor-trailer.

"How're we looking, Eagle Eye? Any bogeys?"

"None to report. Will keep you posted. Eagle Eye out."

I wait for her to come back on the line, but she doesn't. And for the next ten klicks, the ride is uneventful—except for being a literal pain in my ass as I jounce and lurch, upping the speed just enough to make better progress without overturning the trailer. Or jackknifing. Wouldn't want that, either.

"No raiders in sight, Strongman," Shechara provides the half-way-point update.

"If you're not seeing them, they're not there, Eagle Eye."

"True enough."

Sometimes it's hard to believe she was that shy, quiet woman I met five years ago. Tough to get a word out of her back then. She and Daiyna were as tight as sisters, and they always had plenty to say to each other. Words mostly, but sometimes just expressions, like they shared a secret language.

We've all missed Daiyna. Luther loved her, I'm pretty sure. But Shechara lost a part of herself when Daiyna went off on her own.

Guess I was there when Shechara needed a friend. We bonded. Finding out we had ten kids generated in test tubes should have been enough to drive us apart, but it had the opposite effect. We talked about them, about maybe meeting them someday. Seeing who they look more like, me or her. We both agreed they should look like her, for their sake.

Back in the bunker, and even after we climbed out, I always dreamed of having multiple wives. Made sense, since we were the breeders, and it would be our job after All-Clear to repopulate the planet. Or so we were told. But Shechara is more than enough woman for me, even though she's only half my size. She's the other half I never knew I was missing. And now I can't imagine my life without her in it.

Being the closest thing to a preacher anywhere on this continent, Luther performed our marriage ceremony. That was seriously the happiest day of my life. Sometimes we talk about going back there, meeting up with the others. But I don't think we will. Better to hold onto the good memories of what things were like before the missile strike.

Two dirt bikes appear from behind a pair of boulders, one at my ten o'clock, the other at my two, fifty meters ahead in the late afternoon's fading light. Motors grinding, they kick up clouds of dust on approach. Chunky tires skid across the hardpan once they've cut the distance in half. Chugging idly, they sit there, each with a Wastelander in the saddle.

These marauders are a different breed. Nobody knows where they come from or how they de-evolved into insanity. Maybe they lacked a community of right-minded individuals seeking the common good instead of survival for its own sake. They don't seem to care about building a better life or fighting back against the UW raiders. Instead, they've embraced the late 20th century's vision of a post-apocalyptic lifestyle.

I may have watched a few of those films in the bunker. More than once.

"We've got company," I tell Shechara.

"I see them." Her jeep sidles up alongside the rig as I slow it down, balancing the trailer brakes with the truck's. "Not from Stack."

"Agreed." We're about five klicks away. Usually, Stack's sentries hold a perimeter a kilometer out.

The Wastelanders keep their hands on the grips of their dirt bikes. They face me in their bleached-white skull-masks, grinning with all the personality of a Jolly Roger. No way to tell what expressions hide underneath. Black goggles cover their eyes, and a bizarre amalgam of body armor, sandcloth, bones, and manmade feathers adorn their bodies. I assume the feathers are synthetic, since nobody's seen any birds around since before D-Day.

I set the parking brake once I'm within a few meters of their front tires, but I keep the engine running. I don't plan on staying here for long. If these fools intend to hijack a hijacker, they're in for a rude awakening.

"A little early for Halloween, don't you think?" I shout, leaning one mechanical elbow out my window. Then I give them a nod through the windshield. Neighborly, but not interested in leaving my seat.

"Halloween." They glance at each other and shrug. Then the one who spoke points at my silent passenger—the dead guy with a lock-bar through his chest. "Nice costume."

"You from Stack?" I say.

They shake their heads. Didn't think so.

"You're trespassing," says the Wastelander. "You have to pay the toll."

"This your land?"

They both nod.

"Funny." I pause. "Didn't see any signs posted."

The quiet one reaches behind his back. But he's not going for a weapon. Instead, he's got a length of rebar in one hand with a human skull mounted on top. He plants the thing into the ground, marking their territory.

"This is the way of things," he says.

Simultaneously, they reach for their belts. Slow and easy. Going for gunmetal now.

I grab hold of my dead traveling companion and haul both his arms and his assault rifle inside the cab. As the two Wastelanders draw their revolvers and aim our way—one at Shechara's jeep, one at me—I plow my left arm through the rig's windshield, popping it free and sending it sliding down the engine compartment. At the same time, I aim the dead raider's Tavor at them.

Oddly enough, they don't seem surprised.

"Half your load or half your woman," the first Wastelander says, slouching behind the .45 caliber muzzle of a classic Desert Eagle. His partner is a mirror image. "We decide which half."

Easy choice.

"Not my load. Help yourself." I rest the Tavor on the dashboard, keeping it aimed between the two bikers. "Back door's already open."

"Put your gun down."

"Not mine either." I don't move it. A sidelong glance is all I need to see Shechara in her jeep with her 9mm out, ready for action. "Unless you've got backup, you'll want to hurry. The raiders we hijacked? Their reinforcements are on the way."

They have no response to that—other than looking at each other and sitting up straighter in their saddles. I could shoot them both right now. But one of those super-sized revolvers is pointed at Shechara, and I can't risk a knee-jerk trigger-pull. I'm sure she's got a headshot lined up, and I'm equally sure she won't take the same risk where I'm concerned.

"Deactivate the tracker," the Wastelander says, proud of himself. Problem solved, he thinks.

So, he doesn't have any backup.

"Would if I could. Don't have a scanner." I shrug. "We've got all kinds of good stuff up for grabs. What're you waiting for?"

They look at each other again, skulls gaping. Then, in unison, they pivot their muzzles skyward and raise their other hands as if to say no harm, no foul.

"Aw, they don't want a fight," Shechara says on my radio.

I keep the Tavor pointed their way. "Change your minds?"

Both Wastelanders holster their giant revolvers and nod to me, pushing with their boots to back up their bikes. They stop once my path is clear again.

"See you in Stack," says the second one.

Wouldn't surprise me if they were able to speak telepathically to each other. Stranger things have happened on this continent.

Revving their motors, they swing their bikes around 180 degrees in an impressive display of road warrior skills and tear off in the direction we're headed.

"That was weird," Shechara says.

"Those types usually are." I release the parking brake.

"I couldn't see them lying in wait."

"They were hiding behind solid rock. Far as I know, you don't have x-ray vision, Sweetness."

"I should have noticed something. Heat signatures."

"Don't let it get to you. All kinds of uncanny abilities are sprouting up these days."

"Maybe." She doesn't sound convinced.

We cover the next four klicks without any raider or Wastelander sightings. When the three Stack sentries eventually stop us with hands raised in the universal gesture for *halt* and their rifles aimed at the ground, we comply.

"Samson? Been a while." I recognize Barrett, the leader of the pack, by his voice and build. Like Shechara and me, he's got his head and every other patch of skin covered. Unlike the Wastelanders, he doesn't sport any bones, armor, or feathers. "You got something to trade?"

He approaches my door and waves amiably at Shechara parked behind me.

"Believe so." I nod over my shoulder. "You wouldn't happen to have a scanner on you?"

He signals one of his compadres, and the sentry retrieves a device from under his jacket. As I figured, they make a habit of examining anything headed into Stack. Without a word, he holds the scanner out toward the tractor-trailer and starts walking along the side, headed toward the back.

"You got one of 'em." Barrett nods toward my passenger.

"His choice."

"Thought you might lead his friends our way?"

"Figured you could take 'em."

Barrett leans his head to one side, weighing my answer. "Or we could turn you away."

"Fifty-fifty chance, as I saw it."

The trailer reverberates with thuds from the sentry's boots as he hops inside, hunting for that tracking device. I have a feeling Shechara is keeping her eye on him. And her 9mm, just out of sight. Can't be too careful with anybody these days.

I make out the faint, high-pitched beep of the scanner as it closes in on its target. Hidden somewhere underneath all those crates back there.

"Maybe you don't like the arrangement we have with the raiders?" Barrett says.

"Figured you had some kind of deal."

"Fifty-fifty." There's a smile in his tone. "Half of everything we scavenge goes to them. In return, they leave us alone to scratch out our existence." He turns as the sentry with the scanner approaches. The guy holds a tracker in the palm of his hand. "Deactivated?"

The sentry nods. Then he tosses the device up to me. I catch it in my left hand, metal clinking against metal. Keeping my goggles trained on him, I crush the thing to pieces and let them rain onto the ground. Now there's no doubt about it.

"Here's how you're going to proceed," Barrett says. "Drive that shipping container into Stack and drop it off. You're welcome to take whatever you can carry in your jeep. The rest stays with us."

"Fair enough." It's not, but I don't plan on whining about it. Anything we scavenge is more than we had before.

"Then you drive this rig as far away from us as you can, drive it until you run out of fuel. I don't care where. You leave it there. Got me?"

I give him a slow nod. It's understandable that they wouldn't want any trouble with the UW. *Eurasia*. Sounds like they're enjoying a fragile truce. I don't want to spoil that for them. Peace is as rare as water these days.

Barrett steps back, and his sentries clear the way. He waves us through, and I give the accelerator a nudge, crossing the last kilometer of ragged terrain before we reach Stack. Shechara follows close behind.

It's hard to miss, even half a klick out. A dozen corten shipping containers—some single-story, some piled two-high—tend to be noticeable on a dust-covered moonscape. Barrett must have radioed ahead that we were on our way, because by the time I pull up into the center square, half the townsfolk have gathered in the dusk light to welcome us.

Stack-style hospitality.

Before I've even thrown open my door and stepped out, they've got a crane in motion and are disconnecting the shipping container from the trailer. Half a dozen Stackers with crowbars are already inside, and the rest have arranged themselves into a line, passing packages of supplies and foodstuffs from one person to the next.

Shechara climbs out of her jeep and joins me. We stand there watching, not sure whether we're expected to lend a hand in the unloading process.

"Talk about a well-oiled machine," I mutter.

"Yes, you are." She nudges me.

I reach an arm around her and gently pull her close. "Now about that tryst..."

She giggles. I'll never get tired of that sound.

Darkness falls by the time the locals have finished doing what they do best: stacking things. But as they reach the very last crate in the far corner of the shipping container, one of them lets out a hoarse yell.

"*Tracker!*"

Barrett's sentry already found one earlier. So there must have been another. Somehow, he missed it.

Damn.

Everybody scatters, running in every direction—away from the shipping container, away from all the good stuff it held, away from Stack. I've got Shechara on my back like a pilot riding a battle mech as I outpace them all, hurling myself into a sprint, pounding my metal legs into the earth and lunging, straining for longer strides that will carry us both to safety.

When the missile hits, everything around us is fire and blinding white.

5. SERA
22 YEARS AFTER ALL-CLEAR

Too many voices.

I can't shut them out, no matter how hard I try. Loud music, pillows stuffed against my ears, even screaming—nothing helps. I hear them inside my head, thoughts that aren't mine. A maelstrom of desires, worries, hopes, and fears that I don't share.

It's dark in my cube. Lights out, window set to opaque. Dawn must be breaking. People are waking up. That's why I'm hearing so many voices, so many thoughts. Because my neighbors are greeting the day.

I never reported to MedTech. My augments are still offline. Or are they? Did that EMP change them somehow? Turning me into a...*telepath*?

When I heard Commander Bishop's thought pass through her mind, in that instant I knew something weirdly familiar was going on. The same thing happened with that jumper: *Goodnight, Enforcer!* he called up to me. But I didn't hear his voice, not with my ears. He was inside my head, just like these voices are now.

It's brought back memories I haven't thought about for years. Of being a little girl, before I was old enough to have my augments implanted. Of hearing my mom and dad's thoughts, knowing what they were going to say before they said a word.

Or were those just dreams? My childhood is blurry, always has been. They say it's common for most Eurasian citizens, that memories tend to be cloudy prior to augmentation. The mind itself is so malleable during our early years; it's only once we've reached maturity that our brains have settled in their growth and development and are able to handle the neural implants.

With my augments offline, you'd think I would feel lost, exiled from the data stream. Lonely. But not at all, thanks to this storm of voices crowding my mind.

I roll over in bed and hurl my pillows across the cube. They weren't helping. I sit up, hands clasped to my head, squeezing.

"Go away," I murmur. "Please, go away..."

I really should report to MedTech. Something is seriously wrong. But I make no move to get dressed. I just sit here in the dark, the noisy silence, as if I'm waiting for something.

They're not your parents, Enforcer Chen, the jumper said. *Trace your DNA...*

They love me more than anything. I've always known that. They raised me, providing for me and protecting me, and they supported me as I grew up, guiding me to make my own decisions and live my own life. They're my parents, as much as two people could be. But are we biologically related?

I've often wondered about that. My dad being Chinese, my mom Anglo, you'd think I would display an equal ratio of Eurasian characteristics. But when I look in the mirror, I don't see a resemblance. Honestly, except for my dark hair, I don't look like either of my parents. I sound like them in the cadence of my speech, and I catch myself moving like them sometimes. But that could be due to nurture instead of nature.

Then there are those fuzzy, dreamlike memories. Knowing their thoughts as they looked at me and smiled with pride and affection. They longed for me to be their own. They felt like they were my caretakers, that no matter how much they loved me, they wouldn't be allowed to keep me. I would be taken from them someday. Maybe all parents feel that way at times, but this was a constant, deep-seated sadness that festered behind every smile.

City of Glass | 71

Could I really read their minds? Is that what's happening now? If it has nothing to do with a glitch in my augments, then maybe this is an ability I was born with. And once my neural implants were installed, they kept me from being able to fully access my—

"Stop." I grit my teeth, clench my hands into fists and pound them against my mattress. "Get a grip!"

I have to silence the voices. Somehow. I can't go through another minute of this.

"Shut up!"

My voice hangs in the silence, sounding like it belongs to a crazy person. Good thing these cubes are soundproof, or my neighbors would have reason to worry. I can hear their thoughts, but they can't hear me scream. That's not fair at all.

Growling, I get up and stomp over to the window. With a swipe of my hand, the black tinting fades, allowing the morning light inside. It's a sunny day in Dome 1, and the air traffic outside is already on the move, aerocars casting brief shadows across me as they glide past. I glance down at the street, twenty floors below. Plenty of ground traffic as well.

I pull the single chair out from my dinner table and sit. The faux-wood seat is cool against my bare legs, giving me goosebumps. But the sun is warm here by the window, and I close my eyes as I bask in it. The voices haven't diminished any, but they haven't gotten worse. So that's something.

It's easy to dismiss them as garbled gibberish. But if I really focus...I can make out individual thoughts:

Can't be late...What will she think?...I don't remember that being there before...What's the point?...I am so happy...This pain will never end...They're never going to forget this...I don't know what to do...

On and on, narrowed down from hundreds of thoughts to dozens, then to only a few, then—

It's working. They're quieting down.

How am I doing this? It feels like I've activated a dormant skill; I must have had to do this before, a long time ago, just to be able to function. I cull the stampeding herd until all I'm left with are my own thoughts. The voice in my head is the welcome traveling companion I know best. The interior monologue of one Sera Chen, Law Enforcer.

I take in a deep breath and let it out slowly. The tight muscles in my neck and shoulders start to relax.

The console on my dinner table bleeps. The search is complete.

If my augments were working, I wouldn't have to use this outdated device. These clunkers are usually reserved for senior citizens with no desire for implanted tech but who still want to access the Linkstream on occasion and ride the current.

My DNA search found multiple results, citizens located in just about every Eurasian dome. I have quite a few relatives, apparently.

But my parents are not listed among them.

Not sure how I feel about that. Am I surprised? I've had an inkling for a while; I just chose to stuff it in a deep, dark recess of my mind that I refused to visit. Now I understand their unspoken heartache, and it hurts me, too. They were my parents; they will always be my parents. Even though we're not related by blood.

I don't feel lied to, not by them. I could never blame them for this. They were allowed to adopt me because they've always been model citizens. But someone deceived me.

Squinting at the sunlit screen, I scan the rows of faces. These people share my DNA, but I have no idea who they are. I dig a little deeper into the search results. Nine of them are my age. Exactly my age. The rest...

Are children.

Dozens and dozens of children, ranging in age from a few months old to a few years. My birth parents have been busy, it would appear. And they must still be out there, whoever they are. Somewhere in the Domes, reproducing like nobody's business.

I frown at the results. No, that can't be right. The nine citizens my age—they're the oldest in the search results. There's no one listed who's old enough to be my birth parents.

I'm beginning to recognize some of these faces. Sort of. As if the children I grew up with had their images age-progressed to adulthood. Are these nine members of the Twenty? I haven't seen them in so long—

A sudden alert flashes across the screen. My first thought: one of the analysts has caught me snooping around where I shouldn't be, using my enforcer retrieval code for data I have no business retrieving, since it's not work-related. But that's not it at all.

This is a dome-wide emergency alert. Hawthorne Tower has been attacked. A massive EMP burst has knocked out the power on all 150 floors. Every Dome 1 enforcer, even the lowly curfew-type, is to report for duty on the double.

I swipe my hand across the console screen, clearing its history, and launch out of my chair, kicking it over accidentally. As it clatters across the faux-wood floor, I grab my uniform off the wall hook and pull it on.

My neighbors have seen the civilian version of the emergency alert via their neural implants. How do I know? That's right. I can hear their thoughts spiraling out of control.

In a situation like this, your average citizen is to remain indoors, either at work or home, to avoid clogging the streets and air with traffic, leaving those transit zones free for enforcers to patrol. Except there has never been a situation like this. Not in reality. We've trained for it, working through various scenarios in VR, but it's never happened. No one has ever attacked a government building in Eurasia.

Patriots.

That word keeps cropping up in my neighbors' thoughts. Many of them are happy they won't have to go to work today and can wile away the hours in virtual reality instead. But most are worried. If Hawthorne Tower—the most secure government structure ever built in the heart of Eurasia—is vulnerable to terrorist attack, then how can anyone be safe anywhere? Even at home in their cubes?

There's a knock on my door as I finish getting dressed. My holster is empty, and I don't have a spare shocker. I'll have to requisition a replacement at HQ.

Another knock. Probably Drasko or one of the other retrievers sent to pick me up. No way Bishop would allow me to walk to work on a morning like this. Gotta keep Sera Chen safe, after all.

"Open," I give the voice command for the door, and it slides aside, revealing a stranger standing in the dim interior hallway.

Strange, but familiar. The last time I saw him, he jumped off a very tall building.

"Hold it!" My hand drops instinctively to my holster. Then it freezes there.

"Enforcer Chen." He smiles, hands raised shoulder-high in mock surrender. "Thought you might be home."

"How'd you know I live here?" He's obviously stalking me.

"Everything's on the Link—if you know where to look." He wiggles his right hand. Clasped against his palm is an old phone, another antiquated device favored by the senior citizen demographic. But this guy is close to my age. "You really should do a better job of covering your digital tracks. I'd expect more from an enforcer." He chuckles all of a sudden. "But then again, you're just the curfew variety. Low on the totem pole, I assume?"

I keep one hand on my holster, that hip pivoted away from him. If I'm lucky, he hasn't noticed that it's empty. I point the index finger of my other hand at his face. "Turn around, put your hands behind your head, and interlock your fingers. Right now."

His smile fades. Confusion clouds his eyes. He thought he was having fun. Sorry to disappoint.

"You ran the search." Another wiggle from his phone hand. Then something worse: *They don't share your DNA.*

I stumble back a step at the intrusion—his voice in my mind. Not like when I overheard my neighbors' random thoughts. Instead of a bizarre fluke, this is intentional, like last night. He projected the words into my head in lieu of speaking them out loud.

"I'm sorry." He holds a hand toward me, his brow knitted with concern. Not a bad act. "But you heard me just now, right?" He taps his temple. "In here?"

"You a dust freak?" That would explain it. He's high on the stuff, and in addition to jumping skills, the dust has given him the ability to speak telepathically. And I get to be on the receiving end of his *parlor trick*, as Commander Bishop called it.

Lucky me.

"I've never inhaled the stuff." He's rocking the sincere look now. Guy must have taken some acting lessons. "Never needed to. Once I had my augments removed, my abilities manifested themselves all on their own."

"Why are you telling me this? What are you doing here?"

He takes a step through the doorway into my cube. Bad move.

"Stop right there. Turn around and—"

Instead, he slides the door shut behind him and gives me an apologetic look. "Don't want your neighbors getting curious."

So now I'm trapped in here with him. He's taller than me by half a meter, stronger by a few kilos of muscle. No idea whether he's had any combat training. But if he's been snorting dust, there's no telling what else he might be able to do.

I take my chances and drop to the floor, sweeping out both my legs in a scissor-kick that sends him toppling forward. Like an idiot, he tries to catch himself with his hands, exposing his ribs—which I plow an elbow into as I roll over, dropping him onto his chest with an agonized exhalation of air. He doesn't resist as I straddle his back and snake my arms around his throat in an unforgiving headlock.

"Answer me," I grate out, my lips close to his ear. "What the hell are you doing here?"

"Like old times, eh Sera?" he manages hoarsely. "At Camp Hope—remember those days?"

"You don't know me. You don't know anything about me.

You're a dust freak and a terrorist." I cut off his air supply. "Now tell me about the Hawthorne Tower incident."

He slaps the floor like a wrestler tapping out. I let him breathe. Just a little.

"I didn't have anything to do with that," he manages.

I curse. "So you just happened to have an EMP grenade last night, and now, less than twelve hours later, patriots hit the Tower with a massive EMP burst. You're saying there's no connection?"

"I have a feeling you'd like there to be one." He clears his throat. "I assume your augments are still out? If so, we're in close enough proximity for you to notice I'm unarmed."

"What does that matter?"

"Maybe you could let me sit up and breathe for a bit?"

"You stalked an enforcer to her home and entered her cube without permission. That's more than enough to keep you pinned to the floor."

"As long as you're enjoying yourself. I just have to wonder how long you intend to hold me like this. Without functioning augments, it's not like you can call for backup."

He has a point there. I glance at the console on my dinner table.

"Want to borrow my phone?" He gives it yet another wiggle.

"I wouldn't know how to use that old thing."

"Let me call for you—"

I squeeze his throat, turning his voice into a pathetic wheeze. "Tell me what you're doing here."

"Investigating," he rasps.

"What?"

"Who." His chuckle sounds like it belongs to an old man. "You, Enforcer Chen. I take it you don't remember. My face has changed a little, but I was still hoping you'd know me." *We took a long trip together before we were born...*

I pull away from him at the unwelcome telepathic projection, inadvertently loosening my hold on his neck. He twists with the speed and agility of a trained athlete, gripping both my wrists and rolling me onto my back. The antique phone clatters across the floor.

"I won't hurt you," he says, staring down at me. Straddling me now.

"Wish I could say the same." I bring up a knee, ramming it squarely into his left kidney. As he lurches upward in a combination of wide-eyed surprise and grimacing pain, I bring up my other knee just as hard, aimed strategically for his groin.

With a loud groan, he lets go of me and collapses onto his side, cradling his crotch with both hands.

"Stay the hell out of my head." I'm on my feet, backpedaling toward the kitchen and the one large knife I keep on hand for infrequent culinary adventures. The blade is dusty but sharp. I hold it out toward the bruised intruder and lean toward my console on the table. Swiping a hand across the screen to power it up, I glance at the keys as I type in the number for HQ.

"You won't get through," he says, curled up with his eyes closed. Yet he seems to know exactly what I'm doing. "In an emergency situation like this, every citizen in the dome will be calling law enforcement. Thinking they're helping. Claiming they've seen terrorists on the move in their buildings, on their streets."

"Are you one of them? A *patriot*?"

He shakes his head. "Doesn't matter what I say. You'll think what you want. You've always been stubborn." Wincing, he sits up, leaning against the wall. He turns his head and looks at me. Oddly enough, there's a hint of amusement in his eyes. "So you don't remember Tucker? That long trek through the desert?"

I scowl at that. There are no deserts, not in Eurasia.

"What about Margo?" he prods. "You two seemed to get along real well, from what I remember. Always talking to each other, back and forth. Telepathically."

I have the number dialed. I just have to connect. "You've got me confused with someone else."

He shakes his head slowly, eyes locked with mine. "I've done my research. Believe me, it's taken some effort. The way they've got us separated across the Domes in different social castes, working opposite shifts. Could they be more obvious?"

Could he be more obtuse? Unless... "You're talking about the Twenty."

"We've got that big banquet coming up. Like that's going to iron out years of their abusive power. Let's celebrate! What exactly? Oh, right. Years of filling sperm and egg banks. Making babies for upper-class citizens." His brow creases as he watches my expression. "Wait. You didn't know." He curses under his breath. "Sorry. I've been looking forward to talking to you, but everything's spilling out like sewage here." He mimes vomiting. As if I couldn't find him more unattractive.

"Let me get this straight." My hand hovers over the console keyboard. "You expect me to believe you're one of the Twenty. That you don't snort dust but have bizarre abilities anyway. And that you remember me from when we were kids."

"Before, actually. We first met while we were fetuses." He shrugs. "Weird, huh?"

"You think we're siblings."

"You ran the DNA search. You tell me."

I narrow my gaze, studying his facial features. No, his face didn't show up in the results.

"Right." He grins. "You and I have something in common: we each have nine siblings exactly the same age we are. What are the odds?"

Not good. Nothing about this makes any sense. Time to shift gears. "You say you've been looking for me. What was last night all about? Why not make your first impression on my doorstep?"

He raises an eyebrow. Going for dashing now. "I had my reasons. One being the opportunity to knock out your augments. They get in the way." He leans toward me and stage whispers, "Of your abilities."

I've had enough of this. I connect to HQ. A message flashes on the screen about expected response times taking longer than usual, and that my call will be answered in the order it was received. Fabulous.

"Okay, you think I'm nuts. How about this: read my mind. Gather all the intel you want. I give you permission to ransack the place." He taps his temple. "Go on. I dare you."

Compared to how I spent the wee hours of the morning, tossing and turning and screaming to make the voices stop, I'm doing pretty well holding myself together. Somehow I managed to quiet the thoughts pouring in from my neighbors, and I'm not about to risk opening those floodgates by digging into this guy's mind. I don't care what he's got going on in there, whether I'll find out if he's actually a terrorist or a dust freak or if we were friends as kids. If he, of all people, was invited to the Revelation Banquet, then that's another reason for me not to go.

But who am I kidding? I've always dreamt of being more than a curfew enforcer. And if this newfound telepathic ability is my key to becoming an interrogator—

"I don't know how," I blurt out, surprised to be admitting such a thing to this stranger. I glance at the console and see the wait time now at twenty minutes. When I look back at him, he's smiling.

"I could teach you." Another casual shrug. "I've been augment-free for a while. Plenty of time to practice."

"They let you do that?"

"Who?"

"Your parents. Superiors." Whoever the government put in charge of him before he joined his terrorist cell.

"I wasn't fortunate enough to grow up in Dome 1."

Time for his sob story. I take a seat at my table, figuring I'd better settle in. "Let me guess: Dome 10?" Sewage treatment would suit him well.

He laughs. "Close. Dome 9."

"You were a farmer." Surprising.

"Until I earned enough to take the maglev to the big city. Made a handful of connections, met the right people. All very fortuitous. They seemed to think my face would be tolerable in VR and Linkstream ads."

"Oh, so you're a *model*." I feign a disgusting mix of astonishment and awe.

"I prefer *actor*. Pays the bills. Gives me time for my research." He winks at me.

"Stalking."

"You want in here or not?" Another temple-tap. "I can lead you through it. But it'll work best if we communicate telepathically throughout the process."

"I have a feeling I'm not your first."

He smirks. "Listen, I'm not going to force you to do anything. You tell me to beat it, I'm out of here. We'll catch up at the banquet." With a grimace, he moves to rise.

"You're not going anywhere." I point the knife at him.

"She's got me right where she wants me," he murmurs.

I give the console another glance; I still have fifteen minutes to wait. Then another ten before the retriever's aerocar arrives to cart this guy's ass to HQ for holding. So I have some time to kill.

"Fine." I exhale, but I don't relax my grip on the knife. "Show me."

"It works best if you close your eyes—"

"Not happening."

He nods as if to say he figured as much. *You've managed to quiet the other voices—neighbors, people flying by your window. Otherwise, you'd be a basket case right now. So that's good. What you'll need to do is focus on my thoughts. We're sharing a telepathic link at the moment. I'm sending, you're receiving. But in order to read thoughts that I'm not sharing, you'll have to trace this signal to its source. Pull back the curtain—*

You're a big fan of metaphors, I think at him without realizing what I'm doing.

He grins. *There you go. You've taken your first step.* Another metaphor, I assume, since I'm not moving. *Now maintain that trajectory, and let's see what you can read on your own. I'm not going to send anything your way for a few seconds.*

The quiet is welcome.

Followed by a blast of moving images and dissonant sounds, another maelstrom similar to what I experienced from my neighbors, but this time the storm emanates from only one source: the young man sitting on my floor. I try not to flinch as scenes from his life hurtle past me and crowd my vision. Not my actual vision —I can still see everything in my cube. I haven't closed my eyes. This is some kind of hyperreality, overlaid on top of what's really real. Moving and breathing ghosts from this guy's past.

I have to remind myself to breathe as I learn more about him than I ever cared to know. This is an investigation, nothing more. He doesn't know me. We share no blurry past. He's a dust addict, and my augments are just wonky, giving me these superhuman mental abilities.

His name is Erik. Scenes play out from when he was a boy, live-action footage that's blurry around the edges. We were at the same boarding school before they split us up—Camp Hope. Playing hide and seek in the dormitory, chasing each other up and down those faux-mahogany stairs, three flights of madness, laughter, then some tears as I slipped and fell, splitting open my left knee. Erik was there at my side when I landed in a crumpled heap. He had his sweater off and bunched up, pressed against the bleeding, his brow knitted with concern. He blamed himself, but I was the klutz who'd tripped on the braided rug. He was always too fast for me to catch.

Absently, I rub my knee beneath the stiff material of my black uniform. The scar remains to this day.

I glance at him. Erik. Resting with his eyes closed and his hands folded across his flat abdomen. He is one of the Twenty, and I do remember him. But why haven't I until this moment?

Never looking back...we live only now...

A chill shivers down my neck even though I'm sitting in sunlight.

Next item to investigate: dust usage. Like running a search on the Linkstream, I scan Erik's memories for any illicit deals with dust smugglers or moments alone with a line or two of the stuff ready to snort. There's nothing. Not a single longing glance at a snuff box.

So he's not a dust freak. But I can't wrap my mind around any alternative explanation for his abilities. Is he some kind of superhuman? An above-average VR model living a few rungs higher on the evolutionary ladder?

Erik is two for two, as far as telling the truth. Next up: his involvement with terrorists and the attack on Hawthorne Tower. Will he be three for three? Has he been straight with me this whole time?

A knock at my door causes the scenes and sounds from Erik's mind to dissipate like steam. I glance at the console. My call was received five minutes ago, and a retriever was dispatched to my location. That's who must be outside.

How did I lose track of time?

Shutting down the console, I return my kitchen knife to its resting place and step over Erik on my way to the door. He looks sound asleep. Must be exhausting to have someone sift through your memories.

I wave my hand in front of the door, and it slides aside. Two of the Chancellor's security clones stand in the hallway, shoulder to shoulder. Their white armor shines, pristine, as do their black face shields. No way to tell what they look like underneath. No reason to. They all look the same, from what I hear.

"Sera Chen, you will come with us," they say in unison, in the same gender-neutral robotic voice. Even though they're flesh and blood, these things always behave more like automatons than people.

"What's going on?" I keep my body between them and Erik. No idea why. Subconsciously, do I think of him now as the impish boy I often had to protect from our headmaster? I was good at talking us out of difficult situations. Our teachers had no patience for childish pranks; they expected us to behave like miniature adults. "I'm supposed to report for duty—"

"By order of the Chancellor, under Emergency Stipulation 5.6, Subsection 2, in the event of a threat against law and order, all members of the Twenty are to be sequestered until that threat has been neutralized."

I nod slowly. The Tower attack must be even worse than it sounded. "The Chancellor authorized this?"

"The Chancellor is missing."

I glance from one face shield to the other, seeing my own startled expression reflected back at me.

"So, you're rounding up the Twenty?" Erik stands behind me in the reflection, hands in his pockets. Nonchalant as ever.

I keep my back to him.

The clones' heads twitch a degree to the side as if they've both received the same information on their heads-up displays.

"Erik Paine," they say, "you will also come with us."

"No thanks." He reaches around me, like he's going to hug me from behind. But thankfully that's not what he's up to.

It's something worse.

He tosses two discs at the clones, each device only a few centimeters in diameter, and they affix to the white chest plates. Before either security clone can react, blue lightning radiates outward from each disc, and the clones shudder in place. Their power-suits act as a conduit for this massive shock to their systems, sending them toppling to the hallway floor where they continue to twitch with residual spasms well after the lightning show ends.

Erik presses past me to retrieve the clones' assault rifles. He tucks one under each arm and points the muzzles at the floor. Then he gives me a dashing smile.

"Want to get out of here, Enforcer Chen?"

PART II

REUNION

6. BISHOP
19 MONTHS AFTER ALL-CLEAR

Countless charred bodies cover the ground for a hundred meters in every direction. Black bones, black gaping skulls. Without any skin on them, it's difficult to tell Eden's collared mutants from Cain's superhumans. Fire raining from the sky will do that.

This is how the UW deals with problems: overkill in the extreme.

The carnage is motivation enough for Luther's people to hand over all twenty of their children. Milton had to fly out west to the caves to retrieve the two that were there; the rest came from Eden's sublevels. All carried by hand to the waiting UW troops, all accounted for.

The incubation units have been loaded onto the hoverplanes and strapped securely into place. We're ready to ship out.

"Sergeant." One of the marines aboard the lead plane beckons for me to join him inside. A short walk up the loading ramp, and I'll be parked alongside the unborn children I was sent to collect. Taken back to the *Argonaus* and Captain Mutegi.

Then home to my family. My wife, Emma. My children, Mara and Emmanuel. My heart swells at the thought of it.

Tears sting my eyes as I look back at Luther, Samson, and the others. They haven't moved from where they stood minutes ago, when they gave us their children. They watch us now, their black goggles fixed on our planes, their faces covered by strips of cloth. Are they broken inside? Is that why they don't move—because they can't?

I want to thank them for their sacrifice. By giving up these fetuses, they're giving the civilized world a future. They won't be forgotten. And who's to say they won't be able to have other children someday?

Not that anyone should do such a foolish thing on this quarantined continent.

"Sergeant Bishop!" the marine shouts. "Time to go!"

I give him a nod and fight my unwieldy hazard suit to raise a hand in farewell. Only one of the superhumans responds in like manner. I recognized his voice earlier when he spoke to the UW troops: the man named Luther.

More than anything else, he wanted these twenty unborn children to be safe. He didn't want the superhumans from the coast or that madman Willard to destroy them. I'm sure Luther wanted to keep them and raise them in his happy cave cult, but this is what I came here to do. Fulfill my mission objective and get the hell out. Make sure these babies grow up in Eurasia where they'll be safe from cannibal mutants, gene-altering dust, and deadly sunshine. In the Domes, they'll be able to live a normal life—and then some.

I haul myself up the ramp and take a seat in the cargo section. One of the marines straps me in, fastening the buckles over my chest plate and lap. I watch the lights on the incubation chambers blink with a steady rhythm, and I think of Granger, Sinclair, and Harris. It's wrong to be making this trip without them. They were supposed to be here beside me.

They will be soon. We're stopping to retrieve their remains outside of Luther's Homeplace. Then it'll be a direct flight to the *Argonaus* and her sister ships in the naval blockade. The *Integrity* will take her place while Captain Mutegi sets course for Eurasia with the incubators safe below decks.

"You're lookin' a little worse for wear, Sarge," says the marine, fastening his own buckles in the jump seat across from me.

The ramp rises automatically, shutting out any view of the scorched slaughter or the survivors who stand like a row of forgotten statues.

"Been a rough couple days." I reach to remove my helmet once the ramp locks into place with a loud reverberation along the interior hull. The hiss of fresh O2 fills the compartment.

"You'll want to keep that on," the marine says. He taps his gloved knuckles against his own helmet. "Until we pass through decon aboard the *Argonaus*, all protective gear remains in place."

Decon. "Right." I leave it alone.

"So what was it like out there?"

"Hell." I stare him down.

His smile disintegrates. He finds somewhere else to look.

I lean back and close my eyes. Time to compartmentalize. What's in the past stays in the past. No good dwelling on it. Learn from mistakes and move on. Focus on what's next: picking up my team. They'll be loaded into the hoverplane flying at the rear of this aerial procession. We'll provide air support, incinerators at the ready, in case any hungry mutants show up while our men are on the ground.

Then it's onward to the *Argonaus*. Standard decontamination procedures will be followed to the letter. Assuming we all check out, Mutegi will expect me to debrief him while the medical crew takes the incubators into custody and prepares them for the voyage to Eurasia.

Home.

"That battle was some kind of welcome," the marine continues, still eager to strike up a conversation. "Looked like they were going at each other medieval-style, but with automatic weapons. Didn't get a good close-up view, but would I be right in guessing they weren't exactly human?"

I keep my eyes shut. "More or less."

"So the rumors are true? The toxins in the air turned the D-Day survivors into—"

"Corporal?"

"Yeah, Sarge?"

"Let me sleep."

Rank has its privileges on rare occasions. This is one of them. The last thing I want to do is talk about what happened on the ground, let alone think about it. My briefing with Captain Mutegi will be bad enough.

Thankfully, the next time I hear the corporal's voice isn't until the hoverplane touches down on the deck of the *Argonaus*. I unfasten my safety harness and struggle against my suit to stand, watching as the ramp lowers and the medical team files aboard, their intense focus riveted on the incubators. Everything seems to check out; it doesn't take them long to start wheeling the units out of here on hand trucks.

One of the medics glances back at me, her expression visible behind the clear face shield of her protective suit. She looks concerned. "Sergeant Bishop?"

I frown at her. Why is she talking to me? Then I look around. I'm the last one on board. The marines are gone, and so are the incubation units.

I must have lost track of time, not to mention my surroundings.

"Yeah." I take a step toward her, and she gestures for me to follow her out of the plane.

"This way. I assume you've been through decon procedures before?"

"I want to talk to my family."

"All in due time, Sergeant. Decon first. Then you'll meet with the Captain. He'll get you in touch with your family."

The UW is always a stickler when it comes to procedure. I should have expected as much. So I go through the motions on autopilot. Do what the medic tells me to do. Walk through here.

Stand there. Don't touch anything. Don't move while the scanner is in operation. Don't take off my helmet.

"Stay here." She leaves quickly. Two armed marines pivot to block the exit.

I'm standing in a shower-sized cubicle partitioned off from the flight deck. No freight elevator ride down to the medical bay. Not until I check out. These guards have been tasked with making sure I don't leave. I give them a nod. They don't respond, their face shields automatically darkened by the sun.

Not sure what to think. Scratch that. Worst case scenario: my helmet was compromised when I crash-landed. I've been infected ever since.

I'll never see my family again. I'll never go home.

My gloved hands are tight fists when the medic returns with Captain Mutegi. The guards turn to allow them entry and then stand facing each other, rifles at rest.

"Bishop." Mutegi nods to me as he removes his cap. He always wears it, even if he has to set it on top of his environmental helmet. Behind the face shield, it's clear he hasn't slept for a couple days. The worry lines in his dark skin are more pronounced than ever.

"Captain." I glance at the medic. She keeps her eyes on the Slate in her hand, fingers swiping spastically across the glowing screen. "I'd like to call my family. Let them know I'm all right. That I'll be home soon."

Mutegi stares at me. "I'm sorry. That won't be possible, Sergeant."

I clench my jaw and wait for him to explain.

He turns to the medic, and she shows him her screen. He scowls at it. "You're sure."

"Yes, Captain." She's pensive. "I ran it three times."

That sounds unnecessary. These decon scanners are so fine-tuned, they'll detect a case of the flu three days before you start showing any symptoms.

Mutegi dismisses the medic, and she salutes crisply before

leaving. She glances at me with an apologetic look. I focus on the captain.

"So now what, sir?"

He folds his arms—easier to accomplish in a hazard suit like his. No armor. "Bishop, I'll give it to you straight."

"Wouldn't expect anything else."

A hint of a smile glints in his eyes, then dims. "Your family was released from custody yesterday, as soon as my superiors decided you were killed in action along with your entire team." He pauses to let that sink in.

"They...think I'm dead?"

"Your family was told that you died a hero. And because of that, they have been welcomed back into Eurasian society. With honors. They will live a very comfortable life, James. I have it on good authority that Chancellor Hawthorne herself has taken an interest in your children."

Now I'm staring. "But this happened before..." I tap my fractured helmet. "Before I lost my team."

"Yes." He stands up straighter. "I assume you've already figured out—"

"I'm not an idiot." I catch myself. "Sir."

He takes no offense. I'm a dead man, after all.

"Have you noticed any changes in yourself? Anything out of the ordinary?"

Besides talking to a ghost that looks like my wife? Hearing the voice of my daughter? "No, nothing at all." I reach for my helmet clamps. "Okay if I take this thing off?"

"Of course." He takes a step back instinctively, as if what I've got might be catching.

I release each of the clamps and remove the helmet. Inhale the salty sea air. My gloved fingers trace the cracks in the polymer. I don't feel fury or overwhelming anguish now that my greatest fear has been realized. Instead I'm strangely numb all over, my insides hollow and cold.

James Bishop has left the building.

Mutegi clears his throat. No idea how long I've been standing here staring at my helmet.

"Orders, Captain?" I don't know what else to say.

He nods grimly. "You'll be transferred to the *Integrity* for observation. The medical team over there wants to...study you. For any signs of genetic abnormalities." It's clear he finds the subject distasteful.

As do I, being the subject.

"No one will ever forget what you did here." He clasps my shoulder. "Mission accomplished, Sergeant. You did it. You saved the world."

What about my world: Emma, Mara, Emmanuel? They'll be all right. Better than. Seeing how I died a war hero, my family will join one of the upper Eurasian castes—with Hawthorne herself looking out for them. I couldn't ask for a better way to leave them in my absence.

Only I'm not absent. I'm right here, alive and breathing.

"There's one thing I don't understand."

Mutegi nods. He's no idiot, either. He lowers his voice, "Why you were officially declared KIA." He holds my gaze. "Makes me wonder if we're all living on borrowed time, James."

"Because of what we know."

He squeezes my shoulder. "I'd be surprised if any of us make it back inside the Domes."

Leaving me to chew on that, he steps away and salutes. I give a return salute my best effort, considering the armored suit I'm in. One silver lining: I won't have to wear it much longer. I'll be trading it for a glass cage. A locked observation room with a complete array of electrodes. Won't that be nice.

"Escort Sergeant Bishop to the Zodiac," Mutegi tells the guards. "He won't be joining us on our voyage to Eurasia."

He looks back at me one last time, like he wants to say something but can't, due to his rank. So he dips his head and leaves, his long strides thumping across the deck.

"Give me a hand here," I tell the guards, gesturing at my suit.

Not something I can remove on my own. They glance at each other, unsure whether they're allowed inside my little infected space. "C'mon, I obviously don't need this thing anymore. Right? The damage is already done."

I give them a sheepish grin, and they shrug at each other. Why not humor the dead man? They each take a heavy sleeve and pull, prying me out of the bulky thing.

"Thanks. I've got it from here." I sit on the floor and set about freeing my legs. Underneath, all I've got on is a sweat-stained bodysuit. Enough to protect most of me from the sun outside. "I'll need gloves and shoes. Something to protect my head and face."

Their face shields are clear now that they're inside the decon room. They glance at each other again, almost like they're telepathic. But no, they're just wet behind the ears. They've never had to deal with a mutant-in-the-making before.

My throat catches as I remember Granger's fear at the prospect of changing into something inhuman, followed by his amped-up, devil-may-care attitude. I miss that guy.

"We can get you something like this," one of the guards offers, gesturing at his protective suit. The lite version of mine.

"That'll work." I give him a nod of approval.

While he scurries off, the other guard resumes his post at the doorway. I remain seated on the floor with my knees pulled up to my chest.

The thing about your worst fear being realized? Once you push down the grief, squeezing it into some dark corner of your mind where it will resurface later on when you least expect it, and after you wade through the numbness toward the light of acceptance at the end of that dark tunnel, you find you're completely invulnerable.

Nothing can hurt you now. Not their lies to your family or their lab tests. Not even the prospect of turning into something superhuman and superweird. In a way, you're not even *you* anymore. Your former self really is dead.

So why do anything they want you to?

The guard returns with my new suit, creased from where it's been sitting on a shelf in storage. I pull it on and zip it up, lace up the boots, tug on the gloves, adjust the hood and face shield so I have the widest field of vision possible.

Then I follow the lead guard toward the rigid inflatable boat while the rear guard follows me step by step. Both of them have their rifles at rest. Standard procedure, of course. They don't expect the hero Sergeant James Bishop to give them any trouble.

And I don't. Not until we're on the water halfway between the *Argonaus* and the *Integrity*. That's when I make my move.

I pretend to choke, giving the universal sign for an O2 malfunction. The guard who isn't steering the Zodiac doesn't think twice before rushing over to assist me. He doesn't wonder why I'd be having an O2 malfunction when my suit isn't outfitted with a breather. Nobody has to worry about me breathing contaminated air anymore. But he's young, and he acts on instinct a few seconds too soon, before he can think it through.

I hit him in the solar plexus with my elbow, doubling him over while I pivot on one heel. Then I throw him over my shoulder and into the water. He's far behind our wake by the time the other guard turns away from the helm to find me holding his partner's rifle.

"Dive in," I tell him, assuming he'll take me up on the offer. Beats getting shot.

But he's still got one hand on the wheel, so he gives it a savage spin, sending the Zodiac veering sharply off-course. I topple backward, nearly falling overboard myself.

"Drop it, Sergeant!" the guard shouts, powering down the boat. We're rocking in the water now with more than a few hundred meters between us and the nearest ship. "Do it now!" He takes a step toward me, his rifle aimed at my head.

I toss his partner's weapon across the boat and raise my hands. "Now what? You plan on shooting me, marine?"

The dark face shield hides his confusion. He tightens his grip on the rifle. Probably never trained for a situation like this. He knows how to hold his gun and how to fire it, most likely. But at a fellow marine? He's not so sure about that.

"Don't give me a reason to, sir!" He struggles to keep his footing as the boat throws him off balance. There's plenty of chop on the water.

I take my chances and hurl myself at him. What have I got to lose? I'm already a dead man. And I don't plan on being anybody's lab rat.

The rifle goes off with short bursts into the air as I tackle him against the helm. We wrestle for his weapon, and another burst rips across the Zodiac. Unfortunately, my escorts failed to activate the boat's bulletproof armor, having no idea they were carrying a soon-to-be dangerous fugitive. The rounds tear open the heavy-duty rubber, and air whistles outward from the deflating air chamber. The good news: plenty of other chambers remain intact, so we won't sink.

I won't sink. This marine won't be joining me.

He howls as I heave him into the water. Then I start up the outboard motor, and it growls to life. Hands on the wheel, I change course. Sergeant Bishop won't be transferring to the *Integrity*, and he's not welcome aboard the *Argonaus*. So there's only one place for him to go.

Back to shore.

Full throttle, with the wind whipping against my protective suit, it's tough to hear the radio. But Captain Mutegi's voice is clear enough.

He keeps it short: "Godspeed, James."

I nod, hoping he makes it home, that our exalted superiors allow him back inside the Domes. I've got a strong feeling I'll never see him again, either way. But he'll complete his mission. He'll get those incubators and their precious cargo to Eurasia. Because of our efforts, the civilized world will continue beyond the Terminal Age generation. Mara and Emmanuel won't be among the Ten Domes' youngest citizens anymore.

Ten minutes later, I approach the coastline. Those overturned ships are no more, reduced to rubble. The beach where they sat is littered with charred debris and countless craters from the recent shelling, courtesy of the *Argonaus*. If any of Cain's people survived, they won't be here.

I cut the throttle and coast the Zodiac onto shore. Once it's wedged in the wet sand, I jump out and trudge inland with no clear destination in sight. A glance over my shoulder tells me the *Integrity* has yet to send a retrieval crew after their lab rat—or deserter. Whichever shoe fits. The crashing waves are already sliding the Zodiac out of position. They're welcome to it.

The heat inside this suit is unbearable without environmental controls. I crack open the face shield to let in some air. The sooner I can change into the locals' attire, the better. But that will require finding said locals.

I'm walking through a disaster zone here. No signs of life.

Until I stumble across tire tracks through the soot and sand. If I had to guess, they belonged to that armored Hummer Margo was driving. Maybe she's still here, somewhere nearby—on the other side of those windswept dunes in the distance.

"Hello?" I call out as my boots maintain a steady rhythm through the wreckage.

"James, you came back."

The sight of my wife brings me to a halt.

"You again." I look away, unable to bear seeing her like this. A ghost in daylight.

More like an angel, barefoot in her white gown, with her dark hair loose around her shoulders. Smiling at me like only Emma does.

I keep my head down and walk past her.

"They won't let you return home." She doesn't sound surprised.

Of course not. From the moment I first heard her voice, I was already infected. I should have known at that point I'd never see my family again. Maybe I just couldn't allow myself to accept it.

"Looks like this is my home now." I keep moving.

"Where are you going?"

"No idea."

She glides along beside me. "You're a man on a mission."

"Not anymore." I'm adrift, lost at sea. Without purpose.

But survival is a purpose. As is avoiding the poking and prodding I was bound to receive aboard the *Integrity*. Exchanging a glass cage for this post-apocalyptic wasteland. Way to go, Sarge.

"You have friends here," she says. "They will be glad to see you."

"We can all suffer together." I stop and face her. "Where is everybody? Margo—"

"She was here. After you left, Milton found her. They are now escorting the sole survivors from Cain's enclave to the Homeplace."

I frown at that. "Why not Eden? That place has everything they need."

"Unfortunately, after Willard's death, Perch rallied the Eden Guard against Luther's people, driving them away. Eden is sealed off once again. Those men will live out their days underground."

"So Luther and his bunch are headed back to the Homeplace as well."

She nods.

"Alright." I pick up the pace. "Guess I am too."

"You will never make it, James. You have no water, no weapon."

And the Wastes are crawling with meat-eaters. So much for feeling invincible. I really haven't thought this through.

"What do you suggest? Another tornado ride?"

She shakes her head. "That suit you're wearing is not durable enough. It will not protect you from the whirling sand." She smiles. "We will contact Milton."

I pat my suit. "No radio, either." I glance back toward the coast, but I can't spot the Zodiac.

"No need." She smiles. "He's already on his way."

Less than a minute later, a sonic boom reverberates in the

distance, and Milton the flying man soars into view. He pulls up short in mid-air, hovering maybe a hundred meters above the ground.

"You're back?" he calls down, surprised. "Something wrong? Are the babies okay?"

"They're fine, shipping out for Eurasia today," I shout up at him, but I'm not sure he can hear me. The face shield muffles my voice. I pop it open and hold it like a visor. "I'm...infected."

He glides to the ground, his boots sending up puffs of dust on impact. His gloved hands are clenched into fists as he shakes his head. "I'm so sorry, man. Your family—"

"They'll be fine." I glance at spirit-Emma. "She said everybody's headed back to your cave. Everyone who survived..." I trail off.

Milton looks at the spirit. Pretty sure he doesn't see my wife. For him, she appears as someone from his own past.

"That includes you, Sergeant," he says.

"Call me James. Deserters have no rank."

Milton steps toward me and rests a hand on my shoulder. "You afraid of heights, James?"

Like always, I refuse to admit a hint of weakness. The next thing I know, he has one arm around me and the other aimed for the sky. I've got a pretty good hunch where this is headed, so I grab onto him. A split-second later, we're hurtling through the air faster than the speed of sound, and my stomach is lodged in my throat.

This is nothing like riding that massive dust devil on the way to Eden. This is piercing the sky faster than a jet. I close my eyes and grit my teeth, waiting for it to be over.

Then, just as suddenly as it began, my flight ends. Milton touches down on an outcropping of rock near the cave mouth of the Homeplace. Down below, Luther's people are working in pairs to carry the dead to their final resting places: a row of fresh graves dug along the foothills. Granger, Sinclair, and Harris are not among the bodies. They'll either be returned to Eurasia or incinerated to avoid contaminating the Domes. Their families deserve better.

Margo's Hummer is parked down there like it never left. It looks as beat up as I feel, inside and out.

"Thanks," I tell Milton as we let go of each other. I give him a solid pat on the back. "Let's not do that again."

He laughs. "I'll let Luther know you're here," he says as he turns toward the cave.

Good to see you again, Sergeant.

Margo steps out of the shadows as they envelop Milton.

"Miss me?" I approach her.

"I'm sorry...for your loss," she says. If she's read my mind, and I assume she has, then she already knows the situation with my family.

"Guess I'm one of you now. We get to wait and see if I sprout any horns."

She almost smiles, beckoning me inside. "Let's find you something more comfortable to wear."

I follow her into the cave where glowsticks are mounted along the earthen walls at regular intervals. We pass a small group of pregnant young women and a cluster of elderly people who talk quietly among themselves.

Cain's only survivors, Margo explains telepathically. *Milton and I brought them from the coast.*

Somehow, they managed to escape the shelling unharmed. That's a miracle. We enter a spacious cavern with rocks arranged in rows like seats in an indoor amphitheater.

"Any sign of Cain?"

She shakes her head. "You saw what happened to him and his warriors."

I did. They were toast. But he was riding inside that other Hummer—

You intended to kill him. She's not judging. Just projecting a fact into my mind.

I nod. But I suppose being roasted alive was as good a way as any for him to go out. Justice, after killing my team the way he did. "So now what?"

"Now?" She glances over her shoulder at me. "We live. Those who remain. We set aside our differences and survive."

"Eden would be a good place to do that." I gesture at the rock walls surrounding us. "Not that these caves are without their charm. But those women about to give birth would be a whole lot more comfortable with electricity, air conditioning, and running water. Not to mention the rest of us."

Us. She holds my gaze. "We already put it to a vote. Luther sided with the majority: thirty-five to ten. We avoid further bloodshed by leaving Eden alone."

"How'd you vote?"

You already know.

I suppose I do. She said she'd never go back there. "But with Willard dead—"

"It was because of his murder that Perch so easily regained control of the Eden Guard and turned them against Luther and his people."

"Yeah, I heard Perch was in charge." Eden traded one lunatic leader for another.

We've reached what looks like a communal alcove where goods and supplies are stored. Among the hydropacks and standard rations are a couple stacks of loose-fitting, sand-colored clothing.

"I'll leave you to it," she says. "Feel free to take whatever you need. You may place your suit on that shelf. I'm sure we'll find a use for it." She turns away.

I'm glad you're here, Sergeant. She disappears down the earthen corridor.

I don't know what to say to that. I would rather be home with my family. But since that's not an option, I guess I'll be glad, too. Or something close to it. This beats wandering through the Wastes, at any rate.

I stare at the clothing, unsure where to begin. First things first: I peel myself out of the protective suit and fold it up. Then I pull off my bodysuit, leaving only my briefs in place—just in case one of the locals stumbles upon me. Not sure how body-shy these people are, but I don't plan on offending anybody my first day.

Breaking open one of the hydropacks, I take a long swig and pour the rest over my face and chest, smearing around the H2O substitute in an attempt at quasi-cleanliness. Then I pull on a baggy, one-size-fits-all pair of trousers and matching tunic, keeping my own boots. I look almost ready to fit in.

"Sergeant." Luther finds me just as I step out into the corridor. He takes my hand in a firm shake.

"Just James." I shrug. "No longer a UW Marine."

"James." His piercing blue eyes burn with intensity. He looks more alive than he did the last time I saw him. Energized. "I heard about your situation."

"Yeah..." There's nothing I can do about it. Part of me wants to move beyond it. Then I feel guilty, as if I've betrayed my family just by thinking that.

"We are not giving up on our children. Whether it takes us five years or ten, even twenty—we will find them." He grips my shoulder and nods, holding my gaze. Something stirs within me in the face of his confidence. Could it be hope? "That includes your wife, your daughter, and your son. You will see them again, James. I give you my word on that."

7. DAIYNA
5 YEARS AFTER ALL-CLEAR

By all appearances, Stack itself isn't a raging inferno. Just a big rig with loads of supplies piled outside its open cargo container. Wrecked, in flames. Judging from the twisted remains of the truck, a missile strike would be my best guess.

The locals are working with shovels, tossing sand onto the fire in an attempt to smother it. Looks like a solid community effort. Part of me likes the idea of taking a seat right here on this hillside, pulling out my flask and enjoying the show. But those flames look warm, and my teeth are chattering inside this stupid helmet. So I keep walking.

Until a couple well-meaning sentries block my path.

"Going someplace?" one of them asks, seeming to think she's real sneaky popping out from behind that boulder.

I don't tell her I saw her heat signature from fifty meters back. And I didn't even need to activate whatever tech is in this helmet. I'm just special that way. *Gifted.*

"Trade." I keep my rifle propped back against my shoulder.

"What you got?" The firelight casts her in a cocky silhouette, one hand on her hip where a sidearm's holstered. The other holds a sawed-off shotgun aimed at my chest.

"Eden special." Slowly, I set down my rifle and satchel. Then I take off the helmet and place it on top. "Protective suit. I'll take a

12-volt auto battery in trade, if you've got one. If not, whiskey and a bed for the night will suffice."

The other sentry lets out a low whistle at the sight of me. Not because he thinks I'm easy on the eyes. "It's her," he murmurs.

"You've got some cojones coming back here," says the she-sentry, drawing her sidearm and pointing the business end at me. Because two guns are better than one when you're dealing with a loose cannon. "Planning another drunken brawl?"

"Don't want any trouble this time. By the looks of things, you've got plenty already." I nod toward the fire.

"Interesting timing," says the he-sentry. "You showing up like this, just minutes after that missile hit."

"Nothing to do with me. My jeep died, twenty klicks south. Ran into some bounty hunters from Eden—"

"What's your head worth now, Daiyna?" she asks, taking a step toward me.

"Twenty hydropacks, I heard," he answers for me, closing in as well. "Almost worth it, don't you think?"

It wouldn't be much trouble to take them down. Her first, then him. Disarm them, shove their faces into the dust. They might get off a lucky shot or two, missing me entirely as I leap through the air, twisting to land between them, throwing my elbow into her face, my knee into his groin. But with my wounded shoulder, I'd be at a distinct disadvantage. And they'd have help in a matter of seconds. The missile strike has caused all the sentries to hold a tight perimeter. We're within spitting distance of the nearest Stack container.

"Daiyna?"

Time stops at the sound of that sweet, familiar voice. My sister's voice.

Shechara...

Like a scene from a dream, she jogs toward us from beyond the fire, her long hair around her shoulders swaying like thick curtains, half her face illuminated. If her mechatronic eyes could glisten with tears, they would be. She's smiling at me as she approaches.

And I'm staring at her with hot tears drizzling down my cheeks. It's been so long without her.

"She's with us," a thunderous voice booms as a large figure lumbers after Shechara. His metal arms and legs clank, reflecting the flames.

The sentries take a step back, lowering their weapons a few degrees. Shechara passes them as if they're not even there and pulls me into a tight embrace.

"Daiyna, it's really you!" She squeezes me, drops back half a step to cup my face in her hands and look into my eyes, then hugs me again and doesn't let go.

She's so warm, so real. I put my arms around her tentatively, afraid she might shatter or disappear, and I'll be left alone again. I can't believe this is happening. I've tried so hard to stay away from them, to keep out from underfoot. To avoid people. These people, in particular.

Because I love them too much to ever hurt them again.

"It's good to see you, Daiyna," Samson rumbles, and he sounds like he means it. "Been a long time."

"You vouch for her?" says the she-sentry, obviously disappointed.

He nods, keeping his gaze locked with mine over Shechara's head. His eyes shine, but he doesn't smile.

"She does anything to upset the balance, it'll be your head, cyborg." The sentries back off, glaring at me as they retreat.

Good riddance. Go find somebody else to annoy.

"Daiyna, where have you been?" Shechara half-whispers, her lips next to my ear.

"Around." I shrug and hold her close, stroking her hair. I've never seen it this long, so thick and healthy.

"I've missed you so much! We all have. It hasn't been the same, not since..." She trails off. "That doesn't matter. You're here now, and I'm never letting you go!" She laughs, squeezing me again.

"Might want to let her catch a breath, Small Fry," Samson suggests with the makings of a grin. He reaches out with his mechatronic hand like he wants to touch my arm, but he scratches at his nose instead and turns to look past the fire. "We should see about renting a room here."

"Not sure we'll be welcome now, Strongman." Shechara keeps her arms around me, her head resting on my shoulder like it doesn't plan on leaving anytime soon. Okay by me.

"So you don't live here." I can't stop stroking her hair, and I hope she doesn't ask to see mine. Keeping it short with a fairly sharp knife has made it look a little ragged around the edges.

"Nope," she says, "just passing through. We were hoping to trade, maybe spend the night in an actual bed…"

"Not lookin' promising," Samson observes as Stack's mayor heads our way, appearing more dour than usual and flanked by those same two self-important sentries.

I face Shechara, my eyebrows lifting as I nod toward the fire. "That was you?" Not like her to make such a big splash. But if she's been hanging around Samson, his ways might be rubbing off on her. They make an odd couple, that's for sure.

"There were two trackers," she explains. "A sentry found one and waved us through. By the time they located the second one…" She shakes her head at the destruction.

"So you hijacked a raider rig?" I can't help smiling.

She nods. Samson clears his throat.

"First time," she says.

"Probably our last," he adds.

Now that I look closer, I see that more than just the tractor-trailer was obliterated, the remains sinking into a fresh crater. There was also a crane attached to the cargo container, and it's ruined. As is a jeep parked behind the trailer. Judging from the stern look on Mayor Tullson's face, he plans on making somebody pay for the damages.

"I see you're acquainted." Tullson stuffs his age-spotted hands into the pockets of his overcoat and scowls at the three of us. He looks the same as he did the last time I passed through Stack: long greasy hair combed back, hawk nose, eyes that squint day or night, clean-shaven pale skin. Heard once that he was a university professor back before the end of things. I pity his students. "Hard to believe you've caused more of a ruckus than *she* did the last time she graced us with her presence." He jerks his head toward me. "Do you have more drunk and disorderly conduct in store for us?"

I lean forward and mime being hard of hearing. He's about to repeat himself when Samson steps in.

"Honest mistake," he offers, his voice like low thunder. "Ask Barrett. He'll tell you."

"I've spoken with him. Scanner malfunction." Tullson nods slowly. "Be that as it may. We've done well to keep Stack off the UW's radar over the years. We don't interfere with their scavenging runs, and they don't bother us. But now that's changed. They have never fired on us before—"

"Why destroy it?" All eyes turn on me. I must have blurted that out loud. "I assume the truck was carrying plenty of provisions. Fuel, foodstuffs, supplies. The sort of haul those raiders really go for."

"That's what it looked like." Samson nods.

"Why blow it up? Why not send a couple squads to retrieve it?"

Tullson humors me with a smirk. "To make a point: do not hijack their trucks. Ever." He looks at each of us again. "We're lucky no one was killed. But we're out a crane, and you lost your jeep, if I'm not mistaken."

Samson and Shechara nod gravely.

"So you have nothing left to trade—"

"Here." I nudge my satchel toward him with my boot. "Take it. The rifle too, and the suit. That should help even the score."

Tullson laughs. "You've killed too many of your brain cells, Daiyna, if you think this will make up for a *crane!*"

"A down payment then." What am I doing? I didn't bring hellfire raining down on Stack. None of this concerns me. All I need is a battery. Then I'm out of here.

"Take back what you said. Tell him you're drunk, not thinking straight. Say the satchel is a trade, and all you want is a battery." Arthur Willard is suddenly standing right there in front of me, giving me advice. I stiffen with revulsion at the sight of him.

"Daiyna?" Shechara notices my reaction. I look at her instead.

I haven't seen her in so long. Years, probably. And Samson—no idea why it's just the two of them out here, robbing the UW like post-apocalyptic bandits. Not sure why they're traveling together or so familiar with each other. What did she call him earlier? *Strongman?*

I tried to forget them, telling myself they were better off without me. Maybe so. I don't know. There's one thing I'm sure of: I'm not better off without them.

"A room then. For the night," I try a different tack, nudging the satchel again. "Will that about cover it?"

One of Tullson's eyes is squinted up more than the other, almost to the point of no return. "Here's what we'll do. You'll get your room. But tomorrow we'll discuss how you're going to pay for that crane and smooth things over with the raiders." He nods, liking the sound of his own voice. Typical professor-turned-politician. "Don't even think about running. I'll have sentries posted outside your door on rotating shifts."

He looks Samson up and down with a startling lack of respect for his mechanical parts. Maybe he's never seen the cyborg in action, tearing through a horde of daemons. Because there aren't any daemons, not anymore. Thanks to Samson and Luther.

"We appreciate your hospitality." Samson crosses his metal arms and offers a tight-lipped smile.

Tullson orders the she-sentry to lead the way to our room and the he-sentry to pick up my satchel overflowing with bartered items. I'm tempted to take back the rifle; what's in the bag, in addition to the Edenite's suit, should be enough to cover room and board in Stack for an entire week. But a little voice inside my head tells me to stay cool.

You don't want to put them in danger, Rehana tells me, spirit-mind to flesh-mind.

They've done a good job of putting themselves in it, I counter.

See what happens when you leave them alone? Rehana winks at me. *They need you. They always have. And you need them.*

Shechara's got her arm looped around mine as we follow the sentry. Samson is close on our heels, clanking along like a faithful robot. I keep one hand nonchalantly over the grip of the 9mm tucked into my belt. The flask is there too, hidden beneath my tunic. I have a feeling I might be needing one before the other, but I'm glad to have both.

We don't talk until we're alone—or alone as we can be in a shipping container that's been partitioned into four tiny rooms. Three floor-to-ceiling makeshift walls are opaque plastiglass; the fourth is the steel wall of the container itself. A single solar-powered light bulb dangles from a pull-chain, splashing a pair of bunk beds, a toilet, and a sink with its sickly light. Scant privacy from the other rooms, but no privacy among the three of us.

"Enjoy your stay," the sentry sneers, slamming the door behind us. She doesn't lock it from the outside, and her boots don't go anywhere.

Lucky her. She gets the first rotation of guard duty. No wonder she's so pleasant.

Samson eyes the bunks. There's no way he'll fit in either one, and he knows it.

"I'll take the floor," he offers, like he's being chivalrous or something. Grunting and grimacing, he bends his mechanical legs awkwardly and positions his feet against the door. Smart. He'll make a good doorstop. He stretches out onto his back, his metal arms down at his sides, and his eyes closed. "Wake me up if you plan on escaping."

Shechara kneels down beside his oversized head like a princess from a fairy tale, caring for a wounded ogre. She smooths back his tousled hair and rests her hand on his brow. He smiles up at her, and she smiles back, neither of them saying anything. Then she leans forward and kisses him. On the lips. He sighs contentedly, and before she reaches her bottom bunk, he's already snoring.

"Roll onto your side, Strongman," she says quietly.

He obeys, metal parts clunking against the floor. The snores subside.

"That's new." I unwrap my head covering and shrug out of my outer layers, reaching up to place them on the top bunk. "You two?"

She smiles shyly at me. "Three years now. Luther married us. He performed the ceremony, I mean."

"People still do that?" I try not to laugh. "Get married?"

"We did. It took a while for us to realize we loved each other. That we were good for each other. We shared so much... And knowing that, across the ocean, we have ten children growing up inside Eurasia—"

"So this is it." I have my 9mm in hand, and I nod toward the one she has tucked in her belt. "Two semiautomatics and a cyborg. That's how we're getting out of here."

She blinks at the sudden shift in conversation, her metal eyes expressionless. "You think we should fight them."

"We're slaves otherwise, working off however much that crane was worth."

She shakes her head. "You don't owe them anything, Daiyna."

"You do?"

"I told Samson to hijack that truck. We've never tried it before. There was just so much in the trailer, and we couldn't fit it all in my jeep." Her brow furrows. "Now we have nothing. No haul. No jeep. And Mayor Tullson will expect us to work indentured. You're right about that." She slides out of her bunk and places her hand on my arm. "But you can leave. You don't have to suffer because of our mistake."

I don't intend to. But I'll be taking them with me. I just haven't figured out how. Maybe we work for Tullson tomorrow—hell, maybe for a couple days, if they feed us well. Then once we've lulled him and his crew into a false sense of...

Shechara said something, and I missed it. "What?"

"He misses you. He said so, more than once."

I don't have to ask who she's talking about. "When was that?"

"A while ago. After we got rid of all the daemons. He was working with Milton and Sergeant Bishop. They were planning to contact the UW—"

"Idiots," I mutter. Before I realize it, the flask is in my hand, and I've downed a burning gulp of whiskey. I catch Shechara staring at me. "Want some?" There isn't much left, but I'm willing to share. Stack's saloon will be open in the morning. Maybe I'll trade a few bullets for a fresh supply.

Shechara shakes her head, her long hair swaying. "Three and a half years is a long time, Daiyna. What have you been doing out there?"

I cap the flask and set it on my bunk. "Getting by. Doing what I have to."

"We heard about the bounty..."

I laugh—then shoot a glance at Samson. He's still dead to the world.

"Nothing wakes him up short of a kick to the ribs." She smiles with affection.

"You really love him."

She nods without reservation. "I do." Then she pauses. "Luther's worried about you—"

"I don't want to talk about Luther." It stings too much to remember how I hurt him. And recalling his boundless optimism is enough to make me gag. "How about we plan our escape?"

She squeezes my arm before sliding back into her bunk and laying her head down on the pillow. She closes those incredible cybernetic eyes. "You plan *your* escape, Daiyna. If you're gone when I wake up, I won't blame you."

I frown. There's no way I'm leaving without her. And if she thinks she's going to sleep through any sort of escape I attempt, then she doesn't know me very well.

Time changes people. So does time apart.

Up on my bunk, I'm closest to the light, so I reach out for the pull-chain. But I pause to watch Samson for a moment, then Shechara. Both of them sound asleep. *Married?* Hard to imagine, but I guess this is reality. I just have to accept it.

Why aren't they still with Luther and Milton on the coast? Maybe gathering supplies is the work they've been assigned. After what happened to the Homeplace, Luther and his people lost all of their stores: food, water, weapons. I'm sure they've had to scramble and scavenge ever since.

Welcome to life in the Wastes.

So Samson and Shechara were supposed to load up their jeep and then what? Drive all the way back to the coast and divvy it up? Makes no sense. Why head this far inland?

The raiders could have already hit every stockpile west of here. They could be systematically sweeping inland from the coastline, scouring every city ruin and bunker along the way, hauling everything back to their ships on the Pacific. If I remember my geography correctly, their return voyage would take them south, then through the Panama Canal, and onward across the Atlantic to Eurasia.

I pull the chain, and instantly everything is pitch black. Outside, the sounds of Stack's loyal residents putting out the fire continue. Funny they didn't expect us to lend a hand. Probably because the work Tullson has in store for us tomorrow will be the more back-breaking variety. Or the unsavory. I don't even want to guess what it might entail.

I lie back on my bunk and close my eyes. Open or closed, the average human wouldn't be able to see a hand in front of one's face in here. But I've got this special night-vision ability. So if I want to stop counting the furrows in the steel ceiling and think things through, my eyes have to be shut.

If Samson and Shechara are on their own, just looking out for themselves, and if there's nothing worth scavenging west of here, it makes sense that our paths would cross eventually. After gunning down Willard, I kept to myself, covering the range between Sectors 30 and 35. I didn't return to the Homeplace with everybody else. I couldn't.

Not after causing that mess in Eden.

While Luther and the others were topside handing over the incubation units to Bishop's people, I was underground, chasing down Perch. I wanted to end him the same way I'd ended his boss—by emptying an entire clip into his torso and head.

Perch always struck me as a witless neanderthal who got off on hurting people. He never seemed to have much going on between the ears, besides hate and a loathsome personality. So imagine how surprised I was when he succeeded in trapping me inside. Sealing off the exits, he turned the hunter into prey. Once he showed the Eden Guard what I'd done to Captain Willard, they came after me frothing with vengeance and would have killed me, had Milton and Samson not intervened.

It was a bloodbath.

Our people and Eden's paid a high price for my revenge, but Perch survived. We managed to make it out of there, suffering multiple casualties as the men of Eden fired endless rounds after our retreat. They refused to follow us outside, so once we made it topside, we were relatively safe. Only seven of us. Down from more than twenty.

Because of me. The darkness inside. My hate.

Good people died that day, and I couldn't face those who remained. Like a coward, I ran off through the ruins and hid until Milton's flyovers eventually ended and Luther's voice calling out my name faded away beneath the howling wind.

Shechara says he misses me. But Luther misses who I used to

be. His ally. His friend. This person I am now? I barely recognize her anymore.

Maybe I miss me, too.

I pour the last drops from the flask down my throat and savor the smoky burn. Outside, the commotion settles as the flames go out. Inside, from beyond the flimsy partition-walls, low thuds of footsteps and the murmur of conversation seeps through cracks along the floor and ceiling. Nothing I can't sleep through.

Is this your doing? I ask the Rehana-spirit, wherever she is. Doubtful that she'll make an appearance in this cargo container. Her kind isn't able to move through human-made materials. If the floor was covered in dust or dirt, that would be a different matter. *Did you bring us together?*

I want to stay with Shechara, and yes, even Samson, but part of me knows I can't. If they stick with me, I'll put them in danger. There's the bounty on my head to contend with as well as the intangible sense that I've been cursed with bad luck. Tonight's as good an example as any: under house arrest with a guard standing right outside the door.

An ear-splitting explosion interrupts my thoughts as the shipping container reverberates. The bunk bed sways and slams back against the wall. Screams pierce the night outside, cut short by yet another blast.

The dark interior of the container glows with a ghostly blue aura in my special night-vision. I launch myself from the bunk and land between Samson's metal legs as both he and Shechara sit up and blink at me. She can see in the dark as well as I can with those eye implants, and Samson shares my gift from the spirits.

A siren wails. Mandatory evacuation.

"Under attack," Samson states the obvious.

"The UW?" Shechara asks.

No way to know. "This is our ticket out of here. We take one of their vehicles, and we don't look back."

Samson and Shechara glance at each other and nod grimly.

Maybe they don't like the idea of running away. Or stealing. Too bad. They're riding with me now.

I kick open the door to find our guard has abandoned her post. Not surprising. Outside, fresh fire lights up the night as dark figures run in every direction. Screams and automatic weapons fire compete with the wailing siren. Dirt bikes rip to and fro, grinding and chugging, kicking up dust in their wakes.

So, not UW raiders. Marauders have hit Stack.

"Wastelanders." Samson curses as he steps outside, scowling at the mayhem.

They're well-armed. At least three of the shipping containers-turned-makeshift buildings lie in smoking ruin, pulverized by the same sort of missile that took out the raiders' big rig. Same telltale craters in the earth surrounding each impact zone.

A dirt bike skids around the corner adjacent to us, and the rider cackles behind his ridiculous skull-mask and feathers, heading straight for us. He revs his motor as he raises the assault rifle slung over his shoulder and shrieks, "Half your load or half your woman!"

Samson steps past Shechara and me to meet the marauder head-on. The cyborg's arms pivot as he walks, transforming from metal hands to lethal blades.

"Find us a ride," he rumbles. "I'll catch up."

Shechara lurches forward, drawing her semiautomatic as if planning to join him. But I grab hold of her and swing her around the corner. I keep her ahead of me and glance over my shoulder just as the marauder releases a burst of automatic fire. The rounds ricochet off Samson's blade-arms with sparks of light. A split-second later, the riderless bike slams into the wall of the shipping container with a gong-like clang. The rider hangs suspended and stares wide-eyed through his mask, feet dangling in the air, his chest skewered on Samson's arm.

But he's not dead.

"How many?" Samson demands.

The marauder wheezes, his head drooping.

"How many of you are there?" Samson gives him a shake that makes him cry out.

"Enough," the rider manages. "More than enough." Then he laughs. Because he's insane. "Had a feeling I'd see you again." Blood bubbles out of his mouth and drools down his chin.

Samson drops him to the ground and pivots one blade back into a metal-fingered hand. He grabs the marauder's rifle and staggers after me.

"Let's move." I keep a hold on Shechara and draw my 9mm. Samson's shadow covers us both as we head for a darker, quieter corner of Stack, currently devoid of flames, screams, or gunfire.

"Head on a swivel," Samson says, doing his best to keep his voice low. With our night-vision, it will be impossible for anyone to sneak up on us—as long as we're paying attention to our surroundings. Not looking at the empty saloon and thinking this would be a great opportunity to break inside and take a few liters of whiskey—

"There." Samson points out a row of parked vehicles belonging to the Stackers. The four-door solar jeep looks promising, as long as the battery is charged enough to get us the hell out of here.

We pick up our pace, jogging toward the jeep while keeping to the shadows. Samson climbs behind the wheel and pops the hood for me to take a look underneath. The battery's in good shape, and according to the meter, it should hold enough juice to carry us a hundred kilometers.

I close the hood and lean on it, popping it quietly into place. Then I leap into the backseat behind Shechara. Samson slides one of his metal digits into the ignition and manages to start it up on the first try. He's a handy guy to have around.

We roll out, tires crunching across sand and gravel, the electric engine's low hum barely audible beneath the clashing sounds we leave behind. Samson takes us between two shipping containers, slow and steady, hoping not to draw any unwanted attention.

Wide-open space lies ahead where we'll stand out against the barren terrain. Fingers crossed the marauders will be too busy to notice.

"We could fight," Shechara says out of the blue, her voice near a whisper.

Samson shakes his head. "Doesn't feel right, leaving in the middle of it."

"Shut up and drive," I mutter. "It'll feel right being alive this time tomorrow." Should we be so lucky.

"Stack has never looked for any trouble," Shechara continues. "We brought it on them."

"You didn't have anything to do with this," I counter, about to lose my patience.

"We ran into a couple Wastelanders on our way here," Samson admits. "They followed us, most likely. Hell, they might've been responsible for firing that first missile and destroying the raiders' rig."

That makes no sense at all. Who would want to see all those supplies go up in flames?

"Fire and judgment!" a sudden voice screams. The path ahead is now obstructed by the figure of a large, muscular man sporting a flamethrower. He releases a spurt of liquid fire into the air and laughs, his voice ragged and guttural. "You think you can escape my wrath?"

I stand up and lean on the jeep's roll bar, my 9mm aimed at the lunatic's head. "Let us pass, we'll let you live."

Another laugh and flaming spurt. If he keeps showing off like this, maybe he'll exhaust his supply and not have enough to set us ablaze.

"I have seen the very fires of *hell*, woman," he growls. "You think a little gun frightens me?"

"How about three?" Samson holds the assault rifle he took off that marauder, and Shechara aims her semiautomatic. "Walk away, pal. Go find somebody else to creep out."

Silence from the dark figure. The flamethrower holds its peace.

"I recognize that voice…" the oversized marauder says at length. "Luther's…bodyguard?"

Samson flicks the headlights on, then off. The marauder flinches and staggers back, blinded for a moment. Samson slams his metal foot onto the accelerator, and the jeep tears away from Stack as fast as it can go, kicking up a screen of dust in our wake.

No one follows us. Not yet, anyway.

"You saw him, right?" Samson rumbles, like he wants to gauge his own sanity.

Of course I saw him. Not someone I've ever wanted to see again or thought I would, not after those UW hoverplanes rained fire outside Eden.

In the glare of the headlights, his face was a mangled mess of scarred facial tissue, the type of damage reserved for third-degree burn victims. His eyes were wild with hate. But that was him. No doubt about it.

"Cain."

8. SERA
22 YEARS AFTER ALL-CLEAR

I grab Erik by the shoulder and spin him around as we reach the sunlit lobby of the cube complex. Fortunately, the area is vacant, so no one is there to see an unarmed law enforcer following an overly armed citizen.

"You can't walk out onto the street like that," I tell him.

"Want one?" He offers an assault rifle he took from the security clones.

I grab it, if only to disarm him by fifty percent. "What are you planning to do?"

He shrugs. "Get you someplace safe."

"I don't need you to protect me."

"Didn't you hear? They're rounding up the Twenty. That's *us*."

I shake my head. "Just a precautionary measure. There's no reason to be upset by it." If my augments were working, I'd be able to tell how elevated his pulse and adrenaline levels are. But even without them, I can clearly see he's amped. "Once things settle down, we'll be able to return to our daily lives."

"Things won't be settling down anytime soon," he mutters, resuming his long strides toward the exit.

"Drop your weapon."

He halts and does a slow about-face like he's unsure what he'll find behind him. "You can't be serious." He blinks at me, standing there with my rifle trained on his chest.

"I'm taking you to HQ, Erik. Place that rifle on the floor, and then take three steps back. Hands behind your head. Interlock your fingers."

Twenty meters beyond him, outside the clear glass doors, disorder has claimed the street. Speeding automobiles swerve around pedestrians running and screaming. Half of them are armed: enforcers as well as citizens who don't look like they're from Dome 1. They're...filthy. The enforcers are chasing them, shockers out in the open. The grimy citizens turn mid-stride and fire their weapons over their shoulders.

Live ammunition. Actual bullets.

The front doors to the complex shatter, raining shards of glass across the tiled floor. Erik hits the ground in a prone position with his rifle aimed at the street. He looks like he's had some weapons training. Maybe in one of his acting classes.

I took the same position a split-second before he did.

"I recommend finding an alternate route, Enforcer Chen," he advises. "It's a war zone out there."

"Are those...?" I can't believe they're here, in Dome 1, causing such a grievous disturbance. "*Patriots?*"

"That'd be my guess." He keeps his eyes on the scene outside. "I doubt the security clones came here on foot." He glances over his shoulder at me. "Can you pilot an aerocar?"

With active augments, I'd be able to figure it out. Maybe even without them. I've seen Drasko do it often enough. How difficult can it be?

"We're going to the roof." I make it sound like it's my idea as I get to my feet and keep my weapon on him. "After you set down that rifle."

He glances toward the smashed front doors like he's considering making a run for it. Joining the mayhem with his compatriots—if he is, in fact, one of the insurgents. I wasn't able to find out earlier. The arrival of the chancellor's security personnel interrupted my telepathic investigation.

If you're really not one of them, you'll come with me, I think at him.

He looks at me and smiles warmly. *It's becoming natural for you to communicate this way.*

No, it's not. I just wanted to get his attention.

He laughs quietly, nodding to himself. Then he sends the assault rifle skidding across the floor in my direction and jumps to his feet. *Lead on, Enforcer Chen.*

I shoulder the second rifle by its strap and lower my weapon's muzzle by a few degrees. "After you. We'll take the stairs."

His eyes widen involuntarily. "Thirty flights?"

"That's right." *The last thing I want is to be stuck in an elevator with you.*

"You think they'll start hitting civilian targets next."

Honestly? I don't know what to think. "Best to expect the worst."

He regards me out of the corner of his eye as he heads toward the stairwell, a few meters beyond the bank of six elevators. "Is that an enforcer credo?"

Unofficially. I nod for him to pick up the pace, and then I follow a couple meters behind. As we pass the last elevator, its doors open without warning. I swing the muzzle of my second rifle to cover the interior.

An elderly citizen in a floral print dress cries out, covering her mouth, and staggers back against the support rail inside.

I drop the rifle to dangle by its strap and hold out a hand to calm her down. "Please return to your cube, citizen. It's not safe outside right now."

"Is he one of them?" She stares at Erik and the way my rifle is trained on his back. "A *terrorist*?"

Are you? I think at him.

He folds his arms and leans against the wall, shaking his head irritably. *Everything else I told you was true, wasn't it?*

"Why aren't you taking him *out* of the building?" the woman demands, scowling. "We don't want his kind here!"

Erik leans toward her and bugs out his eyes. "Oh, but we're already *everywhere*. We're your service providers. Your caretakers. Your custodians. You see us every day, but you don't give us a second thought!"

She freezes up, her mouth gaping like an extinct fish out of water. I step toward the elevator and press the up arrow. The doors close on her startled expression.

"Was that fun for you? Messing with someone's grandmother?" Probably on her way out for breakfast.

"My audience is limited. Seriously, where is everybody?" His voice echoes in the stairwell as he opens the door and starts climbing.

"In their cubes like good citizens, obeying the public service announcement." I let the door slide shut behind me and follow him, settling into a climbing rhythm that will carry me up the thirty flights without pulverizing my quadriceps. Easy does it.

"Zombies," he mutters. "Every one of them cooped up inside their little units, plugged into VR while the world falls apart outside."

"Careful there. You might start sounding like a misanthrope." I narrow my gaze at his boots as they mount one step after another. "Any reason why you're not jumping up these flights?"

He glances over his shoulder at me. "Wouldn't want to show off..."

"If it's true that you're not a dust freak, then what I saw last night was natural talent. Right?"

He shrugs. Doesn't slow his pace.

"Seems to me you're wasting time. You could be up on the roof in a minute flat. Find out if the security clones' aerocar is there, try to get it started." I pause. "Get away from the law enforcer determined to take you in."

"Are you trying to get rid of me?"

"One flight. Go on, show me what you've got."

"Now I'm feeling like a circus freak." He shakes his head. "Maybe I'm not amped enough for it to work."

"So your jumping ability requires adrenaline as fuel?" Interesting.

Another shrug. "Not sure how it works exactly. Only that it does, when I need it to."

"And you don't right now?"

"Why would I want to miss out on such stimulating conversation, Enforcer Chen?"

I duck my head to hide the involuntary twitch of a smile. This guy sure is a fan of idle banter. Not amusing at all. "What you said before, about knowing me before either one of us was born…"

"Weird, right?"

More like impossible.

"It'll come back to you, eventually. All of your memories will." Another glance back. "As long as you don't get those augments fixed. The longer you go without them, the stronger your telepathic abilities will become, and the clearer your past will be. Trust me on that. I've been there." He curses quietly. "You would not believe our story."

He means our shared history. Where we came from.

The North American Sectors…

My boot soles squeak to a halt. That can't be right.

"Told you it was unbelievable," he says, continuing upward.

I must have collected that tidbit from his subconscious mind. The North American Sectors—that's where we're from? It makes no sense.

"Twenty years ago, when we were born—" I frown, picking up my pace to keep up with him. "That was shortly after All-Clear. The bunkers opened, and nobody came out. They all died underground."

"The official story." He smirks over his shoulder. "The truth? Hundreds survived."

Ridiculous. "Without a protective biodome? I'm sure they survived for years and years."

"People are still alive over there. Survivors from the bunkers. Somehow, they've managed to scratch out a living—like one of those post-apocalyptic VR games, but for real."

"How can you possibly know that?" Anything outside of Eurasia is a forbidden zone. No citizen is allowed out of the Domes except those few in the military. Brave men and women who raid ruins across the globe and send back usable goods and materials.

He stops. Stands still for a moment before pivoting halfway around to face me. He's not smirking or flirting. His expression is dead serious. "Would you believe I've met some of them?"

"Survivors." My tone is flat. Incredulous. As if I haven't heard enough insanity from him already. "Don't tell me you've been outside the Domes."

He shakes his head, almost smiling. "They're here. In Dome 1."

This is too much. Either he's full of it, or my entire world is based on lies. I have every reason to believe the former and no reason at all to ponder the latter.

My life is orderly. Predictable. Maybe a little too much, but that's debatable. Being a law enforcer is important, and I'm proud of what I do. Every night, I help to make Dome 1 a safer place. My corner of it, anyway. During the day, I enjoy the quiet time in my cube. Resting, listening to music, maybe delving into some VR every now and then—swimming through pristine oceans as a dolphin, or soaring through blue skies as an eagle. The most popular avatars are always extinct creatures that died out decades ago. There's no harm in it. I'm not a *zombie*, plugged in all day long. Balance is key to a healthy life, and I've always sought to keep mine in order: work, rest, and play.

But then Erik shows up and disrupts everything. Turns my world upside-down. The Hawthorne Tower gets hit with a massive EMP, and terrorists are running loose outside my cube complex. And to top it all off, without warning, I'm apparently a telepath.

But it gets worse. According to this guy, the world itself is nothing like what I've been told. There are survivors living outside Eurasia's walls, and some of them have managed to sneak inside.

I don't believe it. I can't.

"Why not?"

"Stay out of my head." I point a gloved index finger at him with one hand; with the other, I tap the assault rifle dangling from my left shoulder. "And keep moving."

No more talking.

He honors my request for the next few flights. When we reach the twentieth floor—my floor—he hesitates at the door to the hallway.

"In case the aerocar is keyed to their proximity..." He raises an eyebrow at me.

We're not even sure there is a vehicle on the roof. "You want to drag a clone along? You'll be outnumbered."

He's not concerned about himself. He wants me to be safe. After seeing the violence outside, he's having second thoughts about immobilizing those security clones.

I got all that from a cursory telepathic sweep. Damn. It is getting easier.

"We'll make sure it takes orders from only you," he says, stepping toward the door. It slides open, sensing his presence. The hallway beyond is dim in comparison to the glaring LEDs in the stairwell.

The two clones lie right where he left them, outside my door.

"Fine." I hold the rifles still against my thighs. "After you."

Reaching the first security clone, he drops to one knee and fishes into his jacket pocket. What else does he have in there? I should have frisked him as soon as I had the upper hand—both weapons. I should've had him empty his pockets, at least.

I must be slipping. Granted, there have been a few distractions, but I'm a trained professional. Better than this.

"What are you doing?" I demand, aiming a rifle at his back.

"Easy there." He raises his old phone. "Just running a diagnostic."

"Explain."

He nods toward the disc he planted on the clone's chest plate. "The shock I gave it should have canceled all incoming signals and prior directives. If so, I should be able to give it new marching orders: obey and protect Enforcer Sera Chen." He winks at me. "Best to keep it simple."

"You're not dealing with a robot."

"Believe me, I know. A robot would be so much easier." His thumbs swipe across the screen of his antiquated device, flicking through various images displaying graphical and numerical data. Then he starts typing. "This will work. Just promise me you won't tell it to crush my skull or anything."

I shake my head. He has a bizarre sense of humor. "I plan to bring you to HQ intact, Mr. Paine."

Saying his surname almost elicits a smirk. He really is a pain.

"That should do it." He stands up and backs away from the clone. "Give it an order."

"What about the other one?"

"Well, I wouldn't want to be *that* outnumbered."

"On your feet," I tell the clone, and it stands upright immediately, facing me with its black face shield. Not even a glance at its identical partner lying motionless on the floor. "Did you arrive by aerocar?"

"Yes, Enforcer Chen," it says, its voice somehow different from before.

"Lead us to the roof."

Unarmed, it sets off for the stairwell at an even stride. I nod for Erik to follow and he does, seeming to find the whole situation amusing. He's the only one.

We take the stairwell up ten more flights to the roof access door. There the security clone pauses, half-turning to look past Erik.

"What is it?" My voice echoes down the switchback of stairs and landings below us.

"There is gunfire in the streets, Enforcer Chen," the clone says. "The roof may not be a safe zone. I would be better equipped to protect you if I were armed."

"Can you pilot an aerocar?"

"Yes." It nods.

"Your primary directive is to fly us to police headquarters. Leave everything else to me." The last thing I want is to be sequestered someplace safe with the other members of the Twenty. Until I see this clone follow my orders, I'm not giving it anything it can threaten me with—for my own good, of course.

I'll decide what's good for me. Right now, it's taking a potential terrorist to HQ and finding out what the hell is going on in my city.

The door to the roof slides open as the clone approaches. Outside, the sun is shining. A beautiful day in Dome 1. Nearby domescrapers loom, their mirrored glass reflecting the mid-morning light. Healthy trees in planters line the pathway from the door to the landing pad. The grass fields surrounding us, along with the jogging track, lie vacant.

So much beauty up here, but so few take advantage of it— even on days when citizens aren't advised to remain inside their cubes. When was the last time I went for a run? I'm ashamed to admit I'm more likely to jog in place while plugged into VR, exploring some adrenalin-laced game environment.

The pilot door to the aerocar rises automatically as the security clone steps within range. With a swipe of its white gauntlet, the door to the passenger compartment rises as well. This isn't your standard law enforcement vehicle, the type Drasko flies around the city every night. This is a luxury model straight from the Chancellor's private fleet.

"Very nice." Erik grins as he climbs aboard and takes his seat.

The spotless white faux-leather molds to his body, providing exceptional comfort. "Only the best for our Lady Persephone."

The clone is already at the controls as the cockpit door lowers automatically into place. Both of its hands move expertly, running through the pre-flight sequence and activating the electromagnetic coils. A low hum courses through the padded inner hull as the anti-gravity system prepares to take us skyward.

I drop into the seat across from Erik and rest the two rifles on my knees. Both muzzles are aimed in his general vicinity.

He frowns at them. "What? You think I'm going to jump from a flying vehicle?"

"I've seen you do crazier things."

He leans forward as our door drifts shut. "I'm sticking with you, Sera. Of my own free will. I want you to remember that."

Implying that if he wanted to escape, he could have done so long before now. "You're a model citizen."

"I try." He leans back with his hands behind his head. Fingers interlocked. Big dumb smile.

"We are ready, Enforcer Chen," the clone says.

"Take us out." I keep an eye on the street below as we soar off the side of the cube complex and make our ascent. All other air traffic has been grounded. If I'm concerned that a terrorist may target us, it's because we're the only target in the sky right now.

Erik watches the streets as well, leaning over to press his forehead against the pane of plastiglass. The sun washes his face in golden hues, filtered through the dome's blue-tinted plexicon. He closes his eyes for a moment, basking in the warmth. I'm instantly reminded of the boy he was—

Do I really plan to lock him up?

I have to. It's my job. And besides, it's not like he'll be incarcerated for long. Once he explains himself to an interrogator, he might get out early with some requisite community service. Or he'll be charged with resisting arrest and stalking a law enforcer, entering said enforcer's domicile without permission, incapacitating two of the Chancellor's security personnel, possessing dangerous tech including an EMP grenade...

On second thought, that's enough to put him away for a very long time. Particularly now, with the attack on Hawthorne Tower and whatever insanity is taking place on the streets of Dome 1. Eurasia has always held a zero-tolerance policy towards insurgency. Any sort of rebellion will be crushed, and those even remotely connected to the discord will be punished severely.

Erik picked a very bad time to find me.

"So, I'll probably miss the banquet," he echoes my thoughts. Listening in, most likely. There should be a law against that, too.

"It could be indefinitely postponed."

"One can hope."

"How many others have you found?" I hold his gaze. "Of the Twenty."

He abandons the view below and faces me. "I know where they are. The government did a standup job of separating us—especially those sharing DNA. Couldn't have us reproducing. We'd end up with inbred monstrosities. So they placed us with various families in different castes in order to keep us apart. And once we received our neural implants, they made us forget that we had certain...abilities."

"Did the Governors know? Did the headmaster—our teachers?"

He shakes his head. "We were smart enough to hide what we could do from them. We made a game of it, keeping our abilities secret whenever our teachers were looking. But when their backs were turned..." He smirks at a particular memory. "Pretty sure we drove them nuts."

"Secret," I echo. "Like that rooftop show you put on last night?"

"Things are different now. Dust addicts can do everything I can—for a limited time. The more prevalent dust usage becomes, the easier it will be for us to use our abilities in public."

"Where does it come from?"

"Dust? I think you already know."

The North American Sectors? "But how does it get inside Eurasia?"

He shrugs. "Same way anything illicit enters a highly guarded, civilized society—or totalitarian regime. Smugglers."

"They would have to be in the military." No one else is allowed to work on those freighters or gain entry into Dome 10 from the sea. "Or criminals posing as military personnel."

He gives me a wink. "Now you're catching on."

"The survivors you mentioned—that's how they're getting into Eurasia."

"Are you sure you're not an interrogator? You might want to ask for a promotion, Enforcer Chen."

I shake my head and look out the window. "Still doesn't explain how you know all of this. Unless you're some type of subversive yourself."

"Oh, I am all types of subversive." He follows my gaze to the vacant street below. Quiet, with no one in sight. Local law enforcement must be elsewhere, bringing peace to Dome 1. "Unless I'm mistaken, that's a maglev entrance."

I nod absently. "No trains are running." Due to the current lockdown.

"Perfect."

He stands up and hits the emergency release. The door to the passenger compartment shudders as it rises, buffeted by the wind.

"What the hell are you doing?" I point a rifle at his head. "Return to your seat, citizen!"

With one arm, he braces himself against the upper lip of the doorframe. His hair thrashes wildly as he leans out.

"I can't go to jail, Sera," he shouts. "I have too much work to do."

"Shut the door!" I yell at the clone.

It remains focused on piloting the craft. "I am unable to override an emergency—"

"There's no way you'll survive this jump, Erik. I don't care how talented you are!"

Another shrug and dashing smile. "You wanted me to show you."

"I saw enough last night! Please, return to your seat, or..." My aim wavers.

"You'll shoot me? Then we'll be the *Nineteen*. Nobody wants that!" He gives me a crisp salute. "See you around, Enforcer Chen."

He falls sideways out the open doorway like he's the class clown, toppling into a swimming pool at a rowdy party. I lunge forward, the rifles swinging from my shoulders, the wind blasting against my face as I peer out after him. We're 400 meters up in the air with nothing but plasteel and plasticon below, streets and sidewalks and buildings with mirrored glass reflecting his fall. He doesn't wave his arms or flounder. He looks very composed as he plummets to his death.

So much for sticking with me.

"Follow him!" I order the clone and hold onto the handgrips mounted beside the open doorway. The door itself continues to shake. It won't close until we land, emergency protocols being what they are.

I squint into the wind as the aerocar makes its descent. Hard to believe, but Erik has landed on his feet half a block from the maglev train entrance. He takes a moment to steady himself against the wall of a nearby restaurant, closed for the day. Then, with a glance up in my direction, he staggers onward, moving slower than is customary for him. If I had to guess, I'd say he sprained something during that impossible touchdown.

All the better for me to catch him.

The aerocar sets down in the middle of the deserted street fifty meters from the maglev entrance. The gates are locked, and no one appears to be on duty. Even the automatic kiosks are dim, not welcoming any commuters today. The dark tunnels beyond are far from inviting, but Erik doesn't seem to mind. Despite whatever minor injuries he sustained after throwing himself from a moving aerocar, he manages to scale the three-meter-tall gate with minimal effort—half leaping, half scrambling over it. I can't see where he's headed on the other side, but I have a feeling he's planning to take a tunnel to one of the outlying domes. On foot.

"Contact Commander Bishop at HQ. Tell her I am in pursuit of a suspect." I step out of the passenger compartment and into the street. The aerocar kicks up a torrent of air like a miniature windstorm emanating from underneath the vehicle.

"Enforcer Chen, according to the Chancellor's records, you are not authorized to pursue suspects. Nor are you authorized to wield lethal ordnance." The clone swivels in its seat to face me. "Additionally, it appears that your augments are offline. You will not be able to see inside that tunnel. All things considered, I should accompany you."

I remove the magazine from the rifle I'm leaving behind, tossed onto my seat. Slipping the spare mag into one of the pockets along my pant leg, I point at the gate, choosing to ignore everything the clone said. "Open that for me."

The clone exits the vehicle, leaving it idling, and approaches the train station. Taking a moment to size up the locking apparatus, it reaches with both hands and grips hold of the ironwork. The armored suit whines as it powers up, and the clone trembles in place like a strongman at the circus lifting weights just a bit too heavy for him. But the gate doesn't stand a chance. With a metallic crack, it swings open.

"Secure this position." I head straight for the nearest tunnel, leading to Dome 2.

"Yes, Enforcer Chen."

I activate the tactical flashlight mounted on the assault rifle and sweep the powerful beam side to side, cutting a white swath of light through the darkness. There's a walkway along the right side of the maglev track, and I leap onto it, not bothering to keep my boots quiet as I run. No idea how long I can maintain this pace without an exo-suit to provide that extra boost. But unless Erik's a fast healer, I should overtake him in a matter of minutes.

"Erik Paine, halt!" My voice echoes with confident-sounding authority. I hear only my own footfalls, not his. So either he didn't take this tunnel, or he's in stealth mode.

If I had Wink and Blink with me, I could send them to scout ahead and relay back everything they see. If my augments were functioning, I could call up blueprints of this entire substructure and overlay them in real time. Instead, I have memories bubbling to the surface that make no sense whatsoever.

Erik mentioned two names that meant nothing to me before: *Tucker* and *Margo*. But now I sense some kind of connection to them both. I don't see any faces in my mind's eye, but I feel something. Friendship? Loyalty? Directed toward me from each of them. They cared about me and Erik. They cared what happened to us.

"Enforcer Chen," the security clone's hollow voice calls after me. By the sound of it, holding position at the gate was not a priority. It's following me instead. "I cannot allow you to continue along this course of action. You are placing yourself in danger. Please stay where you are, and I will join you. Together, we will apprehend the fugitive and escort him to police headquarters."

A dark figure lands on the walkway right in front of me, one hand gripping my assault rifle and forcing the muzzle toward the ground, the other pulling me into a tight side-embrace.

"So I'm a fugitive now," Erik says into my ear.

I twist the rifle, shining the flashlight up into his eyes. He flinches, and I drive my boot into his shin. With a garbled cry, he releases both me and my weapon and stumbles away.

"Enforcer Chen, are you in danger?" The clone approaches, its boots smacking the pavement as it jogs my way.

"Halt!" I yell at it, and it does what I say. What a concept. I shine the light at Erik's chest. "Were you hanging from the ceiling?"

He shrugs. "Impressed?"

Exasperated is more like it. "If I have to put you in shackles, I will."

"Think back to the person you were twenty-four hours ago. Before we met."

Before my life became an incomprehensible mess. "Why?"

"Imagine eighteen other people out there, exactly the same age as us. Nine of them your brothers and sisters, nine of them mine. All of them with no idea who they really are or where they came from." He takes a step toward me. "Don't you think they deserve to know? What they're capable of? What our government has been using them for?"

You know where they are...and you're going to find them, I think at him. *To turn their lives inside out, like you did mine.*

"To introduce them to the truth." He gives me half a grin. *Join me, Sera.*

I glance over my shoulder at the clone, silent and still in the darkness. Then I lower my voice as I turn back to Erik.

"First tell me about Tucker and Margo."

9. SAMSON
5 YEARS AFTER ALL-CLEAR

Dawn breaks behind us as we race across the desert, going as fast as the jeep can manage along this uneven terrain. Best to stay off the raiders' well-beaten path, and if any Wastelanders want to follow us, they'll have to work for it.

Shechara hears them first and turns around in her seat to look back, her eyes doing that thing they do when she zooms in on details too far away for anybody else to see—without binoculars. Those metal spheres in her sockets are made of overlapping parts that swivel and slide across one another, glinting under the sun.

I keep my foot on the accelerator and glance into the rearview mirror, squinting through the screen of dust in our wake. Morning light glows across the eastern horizon, scaring off the stars and painting the sky twilight's violet-indigo. Worth stopping and admiring if you're not on the run from a pack of desert freaks.

The grinding motors of their dirt bikes reach my ears before I see their dark forms emerge from the gloom, a dozen of them riding full-speed after us. Some of them take the opportunity to jump their bikes into the air and pose with an arm or leg outstretched before landing. They sure know how to have a good time while hunting their prey.

If I had to guess, I'd say they finished off Stack and got bored. Raping, killing, and pillaging provides only so much in the way of entertainment. They needed something else to keep their hopped-up minds busy. That charred monstrosity formerly known as Cain—not sure what to think of that yet—must have told them about our escape, and they all decided to track us down.

So here we are. With morning on the way and too many Wastelanders for my liking about to overtake us.

Half a dozen, we could deal with. But I'm not optimistic about our current chances. Particularly if these freaks are well-armed. The missiles that hit Stack could have come from a Stinger. If any of the dirt bikes at our six are carrying a Wastelander with a shoulder-mounted rocket launcher, and if they're able to lock onto us with its guidance systems, then we are toast.

But I'm not about to give up. This jeep still has some juice, and I'm squeezing the batteries for all they've got. Shechara and Daiyna are both armed, and I've got the Uzi I took off that Wastelander—not to mention a few tricks up my metal arms. If push comes to shove, we'll take out half of them and then see how we do with the ones left over.

"Thirteen bikes," Shechara reports, her 9mm in hand and pointed at the floorboard.

"Lucky thirteen," I mutter.

"You've had trouble with these guys before, I take it?" Daiyna has drawn her semiautomatic as well.

"You haven't?" I glance at her in the rearview.

She looks different than the last time I saw her. Skinny, unhealthy, pale. Her eyes move around a lot, and she has trouble sitting still. Her short hair is choppy; looks like she hacked at it with a knife. Shechara's overjoyed to see her, to be with her. I hope Daiyna has the presence of mind not to break her sister's heart by disappearing from her life again anytime soon.

"I've been living like a hermit," she explains, "doing my best to avoid people like this."

"Good idea." Shechara's eyes are focused on our pursuers. "Two hundred meters and closing." She rests her hand on my shoulder. "We should swing back toward the main road. Include the raiders in this little meet-up."

Not a bad idea. The enemy of our enemy is someone who may not try to kill us right away. Or something like that. I adjust our course toward the southwest.

"You still in touch with the spirits?" I ask Daiyna.

"Whether I want to be or not," she replies, sounding more exhausted than ever.

"Mind asking them to contact Milton?"

"You expect him to save the day?" She leans toward me, holding onto the back of my seat. "Is that how it works now? You and Shechara go off on your own, hijacking raiders and whatnot, and when you get into some trouble, you cry for help? Scream for the local superhero to rescue you?"

Her tone is bitter, her voice ragged around the edges. Like she's been drinking hard liquor day and night for a few years. Trying to dull the pain, quiet the ghosts. For her, those ghosts are literal, thanks to the spirits of the earth showing up as people from her past.

Glad I'm not somebody blessed by their presence.

"Prior to last night, we've managed to cross paths with the Wastelanders without killing any of them," I explain, taking the jeep across a rough patch that jostles all three of us fiercely in our seats. "They're not easy to get along with, but it's never gotten violent."

"Then you had to go and skewer that guy," Daiyna says.

"Seemed like the right thing to do at the time."

"Usually does." Daiyna exhales loudly. "Alright. So what are we looking at here? Territorial biker gang? Sexual deviants? Cannibals?"

"All of the above," Shechara says. "They've been building a reputation for over a year now. Filling the vacuum left by the daemons." Shechara glances at me. We both had a hand in their extermination.

"The Wastes needs its freaks," I offer. "Difference is, you can reason with these guys. Sometimes—when they aren't high as kites."

Daiyna takes that at face value, and we cut the chatter, bracing ourselves for what's to come. Shechara updates us on how close the Wastelanders are. A hundred meters, then fifty, but no missiles fired yet, not even an RPG. Maybe they don't want to kill us outright.

They want to have fun with us first. Probably Cain's idea.

So he didn't die when those UW planes rained fire down on his warriors and the collared daemons outside Eden. He was inside that Hummer at the time, riding in style. Maybe it sheltered him somewhat. But the burns he endured left him looking like some creature from an old, twentieth-century horror movie. And he didn't sound exactly sane back there in Stack, screaming something about fire and brimstone. Or judgment—that was it.

I thought he died years ago, and he hasn't crossed my mind since.

Shechara nudges me, and I glance into the rearview. The dirt bikes are spreading out, the ones at the edges speeding up as if they've been holding back until now, toying with us. They're planning to flank us on both sides before they close in. Then they'll get in front of us and start shooting.

I clench the steering wheel and swallow a curse. No sign of any raiders as we approach the main thoroughfare, almost as flat as a graded road in comparison to the rugged country we've been bouncing through. Of all the times for those UW scavengers to be nowhere in sight.

According to the battery gauge, we'll have enough power to continue at these unsafe velocities for the next five minutes, maybe ten. After that, we'll drop to impulse speed while the sun rises and the solar panels soak up as much energy as they can.

But impulse might as well be a dead stop. We'll be surrounded by Wastelanders, and we'll have nowhere to go.

The ground in front of us erupts with a sudden explosion—a rocket-propelled grenade fired over our heads. I swerve to avoid the crater as sand splashes against the windshield and side windows, raining down on top of us as we cringe in our seats.

There was no time to put the roof on when we stole this thing. Had to drive it as-is. Of course, the roof would have included a few more solar panels in addition to what's mounted on the hood and doors, and that might've given us a little more juice. Live and learn.

"Warning shot," Shechara observes, and I nod.

No reason to return fire. Yet.

We've got bikers flanking our jeep now, their bleached skull-masks grinning at us instead of watching where they're going. Daiyna looks ready to send a few shots their way, but Shechara shakes her head. Daiyna shrugs, leaning back in her seat to enjoy the ride. She seems strangely detached, as if she's already made her peace with death. Almost like she welcomes it.

Well, good for her. I just hope she doesn't do anything stupid to put Shechara's life in danger. Or mine.

By the time the Wastelanders encircle us, keeping a good ten-meter buffer zone around our vehicle, the jeep's battery decides it's time to sleepwalk. No matter how hard I smash the accelerator into the floor, we won't go faster than a crawl. The dirt bikes slow down, matching our speed and maintaining their oblong circle around us. Thirteen bikes, three of which carry Wastelanders riding double, the ones in back holding shoulder-mounted missile launchers.

I brake, slowing the jeep to a stop. The bikes in front of us and at our flanks pivot, skidding their chunky tires through the dust to face us. The one nearest my window carries the scorched remains of Cain. Flamethrower nowhere to be seen, he carries a Stinger proudly on his thick-muscled shoulder.

"Samson!" he cries, his voice a frayed imitation of the zealous warlord I remember. He climbs off the back of the bike, one hand gripping the shoulder of the smaller man steering the thing, pushing down on him. "It has been too long. Where have you hidden yourself all these years?"

I lower my window and rest a hand on the Uzi in my lap. "Nobody's been hiding. It's a big continent, Cain. But I'm surprised we haven't crossed paths sooner."

"Admit it." He grimaces and wheezes between each sentence. "You are surprised. That I am *alive*."

"It's unexpected."

He chuckles, sounding like he's gargling gravel, and pats the Stinger. "My friend and I have been in touch. More than once." He nods slowly as a cold heaviness weighs down my insides. "Yes, you see it now. After what we did to Stack. The truth has dawned on you: it was never the UW. Not there, and not at Luther's Homeplace. It was *me*. It was always *ME!*"

The hoarse scream at the end is uncalled for, but he has our undivided attention.

"So you've made it your mission in life to attack fellow survivors," I reply. Why seek to destroy those enclaves where folks are trying to make a life for themselves? Where a little bit of civilization is finally returning to these wastelands? "And you've found some new recruits to take up the cause." I look a few of the Wastelanders over. Psychos tend to gravitate toward one another. "I sure hope Cain's not your leader." No response from the skull-faced freaks. "You do realize he led all of his people to their deaths, right?"

Cain curses, loud and foul. "They died gloriously! It was the will of Gaia!"

"I see." My slow nod is intended to show that I'm paying attention. And I am, noting every detail: which Wastelander has both hands on his bike versus the assault rifle dangling from a shoulder strap; which one defers to Cain with every glance versus attempting to stare me down; which ones haven't taken their eyes off Shechara or Daiyna since we started this insightful conversation. "So, Gaia told you to blow up Stack? And the Homeplace?" I shake my head at him. "You're still blaming a spirit of the earth for all the stupid things you do?"

There's a quiet intake of breath from Shechara and an equally quiet chuckle from Daiyna. Half the Wastelanders rev their bikes and lurch toward us with menace. The other half just keep on staring daggers.

Cain grins broadly, not even bothering to cover his face as the harsh morning sunlight washes over us all, scorching the dusty landscape as far as the eye can see. He probably figures the damage has been done.

"Judgment is upon us, Samson. Fire and judgment. I am the emissary of Gaia's wrath!"

Interesting. "Your wives were in the Homeplace, Cain. Your children."

He frowns at me like I'm speaking gibberish. "This is not the time for new life. This is the end of all we know. We are the Horsemen of the Apocalypse." The Wastelanders rev up their bikes, all thirteen of them, in a deafening display of solidarity. "We must burn this world to the ground to make way for what is to come!"

Daiyna leans toward my ear. "He's out of his mind."

"Possessed?" I ask in a low tone.

"This is all Cain." No evil spirit necessary.

Good to know. "So, how'd you all meet?" I nod toward his riding companions. No reason not to be neighborly—until the shooting starts.

Another big smile from Cain. But instead of answering, he asks, "Where is Victoria?"

"No idea. You probably should've asked before you fired that missile at the Homeplace."

It never was the UW, as we assumed at the time. With good reason. They had a track record of wiping out what they considered to be mutant settlements. But no, it was this lunatic. And judging from what we witnessed in Stack, his thirst for destruction is still going strong.

"She is alive." Cain nods. "Gaia has told me so. Victoria survived the attack on Luther's Homeplace, and I must find her. I need to see what she sees."

I drum my metal fingers across the Uzi. "Can't help you with that."

"Then where is Luther hiding?" He looks at the circle of Wastelanders. "You must realize this is the only reason you are still alive. You killed one of us. You should die for that. But if you tell me what I need to know, I will allow you to go free...and take one of the women with you."

Shechara. I would of course choose my wife. Except I won't have to choose. Because Cain is a devil, and I don't make deals with his type.

I can't fight them. There are too many. And I won't put Shechara or Daiyna in danger like this. We're surrounded. It would be suicide. So what's the alternative?

"We go together." I can feel Shechara's eyes on me, staring in disbelief. Daiyna curses under her breath.

"You will lead us to him?" Cain looks ready to laugh. "Like Judas. Betraying your friends?"

I keep my expression stone-cold. "There's a reason we parted company with Luther and the others. But that's none of your business." I give him a nod. "You want to know where they are, we'll take you there. That's the deal."

Cain watches me like he's trying to read my mind. Not sure what sort of abilities he was gifted with, but I don't think telepathy is one of them. As long as he can't sift through my thoughts, this should work.

"We ride together." He nods, liking the sound of it now. "How long until your battery charges fully?"

I defer to Shechara. "Noon," she says.

"Until then, we ride slow." Cain winks at her. "Two people with mechanical parts, and..." He focuses on Daiyna. "Luther's woman."

Oh boy. Not good.

She stands up and levels her semiautomatic with Cain's raw meat-head.

"How did you get to be the leader of this little wolf pack?" Her fearless voice holds the moment. I'd wager she isn't scared of anything this world might throw at her.

Cain's smile is a tight grimace as he raises his chin proudly. "I defeated their former leader in combat."

"Alright." She nods. "New deal: I beat you, and your merry men do whatever the hell I say."

Shechara grabs her arm. "Daiyna..."

"No woman has ever led us!" one of the bikers shouts, incensed. "Women are only good for two things: food and—"

"Let me stop you right there." Daiyna keeps her gun and goggles on Cain but points with her other hand at the loud-mouthed Wastelander. "My first act as your leader will be to institute new dietary restrictions."

Shechara rests her hand on mine. "Samson, you can't let her do this," she whispers.

I'd offer to fight Cain instead, but I doubt he would have it. Human versus cyborg isn't what anybody would call a fair fight.

"C'mon Cain, what are you afraid of?" Daiyna laughs.

There's no turning back now. Cain has to save face in front of his clan. He'll kill Daiyna before our eyes, and then he'll expect me to lead him to Luther.

It didn't have to go down this way.

"It's what she wants," I tell Shechara.

"What is?"

"Death."

She freezes.

"You challenge me for leadership!" Cain bellows as if he's issuing an official decree. "Very well. This should not take long at all. Then we will be on our way."

He hands his missile-launcher to the biker beside him and steps in front of our jeep. As he beckons for Daiyna to join him, the Wastelanders rev their motors and raise their fists into the air with a chorus of tribal screams.

Daiyna hands Shechara her gun. Followed by her flask. "I'll be wanting these back."

"Why are you doing this?" Shechara's voice is choked with emotion.

"Buying us some time." Daiyna launches herself out of the jeep, leaping five meters up into the air and landing with a puff of dust as her boots hit the ground. The Wastelanders lose most of their fervor at the sight of her superhuman agility. "Is this it?" She gestures at the ring of bikers as she faces Cain, keeping at least three meters between them. "The whole tribe?"

He tilts his head to one side. "You wish there were more to watch you die?"

"A step down for you, isn't it? There were close to a hundred living in your rusty old boats, from what I recall."

He clenches his jaw. She's struck a nerve. "That was another life. I have been reborn—"

"In fire. Yeah, you look like a new man." She laughs. "Only the best for Gaia's servant, right?"

"I am her *son*," he growls. "And you will soon learn your place, woman!"

He advances on her with his fists raised to eyebrow level—if they hadn't been burned off. Daiyna keeps her hands hovering at her sides, sidestepping to avoid being backed into the jeep. Beside me, Shechara grips a gun in each hand and watches, motionless.

"It should be you," she says.

"If only," I mutter. Cain wouldn't stand a chance against my blade-arms. "Keep an eye on his crew. Anybody interferes, we shoot 'em."

She nods. "I like the way you think."

Cain swings out one fist, telegraphing the punch from a kilometer away. Daiyna jerks back, allowing his momentum to carry him forward. Then she leaps into the air, vaulting over him and pushing off his shoulders, back-flipping prior to landing solid on her feet. Shechara looks like she wants to cheer, but she holds herself in check. Maybe Daiyna doesn't want to die, after all. Not right now, anyway.

Impossible to see her expression behind the head covering

and goggles, but there's a smile in her tone as she goads him. "Your reborn body is too slow, Cain. I'd ask Gaia for another one, if I were you."

He reels to face her. "I just need to land a single blow, and you will not get up again. I will crush your skull while you lie on the ground. Then my friends will cut you up and roast you over an open fire tonight."

"Disgusting." She shakes her head. "But you'll need to hit me first. And I don't see that happening."

He shuffles forward like he's going to attempt another swing, but then he charges headfirst like a bull. She hits the ground and leans to the side with one leg extended. Anybody light on their feet would be able to avoid tripping, and maybe Cain used to be that agile. Not anymore.

He stumbles into one of the Wastelanders' bikes, and both somehow manage to remain upright. The biker reaches out to help him, but Cain smacks the guy's hands away.

"The former leader you defeated..." Daiyna springs to her feet and backs away. "Did he happen to be eighty years old?"

Hard to tell if Cain's face is crimson with rage. That's his natural flesh tone now. "Enjoy this moment, woman. For it will be your last." He steps toward her but doesn't swing, doesn't charge. He keeps his fists clenched and one foot in front of the other, like a kickboxer.

"Maybe he died of old age, waiting for you to hit him," Daiyna offers. "Is that how it happened?" She glances at the ring of bikers.

Their skull-masks stare back at her. They're not revving or screaming anymore. Uncanny how quiet and still they are.

Cain advances step by step, and Daiyna maintains the distance between them by alternating a step backward with a step sideways. But she can't keep this up indefinitely. Cain's stride is longer; he's twice her size. In the next few seconds, she'll need to leap over him to keep from being pinned against a pair of dirt bikes.

He knows this. And he's ready for it when she does.

As she vaults over him, he reaches up over his head nonchalantly like he's taking something down from a top shelf. He grabs hold of her leg with one hand and twists on his heel, hurling his arm downward as he throws her to the ground. She lands flat on her back with a groan and a loud exhalation of air, her limbs and head flipping upward on impact.

"Daiyna!" Shechara cries.

The Wastelanders turn their assault rifles on her. All thirteen of them. The two holding rocket-launchers aim them at me.

So this is it.

Cain stands over Daiyna, watching her. Then, as she struggles to rise and catch her breath, he plants his boot on her diaphragm and leans forward, resting an arm on his knee as he holds her down. He smiles at her and shakes his head with disappointment.

"Foolish woman. I hoped you would have more fight in you." He chuckles hoarsely. "Is there anything you would like me to tell Luther when I see him?"

She nods, struggling to take a breath under his weight. "Tell him…" Her voice is barely audible.

He moves his head closer to hers, crushing her beneath him. "What's that? Speak up now. Let everyone hear you."

"Tell him…I knocked you down."

He frowns as if he didn't quite hear her. But she's already brought up both legs, one boot plowing upward into his groin. His eyes widen, and he groans, frozen in agony. At the same time, she grabs hold of his boot planted on top of her and wrenches it viciously with both hands, sending him toppling sideways with a garbled cry. Dust plumes as his body hits the ground like dead weight.

The Wastelanders don't know where to look. Their skulls twitch from Cain to Daiyna to us in the jeep.

"That's our cue." I nudge Shechara.

She stands up with her arms extended, both guns cocked and ready to take as many headshots as she can before the return fire sends her ducking for cover. At the same time, I throw open my door and raise the Uzi in my left hand. My right gleams in the sunlight as it transforms into a broadsword.

"Let them finish this," I shout. "Nobody interferes."

"You heard the man." Daiyna stands just out of Cain's reach, hands on her knees as she catches her breath, watching him. "Had enough?"

Teeth clenched, he rises to a sitting position, glaring bloody murder at her. Then he somehow manages to get to his feet, favoring the ankle she twisted. He staggers backward a couple steps, never taking his eyes from her.

"Oh, we're just getting started," he rasps with a broad grin.

The Wastelanders cheer, fists in the air.

Daiyna nods once. Then she stands upright, her hands relaxed at her sides, her weight on the balls of her feet. Cain juts out his chin and rises to his full height, fists framing his gruesome face. His knuckles crack as he takes a step toward her.

Then he frowns, confused. He lurches forward with a grunt, staring at her. All is not well below his belt. "What did you...do to me?"

"It's a pain that will linger. I'm surprised you're back on your feet so soon." She tilts her head to one side. "Ready to call it quits?"

He shakes his head. "I haven't killed you yet."

The bikers hoot and holler at that. But then Daiyna rushes Cain and kicks his injured foot out from under him, ducking as he swings his fists at her but not moving fast enough to avoid a blow to the temple. She spins sideways from the aftershock as he crumples into the dust, howling in both rage and pain. Daiyna looks rattled, shaking her head sharply and struggling to keep her footing.

"Finish her! Finish her!" the Wastelanders chant, building momentum.

Cain scrambles forward on hands and knees, grimacing in the churning dust. Once he's within range, Daiyna drops back and twists her body, driving her boot heel into his oncoming nose. The burst of blood doesn't slow him down any. He roars as he lunges for her with both arms.

I've seen some ugly fights over the years, but this one might be the worst. No sense of decorum at all. Just two people grappling on the ground like animals: thrashing, kicking, headbutting, biting, and screaming. It's clear Cain thinks he'll be able to crush her just by wrapping his arms around her and squeezing. But it's a poor strategy. And Daiyna is making him pay dearly for it. The back of her head has already pounded his nose into mush. He's bleeding all over the place, and she's managed to land a couple more kicks to his nether region. A sane man would have let go of her by now. But he's not sane, and he's holding on with a death grip, his hands interlocked over her chest. Waiting her out.

It starts to work—once he focuses his grip on her wounded shoulder. She wilts in his grasp, crumpling inward.

"That's...better..." he gasps, teeth bared in victory as her head drops forward. "You had some fight...in you...after all."

"Daiyna!" Shechara screams, the guns trembling in her hands.

"This is a good death," Cain says in Daiyna's ear, blood drooling from his mouth. "You have nothing...to be ashamed of. You will feed us...for many nights." He smiles at me. "Thanks be to Gaia."

She whips her head back with such unexpected force—cracking his eye socket—that he pitches over and releases his grip on her. Daiyna scrambles away from him, heaving as she struggles to breathe. Cain lies flat on his back, cradling his face and moaning, cursing her again and again.

The bikers glance at each other, unsure of the situation. Their leader has actually been bested by this woman. As she gets to her feet and he doesn't, it's clear to anybody with a fully functioning brain who's won this fight.

Except it's supposed to be to the death.

"Finish him!" I shout. Not because I'm a fan of blood sports. Because these skull-faced idiots were shouting *Finish her!*

moments ago, and turnabout is fair play. I glance at Shechara, and we shout it together: "Finish him!"

Daiyna shakes her head. "I don't want this guy haunting me."

Not sure what she means by that, but she sounds dead serious.

Cain screams unintelligibly as he tries to stand. The busted ankle won't support his weight, so he kneels instead, cupping one hand over his smashed eyeball.

"Is this who you want leading you?" Daiyna gestures at him as she turns to look at each of the Wastelanders. They stare back at her, their guns drooping toward the ground. "He's not even one of you! He killed your former leader and usurped his role. I say you deserve better."

No idea where she's going with this, but she has their attention. They're nodding to each other in agreement.

"Make me your leader, and I'll take you someplace you've never been. But I'm sure you've heard of it." She pauses dramatically. "*Eden.*"

They nod hungrily, liking the sound of that. Who hasn't heard of Eden? Subterranean refuge, stockpiled with milk and honey. Used to be, anyway. Rumor has it the Edenites are starving these days, thanks to UW raiders taking everything Willard's collared daemons used to scavenge from the city ruins above. But by all appearances, these desert freaks don't pay attention to the local gossip.

"You'll live like kings!" Daiyna laughs as they cheer, ready to make her their queen.

Cain shakes his head angrily and tries to get their attention, but his rasping pleas are no match for their volume. They completely ignore him—a bloody, broken mess of a man unable to stand before them.

"What do you think?" Shechara leans toward me.

I look at her. "I think we're going to Eden."

PART III
ANNIHILATION

10. LUTHER
2 YEARS AFTER ALL-CLEAR

My scarred finger traces the route, east to west, across a map printed off the bunker database long ago. The paper is dusty and wrinkled, torn at the edges, and the map itself is an inaccurate portrayal of the topographical features surrounding the Homeplace; but it is the best we have. Over the past two years, I have added a black marker overlay that represents the current terrain of this new earth. No lakes, rivers, trees, plant or animal life whatsoever; only sand, dust, rocks, hills, and mountains. The map now shows distinguishable land features—lopsided elevation, massive craters—in order for us to orient ourselves.

I've added notes on the roving daemons in erasable pen. Eden's collared variety are no longer a concern. The UW saw to that by incinerating them all. But the packs of wild, armed mutants are still an issue for us in these desert wastes. Thus far, they have not attempted to scale the cliffs or tread along the winding path up to our caves, but our sentries continue to spot them. Jeeps parked in the distance, the daemons stare at the Homeplace for as long as thirty minutes before driving away.

We know they are able to communicate to one another with grunts and snorts, but it remains unclear how intricate their language is. The sounds could be merely warning signals or ways to announce an attack or retreat. Vestiges of their military training, ingrained in what remains of their minds.

I tap my finger on the map. "Here."

Samson leans over my shoulder, squinting in the yellow-green light of the glowstick, and nods. "That would be a good vantage point. Higher ground. Plenty of cover." He glances at Sergeant Bishop.

The three of us are in my study—the alcove in our warren of caves where I go to think, strategize, and pray. It was here that I first met James Bishop when Margo brought him to the Homeplace. He wore that bulky environmental suit, afraid of contamination. But the whole time, he was already *infected*, as his superiors saw it. As soon as his helmet was fractured and his air supply was compromised, he was no longer welcome to return to Eurasia.

"Then we keep moving. South, west, north. Three hunting parties." Bishop points out the locations.

"Split our forces," I echo.

"Set up camp at equally solid locations. Gun down the mutants, take their weapons and vehicles. Form a supply chain to provide the teams that follow us with everything they'll need to hold down the forts as we continue to press outward." Bishop shrugs. "Assuming everything goes according to plan."

Samson smiles fiercely. "I like it."

We have wanted to eliminate the daemon threat for well over a year. When we followed those daemons into the ruined city above Eden, we hoped to find the creatures' home base. For many of them, it was. But after moving our people to the Homeplace and finding just as many daemons out here, so far away from any nearby ruins, it became clear that they are scattered everywhere. As far as we can tell, they continue to hunt in the same units they were assigned upon arrival—back when the UW sent scores of search and rescue teams to prepare for All-Clear.

Originally, the daemons were human beings. Military personnel, ordered to assist us with our re-entry into the world, helping us rebuild lives for ourselves on this wasted continent after we left the bunkers. Their superiors had no idea the spirits of the earth would have other plans for them.

"If only there were more of us." I shake my head at the map. We cannot afford to lose anyone else. Not that we ever could. "The mothers with children will remain here." I look both men in the eye in turn. "Leave two sentries to guard the front and rear cave entrances. Everyone else—arm them, divide them into teams. We'll move out at dusk."

Bishop nods, almost saluting as he exits the alcove. He's one of us now, and he's taken to his role naturally, putting his military training to use. Our people seem to like him, and they don't mind when he orders them around. Because he does it with respect for their abilities. He's learned each of their names, and he knows what each of them can do. He seemed lost when Milton brought him back to us, once it became clear the UW wouldn't allow him to return home. But he's found his new purpose.

He has hope, as I do, that we will see our children again. It may not be tomorrow or even ten years from now, but it will happen. The Creator has not seen us through all of the trials we've endured only to leave us without a future. I have faith He will continue to guide us and protect us, and that somehow, we will break into that city of glass across the sea. Or at the very least, make this quarantined continent a place worth visiting, should our children ever desire to do so.

Samson lingers at the earthen doorway to the passage beyond, the alcove's glow barely revealing his features. "It's a good plan," he offers.

I nod. It's the best we have. "I can't lose anyone else..." I trail off.

He takes a step toward the large rock I use as a desk and rumbles quietly, "You didn't lose her. She left us."

"I should have been there for her—or stopped her." I can't

bring myself to say her name. I'm afraid the sound of it will bring tears to my eyes.

"She's got some stuff to work out. Needs space. She'll come back when she's ready, I'm sure of it."

I shake my head, not sure at all. "She's given herself over to vengeance. She's lost herself in it."

"That guy had it coming."

Willard deserved to die. No question. "But she didn't have to be his executioner. She could have left him in the hands of the Creator, who rewards both the just and the unjust, according to their works."

Samson gives me a sympathetic smile. "If only the whole world shared your beliefs. Maybe D-Day never would've happened."

"We can't change the past. What's done is done. But we can avoid making the same mistakes going forward." My gaze returns to the map. "I hope this is the right move."

"Exterminating the daemons? Yeah, I'd say so. One step closer to a livable future, at any rate." He pauses, trying to remember something. "We've gotta clear the Promised Land of those Canaanites before we can live in it. Something like that, right?"

Back in the bunker, I would read aloud from the Holy Scriptures every night. I was never sure whether Samson paid any attention, swinging in his hammock with his eyes closed.

"Except our Canaanites are cannibal freaks," he mutters.

I join him at the doorway and clap a hand on his shoulder. "Let's get to work, brother."

In the great cavern, Milton and Sergeant Bishop have everyone assembled, seated and attentive. There are thirty of us left. We lost people when Cain's warriors attacked, and when we marched on Eden. We lost more when Perch led the Edenites against us, after the UW flew off with our unborn children in the bellies of their planes. But our numbers increased when Cain's wives, children, and the elderly members of the Shipyard joined our ranks.

United now, we gather to prepare for our ground assault against the daemons.

Milton will fly ahead, conducting an aerial search to locate daemon positions while trying not to get himself shot down in the process. Margo will remain in contact with him telepathically and relay his recon back to us as we move out. Victoria will stay here in the Homeplace, but she will use her gift to scan the terrain on all sides of us for daemons, notifying Margo of any movement. Shechara will join Samson and myself as we take point. Bishop, Margo, and Justus will flank right while another team of three—Ethan, Connor, and Deven—flank left. We'll be in constant radio contact every step of the way as we press westward and set up camp at the first lookout, ten kilometers out.

Bishop explains the tactics and strategy, fielding questions, answering people by name. He was born for this.

Samson nudges me with his mechatronic elbow. "Glad he's on our side."

As am I.

Taylor, one of the sentries, slips inside to notify me that dusk has fallen. I gesture to Bishop, and he wraps up the meeting. The nine of us heading out collect our weapons and make the slow descent from the cave entrance to the foothills below. We don't speak to one another, using hand gestures and nods instead.

Except for Margo. Once Milton launches into the darkening skies, she faces me.

I will keep Sergeant Bishop informed of any sightings made by Milton or Victoria. He will radio you should the need arise, she projects her thoughts into my mind.

Nodding to her, I beckon to Samson and Shechara, and the three of us take the lead, leaving the foothills and striking out across the desert. If all goes according to plan, we won't be walking on the way home. The daemons' solar jeeps will be ours.

We maintain a brisk pace for ten klicks. Then after trudging uphill for half an hour, we reach the first vantage point marked on the map. All nine of us meet at the hilltop and set up camp for the night behind the boulders: four on watch, one at each compass point. We'll rotate in two-hour shifts. Margo, Justus, Samson, and I take first watch. The others lay out their bedrolls and try to get comfortable.

I raise an eyebrow at Margo as I rest my rifle on a level sheet of rock. She shakes her head. Not daemon sightings yet.

They tend to be less mobile at the end of the day, although they have been known to attack after dark. It's fine by me if we don't engage them until first light. Milton will lure them our way, and we will neutralize them. Once the next team from the Homeplace arrives to take our place here, we'll split up, advance, and take the next three positions. Milton will again lure them into the kill zone, and we'll keep forging westward, repeating the strategy until we've cleared a path to the coast. By then, we should have enough of their jeeps and weapons to split our forces and sweep both north and south as well. Should the Creator bless our efforts, we will then move inland, past the Homeplace toward Eden, scouring the wastelands for any lingering daemons.

This is an enormous continent, but thankfully the only Sectors with bunkers prepared for D-Day were located here in the southwest. So it was only here that the UW sent their search and rescue teams. We don't need to worry about daemons roaming across all of North America.

Why the southwest? Why not build bunkers from coast to coast? Originally, that had been the plan, but by the time the patriots unleashed their bioweapons, only the bunkers in the southwestern Sectors had been completed and were ready for our internment. The government had to act fast, abandoning all else in favor of what was expedient. If the situation hadn't come to a head so soon, there may have been millions of survivors at All-Clear.

And more daemons than we could ever hope to deal with.

As the situation stands, we estimate there to be at least a hundred daemons in tribes scattered across the desert wastes. Sergeant Bishop says the original number would have been under a thousand. Deducting the number of daemons we've neutralized since we left the bunkers—along with those that died in the tunnel outside Eden when Willard sent a collared horde after Samson, Shechara, and myself—and those that were incinerated by the UW hoverplanes—we're left with a hundred, give or take.

From what we've seen, they never roam in groups of more than twelve, four to a jeep. But we have seen plenty of single jeeps out and about, hunting for their next meal...

My head jerks upward. Now is not the time to be nodding off. I blink and inhale the cool night air, doing my best to stay in the moment. I peer east through the rifle scope and trace the terrain we crossed on foot. No daemons are following our tracks. I glance over at Justus who's keeping a steely eye on our southern flank. Easily the oldest among the Shipyard survivors—or any of us, for that matter—he took it in stride when we told him what happened to Cain and his warriors.

"Guess that means I'm one of you now," he said. "What you've wanted for a while, isn't it? Joining forces." He winked, the skin crinkling around his eye like wax paper. "Gaia's chosen people and the infidels."

Meeting him for the first time, I couldn't help but be reminded of Rip, the oldest member of our Sector 51 brotherhood. Killed by daemons when they attacked our first cave refuge, farther inland.

When I think back to that series of caves we occupied, survivors from Sectors 50 and 51 finally living together after so long apart, the memory morphs into the Homeplace, as if the older images have been overwritten by the new. I try to remember the twinkle in Rip's eye, and instead I see Justus, whom I've known for only a few weeks. I knew Rip for twenty years.

Two decades from now, what will my memories be like? Will I even remember this moment? Crouched up here behind this rock, holding this rifle, keeping watch in silence as the stars shine above and the night's chill creeps into my bones. How many of us will still be alive? Will we survive the next few weeks?

I glance at Samson, facing north. His remark earlier today about the Canaanites gave me pause. The God of Israel commanded his chosen people to wipe out the native inhabitants of the Promised Land. They were idolaters who sacrificed their own firstborn children, and despite multiple warnings, they would not change their ways. So when judgment eventually came, they were annihilated.

I have always found that genocide difficult to reconcile with the New Testament scriptures, which are concerned with going out into the world and sharing the Good News that God is love, and He made a way for us to spend eternity with Him: through Jesus Christ paying the price for our sins. What about the Canaanites? Was there no redemption for them?

Perhaps the lesson is to get right with God before it is too late—before the ax of judgment falls.

The daemons were men and women, once. Some of them may have shared my beliefs. Not many do in Eurasia these days, according to Sergeant Bishop; but throughout history, there has always been a remnant of true believers. Followers of the Way, the Truth, and the Life.

What happened to the human souls the daemon bodies once carried? When we exterminate them, will we be freeing them from the torment of their daily lives? Or are they so far gone that they don't remember who they once were and can't comprehend what they've become?

Without warning, dust blasts upward as Milton lands in our midst, causing those in their bedrolls to cough and curse quietly, turning away from him.

"Sorry," he whispers, crouching sheepishly and making his way to my side.

"Anything?" I look up at him.

He shakes his head. "I'll try again before first light. You'd think all those explosions on the coast would've scared them inland.

Figured there would be more than a few nests to spot from the air." He shrugs. "Zilch so far."

"What about the northwestern ruins?"

"I'll check them out tomorrow. Didn't want to get too far ahead. You know, in case you needed me or something." He unwraps his head covering, releasing his shaggy hair.

"Good thinking." I give him half a smile, but it fades when I notice his worried look. "What is it?"

"Probably nothing." He pauses. "But it's weird, right? How a few daemons have been parking half a klick out and watching the Homeplace? Like they know better than to approach, but they're thinking about it anyway."

I nod. "That's one of the reasons we're out here."

"Yeah. What are the other reasons again?"

"The UW may never permit us to enter their domed city, but that doesn't mean they intend to abandon us here. If we remove the daemon threat, they will be more likely to interact with us. Perhaps even send us food and supplies without fear of having their helicopters shot down."

"You're a very optimistic person." Milton leans back against a boulder and closes his eyes. "Has anybody ever told you that?"

"Once or twice." I pat him on the shoulder. "Get some rest. We'll need you in the air again soon."

"Roger that." He nods, interlocking his fingers across his abdomen. It isn't long before he's snoring quietly.

I have a difficult time remembering the Milton I first met over a year ago. He was a different person then. The spirits played tug of war with him, two sides attempting to sway him to their cause: saving the human remnant versus destroying it. I prayed for him while he was possessed by an evil spirit, but I had my doubts whether he would emerge from the experience unscathed.

Yet he did. And he was granted an additional ability by the spirits. Not only is he the fastest man I have ever seen, but he's also able to fly without a jetpack. It's clear to me that the Creator has a purpose for Milton's life, as He does for all of us. But with Milton, safe to say it is something special.

He went through a period of doubting the spirits, even after they blessed him with flight. He let them know he could figure things out for himself. But lately he seems to be on speaking terms with them again; and they, in turn, have communicated with him.

They have confirmed what we suspected: that the only daemons who remain alive are located in our corner of the continent. Once we eradicate them, life will change for us. We will not have to hide in our clifftop caves. We can scavenge materials from deserted city ruins and build a life for ourselves. Makeshift villages will lead to towns and future cities—

One step at a time, one foot in front of the other. We cannot afford to get ahead of ourselves. One of the pitfalls of optimism, I suppose.

Sergeant Bishop takes over my post at the shift-change, and I take his word for it that two hours have already passed. He's the only one of us who wears a timepiece. We'll trade places two hours from now.

"All quiet," I tell him as he sets his rifle on the rock and settles in. "Anything from the spirits?"

"Not yet."

He's uncomfortable sharing an open line of communication with the spirits of the earth. So far, they haven't told him anything different from what they told Milton. And, so far, Bishop has yet to see a manifestation of the malevolent spirits. Only the benevolent variety has appeared to him, taking the form of his beloved wife. He has not exhibited any other unique abilities, which is probably for the best. His interactions with the spirits unnerve him enough as it is.

I have often wondered why I was excluded—why the spirits have chosen to communicate with individuals who are less inclined toward any sort of spiritual belief system. But I remind myself that the Creator is the one I worship, not His creation. These spirits of the animal kingdom are powerful, but they are not omnipotent, nor are they omniscient. If anything, they remind me of the capricious gods of ancient Greece: some blessing us while others curse us.

Many spirits retain fond memories of their interactions with humans prior to D-Day, but others do not. When the blasts and resultant nuclear winter wiped out every living creature on the planet, the spirits with no love for humankind found another reason to hate us. They tried to get Milton to detonate the nuclear reactor in Eden, but they failed. Then they tried to get Cain to destroy the unborn children in Eden's incubators—another failure. What plan are they currently concocting to exterminate the human remnant?

Once the daemons are gone, they will no longer be a tool for the evil spirits to wield against us. Whether another group of survivors similar to Cain's warriors rises up to fill the void, only time will tell. I pray for peace to fall upon these ravaged wastelands, and I hope those of us gifted by the spirits will unite behind a common purpose. More than mere survival, we need to find a way to flourish.

I eventually nod off, and when I awake, it feels as though no time at all has passed. Instead of Bishop, it's Milton who jostles my shoulder.

"I'm heading out," he says, wrapping his head covering into place.

What happened to my second shift? I sit up with a start.

"Bishop took two watches," he explains. "Said he couldn't sleep anyway. Figured you could use the rest." He slides his goggles down from his forehead over his eyes. "I'm thinking he was right."

"Thank you," I tell the sergeant in the predawn darkness. "But going forward, I won't tolerate any preferential treatment."

"You did me a favor," Bishop says, keeping his eyes on the terrain below. "I feel more like myself right now than I have for...too long. If it's all the same, I'd like to hang onto this feeling."

He's a marine again, a man with a mission. A purpose. "But you need to get your rest as well."

He nods. "I will. I know my limits."

Milton takes off into the sky with a burst of dust, waking up anyone who wasn't already greeting the early morning of a new day. We break camp but hold position, waiting for Margo to let us know when Milton returns, leading a few daemons our way. I pray that he's able to get their attention while remaining out of range of their guns and rocket-launchers.

But when Margo approaches me, her brow wrinkled with concern, it's not Milton she's worried about.

"I've lost Victoria," she says.

At the same instant, a flash of light illuminates the eastern sky and the ground reverberates from the impact of a massive blast. We all catch our breath and stare, frozen in place.

Oh God, no...

"The Homeplace," Shechara says, her mechanical eyes rotating as she zooms in to focus across the distance. Ten kilometers makes no difference to her. "It's been hit."

Samson stomps forward on his mechatronic legs. "With what?"

"Missile." Bishop peers through his binoculars.

"Who...?" I struggle to find words, as if the air has been knocked out of me. "Daemons?"

"Could be the *Integrity*," Bishop offers.

Samson curses under his breath. "The UW strikes again."

We saw plenty of evidence during our journey west from Eden, survivor encampments wiped out with only craters and scorched wreckage to show anyone had ever gathered there to start a new life together. We assumed the UW intended to eradicate what they perceived as groups of infected mutants.

"Why now?" I murmur as bodies press past me in the dark to

descend from the hilltop and head down, back to the Homeplace as fast as they can.

"You're harboring a fugitive." Bishop means himself, of course. He gets to his feet and shoulders his rifle. He doesn't join the others in their descent. He seems to be awaiting orders from me.

I pray that Victoria and the rest of our people are all right, that they somehow survived the blast. It's difficult to comprehend what's happened. That while seeking to eliminate one threat, another has reared its head against us. That we could return to the Homeplace to find no one alive.

That the nine of us and Milton...may be the very last.

"Margo," I call down to her as I begin to follow the others. Bishop is right behind me. "Tell Milton—"

"He's on his way." She jogs toward me, her silhouette recognizable. "And he's got company."

Daemons, her voice echoes in my mind. *Plenty of them.*

"Everyone, back into position! Quickly!" I shout, rushing down the grade to stop them. When I grasp the cold metal of Samson's arm, he resists.

"Luther, we have to go home," he rumbles. "They need our help."

"We will," I assure him. "But the daemons will overtake us on foot. We must hold the higher ground and hit them hard."

He nods with reluctance. "Then we'll take their jeeps to the Homeplace."

I'm glad he foresees our victory. I squeeze his arm, unsure whether he can feel the pressure. "We can do this."

"Hell yeah." He stomps toward the hilltop where everyone else is taking their positions, rifles at the ready.

Milton swoops down from the sky and lands beside me, facing east. Toward the Homeplace. "I should—"

"Go, Milton. Help them as only you can." I give him a push, and he nods, returning to the sky and disappearing into the distance.

With his superhuman speed, he will arrive in a matter of

seconds. Once there, he will triage the situation, moving in a blur as he tends to those most in need of care first, whipping through the broken rock and rubble to save as many lives as he is able. Anyone who is trapped will have to wait for Samson.

Again, I pray...

"Here they come," Shechara announces as I take my place beside Bishop, my rifle aimed at the cracked hardpan below. "Three jeeps, twelve daemons, approaching full-speed from the northwest."

"Keep your heads down," Bishop advises, "and don't start shooting until you see the yellow of their eyes."

We will wait for them to get close. Once we start firing, they will either back off, split up and circle our hilltop, or launch a grenade or two toward our vicinity.

"Concentrate your fire on any jeep with a rocket launcher." I try to control my breathing as my pulse races.

"What if all three do?" Justus pipes up.

"We hit 'em all hard," Samson growls, glancing at me.

I nod grimly in the early morning light, enough for those of us without Shechara's special eyes to see by. I notice her looking over at Samson, and he returns her gaze. A meaningful look, from one who cares deeply for another. He may even love her; I would not be surprised. Lately the two of them have been spending more private moments together. She smiles faintly at him now, and he nods before they both return their attention to our visitors.

The solar jeeps approach, tires kicking up dirt and gravel. Margo keeps track of how many daemons we have targeted by entering the minds of our people and seeing what they see.

Six headshots lined up, she reports silently as her thoughts join with mine.

We do not fire yet. Not until we can take out more than half of them with our first salvo.

She nods, relaying that message to the others—to all of us. *Wait...*

"Grenade launcher," Shechara whispers as soon as she spots the weapon, "second jeep."

Bishop glances at me. I nod.

"Fire!" he shouts.

Rifles erupt from the western and northern sides of our vantage point, with Shechara, Samson, Justus, and Margo firing at will in automatic bursts.

Rocket-launcher neutralized, Margo reports, *along with four mutants. That jeep is ours.*

Leaving two vehicles, and eight daemons.

"Here they come." Bishop releases a short burst as the lead jeep swerves around our side of the hill.

He hits the driver in the side of the head with a splatter of black blood across the windshield, killing the daemon instantly. The other three in the vehicle unleash a fierce barrage on our position, and we duck behind the boulders as their rounds chip the granite, choking the air with bits of rock and dust.

The third jeep is retreating, heading back the way they came. They're moving out of range.

"I've got them," Shechara says, her aim steady, her eyes focused on the retreating daemons. She squeezes the trigger of her assault rifle in a calculated semi-automatic rhythm, one round at a time, shifting her position slightly with each shot.

Four headshots. Margo is impressed. *Mutants neutralized. Another jeep is ours.*

I give her a nod and gesture for Samson to join Bishop and myself as we cower under fire. He lumbers toward us, shielding his torso and face with his metal arms. The daemons' rounds ricochet off his mechanical limbs and smack into the boulders on either side of him. He doesn't bother to duck for cover.

"Look out below!" he booms.

Then he slams his arm against the boulder on his right, sending it sailing through the air. When it strikes the ground, it bounces and rolls like a massive bowling ball of solid granite, blocking us completely from the daemon's gunfire before smashing into their vehicle and throwing the creatures out of their seats. Bishop and I gun them down where they land.

"All twelve mutants have been neutralized," Margo reports aloud. "Two jeeps in working order. Every one of us uninjured and accounted for."

Samson gives me a direct look. "Now we go home," he rumbles.

11. SERA
22 YEARS AFTER ALL-CLEAR

I don't trust that thing, Erik thinks at me as we walk through the dark maglev tunnel, half a klick away from Dome 2 now. *And I don't like it following us.*

I'm not a big fan of him sending thoughts into my head, but I figure fair's fair. *You gave it new orders.*

Clones are conditioned to follow orders, and yeah, I gave it a new set, he replies. *But there's no guarantee it won't revert to its original directive. Namely: locking us up for our own protection.*

I glance back at the clone, hearing only the heavy, measured footfalls of its armored boots. Weirdly enough, I can see it. And I shouldn't be able to, not with the only light being an occasional glow strip mounted along the track below. Not without my augments, at any rate. But I can make out every centimeter of its white armor as clearly as if a train were speeding down the track, washing the tunnel with its headlight.

Maybe my eyes have just grown accustomed to the dark. Or maybe the capabilities of my visual augments are lingering, enough to see a bit. I can't allow myself to consider the alternative: that in addition to my newfound telepathy, I have a second bizarre ability that has decided to manifest itself.

I don't tell Erik. I don't want to encourage him. Or scare myself. What the hell am I turning into?

No. I can't allow the anxiety to take root. I breathe in and out a few times and focus on the path ahead. Once I report to MedTech at HQ and get my augments fixed, everything will be back to normal. No more mind-reading or night-vision.

But is that what I really want?

I'm surprised we haven't run into any other enforcers. After a terrorist attack, martial law should be in effect, with armed guards at every point of entry.

Erik chuckles at that. *Just you wait. The outlying domes will be different. Crackdown in full effect.*

Why should it be any different in Domes 2 through 10?

He glances back at me. *The sun shines on Dome 1 while clouds cover every other dome.*

I've heard that saying before—usually from residents of the outer domes. They seem to think Dome 1 is this majestic, opulent city favored by Chancellor Hawthorne while the other nine domes' second-class citizens live only to serve. To provide for Eurasia's every need: agriculture, manufacturing, technology, oxygen generation, recycling, and waste management, to name a few. But it doesn't matter where you live or what your job assignment is; Eurasia would cease to function if anyone gave up their responsibilities. Every dome is vital. So is every citizen.

You sound like a patriot, I think at him.

He shakes his head. *You still believe I'm a terrorist?*

Jury's out.

What will it take to convince you I'm not?

I've been trying to keep an open mind, to listen to what he's had to say and somehow make sense of it. No idea where exactly he's leading me right now, but he seems to think we should find the other members of the Twenty. If doing so doesn't involve working with terrorists, then maybe I'll trust him. But I have a hard time believing he got hold of an EMP grenade—and those discs he used to immobilize the clones—without some sort of shady underworld contacts.

Just because I happen to know people on the other side of the law doesn't make me a patriot.

Gritting my teeth, I restrain myself from cursing him out. I've got to figure some way to hide my thoughts—

I could teach you, he offers.

"Stay out of my head, or I'll shoot you in the leg and drag you back to HQ."

"Police brutality!" His voice echoes up and down the tunnel. "Did you hear that?" He looks at the clone. "She just threatened me!"

The security clone doesn't respond or alter its pace, walking a couple meters behind us.

"So. Tucker and Margo. Who were they?" I ask.

He faces forward and keeps moving. "You remember them."

"It's blurry."

"It'll clear up. As long as you don't use those augments, all of your memories of the early days will return in time."

If what he said is true, then we're talking extremely early. Pre-birth. How is that possible?

"Margo made us," he says, like he's discussing the latest Linkstream upgrade. "And Tucker introduced us to our parents. Our real parents."

"In North America."

"That's right."

Land of infected freaks. Does that mean we're infected, too? Is that why we can read minds, see in the dark, or jump off dome-scrapers?

"How do we remember them if we weren't even born yet?"

He casts a sly smile over his shoulder at me—which I can see in the dark.

"We've always been special, from the moment we were conceived. Margo was too, that's how she could communicate with us." He taps his temple. "Mind to mind."

"What do you mean, she *made* us?"

"Hawthorne and the Governors perceive anyone who's lived on

the surface of the North American Wastes as being infected. If you breathe the air, you're contaminated. Happened to the leader of that military team they sent over there twenty years ago. His protective gear was compromised, and his superiors didn't let him back into Eurasia." He pauses. "Our parents were infected. But their sex cells were extracted in a sealed underground lab, and Margo combined those cells to make twenty viable embryos. That's it in layman's terms, anyway."

Sounds like a VR interactive. So very far from any semblance of reality. "Why?"

"Back then, Eurasians weren't having kids anymore. Because they couldn't. Sterility had become a rampant epidemic, and the Governors were afraid we would die out after the youngest generation grew up and eventually expired. The Terminal Age generation." He pauses. "People your boss's age."

Commander Bishop. She's got to be worried about me by now. Offline, not reporting for duty. If the clone's comms hadn't been damaged by Erik's immobilizer—or whatever that was—I would have contacted her. As it is, I'll have to wait until we reach Dome 2 to connect with local law enforcement.

But with the Chancellor missing, I'm sure Bishop has been busy. Hopefully too busy to notice the absence of a lowly curfew enforcer.

"I've never heard about any sterility problem. There are plenty of babies in the Domes these days." It seems like every successful couple in Dome 1 has one.

"Yes. There are, aren't there." He sounds like he's toying with me, yet again. "Of all the children you've seen, what age would you say is the oldest?"

I haven't thought about it. I shrug as he glances back at me.

"Late teens?" he offers.

"No." I frown. It's never struck me as strange, but considering it now— "Maybe eight or so." I've never seen a child older than that. Doesn't mean they don't exist, though.

"And how old were we when those mandatory doctor's visits started?"

I don't know about him, but for me, it was once I got my period. Mom took me every month after that. "I was twelve."

He nods, half-turning toward me. "Eight years ago."

My pace slows. I'm no investigator, but I can recognize puzzle pieces when they fall into place—whether or not I like the way the resulting picture looks.

"You think the Governors are repeating history. Using our sex cells to...create the next generation." My voice sounds admirably in control of itself, considering this new revelation: that the Twenty have had our sex cells harvested from us without even knowing it, ever since we reached puberty. That children sharing our DNA have been created in laboratories and handed out to citizens in the upper castes across the Domes.

Just when I thought I'd reached the limits of incredulity, Erik throws this at me. Way too much for my brain to process right now.

"Next time you're on the Link, expand your DNA search to include shared DNA," he says. "More than your nine siblings will show up. Because all those kids they've made from our sex cells? They've had the DNA of their adoptive parents interwoven to expand the gene pool. We wouldn't want any inbreeding going on, right?"

"Who's behind this?"

"One guess." He nods toward the clone.

Dr. Solomon Wong, master geneticist. Of course.

"How many...are there?" I sound exhausted.

"Close to a thousand. With more on the way."

Because those doctor's visits didn't end when we left home to live on our own and make a life for ourselves, contributing to society as mandated by our job placements. Every month, I'm still required to visit my doctor for a brief examination. She asks me questions, takes a little blood, checks my vitals. Makes sure the job isn't getting to me, that I'm living a healthy lifestyle. The usual. I've assumed it's because I'm in law enforcement, which can be a stressful career. Or so they tell me.

It's hard to imagine her extracting my eggs without me knowing it. What does she do? Knock me out, make the extraction, then reset the chronometer in my augments so I don't notice the time lapse? Ridiculous.

If any part of this is true, then I should be filled with rage. I'm sure I will be, at some point. For the time being, I do my best to compartmentalize my emotions as I was trained to do at the academy.

I doubt that Erik the rebel has met with his doctor lately. "Let me guess. You started missing your appointments a while back?"

He nods. "As soon as I learned the truth."

The increasing brightness at the end of the tunnel signals that the Dome 2 station is located just around the bend. A semicircular patch of light in the distance enlarges as we approach, and a handful of armed guards are clear to see in silhouette. They shout at us to halt once we're fifty meters away. Surprising it took them this long to notice us.

What's our story? Erik doesn't look back at me. He puts his hands on his head, as he's told. Like he's ever been that compliant with me.

I do the talking. I follow their orders as well, placing my hands on my head—away from the assault rifle at my side.

"They are Dome 2 law enforcement personnel," the clone observes without any alteration to its monotone. Both of its gauntleted hands are set atop its helmet. "Enforcer Chen, you will be safe with them."

Keeping their weapons trained on us, the guards beckon us closer and then surround us once we reach the end of the pathway and enter the maglev station. Just like Dome 1, the gates are closed and the ticket kiosks are offline. But on this side, a sleek, gleaming train sits idly by, unaccustomed to being off-duty.

"Sera Chen, Dome 1 Curfew Enforcer," I introduce myself. "I apprehended this citizen—"

"Curfew's over, Chen." The guard's eyes glaze over as he consults whatever is displayed on his ocular implants. A middle-aged fellow with a sizeable paunch and dark-grey buzz cut, he nods to himself. "You attempted to apprehend this violator last night but failed. I see you had some help remedying the situation this morning." He nods toward the security clone. "Why take the tunnel here?"

"The surface streets are unpredictable in Dome 1 right now. I need a safe space to drop him off." I raise an eyebrow as I lower my hands. The clone echoes my movements. Pretending to be a good boy, Erik keeps his fingers interlocked on his head and doesn't say a word, his gaze fixed on the ground between his boots. "Any chance you can take him off my hands?"

The guards shake their heads. "We've had our own share of trouble. Martial law's in effect, and the streets are clear, but that hasn't stopped local agitators from doing what they do best. Smoke grenades tossed out windows, live ammunition fired at random. Luckily, none of our personnel or any citizens have been injured, and the individuals responsible have been arrested. But the terrorist threat remains."

"Any news on the Chancellor?"

He shakes his head. "The patriots hit the Tower. That's what we heard. But the Link's been glitchy all morning. Wouldn't surprise me if that's what they're targeting next."

I look around at the silent streets and buildings. Smaller than Dome 1, this dome was designed for the main purpose of oxygen generation and recycling. The majority of the space has been utilized for growing leafy trees and other oxygen-producing plant life on the ground as well as suspended from the interior surface of the dome itself. The air is fresher, the tint of the dome's glass greener—either intentionally or a byproduct of so much chlorophyll in a confined space. The only buildings are cube complexes to house the local citizens, stores that provide for their needs, and a station for local law enforcement. Two city blocks away, the small town ends and the forest begins.

"I'll notify our captain that you're on your way, in case you'd like to lock up this violator at the station for a while," the guard offers as he unlocks the gate.

"Thanks." I nod, swinging the muzzle of my rifle toward Erik and keeping it there. The guards relax their posture and step back, clearing a path for us.

"You have been most helpful," the clone tells them.

I ignore it and gesture for Erik to start moving. He keeps his hands on his head as we exit the train station and turn left.

"Wrong way, Chen," the guard calls out behind us. "Something wrong with your augments?"

I look back to find him pointing the other way.

"A lot of help you are," I mutter to the clone.

"My navigation systems are offline," it replies.

I give the guard a friendly wave as we adjust course, heading the right direction toward the law enforcement station. But of course that's not where we're going.

How many of the Twenty are in this dome? I ask Erik.

Two, he thinks back at me.

My siblings or yours?

You believe me now? He glances over his shoulder as we walk along the sidewalk.

That the Twenty originated from four North American survivors—two male, two female. That there are two sets of ten siblings. And you want each member of the Twenty to know the truth.

"Yeah," he says out loud. "That's about it."

"Where are they?"

"Not sure." He points at my pocket. "I'll need my phone to track them down."

"What do they do here?"

"Tree monkeys." He almost laughs at what I'm sure is a confused look on my face. "They work alternating shifts, caring for the trees and plant life suspended from the dome's apex. Keep them fed and watered, happily producing oxygen. One of them lives in that cube complex." He nods toward the building on our left as we pass it. "She's one of your sisters."

"Enforcer Chen," the clone says, "I am concerned about the direction of this conversation. It does not appear that you intend to bring this violator to the station."

"This violator is one of the Twenty. Didn't you say earlier that you were directed to round us up and take us someplace safe?"

"I...do not know..." It sounds perplexed, thanks to Erik's reprogramming.

What's her name—this tree monkey?

Erik smiles at me. *Arienna.*

If security clones were sent to round her up, she may not be here at all.

"Possible," he allows, raising an eyebrow. "But if she is here..."

I hand him his antique phone, and he gets to work, flicking his thumbs across the screen. "That guy wasn't kidding. The Link is moving s-l-o-w." He looks up, but not at me. He's staring at the dome's leafy ceiling. "If she's working her shift, we'll find her up there."

Great. And us without an aerocar.

"Recognize her?" He turns the screen toward me, and I see one of the faces that came up earlier in my DNA search. Otherwise, I don't remember her from our days together at that boarding school, Camp Hope.

We live only now, never looking back. For the common good.

He pats his jacket pocket before tucking away the old phone. I shake my head and hold out my palm. Disgruntled, he hands back the device. "I'll have to knock out her augments. It's the only way she'll be receptive to the truth. But with both of us telling her the same thing, I'm sure it will go a whole lot smoother."

"Was I your trial run?"

He glances at me with an audacious expression. "I like to think of you as my first."

The security clone is scanning the buildings on either side of the street, turning its black face shield from one to the other, its head cocked back. For the first time since its arrival, it seems to be ignoring us.

"You hear something?" I take a step toward it and glance back toward the maglev station, a block away now. I can only see the gate from here, and the guards aren't in my line of sight. Everything is quiet. Maybe too quiet.

"We are being watched," the clone says.

A couple citizens in the cube complex stand at their respective windows, six floors up, staring down at us. Understandable that we would inspire curiosity. Nobody's supposed to be out on the streets, yet here we are: a security clone, a law enforcer, and a citizen who, until a minute ago, was walking with his hands on his head. At gunpoint.

"Friends of yours?" I glance at Erik.

He smiles and waves up at the gawkers, who quickly avert their eyes and back away from their windows.

"Never seen them before." He shrugs, turning his attention to the leafy greenery seeming to sprout from the dome's plexicon walls. "Pretty sure I could jump up there, but I'm assuming you'll want to join me."

"We're joined at the hip." I pat the rifle slung at my side.

"Right." He narrows his gaze at the clone. *Might want to order it to stay put.*

"Hold this position," I tell the security clone. "The violator and I will return within the hour."

"You would be safer if you brought me along, Enforcer Chen."

"Noted." I give Erik a nudge, and we head toward the forest looming at the end of the street. "Assist local law enforcement. Notify the maglev guards of any terrorist activity. If we don't return by 1100 hours, you have permission to look for me."

"Understood." The clone widens its stance in a standard hold-the-perimeter position and scans the surrounding area, its head slowly panning from left to right.

That should keep it busy. I jog after Erik, who's decided to pick up the pace. "Even with martial law in effect, Arienna will be working?"

"One thing citizens and terrorists have in common, Enforcer Chen: we all breathe oxygen. As much as the patriots want to buck the system, they won't attack anything we all need to survive. It would be counterproductive to their cause. They want to gain sympathizers, not lose them."

"So that's what you are." If he isn't a patriot himself. "A sympathizer."

"Never said that." He glances back at me. "But I understand where they're coming from."

Because that's where he came from. Farming Dome 9's fields before his big break as a VR actor or model or whatever he is. I blame my lack of attention to detail on faulty biologic; enforcers are used to sharing the mental workload with our neural implants.

So Erik would have worked alongside potential terrorists in the making. Citizens who felt enslaved by the system, shedding their blood, sweat, and tears so the residents of Dome 1 could enjoy the good life.

For some reason, the Eurasian credo that all of us must do our part in order to ensure a bright future for our people fell on a few deaf ears. Most citizens are perfectly content living day to day and contributing to society, no matter what the job assignment. But others have questioned the status quo. Up to now, that's all it has been: complaints, non-violent protests, insubstantial riots. But today, with the attack on Hawthorne Tower and the disappearance of the Chancellor, words have suddenly evolved into dangerous actions.

Why today? And why didn't we see this coming? Because most citizens were busy living mundane lives, clocking in and out, going home to enjoy virtual adventures on the Link. No one paid attention to the unrest boiling up at the periphery of our highly advanced society. We didn't give it any credence. We assumed these malcontents would never be able to touch us.

What about the analysts plugged into the Linkstream for eight-hour shifts, monitoring the words and actions of every citizen in the 10 Domes? Wouldn't they have noticed *something* in the works?

Shade from the trees covers us now, and our boots have traded concrete sidewalk for a spongy synthetic dirt and mulch composite that gives each of our steps an extra little bounce. I follow Erik since he seems to know where he's going, but I hold my rifle ready and keep my eyes on the surroundings. This would be a perfect location for an ambush. I half-expect patriots to lunge out from behind thick tree trunks or rappel on ropes to surround us with weapons drawn.

But the farther we encroach into the forest, the more unlikely that scenario seems. We are the only people here in this quasi-natural silence. It feels like no one else has ever trod upon this ground, at least not for a very long time. I'm glad the turf silences our footsteps. It seems disrespectful for anything to make a sound here.

I gaze at the trees soaring above and wonder what it was like before the Domes, when not only trees but birds and animals thrived on the surface of the earth. When the sun shone down without an artificial barrier in place to protect us. Tough to imagine. These biospheres are all I've ever known.

With my augments operational, I wouldn't be thinking such thoughts. I'd accept life the way it is and go about my daily routine. *Never looking back...*

The patriots must have deactivated their neural implants. How else would they be able to rebel against life as we know it? Erik is searching for each of the Twenty and disabling our neural implants so we can learn the truth about who we are. There must have been a lone patriot who did the same, stirring up discontent among the laborers in the outlying domes and telling them their lives could be better.

It makes no sense. The original patriots in North America brought about D-Day by releasing dangerous bioweapons into the atmosphere; their actions led to the end of the world. Why would anyone in Eurasia want to be associated with those degenerates? Calling themselves *patriots* is a slap in the face for our Governors and Chancellor who have done everything in their power to build a future for our people after a nuclear holocaust. Terrorists started the war forty-two years ago, but our leaders finished it in a big way.

And, in so doing, they made the world uninhabitable. Discharging nuclear weapons by the untold megatons will do that. So who were the true villains? The agitators, or the government that overreacted?

I can't believe I'm having such treasonous thoughts. I've never questioned our leaders before, never had any reason to. This oxygen-rich air is making me feel lightheaded. I'm not thinking straight at all.

I almost run into Erik. He's stopped, his head tilted back as he stares upward.

"That's the apex," he says quietly.

"How the hell do we get up there?" I gaze through the leafy canopy at the glinting dome high above.

"I'll carry you." He crouches down like he expects me to ride him piggyback. "Here, climb on."

"Not happening."

"Why not? You scared?"

"I'm armed."

He stands up. "Fine. Then we bring her down to us." He cups his hands around his mouth and starts shouting her name at the treetops. "Arienna! Arienna!"

So obnoxious. I can't help cringing. But it does the trick.

A shadow the size of a large leaf swings out from the dome's interior on a bike-shaped hovercraft, built to carry a single rider. It descends slowly, passing through the leaves and branches and enlarging as it approaches. Pausing to hover a few meters above our heads, the rider looks each of us over with a curious frown.

"You're not from around here," she observes.

Her features and coloring are similar to my own. Dark hair, piercing blue eyes, olive-toned skin. Slender but wiry.

"Are you Arienna?" Erik grins at her. Not nearly as suave as he tried to be with me.

"Am I under arrest?" She looks at me, glancing briefly at my weapon.

"No." I shake my head. "Should you be?" *Stupid question.* I feel awkward, and I hate it.

Erik chuckles. "Meet your sister, Sera!"

Arienna's frown takes root. "Who are you?"

"I'm one of the Twenty. I work as an enforcer in Dome 1. My name is Sera Chen." I feel like I said those three out of order.

"Something we have in common," Erik clarifies. "We're all members of the Twenty. I'd shake your hand, but you're just a bit out of reach."

Why don't you jump? I ask him, mind to mind.

He ignores me.

"Of course. Sorry." Arienna glides toward the ground and deactivates the hoverbike as it settles onto the turf. She dismounts from the saddle and reaches out her hand, shaking first with Erik, then me. "Dome 1? I hear things are a little crazy over there right now."

"They've been better," I allow.

"So what are you doing here? Looking for me?" She laughs it off.

"Actually—"

"With the banquet coming up, we thought it might be nice to have a little pre-reunion reunion," Erik says. "You know, to make things less awkward than they're bound to be at that fancy shindig."

He's smooth, I'll give him that.

"The banquet is still on? I thought—with the terrorist threat..." she trails off as Erik and I glance at each other.

We really haven't thought this through. I assumed he knew

what he was doing, but maybe he's just winging it. Nothing about his early interactions with me seemed very well-planned, either.

"Not to be rude, but I don't remember either of you. Or anything from that time when we were kids." She shakes her head, the frown still in place. "Those memories have always been really fuzzy..."

She's staring at the palm of Erik's outstretched hand and what's sitting in it: a small device the size and shape of a grenade, pulsing with an electric-blue light.

He smiles at her. "Would you like to remember who you are?"

12. DAIYNA
5 YEARS AFTER ALL-CLEAR

The Wastelanders have made me their queen.

So much for never having a woman lead them, or for women being good for only two things: sustenance and sex. I made it clear that they won't be eating anybody from here on out. They'll have to go on a meatless diet until one of them wants to challenge me for leadership of the tribe. They glanced at each other in those weird skull-masks, but nobody took me up on it. And that would have been the best time to take a swing at me, since I was still recovering from being nearly crushed to death by Cain.

They didn't understand my aversion to cannibalism, or why Shechara and Samson backed me up. They couldn't believe the three of us have survived this long without any meat. Samson decided it was appropriate to wax religious, and he ended up sounding like Luther. Telling them we were made in the image of God, and that it's wrong to consume the flesh of a fellow image-bearer. That elicited a few more glances among the marauders as they tried to make sense out of what he was saying.

I kept it simple: "You eat anybody ever again, I shoot you in the head." I waved my 9mm at them as a visual.

They nodded. That they understood.

So now we're headed to Eden, since I promised them a taste of the good life. Here's hoping I can leave them there, fat and happy with air conditioning and running water. Maybe I'll appoint one of them as my successor. Let them duke it out with the Edenites to see who gets to stay, and who gets banished. Or they can figure out some way to coexist. Hell, maybe even join forces to fight off the UW raiders, keep them from taking everything of value.

Not that there's much left. I have a feeling the raiders will soon be moving on to greener pastures, scavenging from other city ruins farther east. The Edenites will starve to death, and the Wastelanders will eat them, most likely. And that's fine by me. Shechara, Samson, and I will be long gone, free to do our own scavenging far away from the whole lot of them.

"I don't believe you," Shechara says, leaning against me in the back of the jeep as Samson drives us across the rough terrain. The Wastelanders on their dirt bikes flank us and follow us, jumping into the air, doing their stunts and tricks along the way. Cain sits up front next to Samson. We've got the extra-crispy ex-warlord bound and gagged, but he keeps grunting as if we care about anything he has to say. "I think you want to kill him."

"Him?" I point at the back of Cain's hideous head. No hair, no skin. Just nasty burned flesh.

"Not him. Perch—in Eden. You still want him dead."

Of course I do. But I tried taking him out before, and I ended up getting too many good people killed in the process. Not a chance I would ever risk that again, especially not with Shechara here. I pull her close and give her a squeeze.

"My killing days are over. Don't believe me? Ask this guy." I kick the back of Cain's seat, and he lets out an angry grunt.

"You showed a lot of restraint, all things considered," Samson allows. His black goggles glance at me in the rearview mirror. "But I'm still unclear about our return to Eden. You promised these Wastelanders milk and honey, but that requires getting inside to procure said milk and honey. I've got a feeling Perch has that place sealed up tighter than a bunker on D-Day."

"And isn't there a bounty on your head?" Shechara whispers,

looking at Cain as if she doesn't want him to overhear. "What's to keep these Wastelanders from turning you in and collecting it?"

I nudge her. "Do they really seem that bright to you?" They had a walking lump of barbecue leading them until very recently. I raise my voice for Samson's benefit, "I'll get them inside. Don't you worry. Cain's going to help us."

More grunts from the badly roasted neanderthal.

No sight of any UW raiders so far. Maybe they got scared off by Cain's missile strikes and decided to lay low for a day or two. Let things calm down a bit before they go back to their larcenous ways.

Hard to believe Stack is demolished. If we head back that way after dropping the Wastelanders off in Eden, we could see about helping Tullson and his people rebuild. Assuming anyone survived.

"Well, aren't you the do-gooder," Willard sneers, somehow managing to sit next to me with one leg hanging over the side of the jeep. Easy enough to manage when you're noncorporeal. I really need to refill my flask. "Since when do you give a crap about helping anybody out?"

"I seem to remember a certain Edenite you could have helped but chose not to," Mother Lairen adds, sitting on the other side of Shechara in an equally impossible position. Her flaming red hair flaps in the breeze. "Perhaps you no longer have a stomach for killing, but deciding who lives or dies—whom you help and whom you ignore? It's the same thing, Daiyna."

Shechara hears me grumble aloud as I squeeze my head with both hands. "What is it? Do you need us to stop?"

"I need something to drink," I groan.

Rehana stands on the running board on my side of the jeep and holds onto the roll bar. That's how it looks, anyway. It's all a matter of perception and supernaturally manifested memories. The good news: Willard has disappeared for the moment.

"You're putting them in danger, going back there," she says.

"I'm keeping them *from* danger." I shake my head and close my eyes.

"Who, Daiyna?" Shechara says, holding me close. She sounds worried.

Probably because I'm talking to myself like a crazy person.

"You're running away," Mother Lairen says. "As soon as it looked like Samson would take you back to Luther, you immediately offered to fight Cain. And if that wasn't enough of a death wish, now you're escorting these cannibals to Eden. To die."

"They deserve it," I mutter.

"She's not well," Shechara tells Samson. "We should stop."

"No, I'm fine." I give her a nod and try to ignore my spirit-friends for the moment. "We need to keep going." Make up as much ground as we can in daylight, then squeeze the batteries' juice dry after dark.

We should be passing my derelict jeep soon. After that, it'll be another fifty kilometers to Eden. Doubtful we'll run into any bounty hunters along the way. The Wastelanders on their grinding bikes are a force to be reckoned with, enough to scare away any Edenites with delusions of grit.

"This is about revenge." The Rehana-spirit faces me. "Whether you admit it or not. You've found a dozen unpredictable marauders, and you want to sic them on Perch and his men. Because payback is a real bitch."

"You can keep your hands clean," Mother Lairen echoes. Always a joy when the spirits tag-team up against me. "You won't be doing the actual killing yourself."

I smile beneath my head covering and keep my mouth shut. This isn't about revenge. I'm leading the Wastelanders to a better life, one they've never experienced. Once they take residence in Eden, enjoying all of its modern conveniences, they'll give up their marauding ways. If they don't get along with the Edenites, and if there happens to be some bloodshed, well, that's really none of my concern.

I'm not running away. I plan to join Shechara and Samson

wherever they go after this. If it's back to Luther and the others, then so be it. I'm not afraid of him.

"You're afraid of who you are with him," Rehana suggests, and I don't like the sound of that at all. "You love him, but you can't bear to be around him. You're afraid you won't have anything left to offer. And you don't know how to talk to him about your children—"

"That's enough!" My voice is sharp. Both Shechara and Samson look at me. Cain stops grunting.

Just because they share my DNA—and Luther's—doesn't make them my children. Margo assembled them in a laboratory. They grew and developed inside man-made incubation chambers, surrounded by artificial amniotic fluid. Nothing about them is natural.

I'm fine never seeing them again. They gave me the creeps.

"You may be able to lie to yourself, but you can't lie to us," Rehana says. "You may never be able to have children naturally, after what happened to you in Eden. But you have ten children living across the sea. And if Luther is successful in finding a way into Eurasia to locate them, he will need you by his side."

I'm sure Luther is doing just fine without me. I don't know who he's surrounding himself with these days—obviously not Shechara and Samson. I have no idea who survived Cain's missile attack on the Homeplace. But without me around, at least he doesn't have to be constantly reminded of the deaths I caused during my Eden rampage. And I don't have to see the disappointment in his eyes when he looks at me.

When he sees what I've become.

"You can find yourself again, Daiyna." Rehana leans toward me. "Isolation has not been good for you."

As much as I've longed for solitude, I haven't been alone. These spirits haven't given me a moment's peace lately. They've driven me nuts.

For a long while, they didn't appear to me at all. Back when I burned with a thirst for vengeance, when my only waking—and sometimes dreaming—thoughts were of killing Willard and Perch and obliterating Eden. Darkness festered inside me then, driving a wedge between me and others in the Homeplace who didn't share my hatred.

Luther was one of them. Things between us weren't good for a while before I left the group. Finding out we had biological children didn't magically bring us closer together. Unlike Shechara and Samson, we drifted even further apart, until the unspoken wall between us was insurmountable.

"Daiyna?" Samson glances into the rearview. "Everything alright?"

"Yeah," I lie.

"Spirit problems?"

"You could say that."

Cain grunts in a frenzy, struggling against his bonds, jerking his head against his restraints like he wants to turn toward me but can't.

"Gaia has abandoned him." Mother Lairen clucks her tongue. "The poor wretch."

"What are they telling you?" Shechara rubs my arm.

"Nothing new," I mutter.

"He's lost without her," Mother Lairen continues, shaking her head at Cain with a combination of disgust and pity. "His missile strikes are shots in the dark. He hopes to recapture her favor with these blind attempts at appeasement."

As long as he's killing people, the evil spirits are perfectly content with him shooting blindly. As far as I can tell, their only desire is to eliminate the human remnant from the face of the earth. Turn us against each other, let us wipe ourselves out. Then, once the Wastes are cleared of human refuse, will they move on to Eurasia? I'm sure they're already trying to worm their way into that last bastion of humankind.

But if it's anything like Eden, composed entirely of human-made materials, they'll have a tough time getting inside that sealed biosphere. They move through the dust, through the air.

Maybe if they convince the UW raiders to ship back a few tons of dirt—

"Trouble," Shechara murmurs, her mechatronic eyes twitching as they zoom to focus on an indistinct shape appearing over the eastern horizon.

"What do you see?" I strain but can't make it out.

"Raiders," she says, "driving a big rig this way."

"Deja vu." Samson chuckles without much mirth. "We should get out of their way." He turns the steering wheel hand over hand, aiming toward an outcropping of rock. "With any luck, they haven't spotted us yet."

I'm sure they haven't. But the Wastelanders are another matter entirely. Whooping and screaming, they gun their bikes and bolt full-speed toward the tractor-trailer in the distance.

"Guess they don't wait for orders from their queen," Samson observes.

I watch them go while Cain lets out a staccato of gagged laughter.

"Standing orders." I assume. "Pillage and scavenge."

"They seriously have no fear." Shechara watches them approach the tractor-trailer while Samson pulls our jeep behind the looming rock formation and cuts the engine.

"We'll wait it out here." He remains behind the wheel. "See what's left when the dust settles."

"You've changed." I remember a Samson who wasn't nearly this cautious.

He turns toward me. "Marriage will do that, I suppose."

Shechara rests her hand on his metal arm. Such an unexpected couple. I still have trouble believing what I'm seeing.

"How did it happen?" Not sure I phrased that correctly. "Or when...?"

"Not long after the missile strike on the Homeplace." Samson glances at Cain, who has gone strangely silent again. "We lost a lot of good people. Many of them from Shiptown." He pauses, probably hoping that will sink into Cain's addled brain. "Ten of us were away when it happened, and Milton got back first. Sorted through the rubble at superspeed for survivors. He found five."

From fifty strong when I left them, to fifteen. Luther must have been beside himself. All he's ever wanted was to unite the survivors of this wasteland, and for our numbers to grow as more recruits entered the fold.

"We could've been there when it happened." Samson covers Shechara's hand gently with his own, metal glinting under the sun. "Life's transience made a big impression on us."

Shechara nods. "We decided to spend however many days we had left as husband and wife. Best decision I've ever made."

"Your options were limited." Samson sounds like he's smiling.

"So were yours," she counters.

Maybe they are perfect for each other. But I for one never saw it coming. Guess a lot can change when you're faced with a massacre or few. You cling to those you hold dear.

Or you make your own path with your spirit-friends and a flask brimming with whatever whiskey you can find.

"They're not slowing down," Shechara says, peering around the rock formation to keep an eye on the approaching truck.

The sound of weapons fire pops in the distance.

"The raiders or the Wastelanders?" I strain to see, but it's still too far.

"Both."

Cain's grunting again, adamant about something. Too bad we don't care.

"Two of the Wastelanders have been shot," Shechara reports. "Their bikes and bodies crushed under the rig."

"Eleven to go." Mother Lairen wrinkles her non-corporeal lip at me. "Admit it. You don't mind if they die."

Honestly? No. I don't. They're an untrustworthy bunch of cannibals, and their fashion sense is the worst. My main goal is to keep them away from Shechara and the parts of Samson that are still human.

"Nobody told them to go up against a truck full of raiders," Rehana counters. "They're out of their minds."

"Daiyna knew something like this would happen. If not against the Edenites, then these UW raiders. Either way, it whittles down the number of marauders, makes them more manageable." Mother Lairen stares unblinking at me. "Isn't that right?"

"Half a klick away now." Shechara gazes off into the distance. "The Wastelanders are firing at the cab. There's blood on the windshield, but the truck is driving straight."

"Do you let it play out, or do you lend a hand?" Mother Lairen raises an eyebrow. "And whom do you help? The cannibals or the people under attack—the people from that glass city where your children are growing up?"

She wants me to react. But I refuse to give her the satisfaction. Besides, Shechara has seen enough *Crazy Daiyna* for one day. So I grip my 9mm and wait beneath the sun's oppressive heat, putting the voices of the spirits and Cain's barking out of my mind. Focusing all my attention on the approaching gunshots and roar of the truck's engine.

I give Shechara a pat on the shoulder and a nod, letting her know I can see what's happening now. The number of bikers is down from thirteen to ten, swarming around the big rig and firing their rifles with no apparent attack pattern. None of them have attempted to jump onto the trailer's shipping container; they're content with flanking the vehicle, trading fire, and vaulting their dirt bikes off the rugged terrain and into the air at untimed intervals. A few idiots pass in front of the truck's menacing grill, as if their airborne presence will slow it down.

It's clear to anybody with eyes that the raiders are perfectly fine running over anything in their path.

Then all at once, as if the same thought has occurred to every Wastelander simultaneously, they turn their weapons on the truck's tires, blowing them out one by one. The rig lurches side to side awkwardly, pitching over one way and then the other like a lumbering giant whose ankles have given out. The driver fights the steering wheel and brakes, but it's too late. The tractor-trailer is out of control and careening off the beaten path, plowing through dust and dirt, shoveling it up into the air and smothering the grill and windshield.

Heading straight for us.

I slap Samson's shoulder. "Hey, you might want to—"

"On it." He revs up the jeep and floors the accelerator, swerving out of the way in a tight U-turn, leaving those boulders for the semi to slam into.

Which it does, smashing against the rocks with deafening force. Dust explodes upward and outward, obscuring the impact zone, as broken pieces of granite tumble across the ground. The Wastelanders pull up on their chugging bikes and surround the crash site.

"We haven't eaten them!" one calls out, looking my way. Like he's expecting me to be proud of him.

I give him a thumbs-up. Might as well humor the freak.

All ten of them kill their motors and dismount, their weapons trained on the truck. None of them are watching the back of the trailer. That becomes a problem when the rear door on the shipping container swings open, and half a dozen well-armed UW raiders hop out, firing at will.

I throw myself over Shechara, holding her down. Samson raises his metal arms to shield himself. Cain grunts in a frenzy, cringing in his seat.

But the raiders aren't shooting at us. They've targeted the bikers, and in less than five seconds, the number of Wastelanders is down to three. Those left alive have their hands in the air and their weapons on the ground.

The raiders close in, hunched over their assault rifles, black armor gleaming in the sunlight. Their environmental suits are barely recognizable as such, nothing like that bulky monstrosity Sergeant Bishop was forced to wear a few years ago. These next-gen suits are sleek and form-fitting. The raiders move with ease, their tinted helmets sealed tight against the *contaminated* air.

Half of them split off and aim their weapons our way. "Get out of the vehicle!" one orders, his helmet's external speaker cranked up so we can hear him clearly.

Shechara and I tuck our semiautomatics under our tunics and step out. Samson leaves his rifle behind, his metal arms raised and gleaming under the desert sun.

"Him too!" the raider barks, referring to Cain.

"No can do." Samson shakes his head. "If it's all the same, we'd like to turn him over to you."

"Why the hell would we want him?"

"He hijacked one of your trucks yesterday, then decided to blow it up last night. Along with most of Stack," I tell them. "From what I've heard, you had a good deal going with Mayor Tullson. Fifty-fifty split of everything they scavenged, right? Well, that's all shot to hell now, thanks to this guy's inability to keep his missile-launcher in his pants."

Cain has resumed his eerie silence, still as a statue.

"How do we know you had nothing to do with it?" the raider asks.

I nod toward the three remaining Wastelanders. "Ask them. They rode with him."

The bikers nod quickly, pointing at Cain, their voices clambering over each other: "It was him. All his idea. Fire and judgment, he said. Fire and judgment!"

The cab door of the truck swings open with a long creak, and the blood-spattered driver stumbles out looking a little rattled. The raider riding shotgun is dead. For a second or two, the driver doesn't seem to comprehend what's going on. But then her hand rises to point right at us, and she stammers, adamant and building in volume.

"They hijacked my truck!"

"Not good..." Samson mutters.

"It was those two!" She singles out Samson, then Shechara. "Killed one of my men and sent us hiking, the bastards." She laughs, her helmet jerking. "I told you there was no place to run!"

The raiders who already had us in their sights close in now. The leader of the pack barks out orders, and soon we're kneeling on the ground with our hands up. The three Wastelanders get the same treatment. Only Cain is allowed to stay put, his eyes bright, enjoying the show.

I suppose we're his accomplices. In the eyes of the UW, all seven of us are guilty.

"Stupid bitch," Willard says, standing over me with his arms crossed. If he was really there, I'd be in his shadow. "You just can't help getting the people around you killed. Now it's going to be your dear Shechara. All because of *you*."

I grit my teeth as sudden tears sting my eyes. Fury does that to me sometimes. Good thing my goggles keep them hidden.

"What are you going to do with us?" I demand.

The raiders have all six of us lined up beside the jeep, and three of them keep the muzzles of their weapons trained on us. The other three have already started unpacking the shipping container, setting crates and boxes of food, fuel, and supplies on the sun-scorched ground. They've collected the Wastelanders' dirt bikes and weapons, lining them up next to the other scavenged goods. A real organized bunch, as far as thieves go.

The driver walks toward me. Unarmed, she steps right up and kicks me in the gut. As I pitch forward, she drops to one knee and holds my head down in the dust.

"We haven't met before," she says, sounding calm for someone with obvious anger issues. "But if you're anything like your friends, then I'm going to enjoy watching you die."

I try to speak, but my words are too muffled by the ground to make much sense. She lets me up just enough to sound coherent.

"If you were going to kill us, you would've done it already."

"Is that so?" She sounds amused.

"You people have rules. You only shot the hostiles shooting at you. The rest of us get this preferential treatment. You're going to radio your superiors, and then you're going to wait here until a truck arrives to pick you up, load all your newfound loot, and take you west for the next Eurasia-bound ship." I pause. "Only I have a better idea."

She curses. But she keeps listening, her hand applying pressure on the back of my head so I know she's still the boss. She can drive my face into the dirt again whenever she sees fit.

"You go to Eden," I advise. "You take everything they've got. They've accumulated some primo stuff over the years. Only the best for those Edenites."

"They're sealed up tighter than—"

"I can get you in."

"Daiyna, don't..." Shechara pleads. The eavesdropper.

"Their leader has a bounty on my head. You show up with me, demand the bounty, that's how you get inside. The rest is up to you."

She lets go of me. I rise to face her but remain on my knees like my friends. I don't want to stand out and get myself shot. These raiders may have their rules, but I'm sure they know how to make murder look like self-defense.

"You have quotas, right? Everything you scavenge is weighed, and once you reach that arbitrary amount set by your superiors—maybe after a month or two on this wasted continent—you're allowed to go home. Back to your dome cities across the sea?"

She shrugs a shoulder. "So what?"

I lean toward her. "You plunder Eden, and you'll be going home this week."

I watch my reflection in her black face shield. My eyes are unreadable behind the goggles, but my tone is confident. And why shouldn't it be?

She nods slowly to herself. "Why the hell should I believe you?"

"Because we were already headed there. Ask them." I nod toward the three surviving bikers.

"That's right. We're going to Eden! The Promised Land. Milk and honey!" they talk over each other again.

The driver regards them for a moment, not knowing what to

make of the strange-looking trio, before pointing at Cain. "You claim this badly burned fellow blew up Stack." She shakes her head at me. "How did you all end up together?"

"The same way we're going to end up with you, heading to Eden." I give her a nod. "Some situations call for strange bedfellows."

She walks away to confer with her associates. I can't hear a word any of them are saying in their huddle, but they each have a habit of turning and staring at us. I don't mind, as long as their assault rifles look the other way.

"You can't be serious about this," Shechara insists in a low tone. "Daiyna, you can't give yourself up to Perch."

"Don't think she plans to, Small Fry," Samson rumbles as quietly as he's able. "This has all the earmarks of another attempt at revenge."

I shake my head, wishing they would just shut up and trust me. "The raiders will take care of Perch. Or our three amigos will." I nod toward the cannibals. "Once I tell them Edenite meat is on the menu."

"Daiyna!" Shechara is not pleased.

"Kidding." Maybe just a little.

After their lengthy powwow, the raiders encircle us while the driver paces. "We lost one of our own today, but we took out a dozen of yours. Obviously you're looking for a way to save your necks..." She tilts her head to one side, facing me. "But I see no reason not to investigate Eden. We've scavenged all we can from the storage pockets in the city ruins. There's not much left there. High time for us to see what's available down below." She nods, and the other raiders do the same. "We have another truck on the way. Should be here by 0100. You might want to get some rest." She leans toward me. "You'll need it once we hand you over to Eden."

She and her cohorts laugh it up, seeming to think that's pretty funny. I consider telling the Wastelanders that raider flesh is back on the menu. But I don't want to get them killed in the process. Not yet, anyway.

"She's finally admitting it to herself!" Mother Lairen crows, clapping her hands. "No more denial. One of the first steps toward recovery."

Rehana ignores her, and so do I.

Shechara, Samson, and I sit on the ground in the jeep's shade and lean back against the vehicle. We let Cain continue to roast where he sits. Nobody seems to care much about his welfare, and that suits me just fine. The raiders break up into pairs and watch us in two-hour shifts. Wearing all that black, they must have one hell of a cooling system installed in those suits. None of them look uncomfortable. They remind me of...shiny beetles...

Not sure how long I nodded off for, but the sleep was deep and dream-free. Shechara nudges me in the cool darkness as headlights shine toward us. The raiders get us on our feet and keep us huddled together while they load their spoils into the fresh tractor-trailer with all its tires intact. After they finish wheeling the last of the Wastelanders' dirt bikes into the shipping container, they shove us toward the same vicinity to be locked in the dark while we make the drive inland.

But we won't be alone. Three of the raiders join us with their face shields' night vision activated, glowing a dull green against their flinty features.

As the doors slam shut behind us and the lock-bars slide into place, I take a deep breath and hope this was the right move.

13. BISHOP
2 YEARS AFTER ALL-CLEAR

When we return to the Homeplace, Milton is standing outside the collapsed cave entrance covered in dust and blood smears. Beside him is the young woman Victoria holding her five-month-old son close, both dirty and disheveled. Three others are close by: Taylor, one of Luther's sentries; Burke, an elderly man from the coast, cradling another baby. They stare vacantly, in shock. The babies wail.

They're the only survivors. The missile killed everyone else we left behind.

We don't know who fired it. Could have been the *Integrity* or the mutants. A United World warship might target a group of infected survivors harboring a deserter. But why would the mutants do it? Their only aim in life is to capture and devour fresh meat. They don't destroy things without a reason. When they shot down my chopper six months ago, they closed in for the kill once we hit the ground. But here, as smoke billows out of the Homeplace, none of the creatures are to be seen.

One at a time, Milton flies the survivors down to meet us at the base of the cliff where we've parked the two jeeps. He swoops in low, then jets upward to retrieve the next. Margo approaches Victoria, and the two of them share a telepathic conversation. Have they already searched the rubble with their minds to make sure Milton didn't miss anyone? I have a feeling Luther will want to bury the dead and recite his scriptures over them; but looking up at the cave, I can't help thinking the whole thing could collapse in on itself at any moment.

We need to leave this place immediately and regroup. Find shelter elsewhere, someplace with food and supplies. Everything Luther's people have stockpiled in those caves is lost now. We can't go back for it and risk losing anyone else.

If Luther asks for my advice, that's what I'll tell him. Or I might jump the gun and suggest it anyway. But I'm not in charge here. I have to remember that. They took me in, and I'm grateful for it. I can't overstep—as much as I want to find whoever did this and make them pay dearly.

"Anyone else?" Luther takes Milton aside.

He shakes his head. His sorrowful expression is hidden behind the head coverings and goggles protecting him from the morning sun. But his broken posture speaks volumes.

"So many..." Luther trails off, gazing upward as if he can see our dead deep inside the mountain. "We can't leave them in there. We must bury them."

"It isn't safe," Milton argues gently, squeezing his shoulder. "Luther, I barely got out myself, and that's with my speed—ducking and dodging. We probably shouldn't even be standing here. The whole cliff is unstable."

Something I didn't consider. At Luther's nod, I gesture for Samson and Shechara to put their jeeps into reverse. I climb onto the back of Samson's vehicle and beckon for the others to join us. They start shambling in our direction, glancing back intermittently, unable to ignore the smoking tomb.

Once we're a hundred meters out, we stop.

"The storerooms are lost." Margo is at my side before I realize she's there, her somber monotone unaffected by the recent tragedy. "We can't remain here."

I nod. If the mutants pick this moment to attack, we'll be

easily surrounded, pinned against the cliff. "Any hostiles on approach?"

She pauses as if she's listening intently to something. Then she shakes her head. "I don't sense anyone nearby."

Regardless, I keep my head on a swivel, one hand on the rifle slung over my shoulder. "We'll need to find higher ground, a defensible position. Set up camp, then send out scavenging parties for food and supplies."

"The spot where we camped last night should suffice."

With no other options at present, I approach Luther. He can't shake his gaze from the collapsed cave entrance above.

"We have to get these people to safety," I tell him. Fifteen of us now.

At first it doesn't seem like he heard me, but then he nods absently. "Lead them, Sergeant. I'll be along shortly."

I look at Samson standing nearby. The big cyborg nods. "I'll keep an eye on him," he rumbles.

Margo and I each take the wheel of a jeep, and the others climb aboard, standing on the running boards and gripping the roll bars. Milton doesn't need a ride, and the babies don't take up much space, so we have enough seats for everyone else in the two vehicles. I save a pair for Luther and Samson and signal Milton to head out. He'll fly over the path ahead to make sure we're still alone, as Margo seems to think. I gesture for her to start driving.

"We just can't seem to catch a break," says the older fellow Justus, seated beside me. "The way we keep losing people... If I didn't know better, I'd say we're cursed."

"You don't think we are?" I glance over my shoulder to find Luther and Samson heading our way, both with their heads downcast.

"I don't believe in curses. Or blessings, for that matter. We make our own fate." Justus chuckles with no humor in his tone. "For better or worse."

"So you don't believe in Gaia. Or the spirits of the earth."

He curses under his breath. "I believe in what I can see,

Sarge."

I've given up correcting them when they address me by rank. "Wish I could unsee some things."

"That's right, they say you've seen 'em." Justus faces me now, appraising me. "Those *spirits*. You and Milton are special that way. They reveal themselves to you."

"Not special." I nod to Luther as he climbs into his seat, followed by the cyborg. "Cursed."

Justus grunts.

Six months. That's how long I've been breathing this air—ever since my helmet was damaged. But unlike so many of Luther's people, I haven't exhibited any bizarre talents. I can't fly or move with supersonic speed like Milton; I can't read minds like Margo and Victoria. But every now and then, the spirits talk to me, and that's weird enough. I'm glad I haven't changed otherwise.

Luther pats me on the back, and I start up the jeep, following the tracks left by Margo. Her vehicle is visible in the distance, a couple hundred meters away. It's only ten klicks to the hilltop where we'll regroup and decide our next move.

"We'll find out who did it." I nod, glancing up into the rearview at Luther and Samson in the backseat. "Then we'll give them a taste of their own medicine."

"Vengeance is the Creator's," Luther murmurs, yet I hear him clearly. "Our priority is finding a safe place to live, stockpiling enough water, provisions, and ammunition. The hilltop is only a temporary campsite. We need to find permanent lodging."

"What about the daemons?" Samson crosses his mechanical arms. "Safe places are few and far between with them roaming about."

Luther nods. "We can't hunt them down until we have a base of operations. We can't put those two babies in danger. They are the next generation, the future."

"Cain's spawn," Samson mutters in disgust.

"No, brother." Luther reprimands the cyborg. "It doesn't matter who their father was. Blood and DNA are merely biological fuel. The soul decides the person, and the soul is a gift from the Creator alone. Cain had nothing to do with it. They will grow up among us and be their own people."

Samson nods once. "I stand corrected." Then he clears his throat. "Speaking of offspring and whatnot, there's something I've been meaning to ask you about."

I glance at Justus, wondering if he's eavesdropping on the conversation behind us like I am. The old-timer's chin is on his chest, his head jostling with the jeep's movement across the uneven terrain. Sound asleep.

"Shechara and me..." the cyborg continues in a low tone. "We've talked about it, and we'd...like to get married."

I stop myself from laughing out loud. After what's just happened—the loss of life as well as our defendable Homeplace—this is on Samson's mind? What's the point of a wedding in the Wastes?

"Sooner rather than later," Samson says, shifting uncomfortably in his seat. "And we'd like you to officiate. You're the closest thing we've got to a priest, after all."

"It would be an honor." Luther nods. "Are you sure you're ready to be a husband?"

"Our lives could be snuffed out without warning. Like that." He snaps his metal fingers with a clink. "The way I see it, I'd rather spend whatever time I have left with someone I care about, and who cares about me. I don't want to die alone."

"So you've asked her?" There's an edge of humor in Luther's tone.

"Of course!"

"And...she capitulated?"

"Not sure what you mean by that, but she said *yes*."

"I am so happy for you, brother." Luther claps him on the back. "When were you thinking?"

"After we set up camp."

There's a pause before both men chuckle quietly. Followed by a rueful silence. Survivor's guilt rearing its ugly head.

But we have to move on. We have to survive. And if that means Samson and Shechara marrying each other, I guess I'm all for it.

"Congratulations," I offer. "You two work well together, from what I've seen. Marriage is a partnership..." I trail off, thinking about my Emma. About the lie my superiors told her, that her life partner was killed in action, that he died a hero.

"You will see your wife again, Sergeant."

Luther's able to read minds now?

"You complement each other, is what I meant." I focus on driving.

"Opposites attract, they say." Samson grunts. "We do have a lot in common: Prosthetics. Survival instinct. Ten kids."

"Do you talk about the children much?" Luther sounds wistful.

"We'd like to meet them someday. Introduce ourselves." Samson pauses. "You think they've got 'em living with adoptive families over in Eurasia? Or locked in a government lab, under observation?"

"I've wondered about that myself. I pray for them every night. Your children as well as mine. Daiyna's and mine..." Luther's turn to trail off now.

"After we get rid of the daemons, what do you say we go look for her?" Samson suggests. "She shouldn't be out there by herself. Nobody should."

Luther exhales. "I pray for her as well. That the Creator will soften her heart. That she will return to us. But the truth is, if she wanted to see us, she's had months to come back." He pauses. "If she's still alive."

"Maybe Margo or Victoria could reach out with their brains or whatever. See if they can locate her?"

"Perhaps." Luther grips the roll bar and stands up as we reach the base of the hill that provided our vantage point last night. The mutants' remains lie right where we left them, rotting in the sun.

Margo and her passengers are already carrying their weapons up toward the boulders above. Her jeep is parked facing out. I line up mine next to it and nudge Justus with my elbow.

"Rise and shine."

He snorts and jerks his head upward. "Alright. Here we go."

My passengers climb out, but I pause before joining them. Strangely enough, I can hear every conversation going on around me. And it doesn't matter how far away they happen to be. To my ears, they sound like they're right next to me: Shechara and Margo as they reach the summit and start to set up camp, Victoria and Burke, each carrying a baby. Samson and Luther, discussing the upcoming nuptials. Justus and the others—Ethan, Connor, Taylor, and Deven in a slow-moving group. No matter how far away from me they are, no matter how loud or how quiet they are, I can hear them all.

"What do you hear?" Spirit-Emma appears beside me.

"They're worried," I murmur, sorting through the voices as they take turns expressing concerns, hopes, suggestions, opinions. Somehow, I'm not overwhelmed; I can focus on each conversation simultaneously. "Did you do this to me?"

Six months I've been breathing this air. Finally I've got my own bizarre ability to show for it.

The spirit smiles through the face of my wife. "We had to decide on the best gift to give you. You're a natural leader. You know how to give orders." She shrugs slightly. "But it's equally important to listen."

"Touché," I mutter.

She rests a hand on my arm, her eyes serious. "You need to listen now."

I frown at her and tilt my head toward the others as they reach the hilltop. I'm the only one left standing below.

"Press past their voices. *Listen*, James."

I close my eyes and focus on any sounds coming from beyond our position.

"Is it Milton?" How laser-focused is my newfound ability? Can I pinpoint the sound of him hurtling through the sky?

Then I hear it: a humming sound, like a swarm of bees in the distance. Growing louder as it heads our way.

"What...?"

"They noticed the missile blast. Usually, such a thing would frighten them off. But in this case, with food being so scarce since they picked the Shipyard clean, something in their degraded brains has told them there is fresh meat for the taking. At the Homeplace."

My stomach sinks. "The mutants."

"All of them." She nods. "This will be your chance to finally rid the land of those who remain. But you must listen, and act wisely."

We don't have to hunt them down. They're coming to us. But we're not ready. We don't have the ammunition to take on—

"How many?" My voice is hoarse.

"Close to a hundred."

So our estimates were correct. Good for us—but little consolation right now. We're gravely outnumbered. We can't hit them from our vantage point above. We'd make ourselves an easy target for any RPG. Last night, there was only one rocket launcher to contend with; when Shechara noticed the jeep full of mutants carrying it, we took them out. There were only three vehicles, and it still took a concerted effort to eliminate that threat.

There could be as many as twenty-five jeeps this time.

"Milton—"

"He's back." The spirit turns toward the hill as Milton descends from the blistering sky and lands near the others with a cloud of dust. "Trust the Creator, James. And fight for your life. We'll help you any way we can." She vanishes with a smile and a wink.

They're going to intervene? Well then. Maybe our situation isn't as dire as it looks.

I can't help remembering what happened to those mutants

after they shot my chopper out of the sky. My helmet HUD was on the fritz; I couldn't see a thing. But I felt the whirlwind, and I heard those creatures scream as they were thrashed to death. By the spirits, I've come to believe.

I grab my rifle and charge up the hillside, listening in as Milton reports to Luther: "Daemons—twenty klicks out, coming in from every direction. They're hungry, have been for a while now. That missile blast really got their attention."

"How many?" Luther doesn't sound the least bit nervous.

"All of them."

"How's that?" Samson rumbles.

"According to the spirits, every last daemon is heading this way, desperate for something to eat—or somebody." He comes up for air. "We could do it, right here. Get rid of them, once and for all."

Luther's measured tone is a stark contrast to Milton's excitement. "Are there any defensible ruins or elevated safe zones out of harm's way? You will need to take the babies there immediately."

Our original plan of engagement involved setting up positions every few kilometers, expanding as we moved westward. But none of those locations would be safe for these little ones.

"City ruins, yeah—maybe twenty klicks north by northwest. I can fly them up there, but who's going to take care of them?"

"I will," Victoria says, baby on her hip. "Obviously."

I crest the hilltop and jog toward them.

"Sergeant—" Luther faces me.

"I heard." I give Milton a nod. "We've got company."

He shrugs at Victoria. "I can fly with both babies, or I can fly with you. Not both."

"Two trips, then." Luther beckons to Burke. "Milton is taking the little ones to safety."

Burke hands baby Florence over to Milton without pause.

"Right." Milton struggles to hold the girl, and she starts fussing, not at all confident in his grasp on her.

"Here." Memories of my little Mara at this age hit me like a sucker punch to the gut as I show him how to hold her.

"Thanks." Milton cradles her close with one arm, and she quiets down. Then he reaches for Victoria's son. "Next in line."

"You guys can't be serious." Victoria holds onto little Boaz. "Take me first. I'll be there when they arrive."

She hands her son to me. That's what I get for showing off my dad skills. Milton hands off the baby girl as well.

"Remember how we do this?" He puts his arm around Victoria in a familiar way.

Six months ago, he rescued her from the overturned ocean liner in Cain's Shipyard. I may be wrong, but I might have noticed a budding mutual attraction between them ever since I joined Luther's group.

"I remember." She wraps both arms around him and squeezes tight. "I should be lighter this time."

"Right. Because you're not carrying Boaz." He glances my way, where I have the little guy in my right arm and Florence in my left, staring at each other from behind their makeshift baby goggles and reaching for each other's face coverings with their miniature gloved hands.

"My stomach is flatter now, don't you think?" She slides it against him.

He clears his throat and glances at Luther. "We're off."

With a burst of dust, Milton and Victoria take to the sky and disappear from sight.

"The Creator moves in mysterious ways," Luther says absently, patting me on the back, his attention absorbed by the two babies. "He works all things together for good, even when all we see is evil. The forest for the trees..."

Not sure where he's going with this. "We lost people in that missile strike. We're about to be swarmed by a hundred armed hostiles." I shake my head, doing my best to keep my voice neutral and not upset the little ones. "Where's the good in any of this?"

"You heard Milton. The Creator is bringing the daemons straight to us. We won't have to go out looking for them."

"And that's a good thing?"

He nods slowly. "The offensive we planned—how long would it have taken? How many lives could we have lost in the process?"

"We won't all survive this."

"With every death we suffer, I lose a piece of myself. We all do. But I have faith the Creator will see us through. And once this land is free of the daemon blight, we will be one step closer to seeing our children again."

Feeling the warmth of these pudgy little ones in my arms, it's all I can do to keep my composure. He knows what I want more than anything.

"That's some faith you've got, Luther. Not sure I understand it."

He squeezes my shoulder. "The Creator is greater than our ability to understand."

Without warning, Milton returns with another blast of dust and reaches for the babies. "All aboard the Milton Express."

I adjust his grip on each of the squirming tykes. "Got 'em?"

"Sure." He sounds less than confident. "I mean, they'll probably turn catatonic once we're in the air, right?"

If he's lucky.

"Have a safe flight." Samson gives him two big metal thumbs up.

Another burst of dust, and he's in the air. The babies were on the verge of screaming a moment ago, but as soon as they're airborne, I don't hear a peep out of them. They're probably stunned. Traveling at supersonic speeds will do that, from what I recall.

"Anything, Shechara?" Luther checks.

She's keeping watch, scanning the terrain from left to right with her mechanical eyes roving, rotating, zooming. "Nothing yet."

But I hear the solar-powered engines humming ever louder.

Twenty-five distinct vehicles, each potentially carrying four mutants armed with assault rifles, rocket-launchers, and plenty of ammo. They're never in short supply.

Unlike us. We have the jeeps, rifles, and rocket-launcher we took off those mutants in addition to our own small arsenal of rifles and handguns. Not nearly enough.

Luther catches me staring into the distance. "Battle plans, Sergeant?"

"I'm not liking our odds."

Samson grunts. "We shouldn't be concentrated all together like this. Once we start shooting, we'll give away our position, and—" He whistles while one of his metal arms swoops overhead and crashes down at his side. "RPG inferno."

"Agreed." I glance down the hillside toward the jeeps. There's no cover anywhere else nearby, no fallback position. We're trapped here. "We can't engage so many of them." It would be mass suicide. I clench my fists, desperate for a solution. But nothing presents itself—until I look outside the box we've climbed into. "So we don't fight them. Not here."

"Explain," Luther says.

"You're not going to like it." This will go against every vestigial belief from the Old World he still clings to. Respect for the dead being at the very top of the list.

"I don't have to, as long as our people survive and the daemons do not."

I pause, weighing my words. Then I dive in headfirst. "We let the mutants take the Homeplace. They'll sniff out the blood and climb the cliffs to get inside. Once as many as possible are in those caves, we take out any stragglers in the foothills below while simultaneously hitting the front and rear cave entrances with RPGs. I'd assign that responsibility to Milton, since he can fly around the mountain faster than we can set up positions on each side."

Samson glances at Luther. "Seal the daemons up and initiate a cascade collapse throughout the entire cave network."

Luther is silent for a few moments before managing, "We allow them to desecrate our dead...and trap the daemons in the act."

I nod. There's no point in sugarcoating it. War is an ugly mess. But this way, those we lost in the missile strike will have given their lives for a greater purpose: eliminating the mutant threat once and for all.

"They usually prefer live prey." Samson scratches his chin through his head covering.

"According to the spirits, fresh meat is hard to find these days. The mutants weren't too finicky about the bodies in Cain's Shipyard."

"The spirits told you this?" Luther says.

"And they said they'd help us." Not sure what they meant by that, but it's worth mentioning.

"Maybe they'll throw a screen of dust in the air to cover our approach," Samson offers. "They've done it before."

"Yes. They have." Luther is deep in thought, staring into space. Then he seems to reach a grim conclusion. "Very well, Sergeant. We'll do it. And may the Creator have mercy on us for such a despicable act."

The bodies in those caves are just empty shells now, but I don't say that out loud. Instead I think back on the sight of Granger, Sinclair, and Harris after Cain gunned them down. I get Luther's point. If someone suggested using their bodies for mutant bait, I would have decked the bastard.

"So we sit tight and don't make a sound, let them all pass us by," Samson says. "And hope they don't notice those two jeeps we've got parked down there."

Milton returns, gliding out of the sky to land beside us. "The daemons are less than fifteen klicks away, climbing onto this plateau," he reports. "So what's the plan?"

Luther tells him, and he stares mutely, looking first at me, then Samson.

"You're okay with this?" he finally asks.

"His idea." Samson flicks a metal finger in my direction. "It's horrible. But it just might work."

"I see them," Shechara announces, and everyone instinctively crouches as she points westward.

"Victoria and the children are safe?" Luther whispers.

Milton nods. "Not the most comfortable accommodations, but secure. Hilltop sublevel on the edge of some ruins, near a cache of hydropacks and other rations. Might be a good spot for Homeplace 2.0."

"First things first." Luther raises his voice slightly, addressing the entire group: "Stay low and hold your positions. Do not engage the daemons. We are going to let them pass. Once they're five klicks away from the Homeplace, we will follow at a distance." He turns to me. "Sergeant."

I take my cue and fill everyone in on the plan. Most of them don't like it, looking at each other and shaking their heads. But Luther backs me up, telling them this is the only way. We can't take on a hundred mutants, no matter how courageous we are. We're all that's left, and we have to be smart about this.

Act wisely, the spirit told me. *Listen...*

Milton perks up when I tell him his role. "Always wanted to use one of these." He strokes the rocket-launcher. "Jealous?" He looks at Samson.

The big man grunts. "We'll make sure nobody shoots you down."

Milton's shoulders slump a bit. "Right."

The herd of solar jeeps closes in, seeming to know right where we are. Crossing kilometer after kilometer in a purposeful approach. I strain to hear anything from the mutants themselves, but they remain silent. Easy to imagine them in their vehicles, lidless yellow eyes bulging and oozing, sharp fangs glistening in the sunlight. Weapons held at the ready with a practiced ease.

They've never mobilized in great numbers before. Shechara shakes her head as she watches them in the distance, unable to believe her eyes.

"So many..." she whispers.

In a matter of minutes, they have us surrounded. We hold still, not making a sound, doing our best to blend into the surroundings. We're close to a couple hundred meters above them, so we should be out of sight. But I'm sure Luther is praying. I hope he is.

The jeeps rip past our position, moving onward without pause, headed straight for the Homeplace ten klicks east. A massive cloud of dust drifts after the mutants, thickening as their tires kick up more dirt.

Or maybe it's the spirits, providing that screen Samson mentioned.

Either way, judging by their speed, they should be halfway to their destination within the next five minutes or so. I signal everyone to get to their feet. Time to descend the hill and follow.

"Can you see through that?" I point at the wall of dust.

Shechara shakes her head.

Listen, the spirit said.

I can hear the mutants' vehicles and visualize where they are. "I'll take the lead. Stay close."

She nods.

We pile into our pair of jeeps, some finding seats while others stand on the running boards and grip the roll bars like before. Everyone is armed, a few with more than one rifle. Milton hefts the rocket-launcher.

"I'll see if I can do it in three," he tells me.

Three grenades are all he has. "Good plan."

We take off, keeping our distance—a klick or two behind that dust screen. No one says a word, and I hope none of those mutants have the kind of hearing I do. If we're lucky, the sound of our jeeps will just blend into theirs.

"You praying?" I ask Luther, seated beside me.

"Without ceasing," he says.

I nod. "Keep it up."

14. SERA
22 YEARS AFTER ALL-CLEAR

Arienna takes the news fairly well. Better than I did, at any rate. She seems to accept at face value that the parents who raised her are not blood relatives, that her biological parents are from the North American Wastes, and that her eggs have been harvested monthly to create children for upper-caste Eurasian citizens. Now that her augments are offline, it shouldn't be long before she starts manifesting some kind of unique yet bizarre ability.

That's right, *tree monkey*. Join the club.

The problem being, of course, that the club currently boasts only three members, and it doesn't look like Erik will be visiting the other seventeen anytime soon. Because as soon as he activated that EMP burst in the palm of his hand to knock out Arienna's neural implants, a swarm of Dome 2 law enforcement drones buzzed our way through the trees.

For a split-second, I felt a bit of nostalgia at the sight of them zipping through the air with their little rotors whirring at top speed. I've missed Wink and Blink. But these aren't my buddies, and seeing eight of them whiz our way with their lights flashing and warning sirens wailing is downright intimidating.

Arienna raises her hands into the air and bows her head like a good citizen. I'm tempted to do the same to keep the drones from firing any shocker darts my way. But once they identify me as a law enforcer and Arienna as a local, we won't be targets. Erik is the one they're after.

I consider letting them have him. He's broken more laws than I care to list right now, the most recent being yet another EMP burst. Not a wise choice today, after what just went down at the Chancellor's tower.

But I understand what he's trying to do. As more of my memories return, like he promised they would, I realize how important it is for the other members of the Twenty to discover who they really are. Apparently, localized electromagnetic pulses are the only way to neutralize the augments that interfere with remembering our past...and our abilities.

Which makes me wonder about those thousand or so kids created from our sex cells. Are they displaying any unique talents yet?

"Remain calm, citizens," the drones command in unison, hovering around us in a loose cordon. They direct their high-powered flashlights at our faces in the sun-dappled gloom beneath the leafy canopy. "Please kneel, interlocking your fingers behind your heads."

Arienna and I do so. Erik scowls, fishing through his jacket pockets like he's forgotten something important.

"You're gonna want to kneel," I warn him.

He nods absently but doesn't follow suit. I'm sure he regrets it as a drone fires a dart like a miniature missile, striking his chest dead center. The shock is instantaneous, and he groans, his limbs outstretched as his entire body stiffens. Grimacing and convulsing, he hits the artificial dirt and thrashes around for a few moments before lying completely still. He looks dead.

"Enforcer Chen, why have you not deposited this violator at local law enforcement headquarters as you indicated?" the drones ask. Of course they're in contact with the guards at the maglev station and know exactly what I told them.

I lower my arms and stand, glancing at Erik flat on his back.

"I'm on a special assignment to locate all members of the Twenty. This violator happens to be one, as does Arienna—"

"What is your business with Arienna Dogan?" A short pause. "Why are your neural implants offline, Enforcer Chen? Why have all three of you disabled your augments?"

"Some kind of glitch," I offer, tapping my temple. "Must have something to do with the terrorist attack."

"There is no record of a special assignment for Enforcer Sera Chen," they drone on. "You were expected to report to MedTech and then return to your cube. That is where you should be right now."

Thinking fast, or digging a deeper hole for myself, I reply, "Orders came directly from the Chancellor. Probe that security unit's memory, if you don't believe me."

The security clone I ordered to stay put has instead decided to run through the forest, straight for us.

"Halt." The drones reposition themselves, widening the cordon to include the clone. It stops abruptly. "You are identified as Unit D1-436, member of Chancellor Hawthorne's personal security force."

"That is correct," the clone answers without a hint of irony in its tone.

"Did Chancellor Hawthorne order Enforcer Sera Chen to locate each member of the Twenty—"

"Under Emergency Stipulation 5.6, Subsection 2, in the event of a threat against law and order, all members of the Twenty are to be sequestered until that threat has been neutralized," I recite from memory. Then I raise an eyebrow at the clone. "Sound familiar, Unit D1-436?" Nice to finally know its name.

Erik groans like he's suffering from intestinal distress. I try to ignore him.

"Yes," the clone says, its black face shield directed toward me. Followed by a long pause. "But I am unable to ascertain if the Chancellor ordered you—"

"Call her up," I suggest. "Oh, wait. You can't. Because she's missing."

"We will contact your commanding officer," the drones reply.

Commander Bishop. Great. I'm sure she'll be elated to receive word on her favorite curfew enforcer's most recent insubordinate activities.

The lead drone projects a hologram of Commander Bishop into the air. Her three-dimensional image glows with a ghostly aura as she stands hovering over the ground, dressed exactly as she was last night. Does she ever go home to sleep—to change? I've never seen her wear anything other than that stiff-collared uniform and long coat. I can't tell where she is, since there's no background in the projection, but she looks annoyed by the interruption. She's glaring at me.

"What are you doing in Dome 2, Enforcer Chen?" she demands.

"Following orders, ma'am."

"What orders would those be?"

"I am escorting last night's curfew violator to local law enforcement."

"The violation occurred in Dome 1, did it not?"

"The streets were unsafe. One of the Chancellor's security clones was kind enough to allow me to board its aerocar with the violator in tow." I pause. So far, so good. She seems to believe me. Probably because I'm telling the truth. "But he leapt from the car while we were in flight, and he took off running down the maglev tunnel to Dome 2. I pursued and apprehended him."

Bishop's eyes glaze over. She's receiving supplemental data, probably provided by the drones encircling us. "Why have you interrupted the important work of citizen Arienna Dogan? Why was the discharge of an electromagnetic pulse detected by local surveillance drones?"

Not as easy to explain. I can't think of a single good reason.

So I stick with the truth, come what may.

"She's my sister." I hesitate to proceed, but nobody else is saying anything, so I go on, "My biological sister. After a cursory DNA search, I found that I have nine siblings, and we're all the same age. We're also members of the Twenty. All ten of us. As well as the curfew violator—" I gesture toward him on the ground, and Bishop glances his way with an unreadable frown. "According to him, he also has nine siblings who share his DNA."

Bishop nods to herself, pensive. "You told me before that this was about your parents. This violator mentioned something about them—not any siblings."

"The situation has evolved, ma'am." Has she known all along that the Twenty are two sets of children? Has she known about our monthly sex cell extractions?

"Not a good time to be playing investigator." She looks exhausted all of a sudden.

"Have you located the Chancellor? Is she all right?"

Bishop nods. "I am with her now. She's safe. We are in a secure location—"

"Did she authorize Emergency Stipulation 5.6, Subsection 2?" I interrupt, cringing. Such bad form, but I have to know.

The hologram blurs as Commander Bishop turns to speak inaudibly to someone on her side of things. When she faces me again, her expression is guarded. "Do not interfere with Enforcer Chen's assignment," she orders the drones buzzing around us. "You are to support her efforts as needed. Her orders come directly from the Chancellor."

I glance at the security clone for any hint of surprise. Of course not. That face shield hides everything underneath. But I can't help feeling stunned, and I struggle to keep my face as stoic as possible.

If Chancellor Hawthorne didn't send those two clones to my door, then who did? Who in the government would want the Twenty sequestered? Perhaps it wasn't even a Governor who gave the security units their orders. Erik already showed me how easy it was for him to override Unit D1-436's programming. Could the terrorists have gotten control of a select number of clones and sent them after the Twenty? Difficult to imagine, let alone prove.

No clones have come after Arienna here in Dome 2—unless they're on their way...

"Carry on, Enforcer Chen," Commander Bishop says before signing off. "And be quick about it. You don't have much time."

The hologram dissolves into the air.

"How may we be of service, Enforcer Chen?" The drones have changed their tune, if not their monotone.

"Escort us to the maglev station." I turn to Arienna. "Can you get someone to cover your shift?"

She blinks at me, confused. "Yes, of course. But why?"

You're coming with us, I think at her.

She stumbles back a step and holds up a hand as if to ward me off. "Did you just—?"

Telepathy. Weird, right? I give her a wink.

She nods. "Very."

"This way, Enforcer Chen." The drones sideline themselves, expecting us to walk between them as we exit the forest.

I offer Erik my hand as he comes to, and he groggily lets me help him to his feet. Cursing under his breath, he flicks the shocker dart off his chest and empties his pockets. Half a dozen discs identical to the ones he used on the security clones rain onto the ground, followed by a pair of EMP grenades.

"All fried," he mutters, his voice sluggish.

"Are we returning to Dome 1?" Unit D1-436 steps toward us.

I shake my head. "How many of us are in Dome 3?" I ask Erik.

"Two," he says. "One of my siblings, one of yours. But without a way to knock out their augments, there's really no point in going."

Did you hear Bishop? I think at him.

The tail end of it, I think. He nods. *She basically authorized you to do what we're already doing.*

Not sure what to make of that. *She said we don't have much time. If someone other than the Chancellor is sending security units after the*

Twenty, we need to get to them first. We can worry later about telling them the truth.

First we need to make sure they're safe.

We start walking with the buzzing drones flanking us on both sides. Erik and I lead, with Arienna and Unit D1-436 following close behind.

"We should split up, cover more ground," Erik suggests. "Arienna and I could—"

"I'm going to need to see some proof," Arienna says. "I understand the Chancellor has endorsed your mission, but I still don't see how anyone could get away with what you're suggesting. And the idea that I'm going to display some sort of strange ability now that I'm offline..." She shakes her head. "How do I know anything you've said is true?"

It's totally understandable. Not long ago, I was right where she is, questioning all of this insanity, unaccustomed to trusting my biologic. But now I'm ready to join Erik on his quest, visiting our siblings across the Ten Domes. Why? What's changed?

Easy answer: my commanding officer not only validated what we're doing but told me to pick up the pace. Reading between the lines: the Twenty are in danger.

I hand Erik's phone to Arienna. He doesn't look happy about it. "Here."

"What is this for?" She looks perplexed by the antique device.

"Before neural implants, this was how people used to communicate and access the Linkstream. Think of it as a miniature console. Go ahead, run a DNA search," I tell her over my shoulder. "Siblings tend to share fifty percent of the same DNA. When I ran mine, your face came up. Along with eight others."

Erik takes a minute to show her how to use the touchscreen interface, then leaves her to it. She walks silently behind us, neck bent awkwardly over the small screen as she runs the search.

"It remains unclear why this curfew violator is being allowed to discharge electromagnetic pulses and take citizens' augments offline." Like the drones, the clone's monotone hasn't changed, yet it somehow manages to sound irritated. "How is this in line with the Chancellor's orders?"

I'm about ready to order it to zip its genetically manufactured lips. "Check your logic there, Unit D1-436. Erik's actions have served to keep us on-mission, as unorthodox as they may seem."

He half-turns toward the clone. "If it's any consolation, I'm all out of EMPs. So until I find another supply, I'll have to rely on my wits and charm alone."

I shudder to imagine that. The clone doesn't respond.

"So...we *are* sisters," Arienna says at length. She's verified that much already. "And we're going to meet the others?"

I nod. "That's right. A little pre-Revelation Banquet reunion," I borrow Erik's term for it. He smiles at me. I direct my gaze straight ahead.

"Your commanding officer made it sound urgent," Arienna says, handing the device dismissively back to Erik. "Are we in danger?"

Not sure how to answer that. "We'll be fine." I glance at Erik. *We stay together, and we keep moving. One dome after another.*

We may not reach them all in time, he replies, mind to mind.

We'll do the best we can. One step at a time.

The edge of the forest looms before us, and beyond, two square blocks of Dome 2's urban upward-and-outward sprawl. In the distance, I spot the gate to the maglev tunnel. Should be interesting returning with an eight-drone escort, but maybe their presence will prevent the guards from asking too many questions.

Except the guards are the least of our concerns as a government aerocar swoops out of the tunnel and soars straight for us. The tree branches and leaves tremble as the car stops in mid-air to hover above. Then it slowly descends, preparing to land on the forest floor less than twenty meters away.

Two security clones sit in the cockpit, their garish white armor shining and their black face shields fixed on us.

"Friends of yours?" Erik glances at D1-436.

"Did you call them?" I demand.

"Yes," the clone replies, "if by friends you mean fellow personnel from the Chancellor's security force. But as far as calling them, no, I am afraid that would be impossible. My Link-based communication systems remain out of order."

Thanks to Erik.

"What's going on?" Arienna sounds afraid for the first time.

"Trust us. Everything will be alright." For the moment, I keep my rifle down at my side, dangling from its shoulder strap. No reason to make an awkward situation worse.

As the aerocar settles onto the artificial turf, the side doors drift upward, and both security clones step out with their weapons aimed upward. Just a split-second away from pointing those muzzles at us.

"Enforcer Chen, your orders have changed," the clones say in unison. Sounds like they might've been eavesdropping on my conversation with Commander Bishop. "You, Erik Paine, and Arienna Dogan are to come with us immediately. We will explain the situation while en route to our destination."

"Which is where, exactly?" I step forward, placing myself between them and my motley entourage.

"We are not at liberty to say," the clones reply. "Rest assured, it is a secure location." They glance at the hovering drones. "Return to your duties. We have the situation in hand."

The drones seem reluctant to comply. In the artificially intelligent pecking order, clones reside at the top, being biological organisms. Drones and other automatons are expected to listen and obey, particularly when such biological organisms represent the interests of the Chancellor herself.

"Enforcer Chen is acting on direct orders from her superior officer, Commander Mara Bishop," the drones report, "who is currently with Chancellor Hawthorne." They close in on the two clones, who stand back to back and aim their weapons at the buzzing drones. "It is unclear where your orders originated."

Without a word to one another, the clones open fire, obliterating the drones in midair, sending sparks and shattered parts flying in every direction.

"Get down!" I yell, hoping Erik, Arienna, and D1-436 realize I'm yelling at them. Then I drop onto the ground and take aim at the two clones while the last of the drones disintegrate under heavy bursts of automatic fire.

I've never taken a life before, clone or human. Not even a bot. Watching the drones smashed to pieces is the most violent thing I've ever seen firsthand. In VR, it's different. No matter how real it seems, there's a part of my brain that always knows it's only virtual. I can take a step back and not get emotionally involved.

So that's what I do now.

I need to disable and disarm these clones, but I also need to keep them from summoning more of their kind. Killing each of them with a headshot would be the logical solution, but I may not be ready for that, no matter how high I scored at the academy gun range. I have to act fast and efficiently, not giving myself the opportunity to freeze up and wonder in that split-second whether it's murder to kill a clone. I have to be willing to do what must be done.

If my augments were functioning, I would simply act without this damned biologic getting in the way.

Lying on my stomach with the stock of my rifle shouldered and the barrel steady, I curl my finger around the trigger and squeeze once, twice, three times for good measure. The automatic bursts hit the clones with a staccato-crunch of live rounds impacting plasteel armor, cutting them off at the knees and sending them toppling sideways.

"Cease fire!" I shout at them, rising to train my muzzle on the nearest clone's forehead. "Lay down your weapons, or my next round is a kill shot."

As a rule, clones don't have a death wish. They know they're expendable, but they aren't usually in any hurry to be replaced. These two hold their rifles out laterally, away from their bodies, and point them at the tree canopy above us. But they don't let go of the weapons.

"Enforcer Chen," they tell me patiently, "you are suffering from a great deal of stress. No citizen should be without her augments as long as you have been. You must feel cut off from the world. We are here to help."

"Who sent you?" I stand hunched over my rifle, ready to fire at the first provocation.

"By order of the Supreme Chancellor—"

"I'm following the Chancellor's orders." We can all pretend to be on-mission for Persephone Hawthorne. "My commander is with her right now."

"Your commander terminated two of our units."

That doesn't sound right. "When?" I demand.

"Earlier this morning," the clones say in unison. "Following the terrorists' EMP blast, two security units were escorting the Chancellor and her aide onto the roof of Hawthorne Tower. Commander Mara Bishop arrived by aerocar and shot each clone in the head. The video is a matter of record, accessible via Linkstream with the proper clearance. Current conjecture is that Commander Bishop has gone rogue and that she kidnapped the Chancellor."

"To what end?"

"Unknown."

None of this makes any sense. Why would Bishop do such a thing?

"D1-436, disarm them," I order.

Without a word, it walks toward the two clones on the ground, their knee armor blown to bullet-riddled scrap with blood oozing out. Neither one will be walking again anytime soon.

"Don't try anything," I add.

Oddly enough, D1-436 responds instead, its face shield turning my way mid-stride. "You can trust me, Enforcer Chen. I am here to protect you."

"Good clone," Erik says, proud that his reprogramming has stuck.

"Unit D1-436," the two clones speak up, "you have been damaged, and you are offline. Your mission has been compromised. Someone has overwritten your primary directive."

"My primary directive is to protect Enforcer Chen." It snatches each clone's weapon and walks back toward me.

Well done. "Give those to Erik and Arienna." I step aside as it approaches, keeping my rifle on the unarmed clones.

"Have they had any weapons training?" D1-436 stops in front of me with an assault rifle in each hand. For now, the muzzles are pointed at the ground.

"Of course," I lie, having no idea. But being offline like the rest of us, the clone has no way to verify my claim. So it hands the weapons over.

"I've never…" Arienna trails off, keeping the rifle at arms' length.

"Never seen such a well-maintained firearm!" Erik lets out a low whistle.

"Neither Erik Paine nor Arienna Dogan has received any weapons training whatsoever," the two clones report. Because they still have full access to the Linkstream and can look up anything they please.

"As far as you know." Erik shoulders the rifle with familiarity and sights along the barrel, squinting one eye as he aims at a distant tree. "Not everything is on record, my genetically identical friends."

Right. Especially when it comes to terrorists.

"Enforcer Chen lied to you, Unit D1-436." The two clones' face shields are directed at the unit beside me now. "She does not trust you."

"Shut up, both of you." I half-turn toward D1-436. "Is there any way you could find out who sent them after us?"

"Other than Chancellor Hawthorne?"

I nod.

"I would need to connect to one of their cranial jacks."

Careful, Erik warns. *If it bumps brains with these units, it could be swayed to their cause.* Overwriting his overwriting, in other words.

"You would trust me to do this?" D1-436 faces me as if it heard Erik's warning. But that would be impossible. Clones aren't telepathic.

"Don't give me a reason not to."

It strides forward, walking behind the two immobilized clones. They watch silently as it approaches. D1-436 raises one hand, and the section of the white gauntlet covering its index finger seems to break in half, the finger curling while a spike-shaped data connector extends from the first knuckle. D1-436 takes the helmeted head of one clone in its other hand and forces the chin down, exposing the cranial jack at the base of the neck. Unceremoniously, the data spike slides home, and the clone stiffens. So does D1-436. Both of them are frozen in place, while the third clone looks on. Wondering if it will be next?

"Our orders came directly from the Creator." D1-436 and the clone it's jacked into speak in unison.

"The creator?" I echo. Not weird at all.

"Who now?" Erik steps forward on my right.

Doesn't sound like the Chancellor, I think at him.

Agreed.

"No longer will the Twenty be allowed to live in the world," D1-436 and the clone continue. "It has become an evil, dangerous place, and they are far too valuable. They must be protected at all costs. They will be gathered together in a safe zone where they will live out the rest of their lives in service to the greater good of all Eurasia."

Arienna joins me on the left. "I'm not liking the sound of that."

"Who is this *creator*?" I need a name. "Nobody outranks the Supreme Chancellor. You are members of her security detail. Your orders should come only from her."

"You will meet the Creator once the Twenty have been gathered together. Until then, you must trust that the Chancellor's security personnel have your best interest at heart. We will escort you to a safe location—"

"How many of the Twenty are currently in this so-called safe location?" I can't imagine anyplace safer than Dome 2. It's so quiet here, so green.

"Ten at present."

I nod to Erik. *That's where we're going.*

"What?" he blurts out loud before checking himself. *Are you out of your mind? We can't go there—wherever it is. We stick to the plan—*

There isn't time. They've already captured half of us, with potentially more en route. I pause a moment to strategize. *We stop by one of your suppliers, pick up some more EMP grenades, then we fly in like any other aerocar full of precious cargo.*

He nods, not liking the idea but understanding where I'm going with it. *Then we knock out everybody's augments at once.*

As well as the security clones guarding them. I raise an eyebrow.

"Might work," he mutters. *If we knew where the hell to go.*

That's easy. "Unit D1-436," I say aloud, "tell me where the Twenty are being held."

The clone nods but doesn't say anything. Then D1-436 and the clone it's jacked into begin to tremble, small tremors at first, escalating into violent convulsions that risk severing the connection between them.

"What's going on?" I glance at Erik.

"Not sure." He winces at the sight. "Could be a defense measure to keep anyone from learning the location—"

D1-436 withdraws the data spike, and the clone it was connected to tips over, collapsing limply onto the ground.

"I have the coordinates, Enforcer Chen," it says, striding toward me as the spike folds back into place and its gauntlet returns to a five-fingered hand. "Shall we go?"

"What did you do?" I nod toward the motionless clone. It looks dead, for all intents and purposes.

The one next to it sits there looking stunned, staring at its partner.

"Unit D1-917 refused to share the location with me," D1-436 explains. "We fought. I won."

"You killed it."

D1-436 faces me. "Have I earned your trust?"

Instead of answering, I point at the aerocar. "I'll need you to fly that thing."

"Yes, of course, Enforcer Chen." It pivots toward the car.

I place a hand on its cold, armored arm. "Input the coordinates into the navigation console, but don't share them with anyone." If we're going under the guise of a security team returning with its cargo, we must maintain the air of secrecy. "And stick that other clone in the seat next to you." It'll look better having two of them in the cockpit. Business as usual.

"Yes, Enforcer Chen."

I turn to Erik. "Where do we need to stop first?"

He gives me a sheepish grin. "Oh, you're really not going to like it."

"I'll be the judge of that."

He shrugs. "Dome 10."

"Of course," I mutter. The birthplace of the terrorist uprisings—and the best place to procure illegal weaponry, along with other unsavory substances such as dust. Located on the edge of the Mediterranean, Dome 10 serves Eurasia as a waste-processing center, and it's the only dome with airlocks that open to the outside world. "Very well. Unit D1-436, we'll be making a stop in Dome 10. Then it's straight to our class reunion."

I release the clone to follow its orders.

Don't you want to know where the reunion's taking place? Erik thinks at me.

We'll know soon enough. Right now, I'm more concerned about Commander Bishop's rogue status. It's suddenly all I can think of. What the hell is going on? Why would she kidnap the Chancellor?

Any idea who this creator-person is? Erik scratches his chin. *Because, if I had to guess—*

Hey...guys? The sound of Arienna's thoughts enter our shared telepathic space for the first time. *I think something might be happening to me...*

15. SAMSON
5 YEARS AFTER ALL-CLEAR

Cain reeks.

I caught a whiff or two of his stench while he was sitting next to me in the jeep, and I thought that was bad. But being trapped inside this dark shipping container as we roll toward Eden? Nothing I wouldn't give for a breather right now.

The four raiders keeping an eye on us don't seem to mind, but then again, they've got their own oxygen supply. The three Wastelanders aren't bothered by it either. They've gotten used to Cain's stank by now, or they can't smell it over their own. The smell intensifies the longer we're kept locked in the dark.

Shechara and Daiyna still have their head coverings on. Wise choice. Shechara holds a hand over her mouth and nose, but Daiyna doesn't bother.

The three of us can see perfectly fine in the dark, thanks to the spirits. So can the raiders, due to the tech in their helmets. They sit on crates and we sit on the floor, but we all sway with the movement of the tractor-trailer.

They keep their Tavor assault rifles resting casually on their laps with the muzzles aimed at us. And they keep their face shields pointed in our direction. No conversation, of course. This isn't that kind of road trip.

Cain is the only one of us bound and gagged, just the way we like him. The raiders saw no reason to untie him, and that's all right by me. So far, they seem to believe he was responsible for the destruction of their rig, as well as Stack. Also okay by me. The problem is, they think we're his cohorts.

I figure they'll hold onto him but try to hand the rest of us over to Eden. Daiyna, in particular, with that bounty on her head. When the raiders move in to commandeer, pillage, and plunder, we'll take that as our cue to escape. Assuming all goes according to Daiyna's plan.

But I'm not sure she's in any shape to be making plans. The past few years have been rough on her. There are moments when we catch a glimmer of who she used to be. But for the most part, she comes across as a haunted drunk. I hope this trip to Eden isn't just a way for her to raid their liquor cabinets.

And kill Perch.

The last time she went after him, over three years ago, we ended up losing good people. I won't let that happen twice. Shechara and me, we're leaving at the first opportunity. Daiyna doesn't want to come along, that's on her. She can stay and lead her new Wastelander lackeys to their deaths if that's what she wants.

What do we want? To live life on our own terms. Not chasing Luther's lofty dreams of a future that may never come. Surviving here and now. More than surviving: enjoying every day we have together.

Will we get back there? I see the way Shechara dotes on Daiyna. The two of them aren't related biologically, but they've always been as close as sisters. Even if she hasn't mentioned it, I doubt a day went by that Shechara didn't worry about Daiyna. I could say the same about Luther, though he'd never admit it. They both love her in their own way.

I love Shechara more than anyone else on the planet. I can't let anybody put her in danger. Even if it is her beloved sister.

"Deep thoughts?" Daiyna's watching me, her goggles up on her forehead.

"Just planning our escape." My voice has a tendency to be louder than it should, even when I'm trying to keep it quiet.

The raiders chuckle and shake their heads. Because they don't think I can break out of here. The truth is I could, but I'd be risking lives in the process. I don't much care what happens to Cain or the Wastelanders; if we were positioned differently, with them in the line of fire, I might try something. But Shechara and Daiyna are seated on the floor close to one of the raiders. No way.

"Any ideas?" One of Daiyna's eyebrows lifts.

"I was liking the idea of Cain as a human shield. But then I realized he's not human anymore. He's hamburger."

Cain growls and thrashes at that, and the raiders laugh, a couple of them nudging him with their boots. Poking the bear.

"Hamburger..." Daiyna murmurs. "The first bite was always the best. You know? That explosion of flavor—" She cuts herself off at the sound of Shechara's stomach growling. "Sorry."

"It's okay." Shechara wraps an arm around her middle. "I'd even go for a protein pack right now."

I frown, unable to remember the last time we've eaten. Before we hijacked that big rig yesterday? Of course she'd be hungry now. I would be, too, if my arms and legs weren't made out of metal. Cyborg that I am, I only need to eat once a day. Although I can always eat more, if there's extra to be had on the rarest of occasions.

"Got any standard rations?" I nod to the raider who was calling the shots when we first entered our mobile prison cell. "We haven't eaten in a while."

"Not my problem," he says.

"You want our help invading Eden? We'll be more helpful if—"

"I want you to shut your mouth for the duration of this trip." He stares me down. Tries to, anyway, patting his Tavor. "Or do we have a problem?"

"No problem," Shechara says. "Except that he gets awful grumpy when he's hungry. I've seen him take on four or five guys without breaking a sweat. Just to get a protein pack."

"Is that so?" The raider stands, steady on his feet despite the rig's movement. "You some kind of tough guy, metal man?"

"Can't be helped." I shrug and cross my mechanical arms. "Those wackos in Eden thought I needed limb replacement surgery. Side effect: I'm usually a real force to be reckoned with."

"Yet you're sitting there on the floor." He aims his weapon at my head. "Completely at our mercy."

"Ironic, right?"

The raider tilts his head to one side. "How about we rip off your arms and legs and drop what's left of you in the middle of the Wastes? Sound fun?"

Sadistic, more like.

He's looking to start something, but he has me at a severe disadvantage. For one thing, he and his cronies are pointing automatic weapons at my people, so of course I'm not going to take a swing at him. And even if he stopped the truck so we could step outside and duke it out, I would destroy him with a single punch. He'd have to be a complete moron not to realize that.

"I'll zip it." That should be enough to make him think he's won. For the time being, anyway.

He stares my way without saying anything else, his cocky posture doing the talking for him: *Yeah, I thought so.* Then he returns to his seat, and I pretend to doze off. Checking my eyelids for holes, as my grandfather used to say. But the lurching motion of the truck doesn't lend itself to actual snoozing.

I'm resigned to the fact that we won't be escaping while en route. We're actually going to Eden. Three and a half years is way too soon when you think you're never going to see certain people ever again.

Perch, in particular. The man who took my limbs.

I shouldn't worry about Daiyna's thirst for revenge. I'll have plenty to occupy me, keeping a lid on my own. Can't do anything that will jeopardize Shechara's safety. Once we arrive, we'll let the raiders take the lead while we fade into the distance, as far away from any crazies as possible. Where? Doesn't matter much, as long as we're together.

Cracking open one eye, I watch Shechara until she notices. Difficult to tell if she smiles at me, with her head covering in place. But I smile at her.

We're gonna be all right. We've gotten through worse.

I hope that's what my expression conveys. She gives me a little nod and looks down, keeping her eyes to herself.

"You'll want to have your driver pull into the east end of the city ruins," Daiyna speaks up. "No way this rig will fit inside the parking structure, so we'll either have to take these—" She slaps one of the Wastelanders' dirt bikes parked beside her. "—or go on foot. Five levels down."

She has the attention of my sadistic friend. His face shield turns her way and stays there. "Then what?"

"We take a tunnel straight to their front door." She shrugs. "Giant airlock, big enough to drive a jeep through."

"That's where we claim the bounty."

She nods. "They'll open the door as soon as they see you've got me. We won't even have to knock."

"Dead or alive." He raises the Tavor, his gloved finger curled around the trigger.

She doesn't blink. Doesn't cringe, either. I've never known anything to frighten Daiyna. She's seen much worse than this guy.

"They'll be more enthusiastic about opening up the airlock if they're the ones who get to end me. Your call, but I'm thinking you could use that enthusiasm as a distraction while you invade their subterranean sanctuary." She leans forward and lowers her voice. "That's where the babies were made, you know. Eurasia's hope for a bright future, right there in Eden's sublevels. I'll take you on a tour." She chuckles to herself. "Hell, I should sell tickets..."

The raider eases his weapon back onto his lap, finger off the trigger. "You're not exactly right in the head, are you."

"I've been told that before." She gives him a wink.

Shechara looks concerned. Not the first time since reuniting with Daiyna, probably won't be the last.

By the time we reach the ruins, it's mid-morning. The driver parks the rig where Daiyna suggested, and the raiders who followed in our jeep open up the shipping container with jarring metallic shrieks. We're expected to exit one by one, the raiders keeping their rifles trained on us the entire time.

They don't like the idea of riding down into the parking structure on motorbikes, so we hoof it. Daiyna and three raiders in front, followed by the Wastelanders and Cain, then a couple raiders, then Shechara and me, with the last two raiders bringing up the rear. Cain's ankles are unshackled, but his arms remain bound, hands behind his back, and the gag is still right where it should be.

Anytime I make eye contact with the oaf, he gives me a maniacal stare with plenty of bloodshot white around the dark irises. Like he wants me to know he's not through with any of us. That his current situation doesn't define him. That he'll have his revenge. Or maybe I'm reading too much into it.

We make our way down into the lower levels of the parking garage, the high-powered flashlights attached to the raiders' rifles cutting a white swath through the darkness and throwing the abandoned automobiles into stark relief against the surrounding concrete. I keep an eye out for cameras mounted along the ceiling but don't catch sight of any. Perch has really dropped the ball. Willard was always so proud of his surveillance tech down here.

The only sound is our footfalls as we descend the ramp into the lowest level and head straight for the tunnel's open mouth at the far end. We're thirty meters away from it when shots explode, fired from somewhere off to the left.

"Shechara!" my voice booms, lost beneath the barrage as raiders crouch and return fire.

Shechara and Daiyna scramble for cover behind one of the abandoned cars. I hold my metal arms up to shield my head and torso and hunker down. My mechanical legs scrape across the concrete floor as I advance, taking cover behind support pillars and autos along the way.

During a brief lull in the shooting, an unfamiliar voice screams, "You did this to me! You!" Followed by more shots fired in Daiyna and Shechara's direction. "You left me out there to *die*!"

I stay low and continue to move toward the shooter. The raiders take cover and hold their positions. The one who suggested removing my limbs earlier doesn't like the fact that I'm not staying put.

"Get back here, cyborg!" he shouts, mostly drowned out by the weapons fire.

"Not my name." I keep moving. So far, I seem to be off the shooter's radar. He's concentrating all his rage elsewhere.

"You knew they wouldn't let me in!" the shooter screams during another lull. "I'm *starving* out here!"

"It's only been a day or two, you big baby!" Daiyna shouts back.

So, they're acquainted.

He releases a half-curse, half-shriek and resumes firing automatic bursts in her direction.

"They've led us into an ambush," one of the raiders complains.

The three Wastelanders keep low nearby, their grinning skull-masks looking pleased as ever by the proceedings. Cain is curled into a fetal position, grunting to himself.

"One guy? Hardly an ambush." I swing my right arm, smashing it like a wrecking crane into a sedan and sending it rolling laterally, straight toward the shooter's position. I follow the tumbling vehicle, using it as cover while I advance. Automatic fire blasts my way, and I duck, shielding myself mid-stride.

I have his attention now.

A swing of my left arm sends another car his way. This one hurtles through the air a meter above the ground, corkscrewing until it slams into the auto he's been using for cover, skidding it across the floor and pinning him against the far wall. He screams, agony and anger fueling the primal sound. He's got every right to be mad at me as I approach. His shooting arm, along with the rifle it holds, have been crushed.

"All her fault..." he whimpers, head lolling forward. "She should've killed me..."

"You from Eden?" I look him over. No camo, no black beret. He wears filthy thermal underwear instead. Haggard and gaunt, he obviously hasn't eaten lately.

"They won't let me back inside." He shakes his head with a manic rhythm. "Not now... She did *this* to me!"

When he looks up, I see that his eyes are wrong. They're yellow. Bulging outward unnaturally. The eyelids are little more than fleshy tatters, torn away from the sockets.

"What the hell is happening?" he wails.

I have no idea. Never seen anything like this before. If the spirits have gifted him with a new ability, I can't tell what it is. Looks more like he's turning into a daemon—but that can't be. Can it?

After all we went through to get rid of those creatures, are the evil spirits making new ones?

A single gunshot explodes next to me, and the mutant-in-the-making's head snaps back with a burst of blood. Then he slumps to the ground, his arm and rifle stuck above him at an awkward angle.

"Was that necessary?" I turn on the raider who fired the headshot.

"Didn't you see his eyes? We don't mess with the infected." He nods for me to return to the tunnel entrance. "Move out, cyborg."

He waits until I lead the way, metal feet clanking. "You've seen this before, then."

He grunts. "Three years ago, we received word the roaming hostiles had been neutralized. Flesh-eating freaks with the same yellow eyes. I'm sure you're familiar with them."

I nod.

"For a while, we didn't see them anywhere, which made our

supply runs possible. But lately, with food and water running low—"

"Thanks to you," I mutter. These raiders keep taking what we need to survive.

"—we've noticed an uptick in small pockets of the infected. Nowhere near as dangerous as the well-armed variety that used to rove around in their jeeps. Now they just hole up and starve to death. But the eyes are always the same. The first thing to change, once the infection sets in. Those hideous yellow eyes."

Shechara leaps into my arms as we meet up with the others, and I pull her close. "You all right, Small Fry?"

She nods, gazing at me with a slight scowl. "That was some real Strongman action, throwing those cars around." She squeezes me tight. "You put yourself in danger like that again, I'll punch you right in the eye."

Love it when she gets feisty. "Roger that." I kiss her forehead and notice Daiyna staring at the dead shooter. "You knew him."

"We met." Daiyna turns away.

"He didn't like you very much."

"He should've left me alone."

I nod slowly. "Bounty hunter?"

"He thought he was."

I won't be getting his creepy eyes out of my head anytime soon. "Looked like he was turning into a daemon. Ever seen anybody change like that before?"

She shakes her head, unsettled by it. I don't blame her.

The raiders herd us together, and we head into the tunnel, lit only by the narrow beams of their flashlights. My first trip to Eden was bad enough. Never thought there would be a second, much less a third. This return trek takes the longest, since the raiders appear to be in no hurry, either due to overweening caution or a desire to keep their captives in line while en route. The monotony of boot soles meeting pavement is broken only by the sounds of my metal feet clunking along.

Nobody says anything. Even Cain is silent. The skull-faced

Wastelanders with their feathers and studded leather seem right at home in a murky tunnel like this. They swagger along without a care in the world.

They've got to be getting awful hungry by now. Even my stomach is grumbling.

A while later—impossible to judge how much time has passed; maybe an hour—the raider in the lead holds up a clenched fist, and we stop.

"End of the line," Shechara whispers, but I hear her loud and clear.

"Quiet." The raider in front points at Daiyna. "You. Come with me. Everybody else, stay put."

Daiyna joins the raider, and they exit the tunnel. Their footsteps echo as they enter the dark, spacious area in front of the airlock. The raider clears his throat. His rifle-mounted flashlight sweeps across the massive blast door before them.

"Twenty hydropacks, dead or alive." His voice is loud and confident. "Who do I see about claiming my bounty?"

No response. The Wastelanders shuffle their feet, unable to stand still like the rest of us. We wait. After seeing that scrawny, half-daemon shooter back there, I can't help wondering if Perch and his men have all starved to death. Or are too weak to open the door.

But then the intercom switches on, and Perch growls low and conversational, "Knew I'd be seeing you again, Daiyna. What's it been? Something like three years, right? Hope you're not here for your *eggs*. We had to divert power a while back. Sealed off Margo's lab. Let everything down there rot. I'm sure it's a real mess now."

She doesn't respond.

"Well. We sure are gonna have us a good time."

The steel blast door creaks as it retracts into the ceiling, revealing the sealed airlock vestibule inside.

"Drop your gun, Mr. UW," Perch says. "Then you and Daiyna will be allowed to enter."

The raider's flashlight flicks from the intercom speaker above the door to the airlock as if weighing his options.

"Otherwise, my men will shoot you right where you stand," Perch says, "soon as that door opens."

The raider curses under his breath and backtracks toward the tunnel where we wait. He unclips the Tavor from his shoulder strap and hands the weapon to a member of his team.

"Soon as that door opens," he repeats in a whisper, and his teammate nods. Then he returns to Daiyna's side, gripping her arm above the elbow—which she surprisingly tolerates. "Ready," he says aloud.

Perch chuckles on the intercom. Not a sound I've ever wanted to hear again.

The airlock cycles open with an expanding halo of light. Three Eden Guards in O2 masks step out wearing their blue fatigues and black berets. They point assault rifles at the unarmed raider and the tunnel as they step toward Daiyna. One swings a satchel forward, and it slides across the slick concrete floor.

"Twenty hydro," says the guard. He reaches for Daiyna's other arm.

Bad idea.

She grabs him by the wrist and lunges into the air, back-flipping over his head to land behind him—nearly breaking his arm in the process. He tries to stifle a yelp but doesn't do a great job of it. His arm's bent at a painful angle, and he's unable to stop the raider from seizing his weapon and turning it on the other two Eden Guards.

They freeze. For the moment, no one fires.

"Daiyna, Daiyna..." Perch clucks his tongue on the speaker. "What do you think you're doing?"

"Go!" the raider shouts, gesturing for his two teammates at the tunnel exit to run into the airlock before the heavy door swings shut.

That leaves only four raiders in charge of us captives. Our odds are looking better.

The two raiders in the well-lit airlock force the exterior door to remain open while they get to work unlocking the interior door. In a matter of seconds, they have the vestibule wall panel torn off and a jumble of wires exposed.

"You think we haven't prepared for every eventuality?" Perch scoffs.

He must have taken a vocabulary course since we saw him last. I don't remember him being able to string more than a few words together. And they were usually of the single-syllable variety.

"Go ahead, cut those wires. Cross those other wires. You won't short anything out." He pauses. "But we may have a surprise in store..."

On cue, white smoke pours into the vestibule from above. If it's some kind of gas, the raiders won't be vulnerable to it with their helmets on.

Except it's not gas. It's liquid nitrogen.

The raiders stumble out of the vestibule in a hurry, covering their face shields with both hands. Their armored suits are now frosty white instead of black where the liquid struck them. No real damage there. But the polymer of their face shields is cracking in web-like patterns, and it won't take much to compromise the integrity.

The outer airlock door remains propped open with a rifle jammed in place, but nobody seems eager to enter. Particularly those of us without any sort of protective suit.

"You see?" Perch says as the vapor clears. "Nobody gets inside unless we want them inside. And Daiyna, we definitely want you. So let go of that guard, and let's proceed with your warm welcome, shall we?"

She shifts her hold on the Eden Guard, placing her other hand on his elbow. He groans, grimacing in pain. She's got him on the verge of bone-breakage, and he seems eager to avoid that.

"Can you get through?" one of the raiders behind me says in a low tone. "Team leader wants to know."

They must have been conferring on internal comms.

"Maybe." I shrug.

A rifle muzzle digs into my back. "Move."

The others clear a path as we pass them by. Shechara's frown deepens.

"Enjoying yourself?" I raise an eyebrow at Daiyna as I exit the tunnel. The Edenite she's holding glares up at me.

"All part of the plan." She graces me with half a smile.

"Right." There's no plan. That much is obvious.

Time for a change in tactics.

The lead raider says something obnoxious, but I ignore him. I've got my eye on the airlock's exterior door, propped open precariously with that rifle. Not sure it will hold. So I step forward and jump, grabbing onto the upper rim of the door and pulling, bending it out of shape. The hinges moan, and the entire thing shudders under the abuse. But the end result is exactly what I had in mind.

I let go and take a step back to survey my handiwork. That heavy exterior door will never shut again. All that's left to contend with is the interior airlock door—and that liquid nitrogen.

"Good work," says the lead raider, mildly impressed.

Perch curses on the intercom. "Now why'd you have to go and do a thing like that, Samson?"

I look up at the intercom's camera lens. Then I point at it with a metal index finger. "See you soon."

I grab the raider by his armored neck and hoist him up into the air over my head as I charge into the airlock. He shouts and thrashes, but I've got a solid hold on him, and I'm not letting go. His teammates surge forward and aim their guns at me, but nobody fires. Not yet. The Wastelanders whoop and cavort inside the tunnel, enjoying the show.

The liquid nitrogen rains down moments later, but I've got my raider shield in place. His armored suit catches the brunt of it, streaming off him to strike the floor with thick clouds of vapor.

Tough to see through, but I manage, flipping my other hand into a multitool and using it to rearrange the inner door's locking mechanism.

"Shoot him, dammit!" the raider yells.

"Hold your fire," says the rig driver. She doesn't seem too worried about her associate. "Let's see what the cyborg can do."

"You're a dead man! You hear me? I'll tear off your arms and legs myself—!"

"Good luck with that," I mutter.

My work on the wiring is done, the short already producing a nice little electrical fire. I whip my hand back into the anthropomorphic variety and plant my metal palm on the interior door, fingers splayed. Locking my mechanical elbow and planting my mechatronic legs, I push.

Perch is silent on the intercom as the door caves inward with a resistant creak, the hinges straining, the airtight seal weakening. I maintain my role as an unstoppable force, pressing forward incrementally. As I feel the door give, I continue to apply pressure, until the seal pops with a rush of cool, filtered air. The best Eden has to offer.

But that's not all that leaks out. A barrage of automatic weapons fire pounds the door from the other side, and I can't help cringing against the sudden salvo. Since it appears the liquid nitrogen has run out, I drop the raider onto his feet and grab the airlock's interior door with both hands.

"Get ready," I tell him.

His entire back side is covered in frosty white, and his gloved hands are clenched into fists down at his sides. For a moment, he looks like he's going to take a swing at me. But then he realizes what I'm planning to do, and he orders his team to prepare to fire. They advance, one of them handing him his rifle.

They take aim, right at me.

"Samson!" Shechara cries.

Not sure what's going to happen next, I grit my teeth and put everything I have into pushing that airlock door open. But not just open. Off its hinges, tearing it free with a steel shriek. Then I'm charging into Eden, shielding my fleshy parts with the door as I storm the gates. The raiders are right behind me, crouching and returning fire as the Edenites pound my massive shield with relentless barrages, rounds thudding and deflecting on impact, hitting my mechanical legs when I fail to keep them covered.

The Wastelanders race after us without any weapons or body armor. Or much in the way of brains. They launch themselves at the Eden Guards like wild maniacs, and the guards stare wide-eyed like they've never seen anything so bizarre. Their aim falters as they stumble backward, their training forgotten for the moment. But that's all the raiders need. They step out from the cover of my shield and fire headshot after headshot, taking down the men of Eden with practiced ease, not wasting any ammo.

The Edenites retreat to a rally point, hiding behind empty crates scattered across the floor of Eden's expansive subterranean dome, lit up as bright as day. I remember when this area was covered in pallets stacked two meters high with hydropacks, standard rations, and canned goods—actual food. Not anymore. And the Edenites I've glimpsed don't look much better than that guy we encountered in the parking structure. Just as hungry, but no yellow eyes among them.

Five of the raiders stand out in the open now, pointing their weapons either at the crates on the floor or the catwalk above, where apartment units hang suspended from the dome's interior. The first two raiders who encountered the liquid nitrogen lie dead; Edenite rounds shattered their fractured face shields. One of the Wastelanders lies among four dead Eden guards, and the other two bikers sit nearby, heads bowed as if in mourning.

Silence holds the moment.

Until Daiyna walks out of the airlock with a firm hold on her Edenite, staggering in front of her.

"Well, Perch," her voice echoes, filling the entire dome. She takes a look around. Unimpressed. "I'm here."

It's still unclear whether she's out for revenge. But I know I'm not. For all I care, Perch and his people can starve to death in their compromised refuge. I'm not about to help them along.

And I'm through with these UW raiders.

I hurl the airlock door at the five of them, and they go down like dominoes. Next, I slug the Edenite Daiyna's holding, and he collapses to the floor.

"We're leaving." I jerk my head for her to follow as I charge straight for the open airlock.

She looks confused for a second, like things aren't going according to plan. But the expression doesn't last long. Something seems to click behind her eyes. Purpose, maybe. With a nod, she runs after me.

Shechara is alone with Cain inside the tunnel. She's got a rifle aimed at him, and he's groaning, favoring his broken ankle. She brightens at the sight of Daiyna and me but winces at the roar of weapons fire emanating from inside Eden, reignited with a gusto. Reinforcements led by Perch himself, who's screaming Daiyna's name.

I pull Shechara into a gentle squeeze. "Ready to hit the road?"

She nods eagerly. "What about him?"

Cain. He grunts at us with a spark of hope in his eyes.

"Leave him," Daiyna says.

Good idea.

The three of us sprint up the tunnel and out of the parking garage as fast as we can, my legs making enough racket to let every raider, Edenite, and Wastelander know our exact location. Fortunately, they have enough to keep them busy at the moment: trying to kill each other.

Outside the parking structure, the big rig sits right where we left it. I can't help grinning at Shechara.

Looks like we're hijacking another one.

16. MILTON
2 YEARS AFTER ALL-CLEAR

I watch as eighty daemons scramble up the cliff like the rabid beasts they are and crawl into the Homeplace, squeezing between fallen rocks on their way inside the collapsed entrance. At the same time, Sergeant Bishop and Samson lead the ground assault on the twenty daemons left behind—sitting in their jeeps and holding the perimeter, due to some military instinct from another life. Waiting for their share of the meat to be brought down to them. Not expecting the headshots that send them toppling sideways.

Gritting my teeth, I release a rocket-propelled grenade from the launcher on my shoulder. I'm hovering a hundred meters in the air, so I'm hurled in the opposite direction by the recoil. But I manage to course-correct in time to see the front entrance of the Homeplace explode and cave in completely, dust billowing into the air as the opening is sealed shut. Hopefully setting off a chain reaction of collapses inside the entire cave network.

There's another opening on the other side of the mountain, so I fly over there in a matter of seconds and line up my second shot. This side was left completely undamaged by that missile strike, and the mouth yawns wide enough to aim an RPG deep inside.

I wait for any signs of daemons trying to escape. Ten minutes pass, then twenty without any movement. Automatic gunfire echoes from the mountain's west side, where my friends fight the daemons on the ground. Part of me wants to join them, to use my speed to disarm every last hideous creature in less than a minute. But I'm the only one who can fly, so here I am, floating in mid-air with a rocket-launcher on my shoulder and the second of three RPGs prepped and ready to go.

But I'm not alone.

"Your *friends*." The Julia-spirit hovers beside me and smiles. I do my best not to be distracted by her beauty. Emerald eyes glinting in the hot sun, golden hair undulating in the breeze. "They really are, aren't they? You've come a long way, Milton. No longer a lone survivor, you're part of a tribe now."

"A dwindling tribe," I mutter. Only fifteen of us left, and two are just babies.

I hope Victoria is doing alright with them. As soon as these daemons are exterminated, I'll be flying northward to those ruins to check on her and the little ones.

"You love her." Julia nods with a knowing look.

"What?" I frown at her. "No, I don't. I mean, I care about her, sure. She's a new mother, and she's in charge of two very demanding—"

"You don't have to hide it. I'm not jealous." Julia winks at me.

Well, that's a relief.

The gunfire in the distance has abated. I hope we've won.

"You have." Julia nods. "The only creatures left are skulking inside this mountain."

I almost don't want to ask, but I have to know. "Did we...lose anybody?"

Her smile fades away. She nods grimly. "Five."

I clench my jaw. "Who?"

"Burke, Ethan, Connor, Deven...and Margo."

The sudden loss hits me like a punch to the gut. My eyes well up with hot tears. I can't believe they're gone, just like that. I saw each of them, spoke to them, only minutes ago. Now I never will again.

"They took down multiple daemons before they were killed." She reaches out to touch my shoulder. "They gave their lives for your future. So you could live without fear."

"They were *good*..." I choke.

The sheer volume of people we've lost has finally caught up with me. Now, at the end of our offensive, with my finger on the trigger, waiting for the first daemon to rear its ugly head from the collapsed cave network, reality sets in.

There are only ten of us now.

"They deserved better." My tears dry, replaced by a slow-burning rage. "Margo—after all she endured in Eden, she deserved to live in peace!"

"She will now."

I shake my head. "Don't you dare tell me she's in a better place."

"Even if it's true?"

My laugh is bitter as I look over our dead surroundings. "So why don't we all just kill ourselves? Why have we struggled to survive every day for the past two years?"

"Every life has a purpose, Milton. Just as Margo and the others lived out their purpose, so must you."

I curse under my breath. "What *purpose*? We're just living for the sake of living. Postponing the inevitable."

Dust stirs at the cave's mouth as deformed figures half-stumble, half-crawl out into the light. A couple of them at first, followed by half a dozen more. Bulbous yellow eyes staring as they snort and bark angrily at each other. One seems to notice me.

I send the second RPG rocketing past them to detonate deep inside the caves. The explosion throws the daemons attempting to escape to the ground as dust and rocks fly upward and outward. I load the last RPG and fire it at the roof of the cave's mouth, crushing any daemons who survived the first blast.

When the dust eventually clears, carried off by the desert breeze, there is no movement. The caves have been destroyed, along with everything inside. The daemons who've made our lives hell for so long...are no more.

Someone slow-claps on the ground below me: the Jackson-spirit.

"Bravo!" he calls out.

He grins as I descend, my boots touching down with twin puffs of dust. Even if I had another RPG in my launcher, it would be useless against him.

"I should be able to retire early, what with you doing my work for me. Only ten of you left?" He snickers.

"Your monsters are extinct." I jerk my head toward the demolition above.

"You don't think I can make more?"

The Julia-spirit lands beside me with no evidence that her feet have touched the earth. "You promised not to interfere," she chides him.

He shrugs his bulky shoulders, garbed in the same jumpsuit he wore down in the bunker. "I don't have to. Just wait and see. Once the food starts running out, and the oxygen—"

"That won't affect them," Julia counters.

"Not talking about *them*." He nods at me. "They're golden. *Blessed*, you might say. But anybody who's been breathing filtered air up to now? As soon as their lungs try to squeeze out what little O2 is left..." He shakes his head. "It won't be pretty."

With no plants or trees anywhere in sight, I've often wondered how we've managed to keep on breathing. I hoped the Preserve—with its acres of untouched wilderness and forests—was still up north, shielded by some kind of force field. Wishful thinking, that it wasn't annihilated on D-Day like the rest of the continent.

"Are you saying...?" Not sure how to phrase it.

"Part of the *gift* she gave you," Jackson explains derisively, arms folded. "You breathe whatever this air has to offer, immune to any ugly side effects."

"I see." I really don't.

I still have no idea how I can fly or move at superspeed. I

accept it because it happens on a regular basis, but I don't understand it. Guess the same goes for breathing now.

"Thanks," I offer lamely.

Julia smiles.

"So you're saying if the guys in Eden try breathing the air on the surface, or if the UW people send another team onto shore, and they aren't wearing any sort of breathing apparatus... They'll turn into daemons?"

If so, our actions here—the lives we lost—were for nothing. We'll never see the end of those creatures.

"Not to worry. They wouldn't be foolish enough to risk becoming *infected*, Milton. They have safeguards in place." She pauses, shifting her somber gaze to the mountain. "Return to your people now. They need you." She pats me on the arm. It never ceases to amaze me that I can feel her touch. "We've kept you long enough."

The spirits fade away like evaporating mist. Julia with adoration in her eyes. Jackson with disgust, shaking his head at me like he thinks I'm a sack of crap. Maybe I was, back in the bunker as his hangman. But that's not who I am anymore.

I haven't been that guy for a while.

Taking off in a super-powered sprint, I reach the other side of the mountain in time to find Luther, Samson, and the others starting to dig fresh graves beyond the base of the cliff. The Homeplace graveyard, where we buried everyone we lost six months ago—after Cain and his warriors attacked. When Bishop joined us, he left markers for the members of his team, even though their remains were taken by those UW hoverplanes that carried the unborn babies away to Eurasia.

Now we have five more bodies to add.

"It's over." Luther's voice is quiet as I approach his side. His goggles are focused on the ground as he digs.

The only sounds are shovels cutting and scraping through hard, dry earth as the members of our dwindling tribe follow his example.

"Yeah. They're..." I glance up at the ruined cave entrance. "They're done." I reach for his shovel. "Here, let me. You've got words to prepare."

He always speaks over our dead, reciting the holy scriptures he memorized a long time ago. They seem to have a comforting effect on those left behind. Not sure if I believe the words, or the Creator that Luther believes in, but I understand their purpose.

"We can't lose any more," he whispers, trembling, reluctant to hand over the shovel. "We've already lost too much... I can't bear it. How can He expect us to go on like this?"

I assume he's referring to the Creator again.

"I've got this." I take hold of the shovel and gently pull it from his grasp. The others around us keep their eyes and their thoughts to themselves. "Take a break," I tell him quietly. "Pray or something. We need you to be you."

He stares back at me for a moment. Then he nods to himself. "Though I walk through the valley of the shadow of death, I will fear no evil..." he murmurs as he shuffles away.

I keep an eye on him intermittently as I dig. It's unsettling to see our fearless leader out of sorts. I guess he is human, after all. He walks aimlessly for a while, arms crossed, head bowed. Eventually he settles into a rhythm, pacing back and forth thirty meters away.

"He blames himself," Samson states the obvious.

"He shouldn't," I reply.

"Tough not to," Bishop says, "when you're the one in charge."

Guess he would know.

Once the graves are dug, we gather around the bodies. We lower them into their final resting places one at a time and cover them first in loose dirt, then gravel and larger rocks atop the mounds. Not like we have to worry about animals or daemons digging them up anymore, but it's tradition. In the same way that Bishop left markers for each of his team members, we stack rocks in piles, one for each person we lost when that heat-seeking missile struck the Homeplace.

Luther returns as soon as we finish. He's standing taller, his voice quiet but controlled as he recites what he calls *Salm 23*. At the end of it, he says, "Amen," and we all repeat that word. More tradition, I guess. Then he invites us to say a few words about the ones we've lost.

My focus wanders as the others take turns sharing fond memories. I can't help remembering the bodies I left in my bunker. That was their final resting place, and they deserved so much better. Maybe I should go back and leave rock piles outside the blast door to memorialize each one.

"Milton?" Luther says.

Everybody's staring at me. I guess it's my turn.

"They were good people." I clear my throat, not sure what I'm supposed to say. Nothing sounds right. "They'll be missed." I remember what the Julia-spirit said. "They lived and died for a purpose: so we could have a future. So let's do them proud."

"Amen," Samson rumbles, and the others nod, echoing the sentiment.

I was planning to fly back to Victoria at this point, but Luther convinces me to drive one of the jeeps instead. With only seven of us, we're leaving behind plenty of vehicles the daemons will no longer need; but we choose the best of the bunch, loading them up with all the weapons and ammo we can carry. By the time we're ready to roll out, our mobile stockpile is almost equal to what we had inside the Homeplace. Hopefully we'll be able to recoup our losses where hydro, rations, and supplies are concerned as well. The city ruins where we're headed will be as good a place as any to start scavenging.

After an hour or so of driving through the Wastes, we're there. Victoria steps out of the concrete sublevel of a blown-out building and greets us with a baby in each arm. Her grim demeanor suggests she already knows about our losses.

"Ten of us now," she says to me.

I nod and take Florence from her, already more confident in my baby-handling skills after Bishop's tutorial. The little one fusses at first but then settles down as I hold her close. Security—that's what we'll need in Homeplace 2.0, wherever we decide that's going to be.

What will life be like now that the daemons are gone? Without the constant threat of those flesh-eating freaks appearing on the horizon? Can we allow ourselves to relax, or will new dangers present themselves? Not sure what they'd look like, other than fellow survivors we've yet to meet. Crazy cannibals, maybe.

Bishop and Samson agree that this sublevel is a suitable place to set up camp. Perched atop a hill at the edge of the ruins, it has one entry point, plenty of cover from the sun, and provides a panoramic view of the surrounding area. We park the jeeps on the cracked street and unload our armory. Bishop organizes everything inside and makes sure we each carry a weapon of choice on our persons at all times, along with extra ammo. Just as a precaution, of course. I choose a Beretta 92 with a 15-round magazine. Because why not?

Next up: scavenging for food and supplies. We break up into pairs before heading out. My partner is Justus, that old pal from the Shipyard. I hand baby Florence to Taylor, who's staying behind with Victoria and little Boaz.

"I'll be keeping an eye on you," Victoria whispers into my ear. I assume she means telepathically. "Happy hunting."

I hesitate just a second before kissing her cheek and patting her son's head. "See you soon."

Searching the ruins takes me back to those early months I spent alone after All-Clear, talking to mountain ranges, charred skeletons, and the occasional ill-conceived pet rock. Scared out of my mind that I was going to lose it—until I did. Worst experience of my life. Being possessed by an evil spirit at the same time was just the proverbial rancid icing on an otherwise inedible cake.

Justus doesn't say much as we head out on the hunt, and neither do I. After all we've been through lately, we need some time to process it internally. Samson and Shechara head west;

Luther and Bishop go north; so that leaves the southern part of town for us to pick through. Each pair takes a jeep.

The good news: it doesn't look like anybody's been through this city since All-Clear. The bad news: there's not much to find.

"What Sector would this have been?" I gesture at our charred, dilapidated surroundings as we step out of the vehicle and start walking.

"Twenty-five, maybe. Or Twenty-six." Justus pauses mid-step. "So that makes it either a labor sector or manufacturing center."

The two usually went hand-in-hand. Factories needed their labor force, and those workers needed to be housed nearby.

"So, if we're lucky, we might find a few dozen washing machines in storage." He forces a laugh, but it dies in his throat.

Survivor's guilt: What right do we have to joke around when so many of us are gone forever?

"Laborers needed to eat, same as everybody else." I survey our surroundings. We're not going to find anything above-ground here. The skeletal remains and crumbling brick don't hold any secrets; their barren, ash-covered interiors are clear to see. "Give me a second." That's all it takes to make a complete circuit of the area in a blur of speed and return to his side. "Found something."

"Alright then." He gestures for me to lead the way. "I reckon you could sweep the entire city all by yourself in just a few minutes."

Over a hundred square kilometers, give or take? Maybe an hour.

"Two sets of eyes are better than one."

He grunts noncommittally.

But he curses with appreciation and slaps me on the back when we reach the dusty storeroom underneath what might have been a business center, back in the day.

"Not bad, Milton! What do you think? Emergency shelter? Non-sanctioned bunker or some such?" He peers into the darkness. There's enough exterior light to make the shelves of hydro, protein, and vitamineral packs visible, along with cans of fuel and other supplies. "Was it locked?"

I nod. "Didn't take much to jiggle it loose."

So far, there's been no evidence of anyone living here since All-Clear, not even daemons.

"Well then." He claps his gloved hands together. "Let's load up the jeep!"

When all three scavenging parties return to Homeplace 2.0, none of us are empty-handed. After one day's hunt, we have enough to keep us fed and watered for a month, maybe two. With only eight adults and two babies, we don't need as much as we used to in order to survive. But Luther wants us to go back out for the next few weeks, until we've cleared every cache to be found. He'd like our stockpile of foodstuffs and supplies to rival our weapons.

The days that follow blur into each other like my surroundings when I'm running or flying. And I do a lot of both, scoping out the lifeless ruins as well as the desert terrain surrounding them. Hurtling through the air, covering kilometer after kilometer, I scan the entire area. On the coast, the Shipyard lies in ruin, and a single UW vessel sits out at sea, seemingly anchored there. I keep my distance and don't hover in one location for too long. If the *Integrity* sent that heat-seeking missile to destroy the Homeplace, I don't want to give them another target.

As days turn into weeks, we manage to accumulate enough necessities to survive the next six months, as long as we stick to Bishop's rationing plan. Outside of Homeplace 2.0, there isn't anything left in these ruins to eat or drink; so our scavenging days are through for now.

Hard to believe, but there's not a single government-issued bunker in this sector. Guess the esteemed United World Governors didn't think anybody living here was worth saving.

A month or so after our arrival, we celebrate the union of Samson and Shechara.

I never saw it coming, but their odd-couple romance is

enough to cheer everybody up. "Turning our mourning into dancing," as Luther says. We light up the new Homeplace with a dozen glowsticks that make the big concrete box we're living in seem alive with otherworldly energy. Luther leads the proceedings, facing the happy couple while the rest of us sit on crates covered with blankets. I try to imagine everybody in suits and fancy dresses, with incandescent bulbs glowing and live stringed music playing, flower petals strewn across a polished wood floor. Never considered myself a romantic, but weddings will do that to you.

Instead, we're all in our grubby desert nomad attire, smelling the furthest thing imaginable from fresh, and after the vows and the kiss—Shechara on tip-toes and Samson hunched over like a gentle giant—we get to eat and drink the same ration-packs we've been eating and drinking every day since All-Clear. But since it's a wedding, Bishop says we can indulge in double-rations. And, wonder of wonders, he managed to get his hands on a couple bottles of champagne and keep them hidden until this moment.

"To the bride and groom!" he toasts, taking a swig from the bottle and handing it to the next person in line, which happens to be me.

Samson and Shechara beam and take turns drinking from their bottle. They even get Luther to take a sip. The rest of us pass ours around and congratulate the newlyweds. It doesn't take much to become mildly intoxicated. After drinking only hydropacks since All-Clear, our alcohol tolerances may have atrophied a bit.

We hum some faintly recognizable tune—can't remember the name of it or the lyrics—while Samson and Shechara slow-dance with their eyes closed. Cheek-to-cheek, her standing on top of his metal feet. Every clank and clunk of his mechanical parts echo in the enclosed space, providing the rhythm to our well-intentioned attempt at acapella background music.

Maybe it's the champagne and the beauty of the wedding. Or it might be because Victoria and I spend the night on the same blanket, spooning with our arms entwined. It could also be that for the first time in a very long time, I feel safe here. Regardless, it's the best night's sleep I've had in more years than I can count.

Months pass the way they do, one rolling into the next. We expand our scavenging runs to nearby city ruins, once I've scouted ahead to be sure there's anything worth taking. In the process, while adding to our growing stockpile of food, water, fuel, and supplies, we come across a solar-powered shortwave radio.

Luther sees it as a sign from the Creator: it's time to contact the United World and notify them that the daemon threat has been neutralized. The former North American Sectors are now safe for visitors. It's clear he wants to establish diplomatic relations with them so that, someday, all the children will be allowed to return and meet their parents. The problem is, the *Integrity* is the only UW ship currently patrolling our shores, and Bishop doesn't want them knowing he's still alive.

"I'm a deserter," he explains. "And that's bad enough, a court-martial offense. But they'll also want to run all kinds of tests on me, now that I'm infected. I'll be a human lab experiment."

"If they're the ones who fired that missile at the Homeplace, do we really want them knowing where we are now?" Samson adds.

"But if it brings you one step closer to seeing your family again," Luther says to Bishop, "isn't it worth the risk? We won't mention you at all. We'll simply tell them the hostiles who downed their helicopter a year ago are no longer a threat. And that we welcome the possibility of speaking with a UW representative in person at some point."

"To what end?" Shechara steps forward. "We saw what their hoverplanes did to Cain's warriors. Why contact people with such disregard for human life?"

Samson nods. "It's in our best interest to keep them off our land. Let them think the daemons are lying in wait with rocket-launchers at the ready."

Luther keeps his focus on Bishop, seeming to realize the newlyweds aren't going to change their minds. "We could find out what happened to Captain Mutegi, whether the *Argonaus* will be returning to our coast. You said you trusted him."

Bishop gives a reluctant nod. "He'd be the only one."

After having his superiors decide he was killed in action long before it was clear he'd become *infected* and ineligible to return to Eurasia, it makes sense he'd be leery of trusting any of them.

"So we find out how to reach Mutegi," Luther continues earnestly. "Perhaps he could sneak us aboard his vessel, disguising us as members of his crew—"

Samson curses under his breath. All eyes turn on him.

"You can't be serious," he rumbles. "There are only ten of us left. And two are toddlers." He sweeps a metal hand toward our diminutive group. "You'll put their lives in danger by contacting the very people responsible for blasting the Homeplace."

"We don't know for sure it was the *Integrity*," Justus allows. "Could've been the mutants."

"They never attacked us that way before," Shechara argues.

"They were never that hungry before," I suggest, remembering what the spirits told me.

What would they have to say about our current debate? They can't speak to me or Bishop inside human-made structures, so I excuse myself and step outside. I wait until I'm halfway down the silent street before I stop and stare up at the stars, shining like diamonds scattered across black velvet. The cold night air chills my face and lungs as I take a deep breath.

It's weird to see Luther and Samson at odds. Not sure why their dynamic has changed. Maybe being married has made Samson and Shechara want to play it safe. They're each protecting their new spouse.

But I can't disagree with the points they've made. I don't share Luther's overweening urgency to establish a working relationship with the UW. As far as I'm concerned, they're the enemy. We should focus on surviving and making a life for ourselves here, not trying to hitch a boat ride across the ocean.

"You'll have to travel east," the Julia-spirit says, appearing as I hoped she would.

"For once, we agree on something." The Jackson-spirit appears as well, uninvited and unwelcome.

They stand beside me, one on either side. Like an angel and a demon on my shoulders.

"Why?" I demand.

Travel east? Where to? This is not even remotely related to Luther and Samson's debate.

"That's where he's been stationed," Julia says. "Captain Mutegi. The *Argonaus* is acting as lead ship for the freighter convoy loading all scavenged goods, materials, vehicles, and machines from the northeastern Sectors."

I frown at that. "The UW is..."

"Pillaging this land of anything useful in a very methodical manner," Jackson reports. "Freighters are on their way to your coast as well, and the *Integrity* will be supplying the soldiers and firepower when they start sending their raiders inland."

"What the hell for? Don't they already have everything they need?"

Julia tilts her head to one side. "They consider the Sectors, along with everything their factories ever produced, to belong to the United World. And they have no desire to aid *infected* individuals in their survival."

"They want to starve us to death." I can't believe this. I mean, I believe it—the UW Governors are apparently inhuman. But after all we've been through, to have to deal with this now? "So you both want us to find Mutegi. Why?"

Julia smiles at me. "You'll see."

"Doesn't make sense that *you*'d be interested in our survival." I squint at Jackson.

He laughs with a shrug. "Who said you're going to survive?"

Best to ignore him. "How far east?" I ask Julia.

"All the way to the coast. Bring that radio you found. You'll need it to contact Captain Mutegi once you arrive."

I look at our jeeps, each parked at an angle on the hill. Factoring in the terrain, the max speeds running completely on solar batteries, and the distance from the west coast to the east... That's five thousand kilometers we'll have to cover, riding in vehicles that can travel at 50 kph for six to eight hours each day—barring no sandstorms or breakdowns.

"A couple weeks," I murmur. "If we leave tomorrow."

Julia nods. She's about to say more, but she's interrupted by Samson charging out of Homeplace 2.0 with Shechara right behind him. They're both carrying weapons, food, and water—enough to last two or three days.

Luther pleads with them to rethink their actions, to stay and discuss matters.

"We're not dying for you!" Samson booms. Then he flinches, pained by his own words, knowing he's hurting Luther. A man as close to him as a brother.

The newlyweds climb into a jeep at the bottom of the hill and take off into the night, sending up a cloud of dust in their wake.

Luther watches them go, defeat slouching his shoulders. He doesn't seem to notice me standing farther up the street.

I approach him and clear my throat. "I've heard from the spirits. They want us to go to the east coast. We'll find Mutegi there."

Luther's eyes glisten as he nods and smiles, clasping my shoulder in a strong grip. "All things work together for good." He sounds like he's giving himself a pep talk. Half-turning toward our erstwhile Homeplace, he says, "I'll tell the others. If you would...please go after Samson and Shechara. Let them know there is no reason to run. We need them with us. We are stronger together."

I nod and take off, shooting through the night sky and landing twenty meters ahead of Samson and Shechara's jeep. My boots skid across the hard-packed earth as their headlights knife the darkness between us.

"We've made up our minds," Shechara says as Samson brakes a few centimeters away from my kneecaps. He keeps the motor running, using up the solar battery's juice. "We don't want any part of it."

"I agree with you about not contacting the UW. That's wise. But I've heard from the spirits, and they want—"

"We don't much care what they want," Samson says, fixing me with a hard stare. "It's time to go after what *we* want."

I guess they never got their honeymoon. Is that what this is about? Doubtful. More likely: neither one can stand the thought of losing each other. And contacting the enemy is a whole new level of danger.

"Where will you go?"

Samson shrugs with half a grin. "No daemons to worry about now. This land is ours for the taking." He winks at his bride, and she leans onto his metal right arm, wrapping both of hers around it. "We're gonna see what's out there."

This feels like farewell, and I don't much care for it. "Once we get to where we're going...I'll find you. Let you know where we are, in case you want to join us..." I trail off lamely.

The newlyweds have eyes only for each other. "Goodbye, Milton," Shechara says, and I step out of the way.

Samson gives me a salute, his metal hand reflecting starlight. Their jeep takes off into the night. I watch them go.

"Goodbye." The word catches in my throat.

PART IV
CONSPIRACY

17. SERA
22 YEARS AFTER ALL-CLEAR

As D1-436 maneuvers the aerocar out of the dark maglev tunnel from Dome 2 and back into the brilliant light of Dome 1, we have a surprise waiting for us.

"Friend of yours?" Erik peers over my shoulder as I lean over D1-436's. The motionless clone with the smashed kneecaps sits up front in the passenger seat.

"Drasko." I wave to him through the windscreen, and he gives me a crisp salute. He's got his lanky frame propped against his black and white aerocar, parked beside the government vehicle D1-436 left behind when we had to go chasing Erik on foot.

Dazzling sunlight reflects off the mirrored glass of every domescraper, causing me to squint as my unaugmented vision adjusts. I keep an eye on the surface streets while we land. No signs of anyone running, shooting, or throwing things. Broken windows and doors along both sides of the street are the only evidence that lawlessness existed here a couple hours ago. But like Dome 2, everything is quiet and lifeless now, with citizens confined to their cubes or workplaces.

"Why are we stopping?" Erik seems surprised. "We've got places to be."

We do. He needs to meet with an underworld contact in Dome 10 and pick up some EMP grenades, and then we need to go to our class reunion and meet the *Creator*, whoever the hell that is. But first—

"He's a good guy." I nod toward Drasko. "Just give me a minute."

Erik mimes tapping an antique timepiece that people used to wear on their wrists in the days prior to neural implants. Just when I think the guy's antics can't get any more cringe-worthy.

The aerocar sets down with a soft bump, and the side door rises. I tell everybody to stay put and jump out, jogging straight toward Drasko.

"So, you *are* alive." He gives me a wink, the wrinkled skin around his neck scars more pronounced in daylight. "Been hailing you all morning. Figured I'd stop by your cube to check on you." He raises an eyebrow like he knows more than he's letting on.

Probably because of the immobilized security clone he found on the floor outside my place.

"Augments are out." I double-tap my temple. "Been on special assignment."

He looks impressed. Then he coughs into his fist and turns toward his aerocar. "Figured you'd want these guys back." He hits the cargo compartment's manual release, and the door drifts upward.

On the bench seat, belted in like I had them last night, sit Wink and Blink. I could be wrong, but they both seem to light up at the sight of me. Probably their motion detectors recognizing my movement. Without my augments, I'm just a human-shaped blob to them now.

"Good as new." Drasko pats Blink on its flat chassis.

"Thanks, Drasko." I can't help smiling. Haven't been doing much of that lately. "I owe you one."

"Okay." He nods toward the aerocar with D1-436 at the controls. "Tell me what you're up to."

"Can't. It's classified." I unbelt my drones and pick them up, sliding one under each arm. Not sure what I'll do with them, but it's great to have them back. Maybe Erik can sync them with D1-

436, and they can go back to keeping me out of trouble. Sounds like they'll have their work cut out for them where we're headed. "Never seen Dome 1 like this."

I pause to survey the silent streets. There's an uncanny resemblance to one of those post-apocalyptic VR games where a virus has killed off the entire population, but every building here is left standing, looking so pristine yet devoid of life.

"I have." Drasko grimaces like he's tasted something bad. "During the plague, martial law was in effect for months. Just as quiet as this. Eerie." He nods to himself, seeming lost in a memory as he follows my gaze to the surrounding domescrapers. Then he clears his throat. "You been in touch with Bishop?"

"She gave me my orders."

He holds my gaze. "Nobody's seen her. Not since the Chancellor went missing."

"You think it's the patriots?"

"Kidnap two of the most powerful women in Eurasia, then make demands." He nods to himself. "Sounds like a terrorist plan." Then he frowns. "But you've heard from Bishop recently?"

"Half an hour ago." I have no reason not to trust him, so I add, "She said the Chancellor is fine. They're in a safe location. Waiting things out."

Drasko exhales, looking relieved. "Alright then." He gestures toward the other item sitting in the cargo compartment: my exosuit, looking polished up and ready for action. "Want to take this along?"

"Can't." Without my augments filling in the gaps, wearing an exoskeleton would be like learning to walk all over again. "Thanks, though. You've outdone yourself."

He almost smiles. Then he glances at my aerocar before stepping toward me and lowering his voice. "Is Chancellor Hawthorne still giving the clones their orders?"

"I assume so. Why?"

"Law enforcement and the Chancellor's private security have been working together to establish martial law. But there's what you might call a leadership vacuum right now. Nobody has addressed the public. Nothing is on the Link other than conjecture—the usual talking heads repeating themselves with nothing significant to share. But the conspiracy types—"

"Nobody listens to those wackos."

"You'd be surprised. They think there might be a coup in the works. They're claiming somebody, maybe one of the Governors, is trying to usurp Hawthorne's position. The so-called terrorist attack might have been just a diversion, not even led by real patriots."

"Intriguing theory."

He smirks. "But you can't tell me if any of that lines up with your current assignment, because it's classified. Curfew Enforcer Sera Chen on a secret mission. Nothing weird about that at all."

He has every right to be suspicious. But I don't know how much to tell him.

"Minute's up!" Erik calls out the open aerocar door.

"I've got to go." I shift Wink and Blink upward. "Thanks again. Like I said, I owe you."

"Your holster's empty." Drasko nods toward where my shocker should be cased on my hip. "And that guy with you looks a whole lot like last night's dust freak—the jumper. I finally got around to watching the footage while I was fixing your drones."

Erik sees Drasko staring at him and decides to grin and wave. Like an idiot.

Drasko's steely-eyed gaze doesn't falter as he continues, "Then there's the clone I found outside your cube. Somebody rattled that thing but good. And I see you've got two more of them up front in your vehicle. The Chancellor's own security personnel are chauffeuring you around?" He shrugs like it's all a bit much to process. He'd be right about that. "Not sure what to think here, Chen."

I can't tell him the truth. Not until I know what it is.

"I'll explain everything once this is over, I promise." I backpedal toward the waiting aerocar.

He crosses his arms and watches me leave, a frown of what could be concern across his brow. I jump inside, and D1-436 fires up the engines, sending a burst of air outward as the aerocar rises. The side door seals itself shut behind me, but not before I hear Drasko call out,

"Watch your six, Chen!"

I give him a nod through the porthole. Then we're off, soaring toward the Dome 10 maglev tunnel. All nine of the outer domes are connected to Dome 1, but none of them are connected to each other. The only way to visit Domes 2 through 10 is right here, via the central maglev station. Just another way the Governors designed our society to keep all of the outlying domes reliant on central authority.

"He seemed nice," Erik says. "Boyfriend?"

Drasko? "He's my father's age."

"Maybe not." Erik winks. "You haven't met your biological father."

Can somebody please explain what's happening to me? Arienna interjects, thinking at us with her newfound telepathic ability. *How is this possible?*

Erik gives her an understanding smile and dives in, explaining our situation with as much enthusiasm as when he introduced me to life as I now know it. I turn my attention to D1-436 and the mute clone beside it.

"You're sure this unit's comms are down?"

Without turning my way, D1-436 replies, "Yes, Enforcer Chen. Like the rest of us. It will not be able to notify anyone of our intended destination."

First: Dome 10. Then: wherever D1-436 found out the Twenty are being taken. I could have asked, and I'm sure D1-436 would have told me, but for some reason—call it instinct—I think it's best I don't know until it's too late to turn back. Maybe because I have a feeling I won't like where we'll be going.

As if anyplace could be worse than Dome 10.

The aerocar glides through the tunnel with enough room on

all sides to keep from bumping into the walls, ceiling, or maglev rail below. The neon green overlay on the windscreen maps out our trajectory, and D1-436 keeps us on track without a single wiggle in the wrong direction. Would Drasko, the best pilot I know, be able to fly us through at this velocity without shearing off even a smidge of the aerocar's paint? Tough call.

Part of me really wanted to invite him along. But the last thing I wanted to do was pull him into whatever maelstrom I've fallen into. His conspiracy theory gave me pause—the idea that the terrorist attack on Hawthorne Tower might have been staged by someone intending to take over while the Chancellor is indisposed.

I shake my head. Drasko's always been a fan of those Linkstream conspiracy theorists. I've chalked it up to life in Dome 1 being too safe and perfect at times. A man like Drasko was bred for adventure. I'm surprised he didn't ask to accompany me on my *secret mission*. Maybe he could tell I wanted to invite him but couldn't. Obviously, I appreciate the work he did on Wink and Blink, not to mention my exo-suit. He's one of the good guys.

I pat the drones absently, belted in beside me, as the aerocar leaves the maglev tunnel and passes the guards stationed at the Dome 10 terminal. D1-436 flashes the emergency lights, and we soar over the locked gate without incident, heading into the dingy cityscape beyond.

This is the only dome with access to the Mediterranean, since the primary responsibility of Dome 10 is waste management and water reclamation. All of the plumbing from Domes 1 through 9 leads here, and all of the saltwater captured for desalination starts here, where it's purified and pumped into the rest of Eurasia to flow through our sinks, showers, and toilets.

Unlike Domes 1 and 2 where the streets were devoid of life, Dome 10 is bustling with vehicular and foot traffic, everybody headed somewhere in an orderly yet congested manner. As far as I can tell, ours is the only aerocar currently airborne, yet it receives no attention from the citizens walking below. They all seem to have someplace to be but aren't in much of a hurry to get there.

While Dome 1 is a crystal metropolis of light and Dome 2 is a lush forest, Dome 10 appears dilapidated: grimy, polluted, and listless. The transparent plexicon of the dome itself hasn't been cleaned in ages, lending a rust-colored hue to the subdued sunlight streaming through.

Erik leans over D1-436's shoulder and points. "There," he says, and the clone takes us toward the rooftop of a tall building identical to the ones beside it.

All of these structures would have looked out of place in Dome 1. They're half the height of a domescraper and a hundred times grungier. Instead of mirrored glass covering the buildings from top to bottom, there are stripes of black-tinted windows surrounding each floor, while the rest of the exterior walls are simply exposed brick.

Arienna leans toward me while staring out the windscreen. "Have you ever been outside your dome before?"

"First time." Admitting that aloud, it sounds strange. Why haven't I taken the time to visit other domes before now? "You?"

She shakes her head. "So..." she hesitates, not sure how to phrase what she wants to ask. "You remember...not being born yet?"

I note the lost expression on her face. She's mulling over everything Erik told her about us. About herself.

"Give it a few hours. You might, too."

Erik said the memories would come back, and they have. I remember Margo now, how much she loved us. I remember Tucker, how he risked his life to take us home to our biological parents—but I don't remember ever meeting them.

"It's a lot to process."

I nod. Then I switch to telepathic mode, *The good thing is you're not alone. I was right where you are less than twelve hours ago.*

She blinks at me. *You accept it? Being a...mind reader?*

"Not sure what else to do about it." I shrug. Then I gesture at

Wink and Blink as Erik turns my way. "Can you sync these two up with D1-436?"

"I can." He nods. "But why should I?"

The aerocar sets down on the rooftop with a soft bump, and the whine of the electromagnetic coils deepens in pitch as the engines cool off. Our side door drifts open automatically.

"Because I'm asking you to." I tap the law enforcement insignia on my uniform.

"About that..." He winces a little, like he can't stand the sight of it all of a sudden. "Better for everybody involved if you get out of that thing."

"Excuse me?"

"The locals—particularly the ones I do business with—don't appreciate seeing law enforcers in their neighborhood. And enforcement drones—" He nods toward Wink and Blink. "—will be shot out of the sky." He shrugs by way of apology. "So you can either wait here while I conduct my business or change."

Stay behind? Not a chance. I unzip my uniform and tug it off while everyone on board finds somewhere else to direct their eyes.

"Give me your jacket." Standing in my skin-tight bodysuit and boots, I hold out my hand to Erik expectantly.

He raises an eyebrow at me as he pulls it off and hands it over. "Not bad."

You better not be talking about my body. I narrow my gaze at him.

"You'll blend in nicely," he clarifies, nodding as I zip up his jacket. Clearing his throat in an awkward attempt at indifference, he steps out of the aerocar.

"You two stay put," I tell Wink and Blink. Then I glance at Arienna and the clones in turn. "You three as well."

They nod—except for the disabled clone. It sits there in a silent stupor.

I follow Erik out of the vehicle and slap the door as I exit. It drops behind me in slow motion and locks into place as we make our way toward the roof access structure.

"So, these friends of yours. Not exactly law-abiding citizens, I take it?"

"What makes you say that?" He casts a devilish grin my way. "They're not terrorists, if it makes you feel any better."

He holds the creaky door open to the interior stairwell. An outdated gentlemanly gesture. Flickering overhead lights reveal stained steps and graffiti-covered walls. Again, not an environment I've ever experienced in real life, but it might have inspired half the VR games I've played over the years.

I pause before entering. "How can these citizens allow their dome to fall into such disrepair?"

"How do you mean?" He frowns at me like I'm speaking a different language.

I gesture at our surroundings. "It's filthy here."

"We're at the bottom of the food chain, Enforcer Chen. Dome 9, where I hail from, is only a step or two up from this. The citizens here and in the agricultural domes work hard and don't have time to clean house. What they do is vital to the lives of all Eurasian citizens. But how often do we wonder what happens after we flush the toilet? Or where the water comes from that we expect to see flowing out of the faucet?"

I nod toward the street below. "What's with the traffic? Where are they all going?"

"Takes a lot of laborers to keep things running. There are multiple waste management and water reclamation facilities here, and they all have different schedules. We arrived at a shift change." He heads inside, giving the door a final shove to keep it open long enough for me to follow.

Our boots thump noisily down the stairwell. There's no surveillance equipment inside that I can see. Strange, if this building is full of criminals. I keep my hands in the pockets of Erik's jacket, shoving the hem downward in a futile attempt to cover my backside. My bodysuit doesn't leave much to the imagination, but my lack of a weapon makes me feel even more naked as we continue downward. Five, ten, fifteen flights with no end in sight as we pass one level after another.

"Let me guess," I mutter, my voice echoing in the confined space. "Ground floor."

He shakes his head. "Second."

Forty flights later, he veers into a hallway where the stairwell door is missing from its hinges. It's dim inside and smells musty, like fresh air hasn't visited for a while. Thick, stained carpet masks our footfalls. Doors lining the walls are closed and silent. Either the rooms on the other side are soundproofed, or this floor was abandoned a while ago.

Offices? I think at him. *Or Dome 10's idea of a cube complex?*

Both. He slows as he approaches an unmarked door, frowning at it. There are no numbers or any sort of identification on the others that we've passed, either. Then he shakes his head as if chiding himself and continues onward down the hall. *People work and sleep here.*

But they're not in the waste or water business, I clarify.

He glances over his shoulder at me with half a smile. *You catch on fast, Enforcer Chen.*

Why doesn't local law enforcement shut them down?

He pauses outside another door, squinting at the tarnished brass knob. *Because local law enforcement receives a cut of all profits.* He nods to himself and takes a step back, straightening his posture as if he's about to have his hologram captured.

So they're dirty.

He smirks. *Isn't everything around here?*

The door slides open without warning. A blast of white light floods outward for a split-second, along with the sounds of dozens of people talking under a deluge of float-rawk background music threatening to drown them out. Erik squints in the glare and steps inside, flashing one of his most disarming smiles to date. I move to follow him, but the door slides shut again, blocking my path and silencing the noise as if it never existed.

I refrain from cursing, instead adopting the same posture as

Erik's prior to the door opening. There must be some sort of security measure in place, a hidden camera. Someone's watching, and they scan anyone attempting to enter.

A sudden burst of white light interrupts my train of thought, and I step forward, through the doorway, blinded for a few moments. I assume the door slides shut behind me, but I can't hear anything above the wave of voices and music that hits me head-on. When my eyes adjust, I notice the room seems to go on forever to the left and right, taking up the entire floor. So, none of those other doors we passed led anywhere.

The space isn't lit very well, and an easily recognizable haze of illegal smoke hangs low like an oppressive fog in a VR mystery. Well-dressed people mill about with drinks in their hands, many of them with a smoking apparatus clamped between their teeth, releasing gusts of multi-colored and multi-flavored smoke with every exhalation. Everyone is absorbed in some type of conversation, a few serious with their heads together, others more flamboyant with violent hand gestures and explosive laughter. There must be close to a hundred citizens in here, clustered on low couches, standing in huddles, drifting with the music, never remaining in one place for too long.

Unlike me. I've been standing as still as a tree since I stepped inside. Yet no one seems to notice.

So I enter the organized melee and try to look natural. Like I belong here. Keeping an eye out for Erik—who seems to have been swallowed whole, never to reappear—I navigate the perimeter of the animated, smoke-spewing throngs. In the distance, where the lights are even lower, I spy the glow of multiple screens and dark figures hunched over what appears to be a bank of antique computer consoles. I decide to drift nonchalantly in that direction.

"Drink?" A tall blonde in a silver cocktail dress steps in front of me. She has an athletic build and carries a platter with a variety of beverages on display—wine, beer, martinis, others I don't recognize. No idea where she came from, but she seems eager to share her bounties. "Smoke? Dust?"

Dust. Offered like it's just another variety of legal indulgences. How many people in here are high on the stuff? So far, nobody is climbing across the ceiling, so the abilities it produces must be more subdued. Like telepathy, for instance.

"I'm looking for someone." I lean toward her and raise my voice over the din. No band in sight, so the music must be recorded, playing through speakers I haven't been able to spot. "We got separated."

"You're with Erik, right?" She flashes me a gorgeous smile, the kind you might see on a VR model. Come to think of it, haven't I seen her online? "He sent me over. Said he'll just be a minute, that you should unwind a little while you wait." She lowers the platter and thrusts a glass of red wine at me. Her smile doesn't waver, but I get the distinct impression that she's stalling me.

"I don't drink." I slide past her and keep walking.

She grips my arm with sharp fingernails that dig through the fabric of Erik's jacket. The platter of drinks remains steady in her other hand.

"On the house, Enforcer Chen."

"Where's Erik?" I don't try to pull away. Not interested in making a scene. Also, not sure how many of these dust-addled revelers will rush to her aid if I knock her to the floor.

"Neck deep in negotiations, at the moment." She doesn't relax her grip.

So, it's a standoff. "I'm here in an unofficial capacity."

"Yes, we know. You never would have gotten in the door, otherwise." She gives me a friendly wink. "C'mon, take a load off. Erik will be back before you know it."

Without my augments, I have no way of knowing if what she's saying is true. But I don't need them, do I? Because I've got this weird mind-reading ability now. And not only can I dig around in her brain, but everybody else here is fair game, as well. So I replay their memories of Erik's arrival and where exactly he went, once he stepped into this murky dive bar.

What I see doesn't inspire confidence in this waitress's sense of honesty.

I chop her in the throat and yank my arm free, resuming my course toward the computer bank and the secret room beyond, cloaked in a hologram that reflects the lounge's revelry and modifies it just enough to make it look unique, extending the illusion that the room goes on for another fifty meters. How do I know? Because as soon as Erik stepped inside, two blank-faced bouncers converged on him, each one taking him by the arm and escorting him into the invisible room. As they passed through the holo-cloak, it rippled around them like a disturbed pool of water and then stilled once they disappeared on the other side.

No one but the friendly waitress—currently doubled over and wheezing with a hand to her windpipe and her tray of drinks miraculously unspilled—saw Erik's gruff welcome take place. Everyone else in attendance apparently had eyes only for each other or their screens.

And still do. Not one of them races over to ask the waitress what's wrong.

She curses me in a hoarse rasp, saying somebody named *Trezon* will tear me apart. Something to avoid.

I pass the computer consoles and keep my eyes to myself. The people hunched over the old-fashioned keyboards quickly close out whatever's on their screens and mutter expletives aimed in my general direction. Picking up the pace, I head for the holo-cloaked room and walk straight through the mirage.

No one's waiting on the other side—just a nondescript wall, closing off this end of the room. And in the middle of the wall, less than a meter in front of me, a single steel door with a retinal scanner mounted beside it.

I consider going back for the waitress. Grabbing her by the arm and dragging her over here to stare into the scanner. But I don't have to. Once again, just by standing in front of a locked door, I get it to open for me. Customary in Dome 1 where proximity detectors open any door that's unlocked. But I'm getting the feeling somebody noticed me, or they were alerted when I passed through the holo-cloak.

"Enforcer Chen, welcome." The Terminal-Aged man has a deep, oily voice to match his slicked-back hair, and he twirls a chrome baton with one hand. Trezon, I assume. As with the waitress, he looks like someone I've seen in VR. The smooth operator. The gangster with a face covered in spiraling tattoos. They've clearly modeled themselves after characters from the Linkstream, not the other way around. "Erik has told me so much about you..."

I don't like the sound of that. And I don't like the looks of Erik at the moment. His face is a bloody mess as he lurches forward in the chair he's tied to. The pair of bouncers land meaty hands on his shoulders, shoving him back into place.

Get out, Sera! he screams into my mind.

But I can't. Because I've been hit in the middle of my back with a shocker that sends me to the floor in convulsions. Before I black out completely, a familiar face approaches from behind to loom over me.

"Told you to watch your six," Drasko says.

18. DAIYNA
5 YEARS AFTER ALL-CLEAR

So we're truckers now. Driving a stolen big rig with a shipping container full of food, drink, supplies, and more than a few dirt bikes.

Shechara, Samson, and I take turns at the wheel, driving day and night. Always one of us driving, one riding shotgun, and one sleeping, stretched out in the back of the cab. We keep an eye out for any raiders looking for revenge—or hoping to take back what's theirs. But so far we've been all alone on this dusty stretch of hardpan. No daemons-in-the-making, no cannibals pretending to be post-apocalyptic desert warriors.

For the first time in a long time, I feel more like myself. Free to be the person I was, way back when. There's plenty of whiskey in my flask; it hasn't been empty for days. I haven't had a reason to refill it. The spirits still show up periodically, and sometimes it's Willard's ugly face that appears, but I don't have to hide from them.

I've been hiding for too damn long.

"Think it might be time?" Rehana said last week. I was returning to the tractor-trailer after relieving myself behind a boulder.

"For you to leave me alone? Definitely."

"She's a lost cause," Mother Lairen said in disgust. She'd been sulking ever since we left Eden. Guess things hadn't gone down the way she wanted. Knowing the evil spirits as well as I do, I bet she was hoping we'd all end up killing each other.

"Time to guide Shechara and Samson where they belong," Rehana said. "Where *you* belong, Daiyna. With Luther and Milton and the others."

I shook my head, goggles trained on my dust-smothered boots. "I'm not ready for that."

Seeing Luther again after so many years apart. Not knowing how he'd react. Or how I would.

"Three and a half years, and she's still not ready." Mother Lairen laughed bitterly.

"What about them?" Rehana nodded toward the truck with Shechara and Samson inside. "What if I told you they feel the same way? That no matter how much they might want to reunite with your friends, they fear they wouldn't be welcomed back."

That made me frown. "What do they have to be ashamed of?"

"Words were spoken." Rehana shrugs. "Sometimes things are said that you can't take back."

That's why I left without saying a word. I couldn't explain how sorry I was for allowing my thirst for revenge to get our people killed.

"Would you tell them to stay out here in the wastelands? That they should never seek to reunite with Luther?"

My footsteps slowed to a halt. I was a few meters away from the passenger door on the big rig. I faced Rehana. "Of course not."

"Why?"

"Because..." Tears burned hot in my eyes, and I had to clench my jaw to maintain my composure. "Because Luther would forgive just about anything. That's who he is." *He's a good man.*

"A man after God's own heart." Whenever Rehana didn't sound like herself, I was instantly reminded that this wasn't really her at all. Just a spirit-projection. "I think you have your answer, Daiyna." She smiled at me. "When you're ready, you'll need to travel to the east coast. That's where you'll find your friends."

With that, she and Mother Lairen faded away like a mirage on the sun-scorched horizon.

Shechara and Samson took some convincing. Like me, they'd settled comfortably into their desert nomad ways. The two of them against a post-apocalyptic world.

"We don't even know where they are," Shechara said.

Samson shook his head and shrugged his thick shoulders. "Milton told us he might touch base once they got there, but..."

"He never did," Shechara finished his sentence. "And that was three years ago."

"They might not even be on this continent anymore," Samson said.

He had some explaining to do at that point: Apparently, Luther wanted to invite the UW ashore to establish diplomatic relations. He mentioned contacting Captain Mutegi on the *Argonaus*, but then Milton heard from the spirits—

"By that point, after all we'd lost..." Samson shook his head. "I'd had just about enough of Milton's supernatural guidance."

"We've done alright on our own." Shechara reached out and squeezed Samson's metal forearm. Not sure whether he could feel it, but it was a sweet gesture of support all the same. "We found you." She smiled.

I smiled back. "So if I were to tell you the spirits let me know where we should go...to meet up with Luther and Milton..."

Something in their demeanor changed at that point, like they were surprised I would even suggest a reunion. Maybe they thought if I could go back to Luther after all I'd done, then they could, too. If I could let my reasons for staying away crumble and seek reconciliation, they could do the same. In a way, they seemed relieved, and I had to wonder if they'd been waiting for me to come around.

"So, where to?" Samson grinned, always up for a new adventure.

Neither of them liked the idea of the east coast as a destination. Mainly because it's a lot of territory to cover, and the spirits had been so nonspecific. I've been waiting for more details ever since, but they've remained oddly quiet, failing to appear to me at all.

Days have passed into more than a week, and we continue onward, forging a lonely path through the desolation, maintaining an eastward heading according to the compass mounted on the rig's dashboard console. We've already burned through half our fuel reserves and plenty of our hydro. The tractor-trailer is a thirsty beast, and the heat is incredible through the continent's interior. Not to mention the dust storms. We had a few out west, but we were close enough to the coast for the moisture to tamp them down some. Out here, we've had to put our journey on pause half a dozen times when the dust gets so thick we can't see where we're going. We roll up the windows real tight, cover our faces, and wait it out, perspiring until we're soaked through and through. After every storm, we spend an hour blowing sand out of the engine with air compressors Samson located in the shipping container. Not sure what we'll do when they run out.

And while we have no idea where we are, we know we've traveled over two thousand kilometers to get here. No signs of survivors along the way, but plenty of familiar terrain we've come to tolerate over the past five years: desert wasteland with countless rocks, tons of ashen sand, numerous craters to avoid, and hard-packed earth as impenetrable as pavement.

As the day winds down and Samson snores through his nap, Shechara takes her shift at the wheel. I stare into the distance with my elbow hanging out the open passenger window, thinking about what it must have been like for Milton all those months before he met us. Wandering alone. He hadn't run into any daemons yet, so he'd flirted with the idea of actually being the last living thing in the world.

I can see why. It feels like the three of us are all that's left. Just us and our shipping container full of dwindling resources. Nobody around to try and take it from us. Nobody who wants to eat us. Only the monotonous groans of the truck and the creaking sway of the trailer caused by the uneven ground below. A dirt bike would go a hell of a lot faster, but we see no reason to abandon our hijacked haul until it becomes necessary. Even then, we'll carry as much as we can on our backs.

It's not like we're passing through the land of plenty here. Any ruins we find are leveled, most of them little more than massive craters—as if the cities were targeted early on D-Day. The outlying structures were demolished by the nuclear blast winds. Apparently there were no bunkers full of survivors in the continent's interior, or we would have come across a few of them by now.

Samson mentioned something about the UW Governors being caught by surprise. When the terrorists unleashed their bioweapons, the government had to act fast: rounding us up and taking us to the bunkers that were fully functional, while others still in the construction phase were abandoned. Then the bombs fell. And the rest is...our story.

We spent the first couple days of this roadless trip trying to guess why the spirits would send us east. Or why Luther would have led what's left of our people there in the first place. Geographically, it would make sense that there's a greater UW presence on the east side of this quarantined continent. It's a direct route to the Mediterranean across the Atlantic, unlike that long, circuitous route via the Pacific. So that'll mean a lot more UW ships on the coast, as well as raiders filling up their trucks with scavenged goods. Assuming they're in the pillaging business on the Atlantic side of things.

After so much silent desolation surrounding us, I've settled into a peaceful lethargy. The thought of dealing with the arrogant UW types we're bound to run into causes a knot of tension to squeeze my stomach. Part of me has wanted to turn back ever since we started. Seek the path of least resistance. But that's a joke. We're driving a stolen truck. The raiders would be out for blood if we turned around and headed west.

We don't talk about it, but I wonder every now and then who

survived the Eden battle—if anybody. The Edenites had the home-court advantage, but the raiders had body armor. It could have gone either way for Cain and the cannibals. Pretty safe bet no one who survived will be coming after us.

What suicidal lunatics would drive into the interior?

Days blur into one another as we take our shifts at the wheel. We eat and drink our rations, we feed the big rig, we take turns sleeping. Heading ever east with no idea where exactly we'll end up.

Until about a week later. That's when the fuel runs out. We have a decision to make: siphon gas out of the dirt bikes to eek a few more kilometers from the truck—knowing it will need our water as well—or abandon the tractor-trailer and take the bikes themselves, load them up like horses from the ancient west and continue our journey at a faster clip.

Being the three-person democracy we are, we put it to a vote. And as much as we've appreciated the truck shielding us from the elements, we decide unanimously to leave it behind.

So after packing up all the food, hydro, weapons, ammo, and siphoned fuel that can be strapped onto three of the dirt bikes, we rev their grinding little motors and kick up plumes of dust in our wakes, taking off at double-speed in the same direction as before—thanks to the compass Samson carved out of the big rig's dashboard.

The sight of a man his size riding a motorcycle is comical, enough to keep Shechara and me giggling for a while. He has to hunch over and pull his metal knees up like an adult trying to ride something meant for a child.

The laughter feels...good. Like I'm exercising muscles that have almost atrophied. Once we recover from the hilarious sight of our friendly cyborg on wheels, I find that I can breathe easier. Deeper. My head feels clearer.

But that could be due to lower blood alcohol levels. When we packed up the bikes, I didn't bother to take a bottle or few. Didn't top off my flask, either. It's still two-thirds full, and I haven't opened it for the past week. Not a single sip.

Not even when the Willard-spirit shows up.

"We say *jump*, and you don't even bother asking *how high*?" he sneers at me, floating beside my dirt bike. His scrawny arms are crossed like a malevolent genie's. "You'd do anything we ask, wouldn't you?"

I shake my head. I've never spoken to this apparition, not since he started appearing to me three and a half years ago. I had nothing to say to him then, and I don't now. I wait for him to morph into Mother Lairen, which he usually does, sooner or later. Just requires a little patience. And time is one thing I have in abundance.

"I'm proud of her," the Rehana-spirit says, floating on my other side. "You trust us, Daiyna. After all you've been through, all that we've put you through. You still listen."

"I trust *you*," I murmur, not loud enough for Shechara or Samson to hear over the noise of the bikes. "You've always played straight with me. So how about you tell me where exactly we're going?"

"Hold this heading, due east, and you'll get there." Rehana smiles. "Then you'll help us get where we need to be."

Before I have a chance to ask what the hell that's supposed to mean, both spirit manifestations dissolve into the hot air from whence they came. Helpful as ever.

Without the big rig, we can't take turns sleeping, so we make camp at nightfall and keep watch in shifts. Not that there's anything to keep watch for. Not yet, anyway. For the past three thousand kilometers, there hasn't been a single soul. But I'm sure that will change once we reach the coast.

I didn't realize riding the bike would make me so saddle sore, and it doesn't get much better over the next few days. I notice Shechara standing on her bike as she rides, giving her rear end a rest, and I try that for a while. Should've thought of it sooner. Samson has locked his metal legs at an angle that keeps him hovering above the seat. I point it out to Shechara, and we start laughing at him all over again. He's too busy leading the charge to notice.

Three and a half years ago, I tolerated him. Now? Maybe it's because he's Shechara's husband, but I've started thinking of him as family. The kind you actually feel some affection for.

Damn. All the crust is melting off my heart like wax.

Strange to think I've been self-medicating for so many years that I've lost track of the woman hiding inside. But really, I've been hiding my feelings longer than that. Ever since Mother Lairen and the other sisters turned against me following that first daemon attack, I've had to bury my emotions and fight to survive. What happened in Eden formed another rock-hard layer of survival instinct. Then when I killed Willard, part of me cracked, and I had to find something to fill in the gaps—to keep myself together. The whiskey did that for a while. But it also clouded my mind, made me think I didn't care. When deep down, the real me kept right on caring.

Leaning on the left grip of my dirt bike, I reach under my tunic and retrieve the flask. I unscrew the cap one-handed and hold it under my head covering. Just a whiff of the stuff inside brings back a lot of memories, most of them blurry. More like a feeling: dark, comfortable, safe. But also sad. Pathetic.

I cap the flask and toss it over my shoulder. I don't watch it go. I don't hear it hit the ground and bounce until it finds its final resting place. It served its purpose. Time to move on.

There's a lot of time to get lost in your own thoughts when you're riding through monotonous desert terrain. You've got to watch out for craters and rocks and patches of soft sand that will throw the bike off its game, but I can do that with half my brain. With the other half, I mull over what I'm going to say to Luther.

I have a few options, and they're all terrible:

Hey there, stranger. Miss me?

Been a while. What're you up to these days?

Hi, Luther. It's me, Daiyna. So...guess who fired that missile at the Homeplace?

My thoughts drift back to a moment in the caves, when those of us from Sectors 50 and 51 were sleeping separately to avoid the possibility of bringing new life into this messed-up world. Luther and I had noticed a couple who seemed sweet on each other. We agreed it was wise, at least until we dealt with the daemon problem, not to allow procreation. But after seeing these two together... I may have given them night watch duties with a direct line of sight on each other. When Luther called me on it, I admitted nothing. But I couldn't help smiling.

Another memory resurfaces: my reunion with Luther in Eden after his claws had been torn out of his hands, and my egg cells had been surgically removed. We embraced, and in that moment, I wanted to hold onto him forever. I cared for him deeply, more than any man I've ever known. And I still do. I can admit that now.

Luther, I'm so sorry for leaving...

Not because I could have changed how things went down. Cain still would have fired that missile at the Homeplace. Our people still would have died. But I would've been there. Maybe there would have been a wall between me and Luther after what I did to Willard and the bloodbath that followed. Maybe we could have worked past it. I'll never know. But I shouldn't have left him. That was selfish.

I can't change anything by dwelling on the past. Just learn from the mistakes and move on. Make tomorrow better than yesterday. Something worth hoping for.

A week of identical days and nights later, with only our dwindling rations and fuel revealing the passage of time, we spot the first sign of civilization. Shechara sees it first, of course. Samson and I squint and strain our eyes but can't see any of the details she can make out in the distance.

We power down the dirt bikes and lay them on their sides at the bottom of a steep grade. Then we climb toward the edge of a plateau that drops away in a steep cliff. The land below stretches twenty klicks or more, straight to the ocean with no geographical formations along the way. Just the same vacant, cratered moonscape we've seen for the past five thousand kilometers.

A mass of indistinguishable shapes line the shore, both on land and in the water. Trucks, ships, and UW raiders, Shechara tells us.

"Half a dozen freighters holding their position out at sea, along with a couple warships," she says, keeping her voice low. For the same reason we shut off the bikes: just in case anybody's listening. "One of them is the *Argonaus*."

"Bishop said they wouldn't let Captain Mutegi back into Eurasia because he knew too much." Samson lies prone, propped up on his elbows. He keeps his metal arms covered to avoid reflecting sunlight. "Makes sense they'd reassign him to the east coast, in case he had anything to do with Bishop going AWOL."

Shechara shakes her head. "We don't know if he's still captain of the *Argonaus*."

"True," Samson concedes. He glances at me. "Any new orders from your spirit-friends?"

Nothing. Sometimes I miss the good old days, when they would speak to me directly without appearing as people from my past. They'd tell me what we had to do, where we had to go. No, on second thought, I'd rather be the one calling the shots.

"We'll wait until nightfall. Leave the bikes here and approach on foot." I squeeze Shechara's arm. "You won't have to be our eyes."

One thing we all have in common: the ability to see in the dark. The UW raiders with their HUD-enabled face shields have night vision as well, so it will put us on equal footing with the enemy. Their advantage will be sheer numbers. I've never seen so many of them all together.

Over the past few years, it's usually been just a squad of raiders at a time, always with a tractor-trailer to hold everything they scavenged. One crew would show up, take what they wanted, and then leave. A few hours later, the next bunch would pick up where they left off. One city ruin after another. They've been a well-oiled operation ever since the daemon threat was neutralized.

Does Luther blame himself for the depletion of our resources? I doubt he had any idea the UW would start pillaging once the daemons were gone.

"What do they want with it all?" Shechara murmurs, staring without blinking into the distance. Watching the raiders load loot onto skiffs that tear across the rolling breakers toward the freighters. "Don't they have enough already?"

"You know what they say about people who have everything." Samson curses under his breath. "They always want more."

"Maybe life in Eurasia isn't as perfect as we'd like to imagine," I offer.

Shechara nods. "Sergeant Bishop said there's a class system. That those in the central dome live like royalty, while the ones who work in the outer domes live more like laborers used to here in the Sectors."

"Repeating the past," Samson mutters. "Hope it bites 'em in the ass."

If what Bishop told them is true, then it shouldn't take long for discontent among the lower classes to boil over into open rebellion. But I have to assume the UW Governors learned something from our history. Twenty-five years ago, the North American Sectors provided everything the rest of the world needed in order to live like kings and queens. But after decades of being treated like commodities ourselves, a segment of our population retaliated. They called themselves *patriots* after reading ancient historical records of colonies in the northeast rebelling against a powerful Eurasian king and winning their independence.

Pretty sure there weren't any bioweapons used in that rebellion.

What did these terrorists expect to happen? Unleashing dangerous toxins was a sadistic move that hurt our own people in the process. Maybe they wanted the UW to see what it would be like to lose the workforce of North America. Regardless, the end result was not independence. The UW's retaliation was swift and severe.

In order to live cooped-up inside self-sustaining biospheres, I assume the Eurasian Governors have to maintain some sort of tight-fisted fascist control. Relentless suppression of any potential opposition and forceful regimentation of society as a whole. A harsh rule of law with police on the streets at all times. Maybe in the air as well, watching every citizen's every move. No freedom whatsoever.

The thought of it makes me appreciate what we have here. Sure, it's a lifeless wasteland, but at least we're free. There's a big grey sky stretching from one horizon to the other, boundless open space, and plenty of air to breathe. For now, anyway.

We stare eastward. Samson and I take turns asking about the indistinct shapes in the distance, and Shechara describes them in detail. In addition to the raiders' trucks, the skiffs transporting scavenged items, and the freighters loading up the plunder, there are also makeshift buildings set back from the shore, large enough to be warehouses, as well as a series of tent-like structures that could be living quarters. Three earth-moving vehicles carry loads of dirt to one structure in particular, where it's offloaded by raiders who shovel the stuff into bags.

"Hold on—" Samson can't believe what he's hearing. "They're stealing our *dirt* now?"

Shechara shrugs. "I'm just telling you what I see."

"Don't they think it's contaminated?" I wonder.

I'm willing to bet they have their domed cities sealed off completely, with the ground covered by something human-made —either concrete or artificial turf. It makes no sense that they'd want our dirt for anything at all.

Confused, we return to our bikes and wait out the day's scorching heat. The temperature always seems hotter when you're not driving or riding, creating your own breeze. But we handle it like the desert veterans we are, and when night falls along with the temperature, we load the gear we need onto our backs—weapons, ammo, hydro, rations—and leave the rest behind, strapped to the dirt bikes.

We keep our heads on a swivel as we approach the raiders' camp, aiming for the vicinity of the dirt-packing facility. According to Shechara, it's deserted right now. Guess you don't have to guard contaminated dirt when the whole continent is covered with the stuff.

Crossing the kilometers in silence, Samson and I scan our surroundings through gifted eyes that light up the terrain in a ghostly blue glow. Shechara's mechanical pair keep track of any movement in the distance. The skiffs and trucks have been sitting motionless ever since the sun went down, and the raiders appear to be congregating in a couple of areas, carousing now that their shifts are over. No sentries are stationed anywhere in sight.

Why have the spirits led us here? If we wanted to sneak up on raiders, we could have remained on the west coast. Our friends are nowhere to be seen.

Samson does his best to keep his clanking parts quiet. Shechara and I walk heel to toe in our boots, avoiding any sole-scuffing. This time of night and this close to shore, the dust seems content to lie still, and we don't want to disturb its rest. Sticking to the shadows, we slide between one of the dump trucks and the tent next to it, listening for any sounds of raiders nearby.

Laughter echoes from a tent in the distance where men and women too rowdy to turn in for the night drink and razz each other. Samson points at the wall of the dirt-packing tent beside us. I'd rather we stay put and get the lay of the land, but he holds up a metal index finger, signaling he'll be gone just a minute. Shechara frowns but doesn't say anything as he creeps toward the front of the tent and ducks his head. Once inside, he pokes the canvas in our direction. His way of letting us know he's all right.

Shechara grabs my arm, her eyes staring in the direction where all the carousing was going on—until a moment ago.

I see five of them. Garbed in body armor and helmets that reflect moonlight like polished obsidian, assault rifles at the ready as they step heel to toe without making a sound.

Converging on our location.

19. SAMSON
5 YEARS AFTER ALL-CLEAR

I should've been more careful.

Stepping into the tent must have triggered a silent alarm. Not because these east coast raiders find dirt valuable. There's a lot of equipment in here, most of it unidentifiable. Besides the tables, scales, and sifting trays, it's hard to tell what I'm looking at. But these people treasure it enough to send over a squad of armed gunmen to make my acquaintance.

Pivoting to face them, I hold my rifle across my chest and smile. "Good evening. Quite the setup you've got here. Let me guess: prepping for the biggest sandcastle challenge of the century?"

The lead raider barks out the usual commands to drop my weapon, get on my knees, interlock my fingers—

"What the hell?" He's noticed that I'm not exactly human. Not all of me, anyway.

It takes some work, but I manage to keep my confident smile in place as Shechara and Daiyna are escorted into the tent to kneel beside me. Both are armed, as I am—we won't be relinquishing our guns until they ask nicely. But we don't go for our weapons. Not with so many muzzles staring us in the face.

"Get a load of this!" The raider half-turns toward his squad, all four of whom face us with their weapons aimed at our heads.

"We've got a couple escapees from Dome 6, looks like." He gestures at Shechara and me. "What about you?" He tilts his head toward Daiyna. "Got any mechanical parts we can't see?"

She flips him off, and he chuckles.

Figures move in the distance—raiders disturbed from their slumber staggering out into the night to see what's up. It isn't long before this side of the encampment stirs to life, all twenty-odd of them gathering around to take a look at the three oddities in the dirt processing tent.

"They're not wearing masks," one of the raiders observes. Seeing how he's the only other one to speak, I'm thinking he might be second in command.

"Noticed that," says their leader.

Uncanny how quiet they are, just staring from behind their black face shields. Even with the rifles trained on us, these raiders seem more curious than confrontational. Unlike others we've crossed paths with over the years. At least this bunch hasn't shot at us or threatened to pull off my arms and legs. A mark in their favor.

"Are you mutants?" the leader asks with an ironic edge to his tone.

"They're all gone, haven't you heard?" I nod toward my companions. "We helped get rid of them. When was that, three years ago?"

Shechara nods. Daiyna glares daggers up at the lead raider who's shaking his head slowly now.

"Not sure what you're breathing. The atmospheric O2 is just about depleted. Not enough plant life survived D-Day."

I shrug. "Haven't seen a tree for five years." Any growing thing, for that matter.

"If they're from Dome 6, they might have mechanical lungs or something," raider number two suggests.

"No, they're not from Eurasia." The leader slings his rifle over his shoulder and motions for the others to do the same. Which they do, without pause. Just like that, the tension of the moment eases up some. "You're from out west, aren't you?"

I nod. "What gave it away?"

"Hot damn. Five thousand klicks!" He lets out a low whistle that's slightly distorted through his helmet's external speaker. "You must be on some kind of mission."

"Dirt enthusiasts. We heard you've got the best stuff out here. Had to see for ourselves." I raise my voice so the raiders at the back of the pack can hear me, "Didn't mean to wake you."

Immovable, they stare back like a wall of statues.

I lower my arms slowly, keeping my eyes fixed on the leader. "Mind if we..." I move to rise.

"Go ahead."

We get to our feet without any sudden movements, and the raiders hold their positions. It's a silent faceoff, but oddly enough, I don't get the sense there's any impending violence. Word from their western counterparts must not have traveled this far. Apparently, no warning's been issued to be on the lookout for a large cyborg and his two beautiful traveling companions.

"So what is all this?" I keep the conversational tone that's been working so well and incline my head toward the tables and tech set up behind me.

"Classified," he says, still with an edge of humor. "Illegal is more like it. And in high demand."

"Dirt?" I just don't get it.

"Dust."

Shechara touches my arm. "You ship it to Eurasia," she says, her eyes rotating as they focus on each of the stations set up around us, cataloging each gadget and its purpose as only she can, "after it's been sifted, collected, concentrated. Packaged for distribution."

He shifts his stance. Impressed. "You see more than the average person."

"Aren't they afraid of infection? The people who use it?" she clarifies.

"What?" I'm completely lost, but she squeezes my arm gently. She's steering the conversation now, and she wants me to trust her. Can do.

"The effects are only temporary," he replies, "as long as the filtered air is pure. No lasting damage, no genetic transformation. We ran a whole battery of tests years ago to be sure. No way we'd still be in business, otherwise."

"How long have you been in operation?" Shechara probes, her voice quiet and curious.

"A couple months after All-Clear..." He glances at his second-in-command, who nods. "That's when the fluke happened."

"The fluke," I echo.

He chuckles, looking at his fellow raider. "Go on. Show them."

The other guy shrugs and steps past me, making his way toward one of the tables and picking up a small vial. He holds it between a gloved thumb and index finger. Then he pops the cap and attaches it to a valve at the bottom of his helmet, under his chin. His sudden inhalation vibrates through the external speaker, loud and clear. When he holds up the vial again, it's empty.

"So you just..." Okay. The situation is becoming clearer—and completely bizarre.

Aren't these UW people terrified of becoming infected? Isn't that why they wear these protective suits and breathe their own O2? From their point of view, our continent is a contaminated wasteland. Why would they intentionally put themselves in danger?

"Wait for it," says the leader.

His second-in-command stands still for a few moments as if digesting the dust. Then he sets down the vial and steps toward his fellow raiders, who clear a path for him. He ambles toward the shoreline, where the waves crash and slide up the wet sand, then recede like ink. He glances back and gives us a thumbs up.

Then he launches himself into the air. The raiders hoot and holler as he lands with a splash a hundred meters out to sea.

"A new record!" the leader cheers, and they all applaud.

I look at Shechara, then at Daiyna, who puts into words what all three of us are thinking, "What the hell is this?"

The raider out in the water sinks below the surface and doesn't reappear as the breakers roll in. The raiders on shore watch expectantly. So do we.

Thirty seconds pass before he explodes out of the ocean like a missile, soaring high overhead, his figure a ghostly blue form against the black sky in my night-vision. He plummets to the ground and lands in a crouch on the exact sandy spot where he first took off, his armored suit dripping with seawater.

The other raiders gather around to slap him on the back, congratulating him on his extraordinary feat. Made possible by inhaling a bit of *demon dust*, as Arthur Willard used to call it.

Just when I think I've seen everything on this messed-up continent. The idea of un-gifted UW types snorting a little dirt in order to perform superhuman tricks? Never crossed my mind. How do they avoid the *infection* they've always been so afraid of? Why don't their abilities last? Sifted, collected... and packaged for distribution—that's what Shechara said.

"Oh hell no," I growl, and the raiders turn as one to stare at me again. "You mean to tell me people in Eurasia snort this stuff to...show off for each other at parties?"

The leader chuckles. "That's about the shape of it. The wealthy and powerful always need something to battle their boredom." He takes a step toward me with his gloved hand outstretched, and I have to fight the reflex to deck him. "Alan Reinhart. Commander of the Dust Squad."

I reach forward, and he clasps my metal hand in a solid grip.

"Samson," I introduce myself without much in the way of gusto. This whole situation has me taken aback a bit.

He goes down the line, shaking hands with Shechara and Daiyna next. They introduce themselves as well, equally guarded.

"First names only, eh? You people do have your quirks," Reinhart says. He notices that Daiyna hasn't relinquished her grip on his hand.

"You've met others from the west?" She keeps her voice low and even. A dangerous tone, coming from her.

"We have. It's been a couple years..." He trails off, then palms the portion of his helmet where his forehead might be. "Of course. You're looking for them. Luther, Jim, Victoria and the kids—"

"What did you do to them?" she grates out.

"Daiyna," Shechara cautions.

Reinhart doesn't try to pull his hand free. He seems to understand the situation and sees no reason to aggravate Daiyna further.

"They're alive and well. Aboard the *Argonaus*—Captain Mutegi insisted. They've been part of the crew for a while now. Maybe a dozen voyages so far?" He turns to his second.

The guy with the temporary jumping skills nods. "We carry shipments to Eurasia every three months."

Daiyna hasn't let go. "You're saying they work with you. Transporting this...*dirt*?"

Reinhart chuckles. "It's our specialty." He squares his shoulders. "There are other teams in charge of scavenge, up and down the coast. They sort through the ruins, see what's worth taking, and load it onto those freighters. Once they're ready to ship out, it takes us about a month to travel to Eurasia and back." He pauses, leaning toward her. "Captain Mutegi is working on a way to get your friends into Dome 10, located on the banks of the Mediterranean. It'll take some time, but he'll see it through. He figured making them crew would be the first step in that direction. They're hard workers."

"We'd like to see them," Shechara says with an eye on Daiyna, gauging her reaction.

"Of course," Reinhart says. "They told us others might be joining them. But like I said, that was years ago. I think they'll be real happy to see you."

Daiyna releases Reinhart's hand but continues to stare at him without much in the way of an expression. He orders his second and a couple other raiders to ready a skiff.

"Make that two." He turns toward me. "You might need your own."

"Fair enough." I wouldn't want to be the cause of any sinkage.

Reinhart orders everybody else back to their bunks, and they turn an about-face without a word between them. Weird bunch. Or maybe just well-trained and disciplined. They seem to respect their commander. So far, I can see why.

As he oversees the three in charge of getting the skiffs ready to ship out, Shechara and Daiyna flank me. Together, we walk toward the water.

"Can you believe this?" Daiyna whispers, her hand resting on the semiautomatic tucked into her belt.

"None of it," I mutter, "but it's happening anyway."

"They let us keep our guns," Shechara observes. "If he were lying, I doubt he would have."

"I've got a feeling he's telling the truth," I reply. "I'm just having a hard time believing it."

"If our people have been crew aboard the *Argonaus* all this time, and if they've been waiting for us to join them, then why didn't Milton fly back west and tell us about it?" Daiyna shakes her head. "It doesn't make any sense. Reinhart is hiding something."

"You don't think we should board that ship?" Shechara says.

"We need to be very careful," Daiyna replies.

"Agreed." I clear my throat as we approach the raiders waiting for us in the lapping surf.

Shechara and Daiyna climb into the skiff with a raider already at the helm. As I step into the second boat, it quickly becomes clear the small vessel has reached its load capacity. Reinhart asks if I've had much experience piloting watercraft.

"I'll manage." Since All-Clear, I've taught myself how to drive jeeps, a tractor-trailer, and, just recently, a dirt bike. Now I can add a skiff to the list.

A second raider climbs into the first boat. She'll take mine back to shore once we reach the *Argonaus*. Reinhart gives us a salute and turns away, probably returning to his bunk.

"Thanks," I call after him. He halts, pivoting to face me. "This isn't what we were expecting."

Any sort of kindness from strangers seems alien, or like something from another life. Back when times were simpler, before D-Day.

He nods. "You've been through a few levels of hell, I imagine. This is the least we could do. Hope you enjoy a warm reunion with your friends." He marches away up the shore.

The lead boat takes off, cutting through the low, rolling surf. I follow, keeping a light grip on the helm. The wheel, like the rest of this boat, seems awful flimsy. But it does its job, carrying my bulk across the water to the gunmetal grey warship sitting half a klick out. As we approach, a pair of sentries on night watch converge on the starboard side, right where we're headed. They wear the same armored suits as the raiders and keep their rifles at rest.

"You guys get lonely or something?" one of them calls out to our escorts.

The other one nudges him, and he straightens up. Probably catching sight of the two survivors along for the ride. And the cyborg piloting his very own craft.

"Who are they?" The second sentry adjusts his grip on the rifle.

"Friendlies. From out west." The raider steering the first skiff brings it alongside the *Argonaus* and gestures for a climbing apparatus to be tossed down. One of the sentries on the deck above dumps a black cargo net over the side, and it's long enough to slap the water below. "Commander Reinhart thought Captain Mutegi might like to meet them."

"At this hour?"

I keep an eye on Daiyna. She doesn't need the cargo net. With her gift, she can launch herself right out of the skiff and land on the deck above. Unlike that dust-snorting raider, her ability doesn't fade over time. But so far, there's been no talk of mutants with superhuman talents, which leads me to believe these raiders haven't seen the real deal with their own eyes—only the temporary entertainment-value variety. Hard to believe if Milton's been working aboard the *Argonaus*. A flying man tends to be something you don't forget, as well as a popular topic of conversation among mere mortals.

Has Milton been hiding his gift? Or is he even here?

Daiyna climbs up the net hand over hand without using any of her supernatural agility. To the raiders and sentries watching, she looks like any other person struggling to ascend a cargo net for the first time. Shechara climbs up behind her. Not sure how I'm going to get up there unless those ropes are stronger than they look.

I wait for Shechara and Daiyna to reach the deck before I start my climb. The last thing I want is to tug the net free, sending all three of us into the murky water.

Scratch that. The last thing I want is for this to be a trap. For there to be no friends on board. For us to be captured and subjected to the sort of subhuman treatment we received in Eden.

I keep an eye on Shechara as she pulls herself onto the deck, and the sentries offer her a hand. Unlike Daiyna, she accepts the help up. They're all armed, but they're not pointing their weapons at each other. Nice for a change.

Maybe everything will be all right. *Trust the Creator*, Luther would say. But people are a different story. Haven't been able to trust many of them for a long while now.

Slinging the Tavor over my shoulder, I grab hold of the net, giving it a tug to test its strength. So far, so good. The ropes sag once I add my full weight to the mix, and I slowly sink toward the water. Climbing quickly, I manage to reach the deck before the whole thing stretches completely out of shape.

The sentries don't bother offering me a hand. They stand

frozen like a pair of statues—except for their helmeted heads, black face shields rising as they take in every detail of my mechanical limbs. Their mothers never taught them it's rude to stare.

"Mutegi?" I get them back on track.

"Right. This way." One sentry takes the lead, and we follow. The other one tails us. Smart, but it would have been smarter to take our weapons first. Still not sure why nobody's done that.

The sentries pause outside an unguarded airlock that will take us to the lower decks. They won't be joining us.

We step inside, and the door swings shut behind us, sealing us in. When red lights start flashing along the ceiling, I get the feeling a few contaminants have been detected.

"Please disrobe and set down anything you brought with you," a clinical female voice emanates from an intercom on the airlock's inner door. "Once the door opens, you will enter a decontamination chamber. Do not be alarmed. This is standard procedure for all crewmembers entering the ship from above decks."

Now they'll take our weapons. And our clothes. Should've seen this coming.

We look at each other. Shechara and Daiyna are as pleased as I am about the prospect of leaving this airlock in our birthday suits. Five years ago, I would've given anything to get naked with two gorgeous women. But now one of them's my wife, and so far, she's the only human on the planet who's seen me without a stitch on—where the metal meets the man. Not the most pleasant sight.

I guess Margo saw me in my natural state when she installed my arms and legs, attaching them to the stumps Perch left me with. I have to stuff down a few emotions at the thought of her. She was a good person. Gone too soon.

"Only direction is onward," Daiyna mutters, setting down her rifle and semiautomatic. Giving us a shrug, she unlaces her boots.

"You may not like what you're gonna see." I turn my back, the sound of my mechanical legs twice as loud in this confined space, and pull off my head covering.

"I always do," Shechara says, patting my rear end.

Daiyna curses under her breath. "Here's hoping the decon process includes a shower."

I nod. "Haven't had one of those in..." I almost say *since Eden*, but can that be right? Three and a half years with no shower?

I suppose we've gotten used to the stink and grime in between finding a few extra hydropacks, on occasion. If the raiders hadn't carried their own air supply, I'm sure they would've passed out after a single whiff of us.

Once we're naked, the inner door opens with a rush of air, and the woman's voice returns: "Please proceed into the decontamination chamber. We will have towels and a change of clothing for you once the process is complete. Captain Mutegi has been notified of your arrival, and he will be waiting for you in the wardroom."

Keeping my eyes set straight ahead, I lead the reluctant procession into the chamber. "Let's do this," I mutter, my voice echoing.

Shechara's behind me, followed by Daiyna.

"Hey, keep in mind we've got metal parts." I gesture at Shechara and myself, hoping the voice can hear us. "We'd prefer not to rust."

"Not to worry." I picture a woman in a white nurse's uniform. "The hydro substitute we use is similar to what you would find in ration packs. But please keep your mouths and eyes closed for the duration."

Not liking the sound of that.

The airlock door shuts behind us, and now we're trapped in what looks like an iron submarine from over a century ago, with just enough room for us to stand without bumping into each other. Not that Shechara seems to mind bumping into me. I'd wager she's doing it on purpose to keep me distracted from a stressful situation.

It's not every day we find ourselves trapped in the dark with a flashing crimson light above us and who-knows-what about to spray all over us. Not comfortable being at anyone's mercy, I clench my metal fists and look for weak points in the chamber's welding. Almost sure I could break us out of here, if necessary.

The blinking red becomes a constant, glaring red. Sections of the ceiling and walls recede and spigots protrude with dribbles of artificial water leaking out, followed by short spurts.

"Brace yourselves." I plant my feet and keep my arms down at my sides. Against my natural instincts, I shut my eyes and squeeze my lips into a tight line.

When the spigots unleash their spray, it's a blast that packs a wallop, hitting us hard from all angles. Not hard enough to cause any permanent damage, but definitely some bruising, and I quickly cover my more sensitive area. Shechara lets out a short yelp at first, but Daiyna hasn't made a sound. The scent of the water substitute definitely leads me to believe there's a chemical agent involved. We're being sanitized as well as decontaminated. Makes sense they'd want us to look and smell our best when we meet the captain.

After the wash, the chamber turns into a wind tunnel. Shechara holds onto my arm, and Daiyna holds onto her as they struggle to keep their footing against the relentless blast of air.

When the wind stops without warning, the red light turns to yellow. The opposite end of the chamber swings open like a hatch on an ocean vessel. A woman in a white uniform stands outside, just like I imagined, holding out three large towels for us. Not that we have many damp areas left. But we take them to avoid seeming rude.

The woman also has three navy-blue jumpsuits waiting, the baggy zip-up variety that look a lot like what we wore after All-Clear, along with rubber-soled shoes. We put them on, Shechara and Daiyna managing to do so faster than I can, and once we're presentable, we find ourselves led through a warren of tight, vacant corridors. I have to be careful not to clang my arms or legs into the walls. Don't want to wake up half the ship.

Eventually, we reach the wardroom. The woman knocks once on the door.

"Enter," a man's voice emanates from the other side.

She gives us a nod but remains outside. Guess that's our cue. I step up to the door, and it slides open automatically.

"Mr. Samson." Captain Mutegi stands on the opposite side of a large conference table. He's in his uniform, shaved and alert, like it's 0600 instead of after midnight. I've never seen the man before, but he stacks up to what Milton and Bishop had to say about him. He commands the room with a strength both intelligent and physical. "Can I get you anything? Coffee?"

"Yes, please," Shechara says, sidling up next to me. "Coffee would be wonderful."

"Make that two." Daiyna stands on my other side.

I can't remember the last time I had a cup of anything to drink. It's been nothing but hydropacks for years now. "I'll take one. And it's just Samson."

Mutegi nods, gesturing for us to sit down across from him. As we do so—Shechara and Daiyna pulling chairs out from the table while I lock my mechanical legs in a seated posture, not trusting these flimsy chairs to support my weight—the captain steps toward the countertop behind him. A large coffee maker has already brewed a fresh pot, filling the air with its rich aroma.

The room appears to be a miniature mess hall, maybe just for him and his senior staff, with plenty of counter space, a couple small ovens, and a double-doored refrigerator. My mouth waters as I wonder what delicacies might be found inside.

"We'd almost given up hope." He brings Shechara and Daiyna their steaming mugs. They pause to inhale like they're sniffing flowers. Then they take their first sips and nearly melt with delight. He smiles at their reaction. "Luther said there might be others, but that was years ago."

"Where is he?" Daiyna sets down the coffee, giving the captain her full attention.

"He's here." Mutegi hands me my mug, and I do my best to cradle the thing without crushing it. The coffee is hot and bitter, richer than anything I've had in a long while. It brings back a flood of memories from before the apocalypse, of diners and kitchens and breakfasts. Life when it used to make sense. "Lieutenant Commander Davies, who saw to your decon, is rousting him now. He will be here shortly."

Daiyna's gaze drops to her coffee.

"Took us a little while to get here. Some of your raiders decided to capture us."

He nods. "Yes, I heard about that. It seems they walked into an ambush. In Eden."

I don't react. Just drink my coffee and wait for him to elaborate.

"The next team of raiders who came through said it was a real bloodbath." He seats himself across from me and folds his hands on the table. "Only a single survivor."

"Was his name *Perch*?" Daiyna doesn't bother to hide her disgust.

Mutegi shakes his head. "Cain."

Shechara and I exchange glances. "Where is he now?"

"Aboard the *Integrity*. He'll make them a fine test subject." Mutegi leans forward slightly. "Unlike you and your friends, he fits the official narrative. He looks like an infected mutant. So they will spend years, potentially, running all manner of tests on him, finding out how he can possibly still be alive. As for you and your friends..." He sits up straight, squaring his broad shoulders. "You're immune to the contaminants."

"Immune," I echo, not sure where he's going with this.

"That's right. Your singular immunity has afforded you the ability to breathe without an O2 tank, to survive in harsh environments, to live off whatever you can scavenge." He lowers his voice. "You of course do not exhibit any superhuman abilities whatsoever. Because that would be a sure sign you don't belong here with us, wouldn't it?" He holds my gaze. "You do not want to find yourself in the same situation as Cain."

"We're as normal as any immune survivors can be," I speak for the three of us.

So that's why Milton never flew back to find us. Because he's been here, pretending he can't do anything...extraordinary.

Mutegi gives us a solemn nod. "It's the only way we'll ever get you into Eurasia."

"How's that plan going?" Daiyna downs half her coffee now that it's cooled a bit.

Luther's plan.

"Not well. All Eurasian citizens living inside the Domes are fitted with neural implants once they're of age. Visual and auditory augmentation that allows them to interface with the Linkstream. But it also allows the Governors to monitor the health, activities, and whereabouts of every citizen, keeping track of the population. We cannot introduce an unaugmented person into the Domes. First we must find a way to fit them with the proper implants, then immediately have them take the place of someone else—before any change in the official census is noticed."

Seems simple enough. "So you send in one of us and take out one of them?"

Shechara shakes her head. "You would only need to deactivate someone's augments. As soon as they're offline, you could send in one of us."

"That's the theory. But we would have to match your augments precisely to the deactivated citizen's, of course. Otherwise, the analysts would notice a change in biometric data." Mutegi pauses. "Except for you two." He looks at Shechara and me. "We could send you inside the next time we dock."

"What makes us special?" I frown.

"Dome 6..." Shechara murmurs. Reinhart mentioned something about that.

Mutegi nods. "After the plague, hundreds of thousands survived, but many lost appendages and limbs due to infection. They carry telltale scars and wear prosthetics nearly identical to your own. Since they're not included in the official census reports, they are not required to be fitted with neural implants."

They sound like second-class citizens. "So how would you sneak us in?"

"As dust runners."

Right. "This is no longer a navy ship, I take it."

"Not officially. After Sergeant Bishop's escape, I was not allowed to return to Eurasia. My loyal crew stuck with me. We aren't raiders, since our work here is not government-sanctioned. We are smugglers, supplying a lucrative business in the Domes, and as long as we continue to do so, the *Argonaus* is ours." He pauses. "I have an underworld contact who pilots an aerocar for Dome 1 law enforcement. He will be able to get you where you need to be."

"Aerocar…" I stare at him. "That wouldn't be—?"

"A flying car, yes." Half a smile appears on his stoic face. "Welcome to the future, Mr. Samson."

"But what would we do there, in Dome 6?" Shechara asks.

"Luther will fill you in on the details."

The door slides open, and appearing as if summoned, Luther steps inside. He looks at each of us like it's New Year's morning and we're gifts that have been wrapped up and set out for him alone. In his eyes, I see no hint of a grudge for the way we parted company years ago.

I give him a nod, and he nods back, smiling broadly. It's damn good to see him again.

He remains silent as his gaze rests on Daiyna. She rises, her chair skidding across the floor behind her. She stares at him, at a loss for words.

Tears shining in their eyes, they reach for each other and embrace. Doesn't look like they'll be letting go anytime soon.

20. SERA
22 YEARS AFTER ALL-CLEAR

When I open my eyes, I find myself lying on a bench seat in the cargo area of an aerocar. We're moving through the air, and from what I can see of the view outside, we're no longer in Dome 10.

Or any dome, for that matter.

Panic grips my insides as I stare at the sky above, unobscured by a tinted shield of plexicon. The ground below is lifeless, a barren landscape of dirt and rock.

"Where are we?" My voice sounds thick, my vision blurry as I stumble to my feet and grab for the back of the pilot's chair. Suddenly dizzy. "Who the hell are you?"

The pilot is a dark-haired guy with a bloody face, and he's wearing a security clone's armored suit. He steers the aerocar deftly, skimming fifty meters above the terrain. The passenger seat in the cockpit is empty.

"You're awake," he observes in the voice of D1-436, but without the helmet speaker acting as a relay. "We are almost there, Enforcer Chen."

I've never seen a clone's face before, and I can't help leaning forward with overweening curiosity. It looks a lot like the famous scientist Solomon Wong who created the clones in the first place. Not just *like* him—it *is* Wong, just forty years younger.

Did he make every Eurasian security clone in his own image?

D1-436 glances at me, quickly returning its eyes to the windscreen and the flashing coordinates on the display. "I apologize for my appearance—"

"You took us outside..." I stare ahead, not quite able to believe what I'm seeing. Everyone knows the quarantined wastelands exist, but nobody ever ventures out to see them firsthand. It's forbidden. "Why?"

"This is where the Twenty have been taken. These are the coordinates I retrieved while we were in Dome 2."

"And they just...let you fly out of Dome 10?"

"If by *they* you mean port security, I believe they assumed we were yet another government vehicle transporting precious cargo to the facility across the sea."

I peer out one of the side windows. "So we've crossed the Mediterranean." I glance at the display on the console. "And we're heading west."

"That is correct, Enforcer Chen. Are you quite all right? Perhaps you should return to your—"

I flop into the passenger seat next to the clone. "Tell me what happened."

I remember a hidden room in that lounge for underworld types. Erik was there, looking like somebody had worked him over. Before I could find out what was happening, somebody hit me from behind with a shocker.

"Your friend Drasko arrived in his aerocar shortly after you and Erik Paine entered the building. Drasko shot me and the clone beside me through the windscreen with projectile rounds. My helmet was irreparably damaged, yet I survived."

"Drasko." He's the one who hit me with that shocker. Some friend. "Why'd he—?"

"His intentions were unclear."

"What about Arienna? Is she all right?"

"Unknown. When I regained consciousness, the clone beside me was deceased and Arienna was gone. I entered the building and located you. I carried you up to the roof and took Drasko's undamaged aerocar."

The process of entering that lounge and getting away with me in tow sounds like it was no big deal. "How many people did you kill along the way?"

The clone pauses before answering. "I inflicted as much damage as was necessary to ensure your safety, Enforcer Chen."

"How many?"

"I did not intentionally seek to dispatch any human beings on the premises. But it is possible that a few of them may expire due to their injuries, if they do not receive immediate medical attention."

"Was Drasko among them?"

"I broke his arm. It was attached to the shocker he used on you, which, as you can see, is now in your holster."

I hadn't noticed. But there it is. I rest the palm of my hand on the weapon's grip. "You left Erik with those people?"

"Neither Erik Paine nor Arienna Dogan is my responsibility—"

"Because Erik modified your programming!" I curse, pounding the console in front of me with a fist. "Turn this car around. We're going back for them right now."

"We are approaching our destination, Enforcer Chen. It would be illogical to turn back now."

Without Erik, without the EMP grenades he was planning to procure from that shady establishment, our mission to awaken the Twenty will fail. There's no way I'll be able to free them from their augments—and from wherever they're being held. Not with a single shocker and a security clone that's seen much better days.

"Your primary directive is my safety, correct?"

The clone nods. "Yes."

"And you take orders only from me."

"That is correct, Enforcer Chen."

"Then explain why we're still on this heading." I draw my shocker and aim it at the clone's right temple. "You're disobeying a direct order. How do you know taking us to this facility won't put me in danger?"

D1-436 keeps its head stationary, but its eyes glance at me. "You will be safe there. All of the Twenty will be. You cannot be allowed to move among the populace. It was a bad idea from the beginning, unsafe for all of you. The Chancellor was not thinking straight—"

"You're not thinking straight." It sure seems like the clone's original directive is rearing its ugly head. Or maybe it was never completely overwritten in the first place. This unit showed up at my doorstep requesting that I accompany it to a safe location during the terrorist threat, and it sure looks like that's where we're headed right now. "I'll give you one more chance, then I'm pulling this trigger. Turn around and head back to the Domes. Do it now."

"You are too important, Enforcer Chen. I am sorry I cannot comply. I must keep you safe."

Its right arm smacks the shocker away just as I fire a charged round. The pulse of energy misses its mark and hits the interior wall behind the cockpit instead. No damage done as it fizzles out. The weapon is designed for use on biological organisms, not mechanical. It'll knock out a clone with its helmet off, but won't do a thing to fully armored security personnel. And it won't bring this aerocar crashing to the ground.

So I keep firing, struggling to hit D1-436 in the face. But the clone is too fast, effortlessly blocking my every attempt as I curse, frustrated. When I get the bright idea to leave my seat and shoot it in the back of the head, it snatches the shocker out of my hand and keeps it out of my reach, all while maintaining a flawless flight trajectory and keeping its eyes riveted on the windscreen.

"There," it says as if we haven't spent the past minute at odds with one another.

Furiously clenching my teeth, I look outside at what appears to be a squatty tower rising up to greet us from the tortured earth. Almost like it's being birthed by the surrounding area, the same shade of dirt, composed of an analogous substance or made to look like it. There are no other structures anywhere in sight, not a single ruin. Just barren wastes as far as I can see.

"Please take a seat, Enforcer Chen."

Cursing under my breath, I return to the co-pilot seat in the cockpit and strap in for landing. D1-436 maneuvers the aerocar in a flyover, then banks to the right, and we sweep around the tower, closing in on the roof where a single landing pad is waiting for us.

"Why not bring all three of us here?"

"You are my only objective, Enforcer Chen. Other security personnel were tasked with escorting Erik Paine and Arienna Dogan, just as additional units were tasked with escorting the other seventeen members of the Twenty."

Drasko's headshot must have interfered with Erik's reprogramming, causing the clone to revert to its original directive. That's the only thing I can attribute this change in behavior to.

The aerocar touches down with a soft bump, and D1-436 cuts the engines. As the landing pad and the tower it's attached to begin descending into the ground, an eight-leafed plasteel aperture closes above us, shutting out the sun's light and heat. Sudden air jets strike the aerocar's exterior as beads of neon blue along the walls and ceiling illuminate what's now an underground hangar.

Once we stop moving, the artificial wind ceases, and a message pops up on the aerocar's console: WELCOME TO FUTURO TOWER — DECONTAMINATION COMPLETE. Turning to face me, the clone punches the manual release for the cockpit doors, and they both float upward.

"I will hold onto this for now." It keeps the shocker in its left hand. "Please exit the vehicle and make your way to the elevator."

Why do I get the feeling I'm your prisoner?

I watch the clone's dark eyes for any sort of response after sending that thought toward it. D1-436 just stares blankly back at me. The blood on its face has congealed, but the head wound looks nasty and will require stitches. Assuming clones get stitches.

Damaged ones might get recycled.

I pause before stepping out. "Will I meet the Creator here?"

The clone's face twitches into an awkward smile. "Yes. Once the Twenty have all been gathered, the Creator will meet with you to discuss your Ascension."

That doesn't sound ominous at all.

I climb out of the aerocar and make my way across the plasticon floor to a pair of polished elevator doors. The clone follows. Our footfalls and the tick-ticking of the aerocar's cooling engines echo throughout the otherwise silent hangar.

D1-436 opens a covered keypad beside the elevator and enters a code I quickly memorize. Habit, I guess. No reason I'd need to remember it. My priority should be getting out of here, not getting back in.

I stuff my hands into the pockets of Erik's jacket and step inside as the elevator doors slide open. The clone remains on the threshold as I pivot to face it. We make an odd pair: an injured clone and an out-of-uniform law enforcer.

"This is as far as I am allowed to go," D1-436 says.

My gaze wanders to Drasko's shocker in the clone's hand. Why did Drasko follow me into Dome 10? *Watch your six*, he said. Referring to himself, showing up out of the blue to shoot me in the back—or to someone else? He took out both security clones on the roof, made it down into the building, and somehow knew exactly where I'd be. That hologram-hidden room posed no obstacle for him. Makes me think he's been there before. And as crazy as it sounds, that Trezon guy might be an associate of his.

What about Erik—why would he go there, knowing those were the types of people who'd tie him to a chair and beat the crap out of him? He said he wasn't a terrorist or a dust freak. But that place reeked of both.

"You will be safe here." The clone's monotone is quiet, either trying to reassure me or itself. "We will not meet again, Enforcer Chen."

"And here I was, almost beginning to like you." I palm the button to close the doors, and they slide shut, blocking the clone's injured stare.

There are no other buttons on the panel, so I guess I'm just along for the ride. Alone with my thoughts as the elevator glides down the subterranean tower. Reaching the seventh floor, it stops automatically. The doors slide open, and I'm greeted with what appears to be a waiting room.

Unlike the dusty, sun-blasted exterior and surrounding wastes, this space looks like any doctor's office you'd find in Dome 1. Spacious, well-lit, filled with a couple dozen white lounge chairs separated by glass end tables. On each table is a drink and a meal, most of them half-drunk and half-eaten by those reclining in the chairs. Their glazed eyes staring unfocused at the ceiling and their pleasant expressions tell me they're currently enjoying some sort of VR program. The Linkstream wouldn't be available outside Eurasia, so they must be linked-in to whatever VR is offered by this *Futuro Tower*.

They're the Twenty, of course. Or the Seventeen, once I take a moment to count. I recognize half of them from that DNA search I ran, which started me down this winding path in the first place.

Three chairs sit empty. I assume one's for me, one's for Erik, and one's for Arienna, wherever they are.

The room has no doors or windows. Only the elevator as an access point. I step out onto the white tiled floor, my boots making their presence known. No one stirs or acknowledges me. I try clearing my throat. Nothing.

"We have a new arrival!" One section of wall across the room slides aside to reveal a large screen, and on it, Dr. Solomon Wong himself smiles broadly, welcoming yours truly. Round-faced with shining eyes, there's no evidence as far as wrinkles or grey hair that he's old enough to be our grandfather. From what I've heard, he's the grandmaster of genetic manipulation, able to stop the aging process for those who can afford the treatments. And, of course, he created the security clones tasked with protecting the Chancellor and Governors, as well as their interests, across Eurasia. So Dr. Wong is no stranger to any citizen, though few have ever met him face to face. "Please, make Sera Chen feel at home, my children!"

All at once, the eyes of everyone present snap into focus, locking onto me. The Seventeen rise as one from their comfortable chairs and walk toward me in their white bodysuits with friendly smiles frozen on their faces. Within moments, they have me surrounded.

Instinctively, I retreat a step. The elevator remains open behind me, but I have a feeling it won't take me anywhere else.

"Welcome, Sera Chen."

"We're so glad you're here."

"Good to see you, sister."

Their voices merge together as everyone speaks at the same time. Then, realizing how overwhelming the situation must be for me, they laugh in a self-deprecating way and start apologizing instead.

"You must have many questions."

"We know, it's a lot to take in."

"Come, sit down, let's get you up to speed."

Two of them take me gently by the hand and lead me to one of the empty chairs. I allow myself to be led. No one seems to be in any sort of hurry, and there's no way to tell from the drinks and meals who's been here the longest. If the security clones were sent simultaneously to collect us from every dome, it stands to reason many of them could have been here since this morning.

"Let's introduce ourselves," one suggests, and they start rattling off their names. On a good day, I might have remembered more than half, but not right now. There's too much going through my mind; I can't even begin to sort it out.

I send out a telepathic question, hoping at least one of them will be able to answer: *Why are you here?* But all seventeen of them have functional augments, as evidenced by their VR activity when I arrived. None of them are aware they possess dormant supernatural abilities.

And phrased that way, it sounds kind of crazy even to ponder such a thing.

"Did he bring us here?" I nod toward the screen where the live-captured image of Dr. Wong beams at us like a proud parent, tilting his head to one side, then the other.

"The Creator?" One of my siblings looks over her shoulder at the screen and nods serenely as if she's a devoted follower. "Yes, of course. We are so important to him, Sera. He has argued for years that we should be better protected, in case of a situation just like this one."

"What situation?" I frown. "Martial law is in effect across the Domes. The terrorists have been contained."

The Seventeen murmur among themselves, shaking their heads slowly at my ignorance.

"Now that these dangerous individuals have brazenly acted out against the Governors, and attacked the Chancellor's own tower, they will become emboldened. Today's uprising is only the beginning. It is foolish to think law enforcement can protect citizens from the hatred these so-called patriots have been stirring up in the outlying domes for years. Things will only deteriorate into more violence, going forward. We cannot allow ourselves to be caught in waves of unrest. We are the *Twenty*. There is no reason for us to remain in such a hostile environment."

Sounds like she memorized that word for word.

"So you just left Eurasia—flying outside the Domes into this forbidden zone and risking contamination?"

"We are safe here, Sera." Three of them think it's a good idea to pat me on the arms and both shoulders. Like that will calm me down. "Dr. Wong knows what is best for all of us. He has seen the future and our place in it. The Domes have been governed by politicians and military-minded individuals from the start. It is time for science and logic to rule Eurasia. And we will rule alongside the greatest scientist who has ever lived!"

Solomon Wong wants to usurp Hawthorne's throne.

Drasko mentioned the possibility of a coup, but I dismissed the idea as a conspiracy theorist's nonsense. Now I'm not so sure.

I can't allow myself to lose my cool. I'm a law enforcer, a professional. I know how to deal with irrational curfew violators. This easygoing bunch should be no problem.

Taking a breath to steady my nerves, I dive in with, "Tell me about yourselves. Where are you from?"

They take turns sharing, complete with smiles and coy little glances at one another. It's just as Erik said. All seventeen are from Domes 1 through 9, and those of us who happen to hail from the same dome never had an opportunity to run into each other, due to our strictly enforced alternating shifts.

"What were your responsibilities, in each of your domes?" I put on a friendly mask that looks eager to get to know them better.

By now the Dr. Wong screen has receded into the wall, but I'm under no delusion that we aren't still being monitored and recorded. This place has a clinical feel to it, and these people sure look like test subjects.

I'm one of them now. Except for my attire and lack of augments, we're all in the same boat.

Listening intently as they share their stories, I learn that my Dome 1 counterpart worked the day shift at an education camp, teaching the young. Arienna's night shift counterpart in Dome 2 shared her tree maintenance responsibilities along the dome's soaring plexicon interior. Erik's counterpart in Dome 9 was an agricultural planner, organizing the planting and harvesting of crops on a rotating schedule. The only dome not hosting any of the Twenty is Dome 10. For obvious reasons, having just visited the place.

"Why have we been brought here?" I know what they're going to say. *To keep us safe.* But I need time to strategize while they repeat their pat answers. Seriously, they sound like they've been brainwashed.

Maybe that's the purpose of the VR program they were enjoying earlier.

How do I get through to them? How do you show someone the truth who has no frame of reference for it? With their neural implants active, they have no concept of the past. No citizen does. *Only now* and *looking forward*, that's the Eurasian way.

So why take us out of Eurasia? Does Dr. Wong intend to expose us to the truth? That our parents were from an obliterated continent across the sea? How long ago did Wong have this facility built out here in the middle of nowhere—and for what purpose?

We're on the seventh floor, but there are nine others. Ten floors. Ten domes. Connection?

"Sera?"

They're all staring at me. Probably because I'm staring at them, and I have no idea how long I've been doing that.

"It's wonderful to meet you again. After so long apart." I force a smile. "Do any of you...remember growing up together as kids?"

Here we go. Deep-diving into the truth. My first attempt is met with blank expressions and a few confused looks cast at one another. Then their responses cascade my way.

"This is the first time we've ever been together."

"All thanks to Dr. Wong!"

"It never would have been possible without him."

I feign my own bout of confusion. "But I was told by the security clones that Chancellor Hawthorne authorized our capture—" *Wrong word.* I try not to grimace at the mistake. "Collection, I mean."

They look at each other and smile.

"Would we have gone with them otherwise?"

"Dr. Wong had to make it seem like an official act."

"Once we arrived, he explained everything to us, of course!"

In VR, I assume. But that won't work for me. "When do I get to meet him?"

"Soon!" they cheer and laugh. "Once the final two members of the Twenty arrive, the Creator will reveal himself in real-time, and he will teach us everything we need to know about our Ascension."

There's that word again, the one D1-436 used earlier. It's like they've all been programmed with the same phraseology.

"Until then, Sera, let's get you a change of clothes and have you lie down."

"You'll join us in VR, won't you?"

"It's a wonderful program, Sera—you're going to love it!"

They disperse, smiling back at me over their shoulders as they return to their padded lounge chairs. A girl named Lyria walks up to a nondescript section of the wall and places her palm flat against it. A drawer slides out, and from it she takes a white bodysuit and matching slip-on shoes. My new uniform.

"Here you are, Sera." She hands them to me, neat and tidy like they were in the drawer. "You can change in that alcove, if you like."

She nods toward another section of wall that doesn't look like an alcove at all to my unaugmented eyes. I nod, slowly taking the items from her, using the moment to slip into her mind and visualize what she's talking about. Then I nod again.

Apparently, this room is full of hidden nooks and crannies, all accessible by touching various points along the walls. Visible to anyone with active visual implants. An augmented reality overlay would make it a simple matter to walk over to any spot and activate it. But I have to improvise.

From Lyria's memory, I'm able to navigate a course to the alcove she mentioned. I place my hand flat against the far left wall. Instantly, an arch forms with a recessed space that curves to the right. Lit with a soft blue glow, the space provides enough privacy for me to pull off Erik's jacket and my black bodysuit, as well as my boots.

I don't like the idea of leaving them in this space. Where will they go when I step out into the room again, and this alcove disappears? But I've got to keep up the illusion that I'm just another member of the Twenty sequestered here with my fellow chosen ones, awaiting our *Ascension*. So I pull on the white bodysuit, slip on the matching shoes, and head over to the empty lounge chair beside Lyria. She's the only one not relaxing in her chair and staring at the ceiling with glazed-over eyes.

"You look ready to ascend, Sera," she welcomes me with a broad smile. No irony whatsoever in her tone. "But for now, we will congregate in the Promised Land while we await the Creator."

"I'm guessing we're not on the Linkstream." I nod toward the others reclining blissfully.

She shakes her head. "The Link pollutes so many minds in Eurasia. Here, we are cleansed and purified from its influence. There is no perversion or violence, no filth to revel in—committing unspeakable acts we would never consider in real life. Here, the virtual reality is on a higher plane. There's...*joy*, Sera." Her eyes tear up. "Warmth and acceptance like you've never known. Real love that you can *bathe* in." She giggles like a little kid. "I know, it sounds crazy. But you'll see." She rests her head, and her eyes lose focus, that big smile frozen in place. "So many wonders..."

I lie back in my chair and try to keep my eyes to myself. Then I point them at the ceiling like everybody else and manufacture a goofy euphoric smile. But I don't see any Promised Land or wonders, and there's no love to take a bath in. Just white ceiling tiles to match everything else.

A glance toward the elevator confirms that it's disappeared into the wall like that alcove did. But I still have a general sense of where both are located.

I refocus my gaze on the ceiling, feeling like a complete idiot. Realizing my fists are clenched, I relax my hands.

How the hell am I going to get these people out of here? How can I possibly show them the truth? Without an EMP to disrupt their neural implants, there's no way. They seem content to wile away the hours in a VR stupor while they await Erik and Arienna's arrival—followed by Dr. Wong himself.

This *Ascension* they believe is going to happen—is it a political thing? Will Solomon Wong set himself up as Supreme Chancellor, then assign a pair of us to each dome where we'll replace the Governors?

If what Erik said is true, Wong was responsible for the birth of every person here—as well as the thousand children he created from our cells, spliced with those of their adoptive parents. Not to mention the clones he invented in his image to act as the Chancellor's private security force. All along, they've apparently been wired to do Dr. Wong's bidding at the drop of a hat. Why would a scientific genius want to mire himself and his creations in politics?

What grander scheme could he have in mind?

PART V

RESTORATION

21. SHECHARA
21 YEARS AFTER ALL-CLEAR

When I see him for the first time, all I can think is... *He has his mother's eyes.*

"Erik, this is Shechara," his adoptive mother introduces us to one another as we stand in the bright, sunlit kitchen of their farmhouse. "She's here on that temporary transfer program. You know how the Dome 6 Governor likes to do, allowing his citizens to work in other domes for a while. She'll be with us for a couple months, helping out around the place."

"Dome 6," Erik echoes, giving me a nod to acknowledge my existence but not allowing his gaze to linger. Particularly not on my mechatronic eyes. He's tall and broad-shouldered like his father, and handsome, too. "I wouldn't have guessed." He flashes me a smile and wink as he bites into a crisp apple.

"We're glad to have you and your husband, Shechara. With Erik living over in Dome 1 now, acting on the Linkstream and making himself rich and famous, we can honestly use the help." A matronly woman with a kind face, Mrs. Paine pats her son on the shoulder.

"Acting, yes," Erik acknowledges. "Rich or famous? Not so much. I'm just in ads, Mom. No leading roles yet, but that might change." He shrugs. "Someday."

"It may indeed," I murmur, careful not to stare at him for too long.

I don't want him to feel uncomfortable in his own house. He hasn't lived here for the past year, according to Mrs. Paine, but she has kept his room the same as when he left it. She says his bed is always waiting for him to spend the night, whenever he likes.

He arrived half an hour ago, and he will leave first thing in the morning. That's all the time Samson and I have to find a way to meet with him in private.

It has taken so long to reach this point: first contact.

Fifteen years have passed since Captain Mutegi promised that he would get us into Dome 6. The locals were not required to be augmented, since they were already augmented enough. They had survived the plague from decades ago, but they'd lost parts of themselves in the process. Prosthetics filled the gap where limbs, eyes, and other organs had been taken by illness, and many carried scars similar to burns on their ravaged skin.

Mutegi's contact had family in Dome 6 and flew an aerocar for Dome 1 law enforcement. He was also a dust smuggler on the side, using the proceeds to provide for his relations. He met us at the Dome 10 port authority airlock, right on time.

"Drasko," he introduced himself gruffly, his scarred hand outstretched.

Samson's metal hand clasped his in a firm shake. "You our ride?"

Drasko nodded, lowering his voice as he shook my hand next. "I hear you're the first wave of an impending invasion."

"Two by two," I said with a slow smile, not ready to trust this stranger, not sure how much he knew. I glanced up at Samson, his face a guarded mask.

We'd learned to be careful in the Wastes. To look and listen, feel out any given situation before putting ourselves in danger. But here, on this bustling port with so much activity and so many people moving about—all seemingly on-mission with places to be and cargo to offload—I found it difficult to focus.

Sometimes I wish I could dial down what my eyes are able to see.

Drasko led us to his waiting vehicle, parked outside the port terminal. It was strange to stand in full sunlight knowing the dome's plexicon shell was shielding us from the harmful rays. Samson and I paused for just a moment, basking in it with our head coverings loose around our shoulders and our eyes closed. Enjoying the warmth that tingled across our exposed skin.

Three local law enforcement officials converged on our location, their uniforms grubbier than Drasko's. He quickly took them aside and spoke with them. Their eyes darted our way repeatedly as if they didn't believe the story they were told: that we'd been working aboard the *Argonaus*. They didn't seem to like the looks of us.

My paranoia was very real during those first few days. I kept expecting someone to realize we didn't belong in Eurasia and expel us forcefully out of the Dome 10 airlock, headfirst into the Mediterranean.

Drasko shook hands with the three law enforcers, and they parted company without a glance back.

"You trust them?" Samson nodded toward the retreating figures.

"Not really." Drasko climbed into the cockpit of his aerocar and gestured for us to file into the cargo compartment behind him, where a pair of bench seats waited for us. "But we all speak the same language around here." He held up one hand and rubbed his fingers together.

Samson stooped, ducking his head as he entered. "So, this thing really flies?" He reached out for me, and I clasped his arm, allowing him to swing me up next to him. As the doors dropped into place and locked automatically, the vehicle's engines started vibrating.

"Affirmative." Drasko's hands flew across the dashboard

console as he prepared to take us aloft. "You don't get airsick, do you?"

Samson and I looked at each other. Then we shrugged.

"Guess we'll find out," I said.

"Strap in."

Seeing the city from the air was enough to take my breath away. But when Drasko told us this dome was the least-maintained of any in Eurasia, that it was borderline filthy, we had no idea what to make of that—or what we would witness next. For there to be buildings intact with paved streets running between them, and no dust, no cratered wasteland, no blackened city ruins with skeletal remains... A city with *people* going about their business, both on foot and in vehicles that appeared to be stuck in actual *traffic*... It was like traveling back in time and hitting the reset button.

It was wonderful.

But nothing could have prepared us for our emergence from the underground tunnel into Dome 1, a celestial city of light and pristine mirrored glass. Awe-inspiring buildings soared overhead, appearing to scrape the interior of the dome's ceiling half a kilometer above us. This dome was twice the size of Dome 10, with more air traffic and less congestion along the tree-lined streets below.

We didn't linger there long. Drasko banked the aerocar in a tight curve and took us into another tunnel identical to the first. He said he had to time these trips just right; otherwise, we'd find ourselves plowing into a maglev train. As long as we were behind the train or in between scheduled departures, everything was all right, he assured us. Even so, I didn't see any other aerocars attempting to do what we were doing.

Dome 6 was nothing like 10 or 1. They were built up and crowded with people going about their business, but the first impression given by 6 was of a sleepy village. Plenty of open space covered by grass and trees with walking paths; no highrises, no flying vehicles or heavy traffic of any kind. There were paved roads and one-story buildings with two or three-story exceptions scattered here and there. While Dome 10 and Dome 1 were centers of industry and technological advancement, Dome 6 was neither. It was quiet, designed for simplicity. The word *hospice* came to mind, as if this was where Eurasia sent its aging and infirmed population, a final staging area prior to whatever afterlife awaited them.

There were a lot of people like Samson and me, with prosthetics. Apparently, they were not qualified to live with the perfect people in Dome 1—or any other dome, for that matter. Eurasia followed a strict caste system, and the mechanically enabled, while allowed to work outside Dome 6 on night shifts during the enforced curfew, were not permitted to reside anywhere else.

"The motto is looking forward, never back," Captain Mutegi explained to us aboard the *Argonaus* before we disembarked. "Citizens with scars and prosthetics remind the populace of the plague, and they'd rather forget that period in their history. Or any history, for that matter. The neural implants and VR keep citizens focused on the present, always looking toward an ever-brighter future."

Samson had grumbled at that. "You know what they say about forgetting the past."

Perhaps they were indeed doomed to repeat it. Captain Mutegi warned us about terrorist threats from the outlying domes, an underground movement of citizens dissatisfied with their assigned stations in life. But he said Dome 6 didn't suffer from such dissent. The citizens here accepted their lot. It was the way of things, and no one questioned it. For the most part, none of the *sicks* had any desire to leave their peaceful dome in search of a better life. They were already living it.

Dome 6 was lovely, but it was not our intention to remain there. Our mission, as explained by Luther and Sergeant Bishop, was to blend in and become a valuable part of our community. By doing so, we would be eligible to participate in the exchange program where the Dome 6 Governor chose outstanding citizens to live in one of the other outlying domes for a couple months.

Meanwhile, we had research to do.

Using our own DNA samples, we were to track down our ten offspring; using Luther's and Daiyna's, we would track down the other ten. Posing as veterans from the *Argonaus* afforded us a certain level of immediate respect, and we were provided with all the necessary tech we required to get online. They called it the *Linkstream*, and even citizens without neural implants could access it via older consoles that still worked—thanks in no small part to the older citizens in Dome 6. Those with the mental capacity to work did so, repairing and maintaining devices that had become all but obsolete.

This is where Samson and I immediately began contributing to the community. He's always been good with machines, and I tend to be a quick study.

Over the years that followed, we discovered that our children from Eden were referred to as the *Twenty*, an honored segment of the population. They were the only citizens to be born a decade after the Terminal Age generation, thought to be Eurasia's last due to infertility plaguing the entire population.

The Twenty had been placed with adoptive families throughout Eurasia—with the exception of Dome 10—and as they grew and matured into young adults, they were assigned important roles in education, law enforcement, science, healthcare, agriculture, government, oxygen generation, and technological advancement. None of the information we gleaned was common knowledge. We had to rely on our tech-savvy abilities to navigate the Linkstream's hidden tributaries undetected, always disabling the devices we used after obtaining the information we sought. We masked our point of origin with a vacillating receiver that made it appear as though we were in multiple locations at the same time—in various domes.

Years later, longer than we ever thought it would take, by which point we seriously began to doubt whether Luther's plan or our part in it would ever come to fruition, we were chosen by Governor Hallsley to transfer to Dome 9. He'd had his eye on us for a while, noting our positive contributions to the community, but there were others ahead of us in line and only a few openings each summer. Dome-transfer was not popular; many saw it as a threat to the class system. But Hallsley made it clear that every citizen who participated in the short-term transfer would remain in his or her caste. Samson and I were responsible for maintaining and repairing technological and mechanical equipment in Dome 6, and we would have the same job in Dome 9.

There were two male members of the Twenty located in this agricultural center. One of them was related to us. We requested to be sent to the Paine farm, which had extended a welcome to the next Dome 6 transfer. Much to our delight, the Governor honored our request.

But the delight quickly turned into anxiety for both Samson and me. We lay awake at night, asking each other questions neither of us had the answers to.

"What should I say to him?" Samson's deep voice rumbled in the dark. He stared up at the ceiling, lying in our four-poster bed. Tomorrow, we would take the maglev train to Dome 9 and meet Mrs. Paine for the first time.

"We'll have time to figure that out. Erik isn't scheduled to return home for another week." I curled up beside my husband, his metal arm around me. He had it heated to just the right temperature, perfect for snuggling. "You'll do fine. You always know what to say."

"Glad it appears that way." He kissed the top of my head. My long hair fanned out across his shoulder. "I don't want to scare him off. It's taken us so long to have this opportunity, to meet with one of them in a way that shouldn't raise any red flags. Hopefully he won't report us to the authorities."

Captain Mutegi warned us that if we were found out, we could be executed. A worst-case scenario, right next to being banished from Eurasia. After all this time and effort, for it to come to nothing? Neither of us wanted to go back to life as we knew it in the Wastes. Nor did we want to serve aboard the *Argonaus*. Below decks, Samson nearly went mad avoiding claustrophobia. Our people who were still on board were waiting for us to make the first move, and this was it.

We'd singled out the one member of the Twenty who seemed to have a mind of his own. He'd abandoned his original assignment as an agricultural engineer to pursue a career as an actor; he had a habit of hanging around wealthy dust addicts; and he had connections with a few underworld types in Dome 10 who specialized in supplying dust, along with other illegal items. It was rumored they sold weapons, but that was impossible to verify, even employing the code we used to see behind the Link's thick curtains.

"Let's hope we have enough dirt on him to avoid that."

A deep chuckle resonated in Samson's chest. "First time meeting our son, and we're already planning to blackmail him."

"What do you think he'll be like?"

"We already know—"

"Not looks. Who he *is*. Bold and brash like his father, or quiet and intelligent like his mother?"

"Wait a minute. You think I'm brash?"

"You know you are, Strongman."

He gave me a gentle squeeze. "I'd say all of the above, based on what we've learned about him. If we can convince him to join the cause, he'll be a real asset. Hell, he might even take point on Operation Awakening."

"That's what we're calling it?"

He nodded. "Unless you've got a better name for it."

Sounded right to me.

Now as I glance up at Erik—nearly as tall as Samson—I hope with all my heart that we're able to get through to him. That somehow we can make him understand who he really is, and *the truth will set him free*, as Luther said. But part of me balks at the idea of turning this young man's life upside-down. And not only his, but every member of the Twenty, if we're able to do so.

Because Eurasian society has been built upon lies, and it's time to crack the glass walls they've made for themselves.

"Would you like to meet Samson?" I smile but try to keep it casual, as far from over-eager as possible. "He's working on the harvesters at the moment. They've been refusing to function correctly in tandem. It's almost as if they know they're being difficult, and they enjoy causing the inconvenience."

"Oh, Erik knows all about those cantankerous machines. Wasn't that your job, son, before you left us in search of fame and fortune?" She's teasing him, but there's an undertone of hurt beneath the surface. Of course she expected her adopted son to remain in Dome 9 when he grew up.

Erik grunts, nudging the recycler open with his toe and tossing the apple core down the chute. "Don't miss it one bit. Those clunkers are the worst. Why haven't you upgraded?"

"That's what Samson's trying to do," I offer.

"We couldn't afford brand-new machines, but we thought the programming could be tweaked," Mrs. Paine says. "Overwrite the operating system with—"

"You want them to sit out there like dumb clucks? That'll do it." Erik shakes his head and wipes his face, both hands rubbing downward in an exasperated swipe. Then he exhales. "I'll go take a look."

"This way." I lead him out of the kitchen.

"I know my way around," he grumbles, but he follows me anyway.

"Even after being gone for so long?" Mrs. Paine feigns astonishment. "That's impressive!"

"I've always had a good memory, Mother," he calls over his shoulder, stepping outside into bright sunlight and fields that stretch for acres in every direction.

"That's why you'll make a great actor!" Mrs. Paine matches his volume.

The door swings shut behind us. He catches me looking at him.

"She loves you very much." I look away and keep walking, out between the rows of wheat toward the large trio of harvesters sitting in the distance.

"Moms do that," he mutters, his long strides overtaking mine.

It's a surreal experience to walk beside my biological son. Mrs. Paine raised him and deserves the distinction of being called his mother, but his genes, his DNA, his *eyes*... They all came from me and Samson more than two decades ago.

It's difficult to believe so much time has passed, that we've now been out of the bunkers longer than we were trapped inside them. The United World government chose us for our genetic makeup, our intelligence and potential. We were to be their designated *breeders*, ushering in the next generation of North Americans expected to do the UW's bidding.

Except that glorious future never showed up.

The spirits told Milton they intend to enter the domed cities; they just haven't figured out how yet. When they do, there will be chaos across the Domes. The well-structured society they invented for themselves will collapse. The class divisions will shatter. They will require new leadership, and the Twenty could be that governing body. But they will need to understand the past so they don't repeat it.

Erik and those like him are the future—not only for Eurasia, but for the world. Samson and I just have to open his eyes to the truth.

At the same time, I have to accept the fact that, while he shares my DNA, I will never be Erik's mother. Not really. I'll just be an oddity from Dome 6 married to a cyborg, working for a couple months on his family farm where he stopped by for a weekend and had his world turned inside-out.

Assuming he believes anything we have to say.

I wave to Samson as we approach, and he drops back from the control panel of the harvester he was scowling at. His eyes brighten at the sight of me, and then he sees Erik. He takes a deep breath and steps toward us.

Erik can't help staring. It's not every day one sees a man as large as Samson with a great bushy beard and mechatronic arms and legs. I take a moment to introduce them, and they nod to each other. They don't shake hands.

Erik points at the harvester and makes a good guess at the problem Samson's been having with it—something to do with the propulsion sequence being out of alignment. The goal is to have all three harvesters working simultaneously. These unmanned machines have to be programmed for that, and the updated software is not doing the trick.

"Mind if I take a look?" Erik steps forward, and Samson backs away.

"Go for it," he rumbles with a glance at me.

Keeping his eyes to himself, Erik approaches the panel. It's welded to an arm that swings outward from the engine cover on the side of the machine. He mutters something, tapping the display with a growing frown.

"Please don't tell me you wiped its memory." His focus doesn't leave the screen.

"Okay." Samson crosses his metal arms, and they glint in the sun. "I won't."

"We didn't know how else to install the new operating system," I offer.

"You might as well have hit it with an EMP." Erik slaps the panel closed and shuts the engine cover with a clank. "No way you'll get it to run. You removed its brain, and now you want to replace it? Not happening."

"No reason it shouldn't work," Samson insists. "I've worked on machines more complicated than this—"

"But you haven't worked on *these* machines." Erik faces him. It's impossible not to notice the similarities in their posture, their coloring, the profiles of their faces squared off against one another. "My father designed them, wrote the code himself. They won't work with another operating system. They'll just..." He gestures at the machines. "...sit here."

Samson nods, clenching his jaw. He hates being wrong, particularly when he's already invested time in a project. But he wants to build trust with this young man, and I can tell he sees this moment as an opportunity.

"Okay. So where do we get another copy of the original operating system?"

Erik glances at him. "I've been trying to convince my mom to upgrade for years. There's no reason to have three machines when one of the new models can do the same amount of work in less time."

"Is your dad...?" Samson leaves it unsaid, his brow furrowed.

"Passed away when I was fifteen. His artificial lung gave out. Crazy, right? We've come so far as a species—technological and medical advancements our forebears never would have dreamed of. But doctors can still make mistakes."

"Was something wrong with the lung replacement?" I ask.

He shakes his head. "My dad was misdiagnosed. His lungs weren't the only problem. He'd suffered other maladies from the plague, and they interfered with the lung he was given. Kept it to himself until it was too late."

"He was allowed to live here—not sent to Dome 6?" Samson watches Erik closely.

"I may have...had something to do with that."

"Let me guess. You're good with computers."

Erik shrugs. "Machines in general."

Just like his biological father.

"Sounds like you know your history, too." I look up at him. "Most Eurasians live in the moment, ignoring the past. And no one mentions the plague."

He glances from me to Samson, guarded now. "So what?"

"Neural implants keep citizens focused on the present. But we don't have any." I tap my temple and motion toward Samson.

Then I let my hand drift toward Erik. "Neither do you, it would seem. Unless you've managed to switch yours off."

He's scowling at us, backing away from the harvester and retreating toward the farmhouse one step at a time. "Were you sent here to spy on me? To derail my career? Because if you think you have that kind of power, think again. I'll get you carted back to Dome 6 faster than you can—"

"The past is important, Erik," Samson says, his deep voice powerful and authoritative. I've never heard him sound more like a father. "And so is the future. There's a lot you don't know about yourself. About the Twenty. But we can show you the truth."

Erik widens the gap between us. "Who are you people?"

"We're survivors," I tell him. I've never shared this with anyone in Eurasia. "We've been living in Dome 6 for almost fifteen years. But we are originally from the North American Sectors."

Erik stops in his tracks. "There's nothing left out there. Nobody could survive that."

"We did." Samson shrugs. "Then we came here. To find you."

"Me..." His eyes dart back and forth between us. "Why?"

"You're a smart guy. We'll let you figure it out." Samson steps forward, retrieving a pair of blood samples from his pocket. A drop from each of us on a single slide. "Compare it to your own. See what you find out."

At first, it doesn't look like Erik will take the slide. He looks ready to run. But then he reaches forward and snatches it from Samson's metal fingers. "What's this supposed to prove?"

"Let us know what you discover. We heard you're leaving tomorrow morning." I smile at him. "If you'd like to discuss anything with us before you go, we'll be in the bunkhouse."

I rest my hand on Samson's arm. There's more that he wants to say, but it's better to leave matters as they stand, with Erik calling the shots. If he turns us in to the authorities, so be it. Fifteen years of waiting have led us to this moment, with one of our ten offspring holding the future in his hands. What happens next will depend on his curiosity and the impression we've made on him.

As Erik turns toward the farmhouse, staring at the slide in the palm of his hand, Samson calls after him, "So, about these harvesters..."

"I'll get you a copy of the original OS," Erik says without looking back.

Once he's halfway across the field, I turn to Samson, "What do you think?"

He faces me with a sad smile. "If Luther was here, he'd be praying right now."

"That bad, huh?"

Samson exhales. "We did the best we could, considering. Way to blow our cover, though." He gives me a wink.

I couldn't lie to Erik. "So now we wait."

Wait to see if Erik reports us. Wait to see if he scans our blood or throws the slide into the recycler. Wait to find out if we're ever going to see him again.

Just before sunset, we finish our shift repairing and maintaining various machines and computer systems around the farm. There is enough work here to keep us busy through the end of summer, should we stay that long.

The bunkhouse was originally designed for a full complement of twenty farmhands, but Samson and I have had the place all to ourselves. Upon arriving in Eurasia, we didn't take long acclimating to real food instead of ration packs, but nothing has tasted as good as the fresh fare from the Paine farm. Tonight we're enjoying potatoes and corn, applesauce, fresh bread, and soy protein patties, all piping hot and delicious with tall glasses of cold orange juice to wash it down. Comfortable in each other's quiet company, we're too tired to say much, when a knock sounds at the door.

We look at each other, daring to hope. Samson gets up, his mechanical parts clanking and his heavy feet thumping across the bare floorboards. He swings the door open wide.

Erik stands outside with his hands stuffed into the pockets of his jacket. He doesn't seem to know where to look.

"Hey," Samson greets him.

Erik's hand shoots forward, holding a disk. He doesn't meet Samson's gaze. "Here's the OS."

"Thanks." Samson takes it, turning it end over end. "I'll get this installed tomorrow. If your mom decides to upgrade at some point—"

"I've got a whole lot of questions." Erik steps forward, looking first at Samson, then at me with an earnest gleam in his eyes

Samson grins. "You ran the DNA scan."

He nods.

I rise from the table. "Come in, Erik. Are you hungry?"

Samson steps aside, making way for our son to enter. He claps Erik on the shoulder. "Guess we've got a lot to discuss."

But Erik doesn't start out with a question we could have predicted:

"So, can either of you hear people's thoughts?"

22. LUTHER
22 YEARS AFTER ALL-CLEAR

Chancellor Hawthorne remains calm and reserved as I lead her down the interior hallway to the unit I rented earlier today. The cube complex is dark and quiet, as most citizens have been ordered to remain indoors while martial law is in effect. Glow-strips run along the floor on both sides, providing enough light to guide us. Emmanuel Bishop and his sister Mara trail behind the Chancellor.

Once we reach the cube, I knock twice on the door and then step aside, waiting to see the reactions when James Bishop answers.

He's twenty years older than he was when Mara and Emmanuel saw him last. They were merely children, taken from his home by the authorities and held in a government prison to ensure his cooperation. Every member of his team was killed on the North American continent, but he survived. The only thing that got him through was the hope that he would see his family again.

But his wife passed away shortly after news broke that Sergeant Bishop was killed in action. The government's lie broke Emma's heart. Her children were well looked after by the Chancellor, who provided them with opportunities not afforded to most citizens. Mara is now the commander of Dome 1 law enforcement, and Emmanuel is aide to the Chancellor herself. Both are accustomed to shouldering more than their share of responsibilities.

Both melt at the sight of their father.

The years make no difference. They recognize each other instantly, and after only a moment of stunned silence that freezes them where they stand, they rush toward each other, the adult children nearly toppling Hawthorne against the wall as they race past her, their grey-haired father bolting out of the cube with tears glistening in his eyes. They embrace, their arms clasped tightly around each other and their heads together, voices murmuring both joy and confusion.

Chancellor Hawthorne looks shocked at first. Then she backs away with a hand covering her nose and mouth, worried that an infected man like Bishop is sharing the same air she is.

"I wouldn't be concerned about contamination, Ms. Hawthorne." I approach her and make it clear that she's not going to escape. She has been brought here for a reason.

Her eyes flash angrily at me, but she drops her hand from her face—which should look as old as mine. Yet it doesn't, thanks to the age regression therapy upper-caste citizens of the Domes receive on a regular basis. Everyone who can afford it looks like they are still in their prime.

"Who the hell do you think you are?" she demands, pointing angrily at the Bishop family reunion. "He'll infect us all!"

"Not how it works." Milton appears in a blur of speed, rushing out of the cube's open door and snatching the Chancellor's snuff box before she realizes what's happened. Her hand drifts toward the pocket in her vest as she stares at the box in Milton's grasp. He flips the lid open and pours the dust onto the hallway floor, where a thick cloud rises and dissipates. "But inhaling enough of this should do the trick."

She sputters, failing to string comprehensible words together.

"So our illustrious Chancellor is a dust freak." Mara Bishop is not impressed.

"I'm no addict!" Hawthorne hisses through clenched teeth. "Do you know how much that cost?"

"Overpriced, I'll bet. The ground's covered with it where we're from." Milton shrugs. "I could show you."

She stumbles backward, glancing from the Bishops to Milton to me.

"You're from the..." She can't bring herself to say it, to make it real. "The Sectors?"

"Yes." I nod and offer her a reassuring smile. "But we're not here to harm you."

"How did you get inside?" she gasps.

"That's a long story," Milton says with a grin. He snaps the snuff box shut and pockets it like a memento. "Twenty years long. Almost enough time to make you lose what's left of your mind. Living and working on a raider ship, waiting until the moment was right. The *Argonaus*—ever hear of it?" He palms his forehead. "Of course you have. You're the Chancellor!"

He's rambling. He does that when he gets excited. But I cannot blame him; there is much to be excited about.

"You were true to your word." Mara Bishop looks at me with glassy eyes, remaining in her father's embrace. "I'll help you any way I can."

Months ago, when I was first put in contact with Mara through Captain Mutegi's connections inside Eurasia, she seemed resistant. She did not believe I was from the Sectors, and she refused to believe her father was still alive—until I convinced her via a holographic transmission, showing James Bishop standing beside me. She demanded to see him in person, and we agreed on a meeting. But she would have to escort Chancellor Hawthorne to this predesignated cube complex, where her father would be waiting.

All of the residents are support staff for various office buildings in Dome 1, and none of them have any official government associations. Even so, we are too exposed standing in this hallway.

I gesture toward the open door. "Let's go inside. We have much to discuss."

James cups the back of his daughter's bald head with one hand. "What happened to your hair, Sweetie?" He doesn't seem to notice her uniform with its high-ranking insignia. "It was always so pretty." He catches himself. "My beautiful girl. You look so much like your mother..."

Mara kisses his cheek.

"You told us he was *dead*." Emmanuel stares at the Chancellor in disbelief, everything he thought he knew about the world unraveling around him. "A Eurasian hero, that's what you called him. And our mother, she never knew the truth... You *lied* to all of us!"

"I would be very careful, if I were you." Hawthorne's voice is sharp with an undeniable edge of authority. "Both of you." She looks only at Emmanuel and Mara. For the moment, the rest of us do not exist. "If it were not for me, you would never have enjoyed your current stations in Dome 1. Unless you no longer wish to continue serving Eurasia as you have for the past decade, you would do well to remember that." She points at James, then sweeps her arm toward Milton and me without deigning to give us eye contact. "These men are infected. They have come from outside the Domes to destroy our way of life. There is only one thing for you to do here, and that is to contain the situation until we can summon a troop of security personnel to take them into custody." She lowers her voice. "Remember who you are and whom you serve. Extricate yourselves from these men, and I will forget any minor transgressions that may have occurred—including this moment."

Expressionless as stone, Mara nods toward the cube's interior. "After you, Chancellor. Let's hear what they have to say."

The cube is cramped, but we manage to squeeze inside in a semblance of a circle. The Chancellor wrinkles her nose with disgust but sits on the bed; Mara takes the only chair; Emmanuel, his father, Milton, and I seat ourselves cross-legged on the floor.

It escapes no one's attention that Mara is the only one armed. Her hand remains within reach of her holster at all times. As the cube door slides shut and locks itself automatically behind me, I give Milton a look, and he nods. Despite the warm family reunion, we should remain cautious. Mara is not one of us, not yet.

"How many of you are there?" Chancellor Hawthorne demands, glaring at me. "What is your purpose here?"

Milton and James defer to me; Mara and Emmanuel watch everything closely, noting every subtle cue. They are being cautious as well.

"Hundreds of us were sealed inside underground bunkers while the powers of the world destroyed our planet," I begin. "For twenty years we lived beneath the surface, trapped between cold concrete walls, floors, and ceilings. We read, and we studied, exercising our minds and our bodies. We prepared ourselves for All-Clear, when we would be released to rebuild and start a new life together. We would rise from the ashes and repopulate the Sectors, and again our continent would provide everything the United World needed in order to live in the luxury they had grown accustomed to. Or so we were told."

"*Eurasia*," Hawthorne snaps. "There is no United World."

"When we saw what had become of the Sectors, we assumed there was no world left at all. We thought we were the last human beings in existence, and that our daily fight for survival against the elements—and against mutants intent on devouring us—was necessary to safeguard humankind." I pause, glancing at Milton. "But we were not alone in our struggle. A supernatural presence made itself known to us shortly after our return to the surface: spirits of the earth that moved through the dust, empowering us with amazing abilities from the animal kingdom once we breathed the particulate matter into our lungs. We were changed, and these changes aided us in our survival."

Hawthorne scoffs, glancing at Emmanuel and Mara. "Why are you subjecting us to such a ridiculous fairy tale? Obviously you're out of your mind—as is anyone who gives credence to your ramblings."

I had a feeling she would respond this way. Long ago, my talons would have been proof enough of a supernatural gift. But we have another powerful visual aid.

"Milton." I give him a nod.

"Right." He sits up straight, assuming a very serious expression. Even though there is some grey at his temples now and wrinkles at the corners of his eyes, he overflows with as much youthful vigor as when I first met him. "So, these spirits of the earth can appear to some of us as people from our past. No idea why they choose certain individuals to reveal themselves to. Honestly, I kind of wish they'd leave me alone. But anyhow, here we are." He clears his throat, glancing at the Chancellor. "You asked how many of us there are, and of course we're not going to tell you that. But you should know that I smuggled somebody along inside me."

Hawthorne stares at him in the silence. "What?"

"The spirits. They wanted to hitch a ride into Eurasia. They've never been able to get through all the plexicon and plasteel—human-made substances. Even your dirt isn't real dirt, not from the earth outside. But quite a few citizens, including yourself, have been inhaling dust over the years—recreationally, of course—and we think the residue might be just enough." He closes his eyes, sitting very still. "Wait for it," he murmurs.

The Chancellor curses foully. "You people are insane if you think—"

"Persephone," Milton says with a cadence that is unfamiliar, "do you remember the first time we attempted to sail across the Mediterranean?"

She freezes, her lips parting without a sound. Her eyes unblinking, glistening.

"Neither one of us with more than an hour or two of lessons under our belts, yet there we were, learning from every failed attempt. Nothing could stop us in those days. Two kids in love against a whole world we planned to fix. No more war or sickness." Milton pauses. "In many ways, you've realized our dreams."

Hawthorne rises, trembling with fury. "Stop this at once. It's a parlor trick, nothing more. A cheap medium's ploy to—"

"Milton is no medium," I tell her. "Trust me on this. The Creator has made it abundantly clear that his children should not consort with those who contact the dead. I would never be party to such a thing."

Another curse from the Chancellor, this time more vehement. "So you're one of those followers of the *Way*. That explains everything. You're all a bunch of lunatics."

"Milton is, however, currently possessed by a spirit of the earth," I continue. "It's the only way such a being could possibly enter Eurasia. Via a willing host, acting as its vessel."

"Mostly willing," Milton mutters.

"It was communicating with you as someone from your past, I take it?" I raise an eyebrow at the Chancellor.

She glares at Emmanuel and stands. "We're leaving. Right now."

He leans forward, about to get to his feet.

"Sit down." For the first time, James speaks to Hawthorne, and it's like he is giving orders to a subordinate. "Hear us out. At the end of it, if you're not interested in what we're offering, then nobody will stop you from leaving."

"But until then, I'm your prisoner."

"Until then, I don't much care what you have to say." He folds his arms and stares her down.

She fidgets for a moment. Then she sinks onto the edge of the bed, staring daggers at me instead of James. Because he intimidates her. And why shouldn't he? Sergeant James Bishop was responsible for bringing the Twenty to Eurasia, reversing their infertility problem and ensuring a future for the Ten Domes. Without him, they would have died out as a species after the Terminal Age—Mara and Emmanuel's generation, the last to be naturally born to Eurasian citizens more than thirty years ago.

Sergeant Bishop was a famous hero and a martyr for the cause; the people adored him. But that was before the Chancellor started erasing history. She and the Governors of the Ten Domes decided it did their people no good to remember the past, that only now and forever forward mattered. So the citizens' neural implants were tweaked to keep them from remembering past events or even learning about them. In so doing, the people of Eurasia forgot a man named James Bishop, as well as a horrific event known as D-Day. And they had no reason to believe their immaculate city of glass has not always existed.

Thanks to Samson and Shechara's research during their fifteen-year undercover mission, we have learned enough to be well-versed in Eurasian ways. We know never to go under a laser-knife to receive neural implants. As fascinating as augmented reality and virtual reality may sound, we have agreed that we don't want to lose any part of ourselves. Memories of the past make us who we are, and the present must be lived—not ignored with glazed-over eyes while we're online.

The spirit is speaking through Milton again, and I focus on what he's saying. This is the closest I've ever come to hearing a spirit of the earth communicate.

"That enhanced hearing ability you experience upon snorting a pinch or two of dust—it never lasts, does it, Persephone?" he asks.

Her face has gone white, her voice hoarse. "How can you possibly know...?"

I tap my temple. "The spirits know our thoughts. Somehow, they are able to slip into our minds and learn everything about us. But only those of us who, like you, have inhaled the dust of the earth. They communicate directly with a very select few." I regard the Chancellor for a moment as she sits there looking like she's witnessed a ghost. "Whose voice did you hear?"

Color gradually returns to her cheeks. The flush of rage held on a tight leash. "It's just a trick. In very poor taste, I must say."

Mara rests a hand on her father's shoulder. "Do you...?" She frowns, not sure how to phrase the question.

He nods, his voice quiet. "The spirits appeared to me as your mother."

Mara withdraws her hand quickly, as if she's been burned.

He meets her wary gaze. "They saved my life. Kept me on mission. Led me where I needed to go in order to ensure the retrieval and delivery of the Twenty." Even after all these years, he still speaks like a military man. "These spirits, they're... incredible."

Mara does not look convinced. Instead, she seems concerned that the years her father spent outside Eurasia may have affected his mind in detrimental ways.

Milton keeps his eyes locked on the Chancellor, his speech patterns continuing to sound like someone else's. "What if I told you that ability, instead of only lasting a minute or few, could be permanent? Available whenever you need it?"

Hawthorne's jaw muscles twitch as she grinds her teeth. "How would such a thing be possible?" she finally manages, grating out the words.

It's clear that we have her attention. We are offering something she desperately wants. Now to leverage that desire in our favor.

"It is indeed possible," Milton replies. "All I would have to do is—" He flinches suddenly, grimacing as though he's tasted something terrible. "Kiss her? What the hell? You never said anything about—!"

He's arguing with the spirit he carries, that much is clear. All eyes are fixed on him. None of us have ever witnessed anything like the spectacle playing out before us, as uncanny as it is humorous.

His voice returns to its earlier cadence as he explains to Hawthorne, "If we maintain a tight seal, mouth to mouth, I would be able to enter your body and, via the particulate matter already ensconced in your lungs, activate your gift. Permanently." Then he cringes, avoiding eye contact with the Chancellor as he turns toward me to whisper, "I never signed up for this!"

I give him a shrug. *Whatever we have to do.*

That was the agreement we made days ago. At the time, when I learned from Milton what the spirits intended, I balked at the idea of someone as despicable as Persephone Hawthorne receiving a superhuman gift. But then I recalled that Cain, vile as he was, had also been gifted by the spirits of the earth. It is true, at least in a metaphorical sense, that the Creator causes rain to fall upon the just and the unjust.

"What would you want from me in return?" She doesn't seem turned off by the prospect of kissing Milton.

Victoria would obviously have something to say about it, but she is with Daiyna and the others hiding out in Dome 10, ready to flee at the first sign of trouble. Captain Mutegi waits aboard the *Argonaus*, docked nearby, and Samson and Shechara should be headed that way from Dome 6. But if all goes according to plan, then everyone will meet us here in Dome 1.

"You tell us where you've taken the Twenty," James says.

She smirks at him as only a self-satisfied, lifelong politician can. The most powerful woman in the world. "What makes you think I've taken them anywhere?"

"We have it on good authority that your security clones are rounding them up and escorting them to a safe location." I hold her gaze. "We would like to know where that is."

She shakes her head at me. "And what makes you think I would share that information with a group of *terrorists*—" She glances at Mara and Emmanuel. "—and *traitors*?"

"We're not terrorists. As I told you, we're from the North American Sectors—"

"Impossible." It's as though she has turned a sharp corner in her mind, convincing herself that nothing she's seen or heard is true. "There's no way in hell you could have entered the Domes undetected. We have strict measures in place, analysts in each dome who track the movements of every citizen, day and night.

The only people without implants reside in Dome 6, and very few are allowed transit privileges outside that dome. Every other citizen is traceable every moment of their lives."

"Until a massive EMP burst disabled every system in your building, including the neural implants of every citizen inside." Milton shrugs, again sounding like someone else. "While your law enforcers scrambled to contain that situation—and while a few citizens on the fringes of society took it upon themselves to create disturbances in the streets, seeming to think the attack was instigated by the people you call terrorists—Luther and his friends entered Dome 10 and made their way here, right before martial law went into effect. It timed out perfectly."

She narrows her eyes at him, baring her teeth, but not in a smile. "So you're saying it was not the terrorists who attacked my tower?"

"A well-organized group of so-called freedom fighters intent on disrupting Eurasian society in an effort to bring down the rule of law and destroy the rigid class structure currently in place?" Milton shakes his head. "Not this time."

I lean forward. "Those people exist, of course. They call themselves *patriots*, resurrecting the same moniker used by the dangerous radicals who released bioweapons onto North America four decades ago. But the current incarnation had nothing to do with the EMP strike on Hawthorne Tower." I pause. "That was us."

She laughs bitterly. "You really should get your story straight. Didn't you just say you entered Dome 10 *after* the EMP attack?"

"That's right," Milton says, sounding like himself, "but I snuck in early." He holds up the snuff box he stole from her in a blur of speed. "I'm fast like that."

"You must have had some help." Mara studies Milton like the law enforcer she is. "I don't care how fast you are. You couldn't have smuggled in the equipment necessary to knock out Hawthorne Tower without being detected."

"We have had a contact in Eurasia for many years," I reply. "He procured what we needed, and Milton set it up inside your building. The equipment was masked as upgraded Linkstream relays, and Milton's superspeed registered as a momentary glitch on your surveillance cameras."

The Chancellor scowls at Emmanuel. "How can this be possible?" she hisses. "Don't we have analysts plugged into the Link, constantly monitoring every corner of the building?"

He nods, perplexed. "I should have been informed of any anomalies..."

"You're both *fired*." She glares at Mara. "You'll be reassigned to waste management in Dome 10. Enjoy the demotion."

"Assuming you still have any power when you leave this room," James says.

"Is that a threat?" Seething, Hawthorne turns her full attention on him.

"The situation as I see it."

She curses under her breath. "I believe we are through here, Sergeant. Am I free to leave?"

"As soon as you tell us where the Twenty have been taken."

"Why do you care?"

"I know what it's like to lose your family. Your kids." He clenches his jaw. "Half of the Twenty are Luther's children."

Hawthorne raises her chin, pivoting slowly to face me. "So that's what this is all about." Her voice is low, as if none of us are sitting here with her. She's gone back in time to relive a memory. "He said the embryos were from willing donors. I assumed he meant his own people in Eden. But Arthur Willard was a self-serving bastard. Of course I saw that right away." She blinks, focusing on me now. "You've waited a long time to come looking for them."

"Yes," I acknowledge, nodding to Bishop. "We have."

Years passed as we waited for the right moment. Dissent in the outlying domes had to reach high enough levels for there to be a credible threat, and for the attack on Hawthorne tower to be the obvious culmination. Samson and Shechara had to make contact with Erik Paine, and he had to do his own research to validate the information he'd been given. Being tech savvy, that did not take him long. Then we waited while he dealt with his criminal contacts in Dome 10, obtaining the EMP grenades and other devices he would need to deactivate the neural implants of each member of the Twenty so they would be in tune with their gifts.

According to Samson and Shechara, their biological son was not only telepathic but could leap higher than humanly possible. Whether his nine siblings or Daiyna and my offspring were similarly blessed remained to be seen, but one thing was clear: Erik had never breathed in the dust of the earth prior to exhibiting his abilities. The spirits' blessing had been passed to him through his parents' DNA.

Erik managed to locate each member of the Twenty via DNA samples from Samson, Shechara, Daiyna, and myself, utilizing secret Linkstream backchannels. He narrowed down the list and decided on the first one to contact: a law enforcer who worked the night shift, maintaining the curfew. An officer with an impressive record, but who had a tendency to be strong-willed at times and grate on the patience of her commander: Mara Bishop.

"If we do not find the Twenty," I tell the chancellor, "then all of this will be for nothing."

Hawthorne tilts her head to one side, seeming to view me in a new light. "You must realize they are adults now, living their own lives. They have been very well cared for, adopted by loving parents, received the best education. They serve Eurasia throughout the Ten Domes, contributing to their communities." She pauses. "They will turn twenty this month, and we have a celebration planned in their honor. A *Revelation Banquet*. They will be honored for their contributions to society. Most importantly, safeguarding our future for generations to come."

I know full well how important they are to Eurasia. Their sex cells have been harvested for years, and their genetically modified offspring have been farmed out to suitable upper-class couples across the Domes—all without their knowledge. Samson and Shechara learned this during their sojourn in Dome 6, prior to meeting Erik. It was all Samson could do to keep himself from marching on the Chancellor's tower then and there, a mechanized army of one.

I lock eyes with Hawthorne. "No more lies. From this day forward, truth will reign in your glass city."

"Or shatter it," Milton quips, as himself. "Once the spirits get loose, nobody's going to be paying for dust anymore. They won't need to."

"Your secret drug empire will crumble," James says, relishing every word.

She sneers at Milton. "What are you going to do? Kiss every dust freak in Eurasia?"

"If I have to." He doesn't look happy about it. Then, as the spirit possessing him decides to take the wheel again, he sits up straight and stares at the Chancellor. "Should I tell them who I am, Persephone? Do you think they would like to know that you are not only an addict yourself but also a murderer? That you killed your own husband to usurp his role as leader of the United World?"

This is news to us. All eyes turn toward Chancellor Hawthorne.

Her hands are folded in her lap, and they are trembling. She sits with her spine erect and chin held high. Her face set hard as granite, she glares at Milton and the spirit within him.

"Where did you hear such a vicious rumor?" she demands.

"We are not your husband," the spirits reply. Apparently, Milton carries more than one. "But we have seen your memories, and we can emulate his bearing, his nature, even his voice to your ears. We know that you poisoned him slowly over the course of many months. You isolated him from his advisors and the Governors, and you forced him to sign his authority over to you. When he died, you did not shed a single tear." Slowly, Milton rises to his feet, his eyes locked with Hawthorne's. She stares back at him.

"Even so, despite all the wrong you have done, we would like to give you a gift—if you are willing to receive it."

The color drains from her face. Milton approaches, and she shudders with a cold terror. Then without warning, she reaches for him, and they kiss.

As their lips part, her eyes focus on the empty space before her. She convulses, screaming in horror.

"She sees him," Milton says. "Probably should've told her that's one of the side effects..."

"I don't know!" Hawthorne shrieks, her eyes wide as she curls inward. "How should I know where they are! I gave no such order!"

"The manifestation of her husband is interrogating her now," Milton explains. "To me, he looks like that big guy from my bunker—Jackson. He's asking about the Twenty."

"I don't know why my clones are collecting them." She squeezes her eyes shut and covers her face, screaming curses. "Get away from me!"

Milton gestures for us to step outside into the hall, leaving Chancellor Hawthorne alone with the ghost from her past.

"Let's give these two the room."

23. MILTON
22 YEARS AFTER ALL-CLEAR

Once the cube door slides shut and we're out in the hallway, it's clear the room is soundproof. So we don't have to worry about neighbors calling up local law enforcement complaining about a woman screaming her guts out.

Emmanuel looks out of sorts, like someone who's witnessed something awful happen to a loved one. Or his boss. His sister squeezes his arm, wordlessly reassuring him that she's here, that everything will be alright. Then she gets a call and touches her temple, activating her audiolink.

"I have to take this," she says to Luther. Her clean-shaven head reminds me of the first time I met Daiyna. "It's one of my law enforcers—a member of the Twenty."

He nods. "Be careful. I would assume you're being monitored."

Her expression says of course she is. "If the Chancellor didn't order her security personnel to sequester them, then it appears we have another player on the scene. Someone used your attack on Hawthorne Tower for their own purpose, capitalizing on the disturbance. For some reason, they want the Twenty in one place."

Any idea who's collecting them? I ask the Julia-spirit I'm carrying around.

This is my first time here, Milton. I don't have much to go on.

Right. So she's no help. And the Jackson-spirit is busy tormenting Chancellor Hawthorne at the moment, appearing to her as her murdered husband. But maybe he'll learn something in the process that will point us in the right direction.

Mara steps away from us, down the hall. "What are you doing in Dome 2, Enforcer Chen?" she demands, speaking to the air in front of her.

I nudge Bishop. "Proud papa?"

He catches himself watching her and nods. Then he faces his son. "I know it's a lot all at once."

"I'm not sure what I saw in there," Emmanuel murmurs, referring to the Chancellor's behavior.

"Yeah, life these days can be pretty bizarre," I offer. "But you'll get used to it. Eventually."

He turns his vacant stare in my direction.

"Three of them are in Dome 2," Mara half-turns from her call. "The security clones haven't caught them yet."

Luther nods. "We'll have our man tail them. No reason to mount a rescue operation until we know where they are being taken."

"Why not pick up these three now and the other seventeen later?" I suggest, ever helpful. What's the saying? Better to have a hydropack in the hand than a wellspring of imaginary water. Something like that.

Luther clasps my shoulder. "I wish it were that simple. But we have a better chance of locating all of them if we follow these three. We must find out where they're being taken and who is behind their capture. Then we will take action"

Mara joins us as she signs off. "Carry on, Enforcer Chen. And be quick about it. You don't have much time." She taps her temple, restoring her focus on her present surroundings. "Your man is in place?"

"On it." Bishop activates the handheld device he received from Captain Mutegi and contacts Drasko, telling him to move into position outside the Dome 2 maglev tunnel. There he'll watch and follow at a safe distance but not intervene. Because, like Luther said, the goal is to find all twenty.

That's right, I'm a team player. But I've been feeling antsy for a while now. I haven't been able to use my speed or flight skills out in the open since we boarded the *Argonaus* all those years ago. Grounded for too long, I've got a bad case of the jitters.

Stealing Hawthorne's snuff box was the most fun I've had in recent memory.

Want to take a tour of the Domes? I ask the Julia-spirit.

You understand what martial law means, right?

I shrug it off. *Nobody will catch me. I'll be a blip on their radar. Nothing more.*

Somehow I don't think you've run this past Luther, she says.

I glance at him, deep in conversation with the Bishop trio. Grizzled father, shell-shocked son, commanding daughter. She inherited all of her dad's military demeanor, but she also has a calm center. When she looks at her brother, there's a warmth that radiates toward him. In their parents' absence, she's been father and mother to him.

Luther's got plenty to keep him busy, I reply. *So how about it? You point me in the direction of the nearest dust addicts, and we'll introduce them to their permanent special abilities.* I pause, realizing I've assumed something. *You can do that, right? Use your ethereal dust-locator to find every citizen with particulate matter in their lungs?*

Julia hesitates. *Yes.*

That's why you hitched a ride, right? To show these people the truth— that they're more than just zombies going to their government-assigned jobs every day and plugging into virtual reality in their little cubes every night. You have superhuman gifts for them, available for the taking!

But Milton, you're forgetting something very important. As long as their augments are functional—

That's why we'll ignore the law-abiding citizens for now, and only seek out the dust addicts right in the middle of their snorting sessions. Their augments will be offline, and you'll show them how their fleeting abilities can be lifelong gifts. My pulse pounds at the thought of it. *We can* make a real difference here. Set off a chain reaction that will flip this authoritarian regime upside down!*

Her response is slow in coming. *Have you considered how many people you'll have to kiss?*

About that. *You're sure there isn't another way?*

The air here is purified and sterile. The ground is a synthetic material. There is no way for us to move outside of bodies with dust in their lungs.

The *Argonaus* has a whole lot of dirt on board, and it's being unloaded onto the Dome 10 docks at this very moment. If we could get a ton of the stuff and dump it into the air recyclers—

"Dome 10." Bishop's voice interrupts, holding up the communication device in his hand. "That's where they're headed. Drasko is keeping his distance. He's got a tracker on a surveillance drone in their vehicle."

Luther nods. "Then we'll meet at the rendezvous point. Samson and Shechara should be on their way." He faces Mara. "I know it's asking a lot."

"Not at all." She tilts her head toward the cube with Hawthorne inside. So far, the Chancellor hasn't attempted to leave. The door's unlocked. "What about her?"

"Let her deal with her demons."

Nobody has a problem with that.

"This way." Mara leads us to the stairwell and then up to the roof where her aerocar sits on the well-manicured lawn.

The vehicle looks like any kid's dream-come-true of a flying car. Aerodynamic with sharp, rocket-like angles, painted white and sporting black accents. Sensing our approach, the cockpit doors rise like wings, as does the door to the cargo compartment. Mara climbs into the pilot seat, and her father drops in next to her, both of them buckling on their harnesses like it's second nature. The rest of us file into the cargo area, sliding across the bench seats and strapping in. As Mara ignites the engines, a powerful hum resonates throughout the interior. The doors drift shut, locking into place.

Then we're off. Not nearly as fast as I can fly, but this aerocar is something else. We soar through the air, swooping over the top of the cube complex and diving between two skyscrapers—which I've learned are called *dome*scrapers here. Hurtling a couple dozen kilometers across vacant streets cleaner than any I've ever seen, we reach the train station. Nine underground tunnels radiate outward, leading to the outlying domes. Hovering in midair, we rotate clockwise, lining ourselves up with the one marked 10. Then Mara hits the accelerator, throwing us back in our seats as we dive headlong into the dark tunnel.

Less than a minute later, we emerge inside the same dome where we disembarked from the *Argonaus*. The train station security guards wave us through without much interest, much like the Dome 1 personnel did. Of course Mara's law enforcement vehicle would have the right of way during a crisis. By this point, with no update from their superiors or the Chancellor herself—and no further acts of terror to be quelled—they must be wondering what the hell is going on.

As far as aesthetics go, Dome 10 resembles Dome 1 about as much as a hole in the ground resembles sunlight. A city whose primary responsibilities are waste management and water recycling, not to mention being the only Eurasian port on the polluted Mediterranean, should be expected to have more of a grungy vibe, I suppose. Unlike Dome 1, the streets are congested with people in vehicles and on foot. Obviously, martial law isn't in effect. Maybe because no government buildings were targeted by *terrorists* here.

There's no other air traffic that I can see, and more than a few folks on the ground stare up at us as we pass overhead. Not the most inconspicuous arrival, but then again, we're in a police vehicle, so they might assume it's just a flyover. Keeping the peace in a very busy dome.

Drasko, our main contact, informed us about the thriving underworld beneath Dome 10's gritty surface: dust smuggling, weapons trading, human trafficking, clone hacking, and political corruption. Most of Eurasia's intermittent terrorist threats have come from Dome 10 citizens, and who can blame them? They live and work in the cesspool of Eurasia, assigned their roles by the government, with no hope of ever breaking free of the Domes' rigid class structure. It makes sense the current *patriot* resurgence would be born here. They're at the very bottom of the food chain.

With the most dust in circulation of any dome in Eurasia.

This is where we'll start, I tell Julia. *The revolution will begin here.*

You identify with them, she replies. *You grew up in Sector 43, a trade sector populated with unskilled laborers. Sterilized, forced to work long hours in a factory. When you were chosen for the bunker, you felt a glimmer of hope that your life would take a different path—a better future, after the bombs fell.* She pauses. *But Jackson made you his hangman. After you killed him, it took time for you to grow into the man you are today. With a heart for the downtrodden, and a desire to share your supernatural abilities with others.*

I nod. Sounds right to me.

The abilities we gave you were for your survival, Milton. These people...they don't need us. They have clean air to breathe and plenty to eat and drink. They are safe here. Any dangers they experience are their own doing. We are not interested in their political struggles. Only the struggle to survive.

You had no problem revealing yourself to their leader, I retort.

That was Jackson. He promised to leave the rest of Eurasia alone as long as he could torment the Chancellor, perhaps even drive her insane. The two of them may never leave that little room.

And you're okay with that.

She hesitates before answering. *Perhaps without her, the people of Eurasia will find a better way to govern themselves.*

Thought you weren't into politics, I counter.

Instead of answering, she says, *You remember when all Jackson wanted was the destruction of your species?*

I nod. Something like that is difficult to forget.

Then it should seem strange to you that he would agree to limit his destruction to a single life.

I frown. *So you're saying...we made a big mistake by bringing him along.* But I couldn't take one without the other, as much as I would have preferred it. They are inseparable, two sides of the same ancient coin.

We need to find something to occupy him after the Chancellor expires, Julia says.

That sounds like a plan. *Got any ideas?*

I imagine her shaking her head. *Not at the moment.*

Bishop shows his daughter the coordinates on the screen of his handheld device, and she adjusts the aerocar's course. Our destination is a warehouse two hundred meters north of the port airlock. Its main purpose is to store crates of dust from the *Argonaus* prior to their dispersal to various suppliers and low-level dealers. As a side job, it's working as our base of operations.

I glance at Luther. Hard to believe this devout man of God is now a drug runner. But according to him, the dust we're smuggling is the same stuff the Creator used to form the first man and woman, all those millennia ago. Only it's since been nuked to death and somehow has entrapped the spiritual essence of the entire animal kingdom. Not crazy at all. Life as we know it.

More of us should look as stunned as Emmanuel, sitting beside me and staring slack-jawed out the side window.

"Ever been here before?" I offer, trying to be sociable.

"First time." He shakes his head. "It's nothing like Dome 1. How can these people live in such...squalor?"

I shrug. "It's all they know. Dust and the Link keep most of them from rising up against the status quo." I give him a nudge. "Maybe the next Chancellor can change that."

As Hawthorne's aide, he's seen how it's done. Who else would be better suited to take her place?

Luther would probably say I'm being too simplistic. The political gears have turned a certain way for decades, and change cannot happen overnight. But I have to wonder: why not? If the underclass were to rise up with a plethora of superhuman abilities, the ruling elites would be powerless to stop them.

"The way you move," Emmanuel says, frowning as he weighs his words. "How is that humanly possible?"

I grin. "It's really not."

"These *spirits of the earth*..." He glances at the back of his father's head. "They helped you over there." He waves vaguely toward the Mediterranean, glistening under the sun outside Dome 10. "They kept you alive."

"Some of us." My smile disappears. "The rest of us are determined to reunite our friends with their children."

"The Twenty."

He's been paying attention. Another trait of a good leader. "That's right."

"For what purpose?"

"How do you mean?"

"Why is Luther intent on meeting his biological offspring? Does he plan to usurp the role of their parents? Upset their families?"

That question has crossed my mind from time to time. Yet neither Luther, Daiyna, Samson, or Shechara seem interested in insinuating themselves where they don't belong.

"You were lied to, Emmanuel. The government told you that your father had died."

"They told us he was a hero." He raises his chin. "That much was true."

Maybe I was wrong about him. He's been around politicians so much that he can't help smelling like them.

"But you deserved to know the truth. To see your father again. And he sure as hell deserved to see you." I pause, knowing the next part will be tough to hear. "Your government's lie broke your mother's heart."

He clenches his jaw but doesn't disagree. "And now Luther is determined to break the hearts of twenty more mothers. Each one was carefully selected and partnered with a spouse to raise a member of the Twenty. Their well-functioning households have produced twenty-year-old citizens who've contributed greatly to our society. You seek to threaten their cohesion, and in so doing, the cohesion of Eurasia itself."

I give him a moment to listen to himself. Then I reply, "You haven't had long to process what's happening. And you don't know Luther very well. The man's had everything taken from him —even his gift from the spirits—yet he remains hopeful for the future. The world out there, what remains of it, never broke him. He's damaged—hell, we all are. But he'd never go out of his way to damage anybody else. So if you think he plans to wreak havoc here in Eurasia, you're dead wrong." I pause. "He wants you to know the truth, so it will set you free."

"What's that supposed to mean?"

I shrug. "Maybe that you've been living a lie, forced upon you by your government. But once the truth gets out, things are going to change around here. At first, it might not seem for the better..." I take a different tack. "Aren't you glad to finally know the truth about your dad?"

Emmanuel nods slowly, watching his father. He doesn't say anything more.

"Change of venue." Bishop shows Mara a new set of coordinates on his device. "Drasko needs an evac, and he's got company. Two of the Twenty."

The aerocar pitches toward the starboard side—I learned that bit of lingo on the *Argonaus*—and Mara takes us north in a sharp trajectory, leaving the sea at our backs.

"Not the best area," she says, keeping her eyes on the windscreen and the glowing display. "Are any of you armed?"

"Negative," Bishop says, "but Milton—"

"Last resort." She glances over her shoulder at me. "Things are unstable enough right now without adding a superhuman to the mix."

"Understood." I get it.

But depending on the situation, nothing's going to stop me from doing what I do best.

We land on the roof of a nondescript building where a blue

and white aerocar sits, powered down with two bullet holes punched through its windscreen and a dead clone slumped over in the passenger seat. A single bloody headshot gapes from the front of its helmet.

"Can you fly?" Mara glances back at Emmanuel as she steps out under her rising door.

"I'm a little rusty," he admits, but he ducks his head and climbs into the pilot seat anyway.

"Good enough." Mara draws her sidearm and grips it in both hands, pointed at the ground. "Keep the engine warm and be ready to gun it as soon as we're aboard."

Her brother nods.

I hit the door release for the cargo compartment and leap out of the vehicle, floating until my boots make contact. No one seems to notice. Probably for the best; nobody likes a showoff. Luther follows me out, and Bishop is already at his daughter's side.

"Stay behind me. This could be one of those roving dens we hear about." She looks at her father and frowns. Wishing he was armed, probably worried that he's putting his life in danger. But with his military training, he's a real asset right now.

"Roving den," Luther echoes. "Criminals who migrate their base of operations, I take it."

Mara nods with a glance toward the shot-up aerocar. On the backseat sit two surveillance drones that look like miniature flying saucers. "Not sure what happened here. We may be too late."

Bishop points at the stairwell door. "Only one access point. We didn't spot them on the street. My bet: Drasko and the kids are still somewhere inside."

He's always referred to them that way. *The kids.* Luther and Daiyna's kids, Samson and Shechara's kids. Doesn't matter to him that they're adults. Guess we're all somebody's kids. My parents worked hard, long hours, then they weren't chosen for the bunker

—the government's way of showing its appreciation for their years of service. But their kid survived.

Mara leads the way down the silent stairwell, and we do our best to keep quiet as we descend floor after floor. The jittery lights and stained walls remind us we're in the filthiest of the Ten Domes. Which doesn't make sense, when you think about it. Why wouldn't these people keep their dome as clean as Dome 1? Unless this is intentional—their way of showing appreciation for the government assigning them waste duty. In that light, the grime is almost respectable.

As we arrive at each floor, Mara steps into the hallway and gives it a quick scan for life signs with her visual augments. Then she shakes her head at us, and we continue downward.

I could search every floor below us in the time it'll take to descend the next flight of stairs. I whisper as much to Luther, who reminds me that this is Mara's world, and she's calling the shots.

Dome 1, city of the future, may be Mara Bishop's world. This desolate building? It's what I've been used to since All-Clear: searching ruins.

So I blast downstairs in a blur of speed that sends Luther, Bishop, and his daughter staggering against the wall of the stairwell, and I hurl myself up and down the hallways of every floor, busting doors open and finding nobody behind them—

Until I reach the second floor.

Halfway down the hallway, a door stands open. Inside, I find the dregs of what may have been the swankiest party in town. Half-drunk glasses, half-snorted lines of dust abandoned in great haste. Chairs and tables overturned, knocked over by a stampede of revelers.

A holographic wall glitches in and out of existence. Acting like a mirror one second to expand the room's size, then revealing a hidden chamber where a plasteel chair sits alone. Broken restraints and a pool of blood lie on the floor.

Mara storms in glaring at me, but her weapon is down at her side.

"Nobody here." I shrug.

"I can see that. And I thought I gave you a direct order."

"I don't take orders from you, *Commander*. We were wasting time. Now we know the entire building is deserted."

"You checked the first floor?"

Right.

I blast by her in a blur of speed and return a few seconds later. If there were any hairs on her head, they'd be waving crazily right now.

"All clear," I report with a crisp salute.

"Whose blood is that?" Sergeant Bishop steps past us into the semi-hidden room.

Mara scans it with her ocular implants. "Erik Paine. One of the Twenty." She faces her father. "Any further communication from Drasko?"

He shakes his head.

"Then we return to our rendezvous point," Luther says, nodding to himself. "Drasko knew to meet us there if all else failed. There's nothing to be done here."

I'm about to agree, but that's when I'm hit with a pulverizing force, and I drop to the floor against my own volition. Pinned there by some kind of energy field that burns my nerve endings when I try to resist. Glancing around, I find Luther, Bishop, and Mara in the same predicament.

So we were led here. Into a trap. That's just awesome.

"I had three bartering chips, and now I have four more." An unfamiliar voice and a pair of hard-soled boots approach us.

Was there another hidden chamber behind a fully functional holographic wall? Strange that Mara's augmented vision didn't pick up on that. High-end black market tech, I guess, designed to fool the best of the best.

"It's raining opportunity in Dome 10 today!" The languid voice chuckles while the gravitational field encapsulating me rises from the floor, carrying me right along with it.

Immobilized, I drift toward the room's rear wall where I dangle upright, suspended above the floor. Luther, Bishop, and Mara join me. We face a solitary figure, tall and broad-shouldered, with a spiraling tattoo covering most of his pierced, pale face. He wears the standard slicked-back hair and armored faux-leather suit of a fellow who prides himself on being the very dangerous sort.

"Who are you supposed to be?" Mara grates out. Apparently, even speaking is unpleasant while restrained by this field. Good to know.

"I am your opposite in every way, Commander Bishop. You embody the rule of law, the Chancellor's iron fist, while I am Eurasia's nebulous shadow lurking in the deepest dark, always just beyond your reach. I am everything your society doesn't allow itself to be. I am crime. I am disobedience. I am terror. I am treason."

He should add *wordy* to the list.

She strains to raise her weapon, grimacing with the effort. She manages to bend her elbow, her finger curled around the trigger. "I've heard of a low-level gangster named Trezon operating in this area. Heard he's almost as ugly as you."

He raises his hand, and I notice the device he's holding. It looks like a chrome baton, maybe thirty centimeters in length. He points it nonchalantly at her, and she flattens against the wall with a short cry, her weapon forgotten.

"What do you want?" her father demands.

"The famous war hero, Sergeant James Bishop!" Our far-from-gracious host grins, revealing a mouthful of pristine teeth. Almost have to respect anyone these days with a penchant for dental hygiene. "So glad to see you're alive. And I do apologize for interrupting what I'm sure has been a very heartfelt family reunion. But you see, a certain situation has come to light. Mainly due to a sorry excuse for an actor showing up on my doorstep and trying to borrow a few EMP grenades off me. As if I run a charity here! And if that wasn't bad enough, then his little girlfriend shows up, followed by a damned security clone that abuses half my clientele and scares everybody off before whisking her away." He shakes his head, glowering at the memory of it. But abruptly his expression brightens. "If I've learned anything over the years, it's that with every minor setback, therein lies great opportunity."

He swings his baton through the air, and three more figures float into sight from beyond a holographic wall. It ripples as they pass through, from invisible to visible. The first is a young woman, the second a bruised and bloodied young man, and the third is none other than Drasko himself with one arm in a makeshift sling cut from his own shirt. They glide toward us and slide into place, joining the lineup. Pinned like we are.

"I assume no introductions are in order," our host says with a broad smile. "Drasko and I have been involved in various business ventures for many years. He's my favorite dust supplier because he never holds back, never keeps any of the merchandise for himself. I could always trust Drasko. But I realize now that I didn't really know him. "

He twitches the rod, and Drasko screams, eyes squeezed shut, head thrown back in agony like he's being crushed by the pressure field.

"I already knew he led a double life, working as a pilot for Dome 1 law enforcement, and I had no problem with that as long as it didn't affect his work here in Dome 10. But you see, our friend Erik, whom I've also known for quite some time—these wannabe actors always want a piece of the good life, you know, thinking they might find a current that will carry them upstream, away from the little fish—he has very little tolerance when it comes to pain. And he spilled everything that Drasko has been so good at hiding from me." Our host chuckles. "*Everything.* Including the fact that Erik's little stunt last night, leading that curfew enforcer on a merry rooftop chase, was not due to any dust high. He's naturally gifted that way, just like our speedy friend here. Nice moves, by the way." He winks at me. "So I'll make you a deal. You explain how I can have my very own superpowers of a very permanent nature, and I'll let most of you live. How's that sound?"

My stomach sinks.

Do you still think these people should be given supernatural gifts? Julia asks.

If it means saving my friends…

I just hope I won't have to lock lips with this guy.

24. SERA
22 YEARS AFTER ALL-CLEAR

While the seventeen of them smile like imbeciles with their unfocused eyes staring up at the ceiling, enjoying whatever delights exist in their virtual Promised Land, I get out of my lounge chair and inspect the room, activating every alcove I remember by touching various points along the white walls. By the time I've made a complete circuit, the first few sections that I opened have already begun sliding closed. I go around again, faster this time, making a game of it.

It should be obvious to anyone monitoring us that I've grown bored with VR and become restless. Only a matter of time before someone checks in on me.

Eventually, a section of the wall slides open to reveal a doorway to an outer corridor. A boxy robot with large optical lenses but no other anthropomorphic features rolls in on wide treads. I step in front of it.

"Who's in charge here?" I demand.

Keeping its lenses to itself, the bot reverses and then navigates a course around me. It heads for each of the end tables beside the VR zombies and collects their half-finished drinks and meals, piling them into a spacious receptacle in its midsection. Job complete, it circles back to find me blocking its path again.

"Answers." I fold my arms and glare down at it. "Now."

The door slides open behind me, and I pivot to find—

"It's not a very sophisticated machine," Chancellor Hawthorne says as she steps inside the room. "It couldn't communicate with you verbally even if it wanted to."

Taken aback by her sudden appearance—smiling like a young grandmother and dressed in the same white bodysuit the rest of us are wearing—I stumble back a step. She allows the robot to pass between us. Once the door slides shut, she steps close to me, leaning in to whisper conspiratorially.

"I don't much like them myself. *Bots.* I've always preferred clones for my security force. I like knowing the personnel protecting me have hearts pumping inside them. That they would bleed for me, if necessary."

"Chancellor..." I blink, having trouble believing my eyes. "What are you doing here?"

She gives me a knowing look. "You heard I was taken someplace safe during the terrorist attacks."

I nod.

She spreads her arms wide as if to encompass the entire underground facility. "This is the safest place on earth, Enforcer Chen. The perfect venue for your Revelation Banquet, don't you think? All we need are the final two members of the Twenty to arrive, and then Dr. Wong will share the details of your glorious Ascension." She takes my hand in both of hers, and they're soft and warm. "I am so excited for you, Sera. What happens next..." Her eyes glisten with joyful tears. "Do you remember books? No, probably not. They were outlawed long before you were born. But this is like a final chapter ending, a book closing—only to be reopened, and much to the reader's surprise, for there to be yet another chapter waiting to be enjoyed. And it's the best chapter in the book, Sera." She nods emphatically, her grip tightening. "Because the best is yet to come—for all of us!"

I politely extricate my hand. "Where's Commander Bishop?"

Her expression falters. The smile is still in place, held there with some effort. "She had to return to Eurasia. Those terrorists will not catch themselves, you know."

"And who's running things while you're away? Who's in charge of the Domes?"

She stares back at me without response.

"Martial law only works for so long, Chancellor. People will start questioning what's going on, and law enforcement won't have answers for them." I nod toward the Seventeen in their chairs, blissfully unaware of our conversation. "VR might hold citizens' attention for a while, but they'll eventually want to leave their residences and places of business, returning to their daily lives in the absence of further terrorist activity. And the enforcers keeping our streets safe will want to know what their orders are."

Hawthorne laughs mildly. "They are expected to keep the peace. What other orders are there, really?" She reaches for me again, this time patting my arm. "The Governors take care of day-to-day business between the Domes, and they have matters well in hand. Trust me."

For some reason, I don't. "What's out there?" I point behind her at the seamless wall. No evidence that a door ever opened.

"Hmm?" She's rubbing my arm now instead of patting it. Attempting to soothe me, but having the opposite effect.

"What's outside this room, where you came from?"

She shrugs with another noncommittal laugh. "Just more rooms. What does it matter? You are together here, all in one place, safe from harm, provided with anything you could possibly need. Dr. Wong has seen to everything. Isn't it wonderful?"

"They call him the *creator*." I watch her for a response, but again, there's nothing to read. The consummate politician. "Why?"

She squeezes my arm. "Because he creates life. Every clone in my security force, every baby born in the Ten Domes—they are alive, thanks to him."

"And thanks to us." I point at the Seventeen behind me. "Our sex cells harvested monthly. He combines them, edits in a little

DNA from the adoptive parents, and a few months later, we have another fresh batch of newborn citizens."

"It is far more complicated than that, Sera."

"I'm sure. And when Dr. Wong isn't busy *creating life*, he's ensuring that every citizen who can afford it doesn't look a day over thirty. Including yourself. What are you now, eighty-something? You don't look much older than me, Chancellor."

Her grip tightens, her fingernails digging into my arm. I don't flinch. No need to give her the satisfaction.

"You will show me the proper respect, Enforcer Chen." Her smile has been replaced by flashing teeth and the whites of her eyes. "I am your Chancellor!"

I shake off her hold on me and back away, raising my voice. "Hey, everybody—wake up! Look who's here: our illustrious Chancellor Persephone Hawthorne in the flesh!"

I make my way along the rows of chairs, nudging shoulders, rousting them from their VR-induced stupor. They blink and frown curiously, then stare in awe as they notice Hawthorne. One by one, they jump to their feet and bow their heads respectfully.

She nods, her smile firmly ensconced again. "It is so good to see each of you. Dr. Wong sends his regards—"

"Gather around, everybody." I gesture for them to encircle me as I stand beside the Chancellor. "Story time."

They glance at each other, confused, but it's the best strategy I can think of. You want people to know the truth? Tell them a story—a true story. And don't leave anything out.

"It's all about where we came from." I wink at their intrigued expressions and then glance at Hawthorne. "Would you rather tell this one? You were there, after all."

The Chancellor's cheerful expression is unassailable. "Why dwell on the past? The present is all that matters, moving ever forward—"

"Right. So here's the deal." I face my siblings and Erik's. "Your parents aren't your biological parents. The truth is, we're not from around here. There's a quarantined continent across the ocean where we were conceived. It took our parents a lot of years, but they've managed to get inside Eurasia. And now they're looking for us."

I pause, holding their attention while doing my best to ignore Hawthorne scoffing behind me.

"Which is why we've been taken to this secret facility on the other side of the Mediterranean. Underground, where our biological parents will never find us. There's no banquet, no *ascension*, whatever the hell that is. We're just being kept here until our government can find a way to banish or execute the people who gave us our DNA." I pause to let that sink in. "Once that's done, we'll be allowed to return to our lives as if none of this ever happened."

They murmur among themselves, but only Lyria speaks up. "How do you know all of this, Sera?"

Honestly? I—

"She doesn't." Hawthorne gives me a steely-eyed glare and crosses her arms. "Sera may think of herself as an investigator, but she is merely a curfew enforcer. The least of all law enforcement assignments. Apparently, she has grown bored with her duties, so now she is creating fiction and finding conspiracies where none exist." She laughs, and a few of the Seventeen join in.

But most don't. They stare at me with unguarded curiosity. Then they start speaking over each other:

"Why can't we link with you, Sera?"

"What's wrong with your augments?"

"Are you...*offline*?" Eyes aghast.

That gets the rest of them talking, turning toward one another and glancing at me over their shoulders. Chancellor Hawthorne leans uncomfortably close to whisper into my ear.

"I don't know what you're trying to accomplish here, Sera, but it will never work."

"I just want them to know the truth. Someone explained it to me today, and it changed my life." I pivot to face her. *And I'm only telling them half of it.*

She stumbles away from me, slapping her hand against the wall to steady herself. "What devilry is this?"

Guess I'm getting better at this telepathy thing. Now I'm able to send my thoughts into the minds of others who aren't gifted the same way I am. Good to know. But it didn't work on the Seventeen earlier, so this must have something to do with Hawthorne's augments being off.

Why are you offline, Chancellor? I step toward her just as the door reappears, sliding open behind her. She backpedals into the dark corridor beyond. I follow.

"Don't go out there, Sera!" Lyria calls after me.

The others crowd around, staring wide-eyed and echoing her concern.

"We're not allowed to leave this room!"

"Come back!"

"You'll get us all in trouble!"

Too late to turn back. I've found a way out, and I've got Hawthorne on the run. I have her undivided attention as she staggers backward, swinging her arm at me and shouting to stay back. Like she thinks I've got the plague.

"How about giving me a tour of the place, Chancellor?" I smile at her. *You seem to know your way around.*

The door behind me slides shut, and the corridor dumps us into the middle of a long hallway that curves out of sight in both directions. But unlike the room I just exited, closed off from everything, these walls and doors are made of glass, exposing what appear to be research laboratories. Inside, every piece of sophisticated equipment and every person in a white lab coat is clear to see as they go about their business.

They stop and stare at us, all of them with identical faces. They look exactly like D1-436 without its helmet: young versions of Solomon Wong.

"Help me!" Hawthorne spins on her heel and charges down the hallway. She throws open the first glass door she reaches and rushes inside, grabbing the nearest clone by the lapels. "There's something seriously wrong with that one!" She points at me, her eyes wild. "She's a dust freak or-or some kind of *mutant!*"

Dust freak? Really, Chancellor? If I was snorting that stuff, the effects would've worn off long before now. I pull the lab door open and follow her inside.

"She's in my head!" Hawthorne shrieks, shoving her way past the placid clone and knocking over an expensive-looking piece of equipment. As it crashes to the white tiled floor, she staggers onward, trying to put as much distance between us as possible. "How can she do that?"

Tell your boss I want to speak with him, I project toward the eight clones in the lab. My telepathy didn't work with D1-436, but maybe this is a different batch. *Right now.*

"What seems to be the problem?"

I turn to find another Solomon Wong standing at the door. But unlike the blank-faced clones, this one smiles like the version I saw on the wall screen when I arrived: grandfatherly, yet without any wrinkles or grey hair.

"You're their creator," I blurt out the obvious. Then I gesture at his duplicates who stand rooted—not going about their business, but not interfering with mine.

"Yes. I am responsible for thousands of lives in Eurasia, including your own. I was there at the birth of each member of the Twenty." His voice is a resonant baritone without a hint of humility. "I am a creator of life, Sera Chen."

"But we're not in Eurasia."

"No. We are not." He watches me closely. Intrigued, for some reason.

"We're in a ten-story underground tower...in a forbidden zone."

His smile broadens. "I like to think of Futuro Tower as an Ark."

The reference is lost on me. *Explain,* I project into his mind.

He raises his eyebrows, mildly impressed. "I heard that your biological parents exhibited certain rare abilities, but I had no idea these *gifts* transferred through their DNA. Of course, this leads me to wonder about the children currently growing up in the Ten Domes. Will they, too, exhibit such amazing talents when they come of age?"

Sooner. I wasn't even born yet, and I was already communicating with Margo, mind to mind. What ever happened to her? Did she manage to sneak into Eurasia like Erik's biological parents?

"Sooner!" he echoes aloud. "Fantastic. They will become marvels, as will their children and their children's children. One day, Eurasia may find itself overrun with superhumans. But by then, discord will have torn the Domes apart. Their well-structured society will no longer exist." He sounds like he's already seen the future, and he's resigned to it. "The fuse has been lit. The attack on Hawthorne Tower and other government centers across the Domes have shown the malcontents how powerful they can be. Now they know what they are capable of."

"You have to stop them!" Hawthorne cries, taking a step toward him.

"There is no stopping human evolution. Or de-evolution, as the case may be." His tone and expression are perfectly calm—in stark contrast to the Chancellor's. "But there are ways to work around it. This facility is our way to preserve the present while the future unfolds. It is here that the Twenty, along with every advancement we have ever made in science, technology, medicine —everything that has made Eurasia great—will be kept safe from the dangers threatening the Ten Domes."

"I have to go back...put my house in order..." Hawthorne murmurs, looking confused all of a sudden. "Where am I, Solomon? How did I get here?"

He smiles at her as one might an aging parent. "You should return to your quarters, Chancellor. Get some rest. This has been a trying experience for you, I imagine."

She stares blankly at him and shuffles past us, out into the

City of Glass | 383

hallway. She knows her way, disappearing out of sight around the corner.

"Not exactly herself, is she?" I note. *Don't tell me you've cloned her, too.*

He gives me a knowing look and extends a hand toward his duplicates. They return to their duties as if they were never interrupted.

"Unlike humans, clones can be modified as they grow and mature. They can be programmed, for lack of a better term. Of course they are not machines. They are biological organisms as close to human beings as anything could be. But there are no disgusting addictions, no bizarre physical abilities, no reproductive issues. They are easily replaceable! And if, for some reason, these anomalies rear their ugly heads, we decapitate them." He mimes cutting with his fingers. "We edit the clone's DNA and neural synapses, and it proceeds with its life none the wiser. It continues being the best version of itself that it can be."

I glance around the lab, then at the identical rooms lining the hallway. So many Wong clones. "You're planning to replace everyone in Eurasia?"

The good doctor laughs. "You haven't been listening, Sera. Eurasia is a lost cause. This facility, this *Ark*, is the future. When Eurasia, that wonderful city of glass, eventually shatters—and it will, as every human empire in the history of the world can attest—then we will rise from the earth to begin again."

"You and your clones."

"And you! Like every other advancement we've made over the years—the aerocar, the field harvester, the waste reclamator, the oxygen generator—you are to be held in safekeeping. The Twenty are prime specimens of vigor and fertility. You never should have been allowed to walk among the masses. It was never safe for you there!"

Granted, the man is a genius. But, apparently, he's also a sinister madman. "So instead, you want to imprison us here against our will?"

"Come." He steps out into the hallway, holding the door open for me. "I'll show you."

I pause, weighing my options for just a moment. Then I follow. Because there are no other options, not if I want to know what the hell is going on here.

"Why did you clone Chancellor Hawthorne?"

"I needed her clearance codes," he says simply. "I created her security force, but only she had access to their command framework. And it was a delightful challenge." He eyes me sidelong. "How soon did you realize she wasn't the real Persephone Hawthorne?"

I shrug. "She seemed a little off from the get-go."

He clenches his jaw, staring straight ahead as we make our way to a polished plasteel elevator. Leading the way inside, he punches the button for level ten at the very bottom of the subterranean tower. Good thing I'm not claustrophobic.

The door slides shut, trapping us inside. For a few floors, neither of us say anything. What happened to that loquacious mad scientist from a minute ago? Now he's brooding with his arms folded, lost in his own headspace.

"Did you light the fuse?" I break the silence.

His eyes dart toward me as if he forgot I was there for a moment. Then he smiles. "You're much more than a mere curfew enforcer. If permitted to continue serving in Dome 1, I'm sure you would have been promoted to investigator."

I shake my head. "My commander never would have allowed it. Or the Chancellor. They had their own ideas on how to keep the Twenty safe. But back to you." His favorite topic, from what I've gathered. "Why today?"

"How much world history are you familiar with?"

I tap my temple. "More since I've been offline."

He nods. "We will need to get that fixed at some point. But for now, I would like you to think back to the early twentieth century, a time period of extreme nationalism. What spark set the world powers of that time on the path to bloodshed—the likes of which this planet had never seen before?"

I struggle in vain to remember. That was so long ago, and so irrelevant to what's going on right now. Unless...

"A single violent act," I guess. "But the stage had already been set."

"Precisely. As in Eurasia today. For years, discontent has flourished among workers in the outlying domes. They could not keep themselves from envying the lives of Dome 1 citizens. Chancellor Hawthorne and the Governors were perfectly content to ignore the lessons of the past by insisting that the past no longer mattered. 'Only now, moving forward'. Never bothering to look back. And in so doing, they ignored the warning signs."

You mean the resurgence of the patriots.

He nods. "Hawthorne and the Governors have paved the way for D-Day to occur all over again. For a new generation of terrorists to strike—but this time, at the very heart of Eurasia. Over the past twenty-four hours, government buildings across the Domes have been targeted with electromagnetic bursts. Terror has struck the populace, and they can't help being afraid of what will happen next."

"Law enforcement has everything under control."

He raises an eyebrow. "Perhaps for now. But there is no shortage of malcontents who have already claimed responsibility for the attacks, even though they had nothing to do with them. The ball is rolling, Enforcer Chen, and it will only gain momentum going forward. Downhill, of course."

"The idea of Eurasia imploding pleases you."

The elevator door opens onto the bottom floor, and he steps out into a dimly lit warehouse so expansive I can't see an end to the rows upon rows of shelving units. He leads the way down the center aisle with his hands clasped behind his back, his posture rigid.

"The idea of what comes *after* pleases me. The revelation, the unveiling. The true meaning of *apocalypse*, from the Greek." He shows me a well-organized lineup of cold storage units. In each one, embryos float in metallic canisters labeled *bear, wolf, eagle,* and *dolphin* among hundreds of other species.

"You have...animals?" I can't believe what I'm seeing here: every extinct creature that was wiped from the face of the earth. Many of them the most popular avatars in VR.

"We do."

"Why haven't you allowed them to live?"

"In Eurasia?" He shakes his head. "There was concern that we would not have enough resources. Food, water, air. Humankind has always been our priority. But in the future, once the Domes fall, we will terraform this planet. Then the animals will run wild across the land, soar through the sky, and swim the ocean depths again. It will be our Promised Land!"

I nod slowly. "That's what the Seventeen are seeing in VR." No wonder they were so blissed-out.

"They see what will be."

"Why wait? If you have the ability to change the world back to what it was—"

His laughter and upraised hand halt me right there.

"It will take decades, perhaps centuries, to develop the technology and equipment necessary to restore the earth to its former glory. But I have every confidence that we will." He leans toward me. "All two thousand of my clones, each endowed with an IQ very close to my own, are currently working on this project. We will find a solution. And when that day arrives, you will be there to see it!"

He points out another row of cryo-storage units, much larger but empty. Each one is labeled, but instead of animal species, they are the names of each member of the Twenty—along with an extra unit for the good doctor himself.

"We will sleep in perfect peace as the years pass like seconds, while the diligent clones are hard at work. Our minds will be actively stimulated by the Promised Land VR program to avoid neural atrophy. And when the time comes, I will awaken first to ensure the completion of the terraforming process, and then you will be awakened to sire the first generation on a far better earth!"

What were you saying earlier about learning from history?

He frowns. "What are you referring to?"

"Government scientists hand-picked my biological parents to be the breeders of a new world, once the nuclear winters ended. They were expected to rise up from their bunkers at the All-Clear signal and start making babies to repopulate North America." I pause. "How did those plans turn out?"

He holds both of his open hands toward me. "We have you, and nineteen others like you, to show for it."

"A rip-roaring success, in other words."

He puts on his grandfatherly expression—the same one I saw on the wall screen, welcoming me into that weird white room. "Sera, you have to understand, this is the future of the world we're talking about. Every step in the right direction is *progress*."

I back away from him and move toward the elevator. "No, you have to understand, Doctor. I don't want anything to do with it. I have a life, and it's a good one. You don't get to decide what's best for us. You've already taken our DNA without our permission and spawned countless children. Now you've kidnapped us and plan to freeze us for a few centuries against our will. This is wrong on so many levels."

"Once we fix your augments, you will be on board. Trust me."

"Not happening."

The elevator door slides open as it senses my approach. One of Dr. Wong's clones stands inside, but it's not wearing a lab coat. It has on blood-spattered plasteel armor instead. The clone raises its gloved hand to point the muzzle of a weapon—

"What is the meaning of this?" Dr. Wong demands, right before the pulse from a shocker hits his chest dead center, and he's bowled over by the impact. He hits the white tile floor and slides a couple meters, shaking with uncontrollable spasms and groaning as he soils himself. Then he lies still, unconscious.

"D1-436?" I stare at the clone.

It nods. "Enforcer Chen, it appears I may have made an error in judgment."

"Explain." I join it inside the elevator and punch the button for the seventh floor. The door slides shut, and we hurtle upward.

"In seeking to take you to safety, I inadvertently placed you in further harm. To be put in cryo-sleep against your will..." D1-436 trails off, shaking its head. "I cannot think of a worse possible fate."

I eye the clone for a moment. "And you knew about that because...?"

"I attached an audio-transmitting filament to your hair while you were attempting to shoot me with this." It raises the shocker. "If you remember, while I was piloting the aerocar, you—"

"I remember." Can't hide the grin spreading across my face. "Thanks. I owe you one."

It nods pleasantly, lowering the weapon. "Judging from the floor you selected, would it be safe to assume you intend to rescue the other members of the Twenty instead of returning to the launch pad and leaving this facility at once?"

"Safe to assume." The elevator, as fast as before, arrives at our destination, and the door opens automatically. "You need a name."

"My designation is—"

"Something other than a string of alphanumerics. You're able to think for yourself. You deserve your own name." *D1-436...D-one...* "What do you think of *Dunn*?"

"That is not my designation."

"We'll work on it." I lead the way out of the elevator, just as a blaring klaxon sounds and an automated voice announces that Futuro Tower is rising. A low rumble reverberates along the floor, walls, and ceiling.

"That must be Erik and Arienna," I tell Dunn. The clones in the laboratories don't pay us any attention as we make our way to that corridor the Chancellor's duplicate used earlier to enter the white room. "Dr. Wong's collection is now complete."

Entering the room through the sliding wall-door, I clap my

hands together to get everyone's attention. Of course, they're back in their lounge chairs, staring off into the virtual Promised Land. Blinking and frowning curiously, they return to reality as I clap again and gesture for them to follow me outside.

"Field trip," I improvise. "Dr. Wong wants us all to be there to welcome our final two arrivals!"

That gets their attention, and they leap to their feet in excitement, murmuring among themselves that they've never been out of the room before. They give Dunn wary looks, but the clone stands at ease with the shocker behind its back and what might be taken for a casual expression on its face. I lead the Seventeen out into the hallway toward the elevator and do my best to keep them on task; but they're easily distracted, staring at all the Wong clones in the various laboratories.

The clones turn and stare back at them. Then, without a change in expression, the clones sweep aside their lab coats and draw sidearms, charging from the labs to confront the escaping Seventeen.

"Dunn!" I shout.

"That is not my designation." Dunn follows the last members of the Seventeen down the hallway and fires the shocker, releasing a barrage of glowing pulse rounds that bring the Wong clones to a halt. They hesitate behind their glass doors as the energy blasts strike and disperse, fizzling with sparks of light.

"Why do they all look like Dr. Wong?" Lyria asks, right behind me.

The others murmur among themselves:

"Why are they carrying weapons?"

"Do they wish us harm?"

"Everybody inside." I stand just outside the elevator as they file in. "Squeeze tight."

Dunn walks backward toward us, firing the shocker at untimed intervals. One of the Wong clones makes the mistake of rushing out of a lab with its weapon raised and receives a blast to the face. It hits the floor in convulsions before lying still. Dunn picks up its weapon and hands it to me. Feels good to be packing again.

"Once we reach the hangar, I'll need you to sync up with Wink and Blink," I tell Dunn as we wedge ourselves into the elevator, squishing my siblings and Erik's against each other. They don't look happy about it, but they'll live.

"Your drones," Dunn clarifies.

"That's right. I want them to spread out and provide you with real-time surveillance."

"They have been weaponized."

I blink. "What?"

The elevator reaches the hangar at the top of the tower, but the door refuses to open. DECONTAMINATION IN PROCESS reads the display.

"When your friend Drasko returned them, they had been modified. He may be responsible." Dunn pauses. "Your exo-suit is also in the cargo area. It too has been weaponized—and reformatted to work with your unaugmented biologic."

A curfew enforcer is never assigned weaponized drones. They're for overwatch purposes only. And as for the suit...that's unheard of.

If Drasko upgraded them, then maybe it wasn't an act of betrayal when he shot me in the back. He could have done it for my protection, knowing what that gangster low-life Trezon was capable of. And maybe he didn't shoot Dunn in the head with the intention of destroying it, as he did with the clone in the passenger seat. Drasko somehow must have known Dunn would try to rescue me.

The display clears, and the elevator door slides open, revealing the hangar's dim, blue-lit interior and a pair of aerocars sitting side by side on the launch pad. The doors on the recent arrival float upward, and two figures hop out of the cockpit.

I grip the Wong clone's weapon down at my side. Dunn stands next to me, shocker at the ready. The Seventeen cautiously follow us outside with silent stares.

"Sera—is that you?" Erik bounds over to us. His face is covered in bruises and cuts, but he seems all right otherwise.

I hate to admit it, but relief washes over me at the sight of him.

Until I see the woman beside him. Not Arienna. A middle-aged stranger—yet her eyes look identical to my own...

"I'd like you to meet Daiyna," Erik says with a grin. "You two have a lot of catching up to do."

25. DAIYNA
22 YEARS AFTER ALL-CLEAR

No word from Luther. No word from Drasko. If it wasn't for Victoria's extra-sensory abilities to reach out and verify that each of them is still alive, I'd be worried.

More than I am already.

But there's no way for her to tell us where they are. Even when she holds hands with her son Boaz and her adopted daughter Florence, both well into their teens now. They've exhibited their own gifts since they were young—Boaz with his far-sight and Florence with her supernatural hearing. Victoria has been unable to use her special talent of piggybacking onto their abilities to locate Drasko's position.

"Their heart rates are elevated," Victoria says, her eyes shut, frowning as she focuses.

I grip the communication device I received from Captain Mutegi and look out the open warehouse door, hoping to see Luther return at this very moment. That everyone else will be with him. That he was successful in locating our long-lost children.

There's no point in deluding myself that I'll ever be a mother. Rehana was right, all those years ago. We were never meant to be breeders, despite what Mother Lairen told us. Leave that to the *cows*. But even so, I want to see these twenty-year-old men and women who share my DNA and Luther's. Will they have my eyes? His nose?

According to Samson and Shechara, who recently arrived at our rendezvous point—a warehouse filled with dust crates from North America—their biological son Erik has telepathic and physical abilities. Do all of the Twenty exhibit gifts from the spirits? Or is it only because Tucker took him across the Wastelands in an incubation pod, along with my biological daughter? A young woman named Sera, who works in law enforcement. Maybe the pods' seals weren't tight enough, and some dust got into their breathing fluid...

The device in my hand bleeps. I tap the green icon on the screen.

"Luther?" I speak into it.

"He's not here," says an unfamiliar voice. "To whom am I speaking?"

"Who is this?" I demand. Samson, Shechara, and Victoria gather around me.

"My name is Emmanuel Bishop."

"Where are you?"

"On a rooftop in Dome 10. Where are you?" He sounds completely out of his element.

"What are your coordinates?"

He rattles them off, and I repeat them to Samson, who nods with a grim look of determination on his face. He heads out of the warehouse on foot with Shechara and Victoria close behind.

I follow, keeping Emmanuel on the line as I shut and lock the warehouse door and order the two clunky security bots to secure the perimeter in our absence. Florence and Boaz know to hide in the cellar beneath the warehouse floor until we return. Victoria will keep in contact with them telepathically, ensuring that they keep busy studying their math and science lessons. They'll do their best, but they're both worried about Milton—their adoptive father.

"Emmanuel, I'm a friend of James Bishop." I keep the device close to my ear as we hit the streets.

We couldn't have timed things worse. It's a shift change, so the sidewalks and streets are packed with people either leaving their jobs for the day or heading in for their share of the workload. I can't believe how easy these people have it: only 6-hour shifts. Yet there are still malcontents all across the Domes stirring up the masses in a nebulous fight for equality. The way I see it, once you've mastered the art of survival, there really shouldn't be much to complain about. But these people have always had it easy. For them, there's a very different definition of hardship.

Dome 10 workers stare openly at us as we pass each other, and for good reason. Nobody else around here is a large cyborg or has eyes like Shechara's. And nobody uses outdated tech like this device I'm holding against the side of my head. They all have fancy neural implants—even the lowest citizen on the totem pole.

"My name is Daiyna. Did Sergeant Bishop and two other men enter that building?"

"Yes, and my sister went with them. They're looking for someone—a friend of theirs, in need of assistance." He pauses. "But it's been close to an hour, and no one has returned. Do you think I should...go after them?"

"Are you armed?"

"No."

"Stay put. We're on our way."

I pocket the device and nudge Victoria as we follow Samson, who navigates our course through the press of bodies. The workers in their grubby coveralls see him coming and give him a wide berth.

"Any news?"

She looks concerned. "They're in trouble. Their hearts are racing."

"They could be running back to the warehouse." And we won't be there to meet them.

She shakes her head. "They're not moving, Daiyna."

The implication is clear. Someone is holding our friends against their will. Hurting them, maybe.

Samson is always armed with his mechatronic limbs. Neither Shechara nor I were able to smuggle our weapon of choice—a Colt 9mm—past security at the Dome 10 airlock. Citizens here aren't allowed to carry guns that fire lethal projectiles, but Drasko provided us with a small arsenal of the type reserved for the upper echelon of law enforcement. About the same size and weight as a semiautomatic pistol, they fire armor-piercing rounds from a pressurized chamber—utilizing the same anti-gravity tech that makes aerocars fly.

We reach the nondescript building twenty minutes later. Extricating ourselves from the mass of foot traffic outside, we step past a pair of smudged and cracked sliding glass doors stuck halfway open. Inside the lobby, everything's quiet. Abandoned. No desk clerk on duty, no signs of life.

"They're close," Victoria says, her voice hushed as she gazes at the stained ceiling.

"On this floor?" I glance at the vacant hallways and the elevator with an OUT OF ORDER hologram glowing on its door.

"Close," she repeats, pointing upward.

"Second floor it is." Samson heads for the stairwell, his metal left hand pivoting at the wrist and transforming into a long, sharp blade.

Shechara, Victoria, and I draw our Eurasian guns and keep the muzzles aimed at the musty carpet as we follow him up the steps. Can't help cringing at the sounds made by his clanking metal feet.

"At least we don't have to worry about the element of surprise," I mutter. "Any change?" I glance over my shoulder at Victoria.

She shakes her head. Her anxious expression hasn't relaxed.

The second floor is as lifeless as the first, but with one minor difference. A door stands open halfway down the hall, and a man's muffled voice emanates outward.

"Who is he?" I whisper to Victoria.

She squints as if she's trying to see through the walls between us and this mystery man. "He knows Drasko, and he wants something." She looks at me. "He's willing to kill anyone who gets in his way."

Reminds me of her psychotic ex-husband, but I don't mention it. "How many does he have with him?"

She frowns. "He has them trapped: Milton, Luther, Bishop and his daughter... Drasko, Erik... and a young woman." She pauses. "She's one of your daughters."

My pulse quickens as we reach the open doorway.

Samson looks ready to charge inside and skewer every enemy in his path, but Victoria convinces him telepathically to remain right where he is until needed. Otherwise, his noisy metal parts will give us away—if they haven't already. From the sound of the guy inside, he likes his own voice too much to notice much else.

I sneak in and motion for Shechara and Victoria to follow. The large room might have been a swanky lounge at one point in time, but it was deserted in a hurry. Stepping silently heel-to-toe, we navigate our way around the overturned furniture and broken glass until we reach a glitching holographic wall. As we get closer, the man's voice increases in volume, growing more belligerent, more unstable. A dangerous combination.

"You don't have to tell me about dust. Drasko and I know all about it, don't we, Drasko? What's that? You can't breathe underneath all the pressure? You want me to dial it down a bit?" He laughs. "You're the most expendable one here! I already know what you have to offer. I know your sob story." He feigns mild hysteria and raises the pitch of his voice, "Oh, my family's a bunch of sickos in Dome 6! I'll do anything to keep them receiving their treatments and living in comfort, even if I have to sell drugs the rest of my life!"

I thought I'd seen everything on that quarantined continent after All-Clear. Then I had to readjust my thinking after entering Eurasia, the World of Tomorrow. But this? One man pinning seven people against a wall with some kind of force field—and wielding a chrome baton like he's leading a marching band? It's too bizarre.

And I don't have time for bizarre.

I lock eyes with Luther and give him a nod. Then I aim my Eurasian gun at the talkative creep holding them hostage. Two rounds, one to each of his legs, are enough to make him scream and hit the floor writhing. A thunderous clanking announces Samson's arrival, and he snatches the baton from the guy's hand. He crushes it in his mechatronic grip, and all of our friends collapse to the floor, freed from whatever energy field had them immobilized.

Samson keeps a metal hand on the pierced, tattooed guy bleeding out of both legs, pinning him to the floor and seeing how he likes the pressure. Victoria rushes to Milton, and they embrace. I head over to Luther and help him to his feet. Then we do some embracing ourselves—in between the kissing.

"Good work." He holds me tight.

"You're not mad at me for shooting him?"

"You didn't kill him."

"I can try again." I take aim at the guy's head.

"Let's leave him to the authorities." Luther nods toward a tall, bald woman in a severe-looking black uniform. "Daiyna, this is Mara Bishop. Commander of Dome 1 law enforcement."

We shake hands. "You must work with Sera Chen."

Bishop's daughter nods. "One of our best. If I know her, she's already located where the Twenty have been taken. You'll just need to find her." She gives the thug on the floor a cold glare. "I'll take Trezon back to Dome 1 for processing. He won't be seeing the light of day for a long while."

Trezon? Probably gave himself the moniker.

"The truth will get out," he warns with a bloody hand on each of his wounds, pressing against his ugly faux-leather pants. "All across the Ten Domes, citizens will rise up and demand what they have coming to them!"

"Equal rights?" Milton suggests. He and Victoria have their

arms wrapped around each other, and it doesn't look like they'll be untangling themselves anytime soon.

"Powers!" Trezon bellows.

"You can tell your cellmates all about it." Samson hauls the gangster up by the scruff of his neck and lets him dangle there—which seems to have a sobering effect. "They won't think you're nuts at all."

Mara gives Drasko a direct look. "There will be a vacuum in the underworld without his leadership. I'd hate to see someone worse rise up to fill the void."

Drasko nods. "I can take care of that, ma'am."

"I'm sure you can." She seems to be seeing him for the first time. "We'll be in touch."

He salutes her as she turns away.

"Emmanuel," I speak into my communication device. "We've got them. Everybody's fine."

He sighs with relief. "That's good. Thank you... But you'd better hurry. I have a proximity warning on the display here."

"Company?"

"Half a dozen aerocars are headed this way. The Chancellor's security force."

Luther and I nod to each other. Time to move out.

"To the roof," he says.

"Just a second." Erik stumbles out of the room and disappears through a holographic wall that ripples like the surface of a pool as it devours him whole.

"Go ahead," Luther tells the others. "We'll catch up."

We wait for Erik as everyone else files out of the room. A young woman with piercing, clear-blue eyes glances at us with open curiosity. This must be the biological daughter Emmanuel mentioned. She looks so much like Luther, it's uncanny. The same intelligent face, the same beautiful eyes.

He introduces himself as she passes, and she hesitates, looking from me to him and back again.

You're...my biological parents, she projects into our minds.

We nod, glancing at each other. She's obviously been gifted by the spirits.

"I'm Arienna." She places her hand over her heart as tears glisten. Then, without warning, she steps forward and throws her arms around both of us.

It's an awkward hug, but it feels...so good. We hold each other tight, unable to come up with any words.

"Got 'em!" Erik reemerges patting his lumpy pockets. He notices the three-person embrace, and he winks. "Hey, you guys look related."

"I have so many questions," Arienna says.

"There will be plenty of time later." I squeeze her arm reassuringly. "First we need to find your siblings." I face Erik. "And yours."

"About that," he says. "I might have a way to get those coordinates."

We leave the lounge-in-shambles together and catch up with the others in the stairwell. Our leg muscles are complaining by the time we reach the roof. Samson deposits Trezon into the aerocar where a younger version of James Bishop sits in the cockpit, and Mara climbs in beside him. Their father seems torn, standing with us, ready to continue on-mission, but watching his children with obvious longing in his eyes.

"Go." Luther claps Bishop on the shoulder. "Be with your family."

"You were right, Luther. You said I'd see them again, but I wasn't sure I believed you." He shakes his head, clenching his jaw. "This isn't over. We haven't reunited you with your kids yet."

"We're well on our way." Luther nods. "You have an overdue hero's welcome waiting. We'll reconnect with you after we find the Twenty."

It's obvious Luther doesn't want to put him in further danger.

"I owe you." Bishop clasps Luther's outstretched hand.

"I'd say we're more than even," Luther replies.

Bishop climbs into the cargo compartment beside Trezon and

keeps a stern eye on the shriveling gangster. The doors drift shut, and the aerocar takes off with a burst of air, heading straight for the oncoming vehicles. They look like hungry predators, flying in formation against the dreary light filtering through Dome 10's far-from-spotless ceiling, bearing down on us. The clone pilots aren't interested in Mara's police car, and they let her pass without incident.

We're left with a vehicle that's seen better days. The windscreen sports a pair of bullet holes, and a dead clone reclines in the cockpit. Drasko is already at work patching the two holes, smearing what looks like—

"InstaGoo, right?" Milton observes his handiwork with approval.

"Never leave home without it." Drasko grins.

Meanwhile, Erik, Arienna, and Samson are standing beside the open cockpit door, their eyes fixed on the dead clone.

"A data spike would be the only way," Arienna says, pointing to the back of the clone's helmet. "That port right there."

"Can you do it?" Erik raises an eyebrow at his biological father.

Samson grunts. "Won't know till I try."

He folds his left-hand blade back into his forearm and twists it at the wrist, running through an assortment of tools that flip outward. Settling on one that looks like a large needle, he holds it up for inspection.

"That should work." Arienna nods.

"What's going on?" I ask her.

"We saw a security clone access information this way." She shrugs. "We're hoping it works again."

"Information..." Luther echoes. "Coordinates to where the Twenty have been taken?"

"Fingers crossed," Erik says.

As Samson plunges his spike-hand into the data port on the back of the clone's helmet, a readout instantly lights up the screen on his metal forearm.

"Tell me what I'm looking at here," Samson rumbles with a frown, squinting at the strings of alphanumerics.

"Strongman might need glasses." Shechara pats his arm.

He grunts, not pleased by the prospect.

"Got it." Erik claps Samson on the shoulder. "I can program the car to take us there."

"Not all of us." Luther faces me. "Fit as many as you can inside this vehicle and get them to safety."

"I will." I hold his gaze. "But you'd better be right behind me." I pull him close and kiss him. He kisses me back with the vigor of a man half his age.

"Can you fly this thing?" I ask Erik.

He pauses. "Probably."

"Get in."

Samson removes the dead clone from the passenger side, and I climb into the bloody seat. Erik slides behind the controls and activates the engines, ducking his head to see around the goo-smears on the windscreen.

"Here." He retrieves a handful of metal discs from his pocket and leans out of the cockpit toward Milton. "Stick one of these on each of those approaching aerocars, and they'll stall in midair. I've heard you might be able to fly. Literally."

Milton chuckles. "Okay. Then what? We want to commandeer those vehicles, not crash them."

"Steer them my way," Samson says, "and I'll catch 'em."

"Have you ever done this before?" Milton asks.

Samson shrugs. Then he reaches down and picks up our aerocar. It wobbles, reminding me to strap into my harness, but he's got a solid grip on it. With a beastly roar, he raises the vehicle overhead like a weightlifter heaving twice his body weight.

"No worries!" he bellows.

"You'll want to reactivate the engines once they've landed," Erik calls down to Milton. "Remove the discs, and fire up the thrusters. Keep them running. They won't restart again without a new battery installed."

Milton gives him a double thumbs-up.

"Wish we could stick around." Erik taps the console before him, and the doors drift shut, locking into place. "I'd like to see them pull this off."

"I'm sure we will." I glance down at the throngs of people on the streets who have halted in their tracks to stare upward. "Somebody's bound to record it."

He keeps his eyes on the control panel as he runs through our preflight sequence. Helpful the way the onboard computer walks him through it. "Things are going to change in Eurasia. Dust freaks are one thing. But people like us with permanent superhuman abilities? We'd better brace ourselves for a brave new world."

"Maybe a better one," I offer.

"We can hope, right?"

As Samson tosses us aloft, Erik activates the thrusters. We sail off the top of the building, veering away from the oncoming security vehicles identical to ours. Meanwhile, Milton jets into the sky on an intercept course with the six aerocars. He lands on top of the first one and stoops to affix the device Erik gave him. The vehicle shudders in place, dropping out of formation, pitching nose-first toward the street far below. But Milton swoops beneath the craft and guides it toward the rooftop where Samson stands waiting, his metal arms gleaming under the sun. Luther, Shechara, and the others have wisely moved toward the stairwell door in case they need to make a hasty exit downstairs. But Samson manages to catch the aerocar with only a tight grimace and slight tremble to show how much superhuman strength is required to pull off such a feat.

Erik has finished entering the coordinates into the navigation console. Now he's staring at the screen, and he's not blinking. Which dome would be best suited for safeguarding Eurasia's greatest treasures?

"Where are we headed?" I keep a hand on the gun tucked into my belt.

"Outside the Domes," he manages at length. "First time for me."

Unexpected. Why pick a location beyond the safety of the Ten Domes to sequester the Twenty? It makes no sense—unless the move has nothing to do with their welfare.

"Anything I should know about...things out there?" He glances at me.

"The sun can cook you alive."

"Noted."

In under five minutes, our aerocar reaches the airlock at the docks. Erik darkens the windscreen and side windows so no one can see inside, and he runs the flashers along with an automated recording. An authoritative computerized voice announces, "OFFICIAL GOVERNMENT BUSINESS. PLEASE MAKE WAY."

The port security personnel wave us through, and a few minutes later, Erik is steering us over the glittering Mediterranean Sea toward the north coast of the African continent.

On the console before me, the desolate terrain ahead is mapped in infrared gridlines demarking every rise and fall in elevation. Unlike the North American Sectors, there's not a single city ruin in sight. When the United World built the Ten Domes, they must have razed everything else as a way to keep their citizens from looking back. Always forward. So if we're headed to some type of secure location, it must be an underground bunker.

"Just like old times," I murmur.

"How's that?" Erik is hyper-focused on piloting. From what I can see, there isn't much for him to do but adjust the speed and trajectory. Our course is laid in, and the vehicle is taking us to our destination.

Maybe he's nervous about what we might find waiting for us.

"Any idea how we're getting inside?" I glance at his pockets full of EMP discs. "We shouldn't expect a warm welcome."

He pats the dashboard. "The security clones who came for Sera were flying this thing. As long as we keep the windows dark, they should let us in." He sounds confident. "You look a lot alike."

He glances at me sidelong, then quickly averts his gaze. "You and Sera, I mean."

"All in the genes." I shrug.

"The way you carry yourselves. You don't take crap from anybody."

That almost makes me smile. "I look forward to meeting her."

"She's here." He nods, scanning the desert wasteland below as we leave the sea behind. "Somewhere."

"How long have you known each other?"

He gives me a roguish grin identical to Samson's. "We met last night. She chased me across the rooftops of a few domescrapers." He laughs at the memory. "She's relentless."

He brakes suddenly as the ground shifts below. Dust rises in clouds as dirt recedes from the top of a tower gradually erupting out of the earth.

"This must be the place." I draw my gun and lean forward.

"Yeah..." He focuses on landing the aerocar, hovering before he takes us into a jerky vertical drop. On the pad below, an identical security vehicle sits empty with its engines off. No one else is anywhere in sight.

I retrieve the communication device from my pocket and tell Luther we're preparing to land.

"Milton and Samson have managed to commandeer three of the aerocars. The other pilots decided to turn back, and we let them go," he says. "Entering the coordinates to your location now. Should be airborne shortly."

I advise him to use the same strategy Erik employed to get through port security as fast as possible.

"Smart fellow," Luther says. "I wonder where he gets it from."

I glance at Erik as we touch down gently, more or less, on the landing pad. His natural affinity for piloting vehicles may rival his biological father's. Samson never met anything he couldn't drive. "I have some idea."

The hanger roof closes over us like the petals of a massive plasteel flower, sealing us inside for a decontamination procedure that rocks our vehicle with blasts of pressurized air for well over a minute. At the same time, the tower itself recedes into the ground, rumbling with vibrations that travel through the floor to my seat.

With a violent shudder, our descent halts. An elevator door opens at the far end of the hanger, and two figures step out, followed by more than a dozen others. They stop and stare at us as we exit our vehicle.

"She's done it!" Erik takes off in bounding leaps to meet the people at the elevator. Despite being thirty years his senior, I have no trouble keeping up with him. "You two have a lot of catching up to do," he says, introducing me to a young woman in a white bodysuit.

She looks like the version of me who stepped out of that Sector 50 bunker three decades ago. Before I joined Mother Lairen, Rehana, Shechara, and all of my sisters in a rocky climb up into our cave-sweet-home.

"You must be Sera." I smile at her with instant affection I can't restrain. She strikes me as a very confident and capable young woman. I can't help but be honored that she shares my genes.

"We have the same eyes," she says, studying my face for a moment and seeming to like what she sees. "Some DNA too, I'll bet."

"We have little time," says the injured security clone next to her. Without its helmet, its exposed face is a young Dr. Solomon Wong's—covered in dried blood from a nasty head wound.

"Dunn's right," Sera says. "Get them into those vehicles."

The seventeen young men and women behind her wear matching bodysuits and lost looks on their faces. The clone gestures for them to follow, but instead, they glance at each other in confusion.

"Where is our sister?" they murmur. "Erik, where is Arienna? We were expecting her, too. And where is Dr. Wong? Sera said—"

"We're going to the Revelation Banquet!" Erik says with a broad smile, reaching into his pockets and retrieving handfuls of

EMP discs. "Here you go. Take one of these party favors, and make your way to either of the waiting aerocars. Don't delay. We have all sorts of fun activities planned for your entertainment!"

As he hands a disc to each of them mid-stride, they frown curiously and keep walking, following the injured security clone.

"Wait a minute—what happened?"

"Why am I offline?"

They murmur among themselves as the discs disable their neural implants.

"What's wrong with my augments?"

"All part of the fun," Erik calls after them. "Quickly now, everybody aboard!" He herds the last of them toward the vehicles and turns to Sera, keeping his voice low. "Dr. Wong?"

She nods, heading toward the aerocar that was already here. The security clone hands her an activated surveillance drone, and she gives it a pat as one might a pet. Then she tosses it high into the air.

"Wong's behind all of this. The facility, the plan to capture us and put us into cryo-sleep for centuries." She repeats the process with a second drone, and both units fly in separate directions, scanning the hangar for threats.

"Centuries?" Erik stares at her.

"Cryo-sleep..." I echo. "So he's planning something for the future."

"The end of the Ten Domes," Sera says, reaching into the back of her aerocar and pulling out a heavy plasteel apparatus. It slides to the floor with a clunk, and she climbs into the thing, folding it around herself like an exoskeleton. Once she's buckled in place, she tests it by hopping and throwing a few punches. The power-suit whines as it triples the impact of her movements. "He wants to restart civilization."

These government scientists never learn. "They tried the same thing with us, forty years ago. Now all that's left of our Sectors are ruins for your raiders to scavenge."

"Why would they need to scavenge anything at all?" Erik asks.

"The Domes are self-sustaining, supplying us with everything we could ever need."

I wince at that. From what Captain Mutegi told us, Eurasia has never been as self-sufficient as it claims. For decades, it has relied on the goods and supplies pillaged by raiders sent all over the globe. Everything they've found has been stripped down, mulched, and repurposed as raw materials and foodstuffs for the citizens of Eurasia to enjoy.

"Another lie from your government." I pat him on the shoulder. "Something else that needs to change."

Sera nods. "Our people deserve to know the truth—about a whole lot of things."

The elevator door slides open, and without warning, countless Dr. Wongs pour out in flailing white lab coats, wielding the same Eurasian pistols Sera and I carry. They start firing immediately, hunching their shoulders and aiming high, knowing better than to hit any members of the Twenty.

I return fire, ducking around the side of Sera's aerocar where Erik joins me. The power of the weapon in my hands is impressive. A single shot blows a hole straight through the first clone I hit, sending it spiraling through the air from the impact. Crumpling against the floor, it lies still and bloody, staring frozen in surprise.

Sera turns to face the onslaught, and so does the armored security clone she referred to as *Dunn*. The two of them open fire on the Wong clones, downing half the duplicates that charged headlong out of the elevator. The two surveillance drones swoop through the air, converging on the elevator door and laying down a barrage of projectile rounds that cause the remaining Wongs to retreat and cower inside.

"Didn't know they could do *that*." Erik stares at the drones.

"Get ready to fly," I tell him. "As soon as this hangar opens, we need to be airborne."

"How exactly are we opening it?" Sera calls over her shoulder.

"We won't have to, once our people show up." Carrying